Amalia

Amalia

A Romance of the Argentine

José Mármol

MINT EDITIONS

Amalia: A Romance of the Argentine was first published in 1851.

This edition published by Mint Editions 2021.

ISBN 9781513282596 | E-ISBN 9781513287614

Published by Mint Editions®

MINT
EDITIONS

minteditionbooks.com

Publishing Director: Jennifer Newens
Design & Production: Rachel Lopez Metzger
Project Manager: Micaela Clark
Translated by: Mary J. Serrano
Typesetting: Westchester Publishing Services

Contents

Prefatory Note

In this picture of Argentine life during the reign of terror instituted by the Dictator Rosas, Daniel, the hero of the story, represents the spirit incarnate of the best elements of the Argentine people struggling for democracy and freedom, in opposition to militarism and autocracy. It is in fact a social study of a period in Argentine history during which were laid the foundations of the greatness of a people whose soul is revealed in these pages in the vivid and intense emotions and feelings of actual life, portrayed with a master's art by the hand of an actor in its events who himself experienced the feelings he portrays, as event succeeds event, as defeat succeeds victory, victory defeat, but where courage never fails and where confidence in the ultimate triumph of Freedom and of Right is never lost. And over all is spread the magic glamour of deathless love, redeeming the suffering and the bitterness of defeat and exalting and ennobling the vision of a victory still to be won, but to be surely won.

M. J. S.

Introduction

Among the political chiefs of South America Juan Manuel Rosas, the Argentine ruler, for the unscrupulousness of his aims and the ruthlessness of his methods in seeking to attain them stands out a sanguinary figure. Succeeding General Lavalle in 1835 as Governor with extraordinary powers, of Buenos Ayres, his rule was for the country a reign of terror; and the blood-red color which he chose for his own was emblematic of the policy of persecution against his political opponents, the Unitarians, or Unionists, which guided it.

Nor were the political enemies of Rosas, in Buenos Ayres, the only victims of his sanguinary policy. More than one sudden death among the Federal leaders before he finally became chief of the party was rightly, it is believed, attributed to him; and foreign residents were so frequently the objects of his persecution as to draw forth repeated remonstrances from England and France. His policy was one of isolation for the Republic, this policy extending even to its commercial relations with other countries; and for the country itself of retrogression and ignorance. Freedom of speech was interdicted, individual rights were disregarded; and so characteristic of Federalism (in consonance with the tastes of Rosas who, although of noble family, had little culture or breeding), was a contempt for the amenities of life that a regard for these came to be considered a distinctive mark of Unitarianism.

This despotic rule of Rosas had continued for a little more than five years when the opening events of the Romance take place, Rosas having been since his assumption of power not only practically Dictator of the Province of Buenos Ayres, but practically also arbiter of the destinies of the whole Argentine Republic, the other provinces, most of which he had brought under his control, whether by force, fraud or guile, acknowledging tacitly the supremacy of Buenos Ayres. Ambitious of exercising a like control over Uruguay, and eager to gratify his hatred of Rivera, the successor of Oribe, the exiled President of the latter country, for the favor shown the Unitarian refugees in Montevideo, he had, in July, 1839, invaded the territory of that Republic with an army of 7000 men. The defeat of this army and the invasion of Buenos Ayres by the Unitarian chief, Lavalle, which followed, seemed to hold out a hope to the Unitarians of happier days for their country through the downfall of the tyrant. But this hope was for the time and for years to come, destined to prove illusory. General Lavalle was defeated; the Unitarian chiefs of the interior were relentlessly persecuted and a price was set on their heads; and General Oribe, at the head of 14,000 men, again invaded Uruguay and laid siege to Montevideo. But the tide slowly turned. France and England intervened in favor of Uruguay. The French fleet, which had more or less continuously blockaded Buenos Ayres, since 1838, was joined by the English fleet, and both fleets combined began the blockade of Buenos Ayres, on September 18, 1845. The siege of Montevideo, however, was still maintained and Rosas refused to accede to the terms of the allies. The treaty of peace which he finally concluded with them, in November, 1849, by its favorable terms to the Dictator, in the end brought about the overthrow of Rosas. The navigation of the La Plata, Uruguay and upper Paraná rivers was left in the control of Buenos Ayres to the exclusion of the interior provinces, not excepting even the river provinces of Corrientes and Entre-Rios. The dissatisfaction of the excluded provinces was profound, and General Urquiza, Governor of Entre-Rios, issued a manifesto on May 1, 1851, calling on the other provinces to rise against the dictator. An alliance, offensive and defensive, was formed with Brazil and Uruguay, and Urquiza, aided with money and men by the former country, marched against Oribe's army in Uruguay. Oribe was defeated, the siege of Montevideo was raised, and Urquiza, reinforced by the troops of Oribe, who had abandoned their leaders after his defeat, marched against Buenos Ayres. The Dictator, then intrenched at Palerno and Santos Lugares, encountered the allied forces and was defeated by them at Monte Caseros, on February 3, 1852. Taking refuge on a British man-of-war he was carried to England, where he lived in retirement on an estate which he purchased near Southampton, until his death, on March 14, 1877.

I

Treachery

On the night of the 4th of May, 1840, at half-past ten o'clock, a party of six men might be seen crossing the inner courtyard of a small house in the Calle de Belgrano, in the city of Buenos Ayres. On entering the hall which led to the street door and which was dark, like the rest of the house, one of the party stopped and said:

"We must not all leave the house together. There are six of us; let three of us go first, taking the opposite side of the street; a few minutes afterward let the other three follow, taking this side and let us all meet at the corner of the Calle de Balcarce."

"A good idea."

"Well, then, I will go first with Merlo and my friend here," said a young man who wore a sword and who seemed to be the youngest of the party, indicating by a gesture the man who had first spoken. And unbolting the door he opened it and muffling his face in his long blue cloak crossed to the opposite side of the street, accompanied by the two men whom he had designated and walked in the direction of the river.

A few moments later the other three men left the house and fastening the door behind them took the same direction, without crossing the street.

After walking a short distance in silence the companion of the young man with the sword said to him, while the one whom they had called Merlo preceded them, muffled in his poncho:

"It is a sad thought, my friend, that this is perhaps the last time we shall ever walk through the streets of our native city. We are leaving it to join an army that is to see hard fighting, and Heaven alone knows what fate may befall us in the war."

"I feel only too deeply the truth of what you say," returned the other, "but the step we are taking is unavoidable. And yet," he continued, after a few moments' silence, "there is one person, at least, who is of a different way of thinking from us."

"What do you mean?"

"That is to say, who thinks that it is our duty as Argentines to remain in Buenos Ayres."

"Notwithstanding Rosas?"

"Notwithstanding Rosas."

"And that we ought not to go join the army?"

"Just so."

"Bah! Then he must be either a coward or a Mashorquero."*

"He is neither the one nor the other. On the contrary, he is brave to rashness, and there is not among all the young men of our day one who has a nobler or purer heart than his."

"And what would he have us do, then?"

"He would have us all remain in Buenos Ayres," returned the young man with the sword, "because the enemy we have to fight is in Buenos Ayres, and not in the army; and he argues with a great show of reason that fewer of us would die in the streets on the day of a revolution, than on the field of battle during five or six months' fighting, without the slightest probability of conquering in the end. But let us drop this subject for in Buenos Ayres the air hears, the light sees, and the stones and the dust repeat our words to the destroyers of our liberty."

As the conversation had become more animated and they were approaching the barrancas bordering the river, Merlo had from time to time slackened his steps or stood still for a moment, ostensibly to muffle his face more closely in his poncho. When they reached the Calle de Balcarce he stopped and said:

"We are to wait here for the others."

"Are you quite certain about the place where we are to take the boat?" said the young man with the sword.

"Perfectly certain," answered Merlo. "I have promised to take you to it, and I will keep my word, as you have kept yours, giving me the money agreed upon—not for myself, for I am as good a patriot as anyone, but to pay the men who are to take you over to the other side; and you shall soon see what sort of men they are."

The young man's penetrating eyes were fixed on those of Merlo when the other three men of the party arrived.

"Now we must not separate again," said one of these. "Go you in front, Merlo, and show us the way."

Merlo took the lead accordingly and following the Calle de Venezuela for some distance finally turned into the lane of San Lorenzo,

---

* Member of the Mashorca, a political society whose union was symbolized by an ear of corn (Mazorca) and whose object was the propaganda of mas-horca (more gallows).

JOSÉ MÁRMOL

down which he proceeded in the direction of the river, whose waters here wash gently the verdant shores of Buenos Ayres.

The night was calm and starlit and a fresh breeze from the south already announced the approaching frosts of winter.

By the faint light of the stars the Plata could be seen, wild and deserted as the Pampa, and the murmur of its waters, breaking gently on the level beach seemed like the tranquil breathing of this colossus of American rivers whose bosom was laden with thirty French vessels at the time at which the events we are relating took place.

While our fugitives are silently pursuing their way we will avail ourselves of the opportunity to make them known by name to the reader.

The man who walked in advance of all the others was Juan Merlo, a man of the people; of that people of Buenos Ayres who are connected with the civilized races by their dress, with the gaucho by their antipathy to civilization, and with the Pampa by their idle habits. Merlo, as we know, was the guide of the party.

A few steps behind him walked Colonel Francisco Lynch, a veteran of the war of 1813, a man of culture, of high social standing, and remarkable for his personal beauty.

Immediately behind him walked Eduardo Belgrano, a relation of the general of the same name, and the possessor of an ample fortune in his own right—a young man of a brave and generous heart, with a mind highly gifted by nature and enriched by study. This is the young man with the sword whom our readers already know.

Behind him walked Oliden, Riglos and Maisson, all Argentines.

In this order they arrived at that part of the Bajo situated between the Residencia and the lofty barranca overlooking Barracas; that is to say, they were at a point parallel with the house of Sir John Henry Mandeville, the English Minister.

Here Merlo stopped and said:

"It is somewhere here about that the boat is to put in."

His hearers all looked toward the river, endeavoring to discover in the darkness the boat of salvation, while Merlo, on the contrary, seemed to look for it on the land, for his eyes were turned, not toward the water on which those of the fugitives were fixed, but in the direction of Barracas.

"It is not there," said Merlo, at last; "it is not there; we must go on a little further."

The party followed him accordingly; but they had not been walking two minutes when Colonel Lynch, who was immediately behind Merlo, perceived directly in front of them, at a distance of thirty or forty yards, a troop of horsemen, and as he turned to inform his companions of the fact, a "Who goes there?" broke the silence of the solitary region, filling the minds of all with sudden alarm.

"Make no response; I will go on ahead and find out if I can how many of them there are," said Merlo; and without waiting for an answer he walked on a little distance and then set off at a run for the barrancas, at the same time giving a shrill whistle.

A confused and terrific noise immediately responded to this signal— the noise made by the charge of fifty horsemen, who in an instant had descended like a torrent upon the unfortunate fugitives.

Colonel Lynch had hardly time to take one of the pistols he carried from his pocket, and raise it to fire before he was trampled to the ground by one of the horses.

Maisson and Oliden succeeded each in firing a shot, and then they too were trampled down, as Colonel Lynch had been.

Riglos attempted to defend himself by thrusting the point of his dagger into the breast of the horse bearing down upon him but he too was thrown to the ground by the irresistible shock, horse and rider falling over him. But the horseman, rising quickly to his feet, plunged his dagger thrice into the breast of Riglos, making the unhappy man the first victim of that fatal night.

Lynch, Maisson and Oliden, trampled under the horses' hoofs, stunned and bleeding, were soon dispatched by the knives of their assailants.

And while the latter, dismounting, gathered around the bodies of the slain to rifle them of their jewels and money, and all was darkness and confusion here, a hundred paces away Eduardo Belgrano was defending himself desperately against four of the assassins.

At the moment when the attack had been made upon the fugitives, and just as Colonel Lynch fell, Eduardo, who was directly behind the latter, had run toward the barrancas, thus escaping the onset of the horses. But if he had escaped the onset of the horses he had not escaped being seen. His left shoulder grazed the thigh of one of the horsemen, the latter turned his horse around quickly, one of his companions followed his example, and both, sword in hand, attacked Eduardo.

The latter, who had unsheathed his sword and torn off his cloak and wound it around his left arm, flung himself between the two horsemen and shielding his head with the arm thus protected plunged his sword in the breast of the man on his right, killing him instantly. Before the body of the dead man had reached the ground Eduardo had retreated a dozen paces more in the direction of the city.

At this instant three others of the assassins came to the assistance of their companion, and the four charged together upon Eduardo.

He in turn slipped quickly to the right, to avoid the shock, at the same time dealing the horse nearest him a tremendous blow with his sword, on the side of the head. The animal reared and fell back upon the horses behind him, and his rider, thinking that his horse had been mortally wounded, threw himself to the ground to escape falling with him. The other men dismounted at the same time, imitating their companion's action, of the cause of which they were ignorant.

Eduardo now flung away his cloak and retreated ten or twelve paces more. For an instant he thought of taking to flight, but he quickly comprehended that flight would exhaust his strength without profiting him anything, since his pursuers would assuredly remount their horses and quickly overtake him.

This thought, however, had scarcely flashed through his mind before the assassins were upon him, three of them armed with swords and the fourth with a butcher's knife. Eduardo received their attack with coolness and courage and alternately parrying their strokes and dealing blows around him he continued to retreat in the direction of the city, drawing his assailants at every step farther and farther away from their companions, from whom they were soon hidden by the darkness.

Thus, fighting and retreating, he had slain another of the ruffians, and was raising his sword to bring it down with all his force upon the head of a third, when, simultaneously, the point of a saber penetrated his left side and the edge of another saber made a deep gash in his right shoulder.

Collecting all his remaining strength he succeeded in parrying a blow aimed at him by his nearest antagonist; but, losing his balance, he fell forward upon the ground, dragging with him his opponent, whose heart his own weapon had pierced.

The two men who still continued fighting now advanced toward Eduardo, thinking to dispatch him at once, but the latter, raising himself with an effort and resting his right elbow on the body of the dead man beside him, grasped his sword in his left hand and placing himself on the defensive, prepared to sell his life dearly.

Even in this helpless condition his assailants advanced toward him cautiously. One of them approached him from the side and dealt him a powerful stroke with his saber on the left thigh which, even if he had had the time and the strength to do so, he was unable from his position to parry; while the other, seizing him by the hair, as he made a last desperate effort to rise, and pulling his head backward by it, was about to draw his knife across the young man's throat, when the sound of a dull blow was heard, and the ruffian fell face downward upon the body of his intended victim.

"You shall have your share, too," said the calm, stern voice of a man who, appearing upon the scene as suddenly as if he had dropped from the sky, advanced with uplifted weapon toward the last of Eduardo's assailants, who was holding the young man by the feet, not venturing, in spite of his almost lifeless condition, to come within reach of his hands. But the ruffian, without waiting for the newcomer's approach, sprang to his feet, retreated a step, and then ran swiftly in the direction of the river.

The man thus sent by Providence, as it seemed, to the scene, without making any attempt to pursue the fugitive returned to the group of dead and wounded of which Eduardo formed the center.

Uttering the name of the latter in a tone of mingled anxiety and affection, he lifted in his arms the body of the ruffian who had fallen upon him, laid it on the ground, and, kneeling on one knee beside Eduardo, raised the young man to a sitting position and supported his head gently on his breast.

"He is still living," he said aloud, after satisfying himself that the wounded man still breathed. And taking Eduardo's hand in his a slight pressure told him that the wounded man was indeed still living and had recognized him.

Hesitating no longer, after casting an uneasy glance around he rose to his feet, and passing his left arm around Eduardo's waist he lifted him to his shoulder and took the road to the neighboring barranca, on which the English Minister's house was situated.

The firmness and security of his step showed that the path he trod was familiar ground.

"Ah!" he cried suddenly, "it's hardly a couple of hundred yards more, but I must stop to rest, for—" And feeling Eduardo's body slipping in the blood which covered them both, from between his arms to the ground, "Eduardo!" he cried, putting his lips close to the latter's ear, "Eduardo! it is I! Daniel, your friend, your companion, your brother, Daniel!"

JOSÉ MÁRMOL

The wounded man slowly moved his head and half opened his eyes. Revived by the cool night breeze, the faintness caused by loss of blood, which had come over him, was beginning to pass away.

"Fly—. Save yourself, Daniel!" were the first words he uttered.

"Don't think of me, Eduardo," answered Daniel. "Think of—there—pass your left arm around my neck; now, lean all your weight—But what the devil is this? Have you been fighting with your left hand that you still hold your sword grasped in it? Ah, my poor friend! those miscreants must have disabled your right hand. And to think that I was not with you!" And as he spoke thus, wishing to draw from Eduardo's lips some word in response which would enlighten him in regard to the wounded man's real condition, although he dreaded the knowledge, Daniel again lifted Eduardo in his arms and continued on his way.

After they had proceeded a short distance the wounded man, revived by the motion and the breeze, said in affectionate tones:

"Enough, Daniel; with the support of your arm I think I can walk a little now."

"That will not be necessary," answered the other, putting him gently on his feet; "we have reached our destination."

Eduardo remained standing for a moment; but the wound in his thigh reached almost to the bone, and the excruciating pain which he felt in this position made his knees bend under him.

"I imagined you would not be able to remain long upon your feet," said Daniel, with feigned naturalness, for the blood froze in his veins at the thought that Eduardo's wounds might be mortal. "But fortunately," he continued, "we are now in a place where I can leave you in safety, while I go in search of a means of taking you somewhere else."

So saying, he lifted his friend once more in his arms and descended with him to the bottom of a trench, four or five feet in depth, which had been opened a few days before, some twenty feet distant from the side wall of a house situated on the barranca which Daniel had just climbed with his heavy but precious burden—a house which was none other than that of the British Minister, Sir John Henry Mandeville.

Placing his friend in a reclining position at the bottom of the trench Daniel asked him where he was wounded.

"I don't know, but I feel excruciating pains here and here," replied Eduardo, taking Daniel's hand and placing it first on his right shoulder and then on his left thigh.

Daniel once more breathed freely.

"If you are wounded only there it is nothing, my dear Eduardo," he said, pressing him in his arms with the effusiveness of one who has just been relieved from a painful uncertainty; but at the pressure of his arms Eduardo uttered a sharp cry of pain.

"I must be wounded—yes—I am wounded here," he said, placing Daniel's hand on his left side—"but the worst is the thigh; the wound in the thigh pains me horribly."

"Wait a moment," said Daniel, taking from his pocket a handkerchief and proceeding to bind the wounded limb tightly with it. "This will at least stop the bleeding in some degree," he continued. "And now let us see to the side. Is it here you feel the wound?"

"Yes."

"Then—my neckcloth will do for that," and taking off his neckcloth he bound his friend's chest tightly with it.

All this he said and did feigning a confidence which had begun to desert him as soon as he learned that Eduardo had received a wound in the breast, which possibly extended to some vital organ. And as if in mockery of the tragically romantic situation of the two young men, the strains of a piano at this moment reached their ears—Sir John Henry Mandeville was on this night entertaining a small party of friends.

"Ah!" said Daniel, as he finished binding his friend's wound, "his Excellency, the British Minister, is diverting himself."

Eduardo was about to say something in reply when suddenly Daniel placed his hand upon the young man's lips.

"I think I hear a noise," he said, feeling for his sword.

Nor was he mistaken. The noise of horses' hoofs could now be plainly heard and a moment later the sound of voices, conversing, reached the ears of the two friends.

The sounds grew momently louder; and soon the words of the speakers were clearly distinguishable.

"See," said one of them, when they were within ten or twelve paces of the trench, "let us light a cigar and count the money by its light here; for I have no desire to go to the Boca; I want to be getting home."

"Let us dismount, then," answered the other; and the two men dismounted from their horses, the brass scabbards of their swords clanking, as their feet touched the ground.

Leading their animals by the bridle, they walked to the trench and seated themselves close to the edge of it, a few paces distant from Daniel and Eduardo.

JOSÉ MÁRMOL

One of the men, taking his smoking outfit from his pocket, struck fire, lighted a cigar, and then said to his companion:

"Here, give me the bills, one by one."

The other, taking off his hat, drew from it a roll of bank-notes, one of which he handed to his companion who, holding it close to the lighted end of the cigar which he held between his lips, puffed vigorously, illuminating the note with the light thus obtained.

"100!" said the other, who had placed his face close to his companion's, in order to see the figures on the note for himself.

"100!" repeated the man with the cigar, sending a cloud of smoke from between his lips.

And the same operation that he had performed with this note was performed with thirty others of the same denomination. After each of the men had taken as his share 1500 dollars, one half of the 3000 dollars to which the notes amounted, the man with the cigar said:

"I thought it would be more! If we had dispatched the other we'd have had the bag of ounces."

"Well, for my part, I am not going to look for him."

"Look for him? No, indeed! As for me, I am going to the Boca," responded the man who had carried the notes in his hat, rising and tranquilly mounting his horse, while his companion remained seated on the ground.

"All right," replied the latter; "I will stay here and finish my cigar. Tomorrow I will call for you at daybreak, so that we can go together to the barracks."

"Till tomorrow, then," replied the other; and turning his horse's head, he set off at a trot for the Boca.

A few moments later the man who had remained behind put his hand into his pocket and drew from it an object which he examined by the light of the cigar in his mouth.

"And the watch is gold!" he said. "No one saw me take this, and the money I get for it I'll divide with no one."

And he again examined the watch closely by the light of his cigar.

"And it is going, too!" he continued, putting it to his ear; "but I don't know how to tell the time by it—" and he illuminated his treasure again—"it takes the Unitarians* to do that; but what I do know is that it must be after twelve o'clock, and that—"

---

* See introductory note.—*Trans.*

"This is your last hour, scoundrel!" cried Daniel, giving the ruffian a blow on the head with the same instrument with which he had struck the head of the man who had been about to cut Eduardo's throat; an instrument which seemed as fatal in its effect as a ball fired from a cannon, each of the men struck by it having fallen lifeless to the ground without uttering a single sound.

Daniel, who had ascended from the trench and had approached the ruffian as silently as a shadow, now took the dead man's horse by the bridle and led it to the edge of the trench, into which he descended again, still holding the bridle; and embracing his friend he said:

"Courage, courage, Eduardo; now you are free—safe. Providence has sent us a horse, which was the one thing we needed."

"Yes, I feel a little better, but you will have to help me still. I cannot stand."

"Don't tax your strength," said Daniel, taking Eduardo once more in his arms and lifting him up to the edge of the trench. After which, vaulting up himself, by an incredible effort of strength he succeeded in placing Eduardo on the back of the horse, which had been made restless by the proceedings at its side. Then taking his friend's sword in his hand he seated himself at a bound on the crupper of the horse, clasped his arm around Eduardo's waist, and taking the reins from his nerveless grasp directed the horse up the barranca.

"We must not go to my house, Daniel," said Eduardo. "We should find it closed. I gave my servant orders not to sleep there tonight."

"No, of course not; I had no idea of parading you at this hour through the Calle del Cabildo, where there would be twenty watchmen to throw the light of their lanterns on our persons, clad in the bloody livery of the Federals."

"But we must not go to your house either."

"Still less, Eduardo. I don't think I have ever shown any signs of insanity, and to take you to my house now would be nothing less than the act of a madman."

"Then where shall we go?"

"That is my secret for the present. But ask me no more questions. Talk as little as possible."

While he was speaking, Daniel felt Eduardo's head sink heavily on his breast. A second attack of vertigo had clouded the young man's vision and had made him feel faint; but happily the faintness soon passed away.

JOSÉ MÁRMOL

Daniel now slackened his horse's pace to a walk. When he reached the Calle de la Reconquista, he turned into the road leading to Barracas; crossed the Calle del Brasil and, turning to the right, entered a narrow, unpaved street, without a single house, but bordered on either side by the brick walls and the nopals at the rear of the houses with which the city terminates on the barrancas of Barracas.

Arriving at the street leading from the Boca to Barracas he turned again to the right and keeping close to the edge of the road at last reached the Calle Larga of Barracas without having encountered a single individual on the way. Taking the right side of the street and keeping as close to the houses as possible he put his horse to a trot, for he was anxious to get quickly out of this street, which was visited at night by several police patrols.

After riding for a few minutes longer he halted, looked around, and having satisfied himself that there was no one within sight or hearing, he again slackened his horse's pace to a walk, saying to Eduardo:

"You are now secure from pursuit and you will soon be in a place of safety, where your wounds can be attended to."

"Where?" asked Eduardo in a faint voice.

"Here," answered Daniel, guiding his horse up a pathway leading to a house through whose latticed windows, shaded by thick white muslin curtains, they could perceive the lights within. As he spoke he rode up to one of the windows of the house, and putting his hand between the bars and through the lattice, he tapped gently on the glass. No one responded, however. He knocked a second time when a woman's voice asked in suspicious tones:

"Who is there?"

"I, Amalia. I, your cousin."

"Daniel!" cried the same voice, the person within drawing nearer to the window.

"Yes, Daniel."

On the instant the window was opened, the blind was raised and a young woman dressed in black leaned forward and rested her hand against the grating. But on seeing two men seated on one horse, she drew back, as if in surprise.

"Don't you know me, Amalia? Listen to me; open the street door at once; but do not waken any of the servants; open it yourself."

"But what is the matter, Daniel?"

"Don't lose an instant, Amalia; open the door at once while there is no one near to observe us. My life is in question—more than my life.— Do you understand now?"

"My God!" exclaimed the young woman; and, hastily closing the window, she hurried from the room, went to the street door, which she threw wide open, and going out to the path said to Daniel: "Come in!" with that sublime spontaneity of which only the tender and generous soul of a woman is capable when she is performing some deed of heroism, that is with her always the result, not of reflection, but of inspiration.

"Not yet," returned Daniel, who had by this time dismounted with Eduardo, whom he was supporting by the waist. And thus supporting him and leading the horse by the bridle, he gained the door.

"Take my place, Amalia," he then said; "and support this man, who is unable to walk alone."

Amalia, without a moment's hesitation, took the arm of Eduardo, who, leaning against the jamb of the door, was making desperate efforts to move his left leg, which seemed to him of enormous weight. "Thanks, señorita, thanks!" he said, in a voice full of grateful emotion.

"Are you, wounded?" she asked.

"Slightly."

"My God!" cried Amalia, who felt her hands wet with blood.

While they were exchanging these words, Daniel led the horse to the middle of the road, and turning his head in the direction of the bridge and throwing the reins over his neck, he gave the animal a vigorous blow on the haunch with the flat of Eduardo's sword, which he still held in his hand. The horse did not wait for a second signal but started off at a gallop in the direction indicated.

"Now let us go in," said Daniel, returning to the house; and, putting his arms around Eduardo's waist, he lifted him into the hall and closed the street door. In the same manner he carried into the salon, and laid on a sofa this man to whose rescue he had so providentially come on this bloody night; this man whose soul was still resolute and courageous, but whose body could not support itself alone for a single second.

JOSÉ MÁRMOL

II

The First Dressing

When Daniel had laid Eduardo on the sofa, Amalia hurried to a small room adjoining the salon and separated from it by a glazed partition, took from a black marble table a small alabaster lamp by whose light she had been reading when Daniel knocked at the window, and returning to the salon set down the lamp on a round mahogany table on which were some books and a vase of flowers.

At this moment Amalia was excessively pale, owing to the sudden shock which she had just received. She had pushed back her light chestnut curls behind her ears a few moments before and Eduardo now saw revealed in all its loveliness the enchanting countenance of a woman of twenty, with a beautiful and noble forehead and expressive gray eyes, whose black dress, defining closely the contours of an admirably moulded figure, might have seemed chosen to set off to advantage the dazzling whiteness of her neck and shoulders if the material of which it was made had not shown it to be the garb of mourning.

Daniel approached the table as Amalia placed the lamp upon it, and taking his cousin's hands in his he said:

"You have often heard me speak, Amalia, of a young man to whom I am bound by the ties of a close and fraternal friendship; that young man, Eduardo, is the man you have just admitted to your house, the man who lies there dangerously wounded. But his wounds are *official,* they are the work of Rosas, and he must be kept in concealment until they are cured; he must be saved."

"But what am I to do, Daniel?" asked Amalia, in a voice full of emotion, turning her eyes toward the sofa on which lay Eduardo, the pallor of whose countenance, contrasting with the jet-like blackness of his eyes and of his hair and beard, seemed like that of death.

"What you are to do, Amalia, is one thing only. Do you doubt that I have always loved you as a sister?"

"Oh, no, Daniel; I have never doubted that."

"Well, then," said the young man, pressing his lips to his cousin's brow, "what you are to do is to obey me in everything for this one night; tomorrow you shall again command your house and me, as always."

"Act freely, give your orders. And in truth I am at this moment incapable of a single thought," said Amalia, whose naturally rosy color was now beginning to return.

"My first order is that you shall go yourself, without wakening any of the servants, and bring me a glass of sweetened wine."

Amalia, without waiting to hear the end of the sentence, hurried away to the interior of the house.

Daniel then approached Eduardo, who was beginning to recover from the faintness caused by pain and fatigue, and said to him:

"That is my cousin, the beautiful young widow of whom I have so often spoken to you, who has been living alone in this village, since her return from Tucuman, four months ago."

"But this is a cruel proceeding," said Eduardo. "I shall compromise the safety of that young creature."

"Her safety?"

"Yes, her safety. The chief of police of Rosas has as many agents in Buenos Ayres as there are men in it sick with fear. Men and women, masters and servants, all endeavor to secure their own safety by denouncing others. Tomorrow Rosas will know where I am and that young girl's fate will be involved in mine."

"That remains to be seen," answered Daniel, smoothing Eduardo's disordered hair. "I am in my element when I am surrounded by difficulties. And if, instead of writing to me to inform me of your intended flight, you had only told me of it this afternoon, a hundred to one you would not now have a scratch upon your person."

"But how did you know at what point on the coast I was going to take the boat?"

"I will tell you that later," answered Daniel, smiling.

At this moment Amalia reëntered the room, carrying a glass of sweetened Bordeaux on a china plate.

"You must drink this, Eduardo," said Daniel, taking the glass from the plate; "a little wine will help to sustain your strength, until the doctor comes." And while he supported his friend's head and held the wine to his lips, Amalia had leisure for the first time to look at Eduardo, the pallor of whose countenance, added to the expression of suffering which it wore, gave him an indescribably pathetic and, at the same time, virile and noble air; and also to observe that both Eduardo and Daniel presented a spectacle such as her imagination had never conceived, covered as they were from head to foot with clay and blood.

"And now tell me," said Daniel, taking the plate from Amalia's hands, "is old Pedro in the house?"

"Yes."

"Go and waken him, then, and tell him to come here—or stay; let us do several things at once in order to save time. Where can I find writing materials?"

"There in the library," answered Amalia, pointing to the door of the adjoining room.

"Now, then, go and waken Pedro," said Daniel, and entering the library he took a light from a corner stand, passed into the next room, which was his cousin's bedroom, and thence into a small and elegant dressing-room where, going to the toilet-table, he poured some water into a basin, and proceeded to wash his hands, spattering as he did so the china and glass with the blood and clay which covered them.

He then returned to the library, seated himself at a small writing table and, with an expression of gravity on his countenance that seemed foreign to the young man's nature, he wrote two letters, folded them, placed them in their respective envelopes, and then went back to the salon, where Eduardo was answering an anxious inquiry of Amalia as to how he felt. At this moment the door of the salon opened, and a man of about sixty, tall and still vigorous, with perfectly white hair and a mustache and beard of the same color, dressed in a jacket and trousers of blue cloth, entered the room, holding his hat in his hand and with a respectful air, which changed to one of surprise on seeing Daniel standing in the middle of the apartment and a man covered with blood lying on the sofa.

"I think, Pedro," said Daniel, "that you are not the man to be frightened at the sight of blood. What you see means nothing more than that a friend of mine has just been attacked and seriously wounded by some ruffians. Come here. How long did you serve under my uncle, Colonel Saenz, Amalia's father?"

"Fourteen years, señor, from the time of the battle of Salta to that of Junin, in which the Colonel fell dead into my arms."

"For which of the generals under whom you served had you most affection and respect—Belgrano, San Martin, or Bolivar?"

"General Belgrano, señor;" answered the old soldier, without a moment's hesitation.

"Well, Pedro, here you see in Amalia and in me a daughter and a nephew of your colonel, and there you see a nephew of General Belgrano, who at this moment stands in need of your services."

"Señor, I can give nothing more than my life, and that is always at the disposal of those in whose veins flows the blood of my general or my colonel."

"I believe it, Pedro; but here we have need, not of courage only, but of prudence, also, and, more than all, of discretion."

"Very well, señor."

"That is all, Pedro. I know that you have an honest heart, that you are brave; and above all, that you are a patriot."

"Yes, señor, an old patriot," said the soldier, lifting up his head proudly.

"Very well; go now," continued Daniel, "and without wakening any of the servants saddle one of the carriage horses, take it to the door with as little noise as possible, arm yourself, and return here."

The veteran saluted as if he were in the presence of his general, and left the room to carry out the orders he had received.

Five minutes later the sound of a horse's hoofs was heard outside, followed by the noise of the door turning on its hinges; and a moment afterward the veteran soldier, enveloped in his poncho, reappeared in the salon.

"Do you know where Dr. Alcorta's house is, Pedro?"

"Back of San Juan?"

"Yes."

"I do, señor."

"Go there, then; knock at the door and give this letter to the person who opens it, saying that while the doctor is dressing you will go and attend to some necessary business outside and will return for him. Then go to my house, knock softly at the door, which my servant, who will be up waiting for me, will open at once, and give him this letter."

"Very well, señor."

"One thing more. It is now a quarter to one," continued Daniel, glancing at a clock that stood on the mantel piece; "you can be back here with Dr. Alcorta by half past one."

The soldier saluted as before, and left the room. A few moments later they could hear the rapid galloping of a horse, whose hoofs striking against the pavement awoke the echoes of the solitary Calle Larga.

Daniel motioned to his cousin to retire to the adjoining room, and after recommending Eduardo to keep as quiet as possible until the doctor should arrive he said to him:

"You know the choice I have made, and indeed whom could I have sent for who would inspire us with greater confidence?"

"But, good heavens! to compromise Dr. Alcorta in this way!"

"You are sublime tonight, my dear Eduardo. Listen to me. You, I, every one of our friends, every man of the generation to which we belong and who has been educated in the University of Buenos Ayres is a living, breathing, eloquent compromise of Dr. Alcorta. We are his ideas in action; we are the multiplied reproduction of his patriotic virtue; of his humanitarian conscience; of his philosophic thought. From his professor's chair he has kindled in our hearts an enthusiasm for all that is great—for goodness, for liberty, for justice. Our friends who have gone to join Lavalle, who have thrown down the white glove to take up the sword, are Dr. Alcorta. Frias is Dr. Alcorta in the army, Alberdi, Gutierrez, Irigoyen are Dr. Alcorta in the press of Montevideo. You yourself, lying there bathed in your blood, who have just risked your life to fly from your country rather than submit in it to the tyranny that oppresses it, are nothing else, Eduardo, than the personification of the ideas of our professor of philosophy, and—But, bah! what nonsense I am talking! There! there! Let us drop the subject. Rest for a moment while I go and say a few words to Amalia."

So saying he went into the library, where he found Amalia standing in a thoughtful attitude beside the marble table on which her white hand rested. Leading her to a seat on the sofa and sitting down on it beside her he said:

"Tell me, Amalia, in which of the servants have you entire confidence?"

"Pedro, Teresa, a maid whom I brought with me from Tucuman, and little Luisa."

"And who are the others?"

"The coachman, the cook and two old negroes who take care of the villa."

"The coachman and the cook are white men?"

"Yes."

"Then you must dismiss them all in the morning, as soon as they are up—the black because they are black, the white because they are white."

"But do you believe—"

"If I do not believe, I suspect. Listen, Amalia; your servants are no doubt greatly attached to you, for you are kind, rich and generous. But in the state in which our country is, an order, a harsh word, an angry look converts a servant into a powerful and deadly enemy. The door has been opened to denunciations, and on the sole authority of some wretch the fortunes and the lives of an entire family are placed under the ban of the Mashorca. In the lower classes the mulattoes only are to be trusted. The negroes have grown arrogant; the white basely mercenary; but the mulattoes, from the tendency which every mixed race has to elevate and ennoble itself, are almost all hostile to Rosas, because they know that the Unitarians are the educated and cultured class, whom they always take as their model."

"Very well; I will discharge them all tomorrow."

"Eduardo's security, mine, your own, demand that you should do so. You cannot repent of the hospitality you have given to an unfortunate man, and yet—"

"Oh, no, Daniel, do not speak of that! My house, my fortune, all that I have are at your disposal and your friend's."

"You cannot repent of it, as I said, but at the same time you must take every means possible to prevent your goodness, your self-abnegation, from furnishing our oppressors with weapons to use against you. For the sacrifice you make in discharging your servants, indeed, you will soon be able to indemnify yourself. Besides, Eduardo will remain in your house for as long only as the doctor may think absolutely necessary. He will leave it in two or three days at furthest."

"So soon! Oh, impossible! His wounds may be serious, and to let him rise from bed so soon might cause his death. I am independent; I lead a solitary life, because my nature inclines me to solitude; the few women friends I have visit me very rarely; and in the left wing of the house we can arrange comfortable rooms for Eduardo which will be entirely separate from mine."

"Thanks, thanks, my Amalia! But it is possible that it may not be expedient for Eduardo to remain here. It will depend on many things which I shall know tomorrow. Now we must go and get the bed ready which he is to occupy after his wounds have been dressed."

"Yes—come this way;" and Amalia, taking a light, preceded Daniel into her bedroom and thence into her dressing-room. Opening a door in this room she entered through it another room, which was that of her little maid Luisa, who was asleep in bed, and taking a key from a table she opened a door leading into the courtyard which she crossed with as little noise as possible, and unlocking a door in a corridor running at right angles with the corridor into which Luisa's room opened and still holding the light in her hand and followed by Daniel, entered another bedroom.

"This room has been occupied by a relation of my husband's from

Tucuman, who returned home three days ago. It is provided with everything that Eduardo may require." And so saying Amalia opened a wardrobe and taking from it some bed-clothes she herself made the bed and arranged the room, while Daniel occupied himself in examining carefully the adjoining room and the dining-room beyond it, which opened into the hall through which, an hour before, Daniel had entered the salon, carrying Eduardo in his arms.

"What does this window look out upon?" he said to his cousin, pointing to a window in the room which Eduardo was to occupy.

"On the corridor facing the street. You know that the inner part of this house is completely separated from the servants' quarters by an iron railing, and when the door of this railing is locked the servants can go in and out of the house by the street door without passing through the inner rooms. It was by that door that Pedro left the house."

"True; I remember; but—do you not hear a noise?"

"Yes."

"It is—"

"It is the sound of horses' hoofs," and Amalia's heart began to beat violently. "My God! who can it be?"

"It is Alcorta and Pedro," said Daniel, who had been holding his face pressed close to the window pane. "They have stopped at the street door. Oh, the good, the noble, the generous Alcorta!"

It was, in fact, the veteran of the War of Independence, accompanied by Dr. Alcorta, a man of about thirty-eight years of age, who was at the same time a learned professor of philosophy and a skillful surgeon and physician.

Pedro admitted the doctor through the street door, led the horses to the stable, and then opened the door of the iron railing, of which he had the key.

"Thanks, señor," said Daniel, who had gone out to the courtyard to meet Dr. Alcorta, pressing the latter's hand warmly.

"Let us go see Belgrano, my friend," said Alcorta, hastening to cut short Daniel's expressions of gratitude.

"In a moment," said the latter, leading him to the room in which he had left Amalia, while Pedro followed, carrying a wooden box under his arm. "Have you brought everything that you will need for the first dressing, señor, as I requested you to do in my letter?"

"Yes, I think so," answered Alcorta, bowing to Amalia; "with the exception of the bandages."

Daniel glanced at Amalia and the latter left the room quickly.

"This is the apartment which Eduardo is to occupy. Do you think we should bring him here for the examination?"

"That will be necessary," answered Alcorta, taking the box of instruments from Pedro's hands and placing it on a table.

"Pedro," said Daniel, "wait outside in the courtyard; or rather, go and show Amalia how to cut bandages; you ought to be an expert at that. Now, señor, I must tell you what I did not say in my letter—Eduardo's wounds are official."

A sorrowful smile crossed the pale, noble and melancholy countenance of Dr. Alcorta.

"Do you suppose that I did not know that already?" he said. "Let us go see Belgrano, Daniel," he repeated after a moment's silence.

And crossing the courtyard together they entered the salon through the door leading into it from the hall.

At this moment Eduardo was apparently asleep, although it was not sleep, properly speaking, but rather the stupor of exhaustion that weighed down his eyelids.

At the noise made by the opening of the door the young man turned his head with a painful effort; and seeing Alcorta standing beside the sofa, he attempted to sit up.

"Lie still, Belgrano," said Alcorta, in affectionate and sympathetic accents; "here there is no one but the physician." And seating himself on the edge of the sofa he proceeded to feel Eduardo's pulse.

"Good!" he said at last; "we will take him now to his room."

At this moment Amalia and Pedro entered the salon through the library.

The young woman had in her hands a number of linen bandages which she had just cut according to the veteran's instructions.

Alcorta and Daniel now placed Eduardo in an armchair and with Pedro's assistance carried him to the room assigned him.

Leaving Amalia engaged in endeavoring to reduce to order the confusion of her thoughts and sensations we will accompany the doctor and Daniel to Eduardo's room.

After the latter had been undressed with a great deal of difficulty, for the blood had caused the clothes to adhere to his body, Alcorta proceeded to examine his wounds.

"This is of no consequence," he said, after sounding the wound on the left side; "the sword grazed the ribs without penetrating the breast. This other is not serious either," he continued, after examining the wound on the right shoulder; "the weapon was sharp and did not mangle the flesh. Now let us see the thigh." But at the first glance which he gave this wound, which was at least ten inches in length, an expression of dissatisfaction stamped itself upon Dr. Alcorta's eloquent countenance. For fully five minutes he examined with the greatest minuteness the severed muscles in the wound, which ran lengthwise on the thigh.

"It is a terrible gash!" he said at last, "but not a single blood vessel of importance has been severed; the flesh, however, has been greatly lacerated." And he at once proceeded himself to wash the wounds; after which he dressed them by making use neither of the simple cerate nor the lint which he had brought in his box of instruments, but only of the bandages.

At this moment the sound of a horse's hoofs stopping outside the street door was heard, arresting the attention of everyone, with the exception of Alcorta, who went on bandaging Eduardo's shoulder apparently undisturbed.

"Did you give the letter to my servant himself?" asked Daniel turning to Pedro.

"Yes, señor, to himself."

"Go see who is outside, then. It must be he."

A moment later Pedro returned, accompanied by a young man of eighteen or twenty, with a fair complexion, black hair and eyes, and an intelligent and expressive countenance, and who, notwithstanding his boots and his black necktie, was manifestly a legitimate child of the plains—a true gaucho.

"Have you brought everything, Fermin?" Daniel asked him.

"You will find everything here, señor," answered the young man, placing a large bundle of clothing on a chair.

Daniel hastened to take from the bundle the linen required by Eduardo and to put it on him, for Dr. Alcorta had now finished the first dressing. This done, the doctor and Daniel lifted up the wounded man between them, and laid him gently on the bed.

Daniel then went into the adjoining room, accompanied by Pedro and Fermin, and proceeded to wash himself and to change his clothes from head to foot, for those which Fermin had just brought him, without ceasing for an instant, as he did so, to give instructions to Pedro, regarding the other servants, removing the traces of blood from the salon, burning the blood-stained clothing, etc.

Eduardo meanwhile informed Alcorta in a few words of the events that had taken place three hours before, and Alcorta, with his head leaning on his hand and his elbow resting on the pillow listened to the horrible details of the occurrence in which he foresaw the beginning of an epoch of blood and crime that was to bring mourning and terror to unhappy Buenos Ayres.

"Do you think this Merlo knows who you are?" he asked Eduardo.

"I do not remember whether any of my companions addressed me by my name before him or not. But unless they did, he cannot know it, for Oliden was the only one who held any communication with him."

"That makes me a little uneasy," said Daniel, who had heard the end of Eduardo's narration; "but we shall know all tomorrow."

"Meantime, it is necessary that Belgrano should take some rest," said the doctor. "I will return at noon," he added, passing his hand over Eduardo's forehead, as a father might have done with a son, and pressing his left hand in his as he did so.

Then he went out into the courtyard, accompanied by Daniel.

"Do you think, Doctor, that Eduardo's life is in any danger?" asked the latter.

"Absolutely none; but his recovery may be slow."

Exchanging these words, they reached the salon, where Alcorta had left his hat and where Amalia was awaiting them.

Leaving the doctor to give Amalia the necessary instructions with regard to the patient Daniel hurried back to the apartment of the latter to bid him good-bye.

"I must leave you now, Eduardo," he said; "I am going to the city with Dr. Alcorta. Pedro will remain here with you, in case you should require anything. I shall not be able to return before tomorrow night, but I will send my servant to inquire for you. Will you allow me to give yours whatever instructions I may think necessary?"

"Do all that you wish, Daniel, provided you do not involve others in my evil fortune."

"Are we going back to that? Let me do as I think best, Eduardo. Have you any special instructions to give me?"

"None. Have you made your cousin go to bed?"

"There! Now you are beginning to distress yourself about my cousin."

"Foolish boy!" said Eduardo, smiling. "Go home and take care of yourself for my sake."

"Until tomorrow, then."

"Until tomorrow!"

And the two friends embraced each other, like two brothers.

Daniel, motioning to Pedro and Fermin who had remained in a corner of the apartment, went out into the courtyard, followed by them.

"Fermin, take this box of the doctor's and get the horses ready. Pedro, I leave Eduardo in my cousin's care, and to you I leave it to defend his life, if it should be necessary. It is possible that Eduardo's assailants are members of the Sociedad Popular, and it is possible also that some of them may wish to avenge the death of the men slain by him, if by an evil chance they should discover his place of concealment."

"That may all be so, señor, but no one shall enter the house of my colonel's daughter to assassinate anyone without first killing old Pedro, and to do that he will have to fight a little."

"Bravo! That is the sort of man I like," said Daniel, shaking the old soldier's hand. "With a hundred like you I would answer for everything. Until tomorrow, then. Fasten the gate and the street door after we go out. Until tomorrow."

"Until tomorrow, señor."

Alcorta was standing taking leave of Amalia when Daniel returned to the salon.

"Are we going now, Doctor?" he asked.

"I am going; but you ought to remain, Daniel."

"I cannot remain, Doctor; I am obliged to return to the city, and I will avail myself of the opportunity to go with you, if you will permit me."

"Very well, let us go, then;" responded Alcorta.

"A moment, Doctor.—Amalia, everything is settled. Fermin will come tomorrow at noon to inquire after Eduardo, and I will be here at seven in the evening. Now go to bed. Early in the morning do as I have advised you and fear nothing."

"Oh, I am afraid of nothing except on your account and on your friend's," answered Amalia with spirit.

"I believe it, but nothing will happen."

"Oh, Señor Daniel Bello has a great deal of influence!" said Alcorta with good-humored irony, fixing his soft and expressive eyes on his pupil's countenance, on which shone the light of imagination and genius.

"Protégé of Messrs. Anchorena, Counsellor of His Excellency the Minister Don Felipe, and Corresponding Member of the Sociedad

Popular Restauradora!" added Daniel, with such well-feigned gravity that neither Amalia nor Dr. Alcorta could help laughing.

"You may laugh," continued Daniel, "but I will not laugh; for I know how greatly those titles serve me to—"

"Come Daniel, let us be going," interrupted Alcorta.

"I am ready, Doctor. Till tomorrow, Amalia," and he pressed a kiss on the hand which his cousin extended to him.

"Good-night, Doctor," said Amalia, accompanying the two men to the hall.

At the door of the villa Dr. Alcorta and Daniel found Fermin waiting for them with the horses.

Mounting in silence, master, pupil and servant rode at a quick pace up the dark and deserted Calle Larga and, entering the city by the Barranca de Balcarce, drew rein only when they reached Dr. Alcorta's house in the Calle del Restaurador.

There master and pupil took leave of each other, after exchanging a few whispered words; and Daniel, followed by Fermin, crossed the market place, emerging at the Calle de la Victoria, and then turned to the left. After riding a short distance Fermin, alighting from his horse, opened a gate leading into the courtyard of a house, which Daniel entered without dismounting. The house was his house.

III

The Letters

In the courtyard of the house Daniel gave his horse to Fermin, telling him not to go to bed but to wait up for further orders.

Then, raising the latch of a door opening on the courtyard, he entered a large room lighted by a bronze lamp. Taking the lamp in his hand, he passed into an adjoining room whose walls were almost entirely lined with shelves filled with books; these rooms were the bedroom and study of Daniel Bello.

This young man of twenty-five, of medium height, with a well-proportioned figure, warm dark skin, chestnut hair and gray eyes; a broad forehead; a slightly aquiline nose, lips somewhat full, and white and regular teeth, was the only son of Don Antonio Bello, a rich planter of the South, associated in business with the Messrs. Anchorena who, owing to their immense fortune and their family and political relations with Rosas, enjoyed at this period high consideration in the Federal party.

Don Antonio Bello, although himself a good Federal, had a profounder affection than that which he entertained for the Federation—his love for his son. His son was his pride, his idol, whom from a boy he had trained for the profession of letters—to be a doctor,* as the good man expressed it.

At the period at which he is introduced to the reader Daniel was in the second year of his course of jurisprudence. But for reasons which will appear later he had some months before ceased to attend the University.

He lived entirely alone in his house, except on the rare occasions when, as was the case at present, he had guests from the country, friends of his father.

Placing the lamp on a writing-table, he sank into an easy chair, and throwing back his head remained absorbed in thought for fully fifteen minutes.

"Yes," he said, suddenly, rising to his feet and pushing back his straight hair from his forehead, "there is nothing else to do; in this way I shall block up every avenue to them!"

---

* A title given in South America to lawyers and professional men in general, as well as to physicians.—*Translator's note.*

And without haste, but apparently without the slightest doubt or hesitation, he seated himself at his desk, and wrote the following letters, each of which he read over carefully after he had finished it.

> May 5, at half-past two in the morning
>
> Today I have need of your tact, my Florencia, as I always have need of your love, your caprices, your anger and your forgiveness, to be supremely happy. You have sometimes told me, in your more serious moments, that I have educated your heart and your head; let us see now how my pupil has turned out.
>
> "I desire to know what they say at Doña Agustina Rosas' and at Doña Maria Josefa Ezcurra's about an event which took place last night at the Bajo de la Residencia; what names are mixed up in it; the particulars of it; everything, in short, relating to this event.
>
> "At two in the afternoon I will be at your house, where I hope to find you already returned from your diplomatic mission.
>
> "Be on your guard with Doña Maria Josefa; above all, do not betray before her the slightest interest in knowing that which you desire to learn, and which you must make her reveal to you herself; in that will consist your tact.
>
> "You will have already comprehended, soul of my soul, that this matter is of very serious moment to me, and your displeasure last night, your girlish caprices, should have no part in what concerns the fate of
>
> DANIEL

"My poor Florencia!" cried the young man when he had read over this letter. "Ah, but she is as bright as the day, and no one can penetrate her thoughts when she wishes to conceal them! Now for the next letter," he continued; "but for this one it will be necessary to put the clock forward a few hours." And he wrote as follows:

> May 5, 1840, at nine in the morning
>
> Señor Don Felipe Arana, etc., etc.
>
> My distinguished friend and señor
>
> "While you pass sleepless nights and brave with the courage and determination which characterize you the dangers that threaten the government on all sides, owing

to the opposition and the intrigues of its enemies, certain functionaries, who, although your subordinates yet wage secret war against you, neglect the fulfillment of their duties.

"The police, for instance, are more anxious to show their independence of you than vigilant in what should alone concern them.

"You are aware that last week more than forty persons left the country without the slightest interference from the police, notwithstanding the abundant resources at their command; and that his Excellency the Restorer learned of the fact through you, to whom I had the honor of communicating it. But it was enough that you should have communicated it to his Excellency for Señor Victorica to refrain from taking any step in the matter.

"Last night at about half-past ten as I was returning from the Boca to the city by the Camino del Bajo, I observed, near Señor Mandeville's house, a party of men who from their proximity to the river I believe to have had the intention of leaving the country, an intention which they no doubt carried into effect. And this is the time for you to take your revenge on Señor Victorica, communicating this fact to his Excellency, who, I almost venture to affirm, if he knows of the occurrence, does not know the names of the fugitives, which he would be in possession of by this time if the police imitated you in your activity and zeal.

"I shall have the honor of speaking to you in person on the subject this afternoon, when I trust that the high opinion which I entertain of your ability and your energy will be confirmed by finding that you have already ascertained without the assistance of the police, all that occurred last night, including details and names, if, as I believe, I am not mistaken in my supposition.

"Meantime, receive the respectful salutations of your faithful and obedient servant,

DANIEL BELLO

"Ah, my good Don Felipe!" cried Daniel, laughing like a boy, when he had read over this letter, "who could ever have imagined that even in jest anyone would extol your energy and ability! But there is no one in the world who is entirely useless and you will be of great service to me one of these days. Now for the next."

May 5, 1840

Señor Colonel Salomon:
Compatriot and friend

"No one knows better than I that the Federation has no stronger pillar than yourself and the heroic Restorer of the Laws no more faithful and determined friend. And it is for this reason that it vexes me to hear it said by certain persons whom I visit—and I think you can guess to whom I refer—that the Sociedad Popular, of which you are the worthy president, does not aid the police as efficiently as it should in watching the Unitarians, who fly the country every night to join the army of Lavalle.

"The Restorer must be greatly displeased by this; and I, as your friend, desire to advise you to call a meeting in your house this very day of the best Federals of the Society, as well that you may ascertain from them all that they may know with regard to the persons who have recently left the country, as for the purpose of taking measures to pursue and punish those who may attempt to leave the country in the future.

"For myself, it would give me great pleasure to be present at this meeting, and to prepare for you a Federal discourse to arouse the enthusiasm of the defenders of the Restorer, as I have done on other occasions, notwithstanding that you are very capable of acquitting yourself without assistance of your obligations, whenever our sacred cause of the Federation and the life of the Illustrious Restorer of the Laws are in question.

"If you should decide upon holding the Federal meeting, be pleased to answer me before twelve o'clock, and command your obedient servant who salutes you Federally,

Daniel Bello

"This man will do whatever I tell him to do," said Daniel to himself, in a tone of complete conviction. "This man and all the rest of his kind, would ruin Rosas without even suspecting it, if there were only three men like myself to lead them—one in the plains, another in the army, another near the person of Rosas, and I everywhere, like God—or like the devil. I have still another letter to write," he continued, opening a secret drawer in his desk and taking from it a paper filled with conventional signs which he consulted continually as he wrote with them the following:

Buenos Ayres, May 5, 1840

"Last night five of our friends were surprised as they were about to embark. Lynch, Riglos, Oliden and Maisson, have fallen victims—at least up to this moment I believe so; one escaped miraculously. If you should learn of this event through any other channel mention no other names than those I have written here."

And signing this letter with a special sign he wrote on the envelope:

"A. de G3—Montevideo."

Enclosing this in another envelope he placed it under his bronze inkstand and then pulled the bell-rope.

Fermin appeared on the instant.

"Things are going badly, Fermin," said Daniel, feigning a certain air of abstraction and indifference as he spoke. "The enrollment is general, and I shall have to use my influence again with General Pinedo to obtain your certificate of exemption—unless you wish to enter the service."

"And how should I wish to enter the service, señor!" said the young man, with the indolent intonation peculiar to the children of the plains.

"Especially," continued Daniel, "as the campaign is going to be a terrible one. It is probable that the army will have to march through the entire republic, and you are not accustomed to such hardships. You were born in my father's house and you have been brought up with every comfort. I think I have never given you any cause for discontent."

"Discontent, señor; no indeed!" said Fermin with tears in his eyes.

"I have made you my personal attendant, because I have complete confidence in you. You are the master of my servants, you spend as much money as you choose; and I think I have never found fault with you; is not that true?"

"That is true, señor."

"I never send for a horse for myself without asking my father for another for Fermin; and there are few men in Buenos Ayres who might not envy you the horses you ride. So that you would have a great deal to suffer if they took you from my side."

"I will not go into the service, señor. I would let myself be killed rather than leave you."

"And would you let yourself be killed in my service if it were necessary; if I should find myself at any time in danger?"

"Of course I would, señor!" answered Fermin, in the candid and sincere accents of a youth of twenty who has within him that consciousness of his valor which seems innate in those who have drawn their first breath of life in the Pampa.

"I believe it," said Daniel, "and if I had not penetrated into the recesses of your heart long before this, I should well deserve misfortune, for fools ought not to conspire." And with these last words, spoken as if to himself, Daniel took up the three letters which he had first written, and continued: "Very well, Fermin; they will not put you in the army. Now listen to what I am going to say to you: Tomorrow morning at nine o'clock you will take a bouquet of flowers to Florencia and when you are giving it to her you will give her this letter also. You will then go to the house of Señor Don Felipe Arana and leave this letter there. Then go to Colonel Salomon's and deliver this other letter. Be very careful to read the address on each letter before delivering it."

"Have no fear, señor."

"One thing more."

"What is it, señor?"

"On your way back you will pass by Marcelina's house."

"The woman that—"

"The same, yes; the woman that you warned, for certain reasons, not to enter my house in the daytime. You will tell her, notwithstanding, to come at once to see me."

"Very well."

"You will be back by ten and if I am not up then you will waken me yourself."

"Yes, señor."

"Before you go out give orders to waken me if anyone should desire to see me, no matter who it may be."

"Very well, señor."

"One word more and then you may go to bed. Do you not guess what that word is?"

"Yes, señor, I do," answered Fermin with a look of intelligence.

"I am very glad that you do; see that you keep it in mind. To deserve my confidence and my generosity, and to avoid the disagreeable consequences that any indiscretion on your part might entail upon you, you must either not speak at all, or else be more than cautious about what you say."

"Never fear, señor."

"Very well, you may go now."

And Daniel closed the door opening on the courtyard, at a quarter past three in the morning, to seek the rest which he so greatly needed after the superhuman exertions, mental and physical, which he had made on this eventful night.

IV

THE DINNER HOUR

While the events which we have related were passing, on the night of the 4th of May, others of no less importance were taking place in a well-known house in the Calle del Restaurador. But for their complete understanding it will be necessary to recall to the reader the political situation of the republic at the period of which we speak.

It was the critical moment in the dictatorship of General Rosas, when he was either to be utterly annihilated, or to rise up stronger and more despotic than ever, according as events should determine.

The dangers by which Rosas was menaced came from three sources—the civil war, the war in the East, and the French Question.

The insurrection that had broken out in the South, six months previous to the time at which our story opens, had placed Rosas unexpectedly in the greatest danger that had ever threatened his political existence. But the unfortunate issue of this spontaneous insurrection, without plan or direction, had only added, as happens in such cases, to the strength and the arrogance of the conqueror Rosas; of that favorite of fortune who owed his power and his success to the mistakes of his adversaries.

Two severe blows, however, had shaken the edifice of his power to its foundations—the defeat of his army in the Eastern State and the attack of General Lavalle on the Province of Entre-Rios.

By a decree passed on the 7th of April, 1840, the Chamber of Representatives of Tucuman had withdrawn from Rosas their recognition of him as Governor of Buenos Ayres and divested him of the powers which it had conferred upon him as Minister of Foreign Affairs.

On the 13th of April, the people of Salta had deposed Rosas from his office of Governor of the Province and elected another Governor provisionally in his stead, and withdrawn from him their recognition of him as Governor of Buenos Ayres.

La Rioja, Catamarca and Jujuy were about to pass decrees similar to those of Tucuman and Salta.

So that of the fourteen provinces composing the Republic seven were hostile to Rosas.

In order to reinforce his army in the Province of Entre-Rios, Rosas had caused a levy to be made of the citizens without distinction of age, rank or occupation, not known to be Federals, who were obliged to choose between marching to join the army, like veteran soldiers, or paying for two, ten or even as many as forty substitutes, remaining in the meantime in the prisons or the barracks.

This first announcement of the reign of terror, on the one hand, and on the other, the enthusiasm, the patriotic fever which agitated the minds of the youth of the country, at the news of the victories gained by the Liberating Army, together with the propaganda of the press of Montevideo, caused the emigration of many distinguished persons, who escaped from the shores of Buenos Ayres braving the daggers of the Mashorca.

The city was deserted. Those who could not pay for substitutes concealed themselves; those who had the means and the courage to do so, emigrated.

The French preparing for action on the Plata; the Eastern provinces of the Republic threatening an armed invasion; General Lavalle on the Paraná, with the prestige of two victories behind him; in the north, Tucuman, Salta and Jujuy, in the west, as far as the slope of the Cordillera, Catamarca and Rioja in arms, proclaiming and supporting the revolution; the northern part of the Province of Buenos Ayres ready to move at the first sign of aid that should present itself; the city, galled by oppression, sending across the Plata emigrants to the opposite shore—such were the dangers by which the dictator saw himself menaced. The whole political horizon was fast growing dark. And only an occasional word of consolation did he receive from England, through the mouth of the English Minister, Sir John Henry Mandeville, in regard to the French blockade. But England, in spite of the good-will which animated her representative in Buenos Ayres, could not refuse to recognize the right of France to maintain the blockade in the Plata, even though English commerce should suffer by this long interdiction of one of the richest markets of South America.

Such was the situation of Rosas on the night on which the events which we have just related took place. And it is while these events were taking place, that is to say at twelve o'clock on the night of May 4, 1840, that we ask the reader to accompany us to a house in the Calle del Restaurador.

In the hall of this house, which was quite dark, two gauchos and eight Indians of the Pampa, wrapped in their ponchos and armed with carbines and swords lay stretched on the floor, like so many bull-dogs, guarding the insecurely fastened street door.

Beyond the hall was a spacious quadrangular courtyard, without any light save that which came from a half-open door on the left that gave entrance to a room, in the center of which stood a table on which was a candlestick holding a tallow candle. In a few common chairs were lounging three men with heavy mustaches and a sinister expression of countenance, wearing ponchos and carrying swords at their sides.

On the right of the hall was a door which opened into a sort of ante-chamber that communicated with another room of larger dimensions, containing a square table covered with a red baize cloth, at which four men were seated; several chairs ranged against the wall; a saddle and the trappings of a horse, lying in a corner. This room was lighted by two latticed windows which looked out on the street, and communicated by a door in the partition on the left with a bedroom that communicated with several other rooms which opened on the courtyard to the right. In one of these rooms, which was lighted as were all the others by tallow candles, a woman completely dressed lay asleep on a bed.

The eldest and the most distinguished in appearance of the four men seated at the table in the room to the right was a stout man of some forty-eight years of age, with fleshy red cheeks, compressed lips, a high narrow forehead and small eyes with drooping lids; but on the whole rather agreeable than repulsive in appearance. He wore wide trousers of black cloth, a raisin colored jacket, a black necktie and a straw hat, whose wide brim would have concealed his countenance from view had it not been at this moment pushed back from his forehead.

The other three men, ranging in age from twenty-five to thirty, were plainly dressed, and two of them were excessively pale, and bore on their faces traces of fatigue and lack of sleep.

The man with the straw hat was occupied in reading letters, a heap of which lay before him on the table, and the young men were writing.

Sitting on a chair in one corner of the room, was an old man of about seventy years of age, with a lean and shriveled face, over which fell the tangled locks of his unkempt gray hair, and whose spare and slightly deformed figure—the left shoulder being higher than the right—was buttoned in a military coat of scarlet cloth, the gold fringes of whose epaulets, still more dilapidated than their wearer, hung, the one down his breast, the other down his back. A red silk sash, worn and soiled like his coat, served to attach to his waist a short sword that seemed to have come down from the days of the vice-royalty; and trousers of an undefinable color and muddy boots completed the costume of this man who gave signs of life only by the spasmodic movements of the head which he made from time to time in the desperate battle which he was waging with sleep.

In the opposite corner of the room, behind the man with the straw hat, another man lay coiled up on the floor like a boa-constrictor. This individual was a mulatto, stout and apparently short of stature, who was wrapped in a priest's cloak and was sleeping, with his knees drawn up to his chest, profoundly and peacefully.

A sepulchral silence reigned in the room. Suddenly one of the clerks raised his head and placed his pen on the inkstand.

"Have you finished?" asked the man with the straw hat, who was no other than Don Juan Manuel Rosas, the Argentine Dictator.

"Yes, your Excellency."

"Read, then."

The clerk read aloud:

"'Long live the Argentine Confederation!

"'Death to the Unitarian savages!

"'Buenos Ayres, 4th of the month of America, 1840. Year 31 of Liberty, 25 of Independence, and 11 of the Argentine Confederation.

"'The General Aid-de-Camp of his Excellency to Colonel Don Antonio Ramirez, Commander-in-Chief of the 2d.

"'The undersigned has been commanded by his Excellency, the Governor of the Province, our Illustrious Restorer of the Laws, Brigadier Don Juan Manuel de Rosas, to inform you that his Excellency has ordered that for the future in stating in your communications the number of the troops composing a division you are to set down double the actual number, saying that half are of the line and that all are animated by sacred Federal enthusiasm.

"'All which you are to bear well in mind hereafter.

"'God preserve your Excellency many years.'"

"Good," said Rosas, taking the paper from the clerk's hand. "Hey!" he cried, a moment afterward, turning toward the old man in the red coat, who was nodding in his corner and who, starting to his feet at the sound, as if he had received an electric shock, walked toward the table, his sword pointing backward and one epaulet falling over his breast, the other over his back. "You were asleep, you lazy old man, were you not?"

"Forgive me, your Excellency."

"Never mind the forgiveness but come sign this."

The old man, taking the pen which Rosas handed to him, wrote at the bottom of the document in a tremulous hand:

"Manuel Corvalan."

"You might very well have learned to write a better hand than that when you were in Mendoza," said Rosas, laughing at the writing of Corvalan, who stood motionless as a statue beside the table without answering a word.

"Have the abstracts of the communications from Montevideo been made?" continued Rosas, turning to one of the clerks.

"Yes, your Excellency."

"The information received by the police?"

"It has been noted down."

"At what hour was the embarkation to have taken place tonight?"

"At ten o'clock."

"It is a quarter past twelve!" said Rosas, looking at his watch. "They were probably afraid. You may all go now. But what the devil is this?" he exclaimed, suddenly, observing the man who was coiled up asleep in a corner of the room, wrapped in a cloak. "Ah! Father Viguá! Wake up, your Reverence!" he cried, giving a vigorous kick in the side to the man whom he had addressed as "your Reverence," who started up with a shrill scream, entangling his feet in the folds of his cloak. And the clerks left the room one after another applauding with smiles the wit of his Excellency the Governor.

Rosas remained face to face with a mulatto of short stature, broad shouldered and fat, with an enormous head, a narrow flat forehead, plump cheeks and a short nose, and whose shapeless features expressing the extreme degeneration of human intelligence bore the stamp of imbecility.

This man, such as we have just described him, wore the sacerdotal garb and was one of the two buffoons with whom Rosas diverted himself.

The poor mulatto, stupefied and smarting with pain, rubbed his side while he looked reproachfully at his master, who turned with a laugh to General Corvalan, saying:

"What do you think of that! His Reverence was sleeping while I was working."

"Very ill done," responded the aid-de-camp, with the same immovable countenance as before.

"And he is vexed because I wakened him."

"He struck me," said the mulatto, in harsh and querulous accents, disclosing to view as he opened his liver-colored lips two rows of small, sharp teeth.

"That is nothing, Father Viguá; the dinner we are going to eat presently will cure your Reverence. How is the house, Corvalan?"

"There are eight men in the hall, three adjutants in the office, and fifty men in the yard."

"Good; you may go now to the office."

"If the chief of police should come—"

"Let him tell you his business."

"If—"

"If the devil should come let him tell you his business," interrupted Rosas brusquely.

"Very well, your Excellency."

"Listen."

"Señor?"

"If Cuitiño comes let me know."

"Very well."

"You may go now—Will you stay and dine?"

"Thanks, your Excellency; I have already supped."

"So much the better for you."

"Manuela!" called Rosas, when Corvalan had left the room, passing into the adjoining apartment in which burned a tallow candle whose soot-clogged wick shed around a dim and yellowish light.

"Papa!" answered a voice from an inner room, and a moment later the woman whom we saw lying asleep on a bed made her appearance.

This woman was between twenty-two and twenty-three years of age, tall and rather slender, with a graceful and finely moulded figure and a countenance that might be called beautiful were it not more adequately described by the word interesting.

Her complexion was of that dark, pale hue peculiar to persons of a nervous temperament who live more in the spirit than in the body. Her forehead, although not broad, was rounded, and delicately modeled, and her dark chestnut hair, drawn back behind the ears, defined the outlines of an intellectual and finely shaped head. Her eyes, a shade darker than her hair, were small but animated and restless. Her nose was straight and delicately chiseled; her mouth large but fresh and well-formed; and, finally, a piquant expression of countenance made her one of those women at whose side men are apt to forget prudence in passion, and who fire at the same time, the senses and the imagination.

Her closely-fitting gown of cherry-colored merino defined the outlines of a round and slender waist, leaving bare her smooth and polished shoulders.

Such was the woman who now appeared before Rosas, whose daughter she was and who greeted her with the words:

"You were sleeping already, eh? One of these days I'll marry you to Viguá so that you may sleep away your lives together. Was María Josefa here tonight?"

"Yes, papa; she stayed until half-past ten."

"And who else was here?"

"Doña Pascuala and Pascualita."

"And the gringo did not come?"

"No, señor. Tonight he has a small party in his house to hear I don't know who play the piano."

"And who are the guests?"

"I think they are all English."

"A pretty sight they will be at this hour."

"Do you wish to dine now, papa?"

"Yes, tell them to put the dinner on the table."

Manuela left the room and in a short time returned to announce to her father that dinner was on the table.

It was served in the adjoining room, and consisted of a large roast of beef, a roast duck, a pudding, and a dish of preserved fruit. For wines, two bottles of Bordeaux had been placed before one of the covers. An old mulatto woman stood near ready to wait at the table.

Rosas called to Viguá who had fallen asleep again leaning against the wall of his Excellency's study, and then went and sat down with his daughter to his nocturnal dinner.

"Will you have some roast beef?" he said to Manuela, cutting an enormous slice and putting it on his plate.

"No, papa."

"Take some duck, then."

And while the young girl cut a wing off the fowl and began to cut the meat off it and eat it slowly, rather to pass the time than anything else, her father ate slice after slice of meat, washing down each mouthful with copious draughts of wine.

"Sit down, your Reverence," he said to Viguá, who was devouring the viands with his eyes, and who did not wait for a second invitation.

"Help him, Manuela."

Manuela put a rib of the roast beef on a plate and handed it to the mulatto who looked at her as he took it with an expression of savage resentment that did not escape the notice of Rosas.

"What is the matter, Father Viguá? Why do you look at my daughter with that angry expression?"

"She has given me a bone," answered the mulatto, cramming an enormous piece of bread into his mouth as he spoke.

"How is this! You won't help the man who is to pronounce the benediction over you when you marry the illustrious Señor Gomez de Castro, Portuguese Hidalgo, who gave his Reverence two reals yesterday? You have done very wrong, Manuela; get up and kiss his hand to make amends to him."

"Very well; tomorrow I will kiss his Reverence's hand," returned Manuela, smiling.

"No, this very instant."

"What an idea, papa!" responded the young girl, half angry, half smiling, as if in doubt as to her father's real intentions.

"Manuela, kiss his Reverence's hand."

"Not I."

"Yes, you shall."

"Papa!"

"Father Viguá, get up and kiss her on the mouth."

The mulatto rose, tearing with his teeth a strip of meat from the rib which he held in his hand, while Manuela looked at him with her eyes sparkling with pride, mortification and anger, eyes that would of themselves have sufficed to fascinate this stupid and abject creature, even without the encouraging presence of Rosas. The mulatto approached the young girl who, passing from the indignation inspired by wounded dignity to the dejection produced by the consciousness of her helplessness, hid her face in her hands to protect it from the profanation to which her father had condemned it. But this frail and insufficient defense did not extend as far as her head and the mulatto, who was more desirous of eating than kissing, contented himself with pressing his greasy lips on the young girl's fine and lustrous hair.

"What a fool your Reverence is!" cried Rosas, bursting into a laugh. "That is not the way to kiss a woman. And you, bah! what a prude!

If he were a handsome young fellow, I wager you would be willing enough!" And he tossed a glass of wine down his throat, while his daughter, crimson to the tips of her ears, winked away the tears which mortification caused to start in her angry and sparkling eyes.

Rosas meanwhile continued to eat with an appetite which gave evidence of a vigorous digestion and of the perfect health of this privileged organization in which mental labor supplied the want of the physical activity from which he was at this time debarred.

After the roast, he ate, in turn, some of the duck, of the pudding and of the preserved fruit, without ceasing to converse with Viguá, to whom he threw a morsel from time to time. At last, turning to his daughter who had kept silence with her lips while the conversation which she held with herself was plainly to be read in her swiftly changing countenance, he said:

"The kiss displeased you, did it?"

"You knew it did. You seem to take pleasure in humiliating me before the most degraded beings. What difference does it make that he is a fool? Eusebio is a fool, too, yet through him I was made an object of public ridicule because he insisted, as you know, on embracing me in the street without anyone daring to prevent him because he was the Governor's favorite fool," replied Manuela, with a nervousness of intonation and an animation of face and voice that showed plainly the effort it had cost her to bear without complaining the humiliation which she had just endured.

"Yes, but you know that I ordered him to be given twenty-five lashes, and that I shall keep him in Santos Lugares, until next week."

"And what does that matter? Because he has been punished are people going to forget the ridiculous position in which that imbecile placed me? Because you ordered him to be given twenty-five lashes will people cease to make me, and justly, a subject of gossip and ridicule? I can understand that you should divert yourself with your fools; they are, it may be said, the only distraction you have; but from the liberties you allow them to take with me in your presence they get to think that they are authorized to treat me with disrespect wherever they meet me. I would consent to their saying whatever they please to me, but what amusement can you find in their touching me and irritating me?"

"They are your dogs caressing you."

"My dogs!" exclaimed Manuela, whose anger increased with every word that fell from her rosy lips; "dogs would obey me, a dog would be more useful to you than that idiot, for a dog would at least guard your person and defend you if the dreadful occasion should arrive which everyone is bent upon prophesying to me; in ambiguous terms, indeed, but whose meaning I can very clearly understand."

Manuela ceased speaking and a dark cloud overshadowed the brow of Rosas at his daughter's last words.

"And who talks to you in that way?" he asked quietly, after a few moments' silence.

"Everybody, señor," answered Manuela, recovering her habitual calmness. "It seems as if everyone who came to this house conspired to fill me with terror of the dangers which they say surround you."

"Dangers of what kind?"

"Oh, no one speaks to me, no one would venture to speak to me of the dangers of war or of political dangers but they all paint the Unitarians to me as capable of attempting your life at any moment; they all charge me to watch over you, not to leave you alone, to see that the doors are securely fastened; always ending by offering me their services which perhaps not one of them is loyal enough to offer me with sincerity; for their civilities are more a boast than a mark of good will."

"Why do you think so?"

"Why do I think so? Do you suppose that Garrigós, that Torres, that Arana, that García, that any of those men whom the desire of standing well with you brings here would be capable of risking his life for anyone in the world? If they are afraid of a disaster it is not on your account but on their own."

"It is possible that you are right," said Rosas, quietly, twirling around on the table the plate before him; "but if the Unitarians do not kill me this year they will not kill me in any of the years to come. Meantime, you have changed the conversation. You were angry because his Reverence wished to give you a kiss, and I desire that you should make up with Father Viguá," he continued, turning to the mulatto, who held the preserve dish close to his face and was occupied in licking it clean. "Father Viguá, give an embrace and a couple of kisses to my daughter to content her."

"No, papa!" exclaimed Manuela rising to her feet, in an accent of mingled fear and irresolution difficult to describe, for it was the expression of the multitude of emotions which at that moment agitated her soul, as a woman, a young girl and a lady in the presence of the repulsive looking object whose monstrous mouth her father wished to bring in contact with her delicate lips, solely because he made it a point never to allow his will to be thwarted by another's.

"Kiss her, Father."

"Give me a kiss," said the mulatto, turning to Manuela.

"No!" cried Manuela, running away from him.

"Give me a kiss," repeated the mulatto.

"Catch her, Father," cried Rosas to him.

"No, no!" exclaimed Manuela in a voice full of indignation.

But in the midst of the efforts to escape of the daughter, the vociferous laughter of the father, and the mulatto's pursuit of his prey, this slim girl who, pale, mortified, impotent to defend herself in any other way than by flight, succeeded always in eluding his grasp, the clatter of horses' hoofs on the stone pavement of the street suddenly arrested the movements and the attention of all three.

V

Commandant Cuitiño

The horses stopped outside the door and after a moment's silence Rosas nodded to his daughter, who comprehended at once that her father desired her to go and see who it was that had just arrived. She left the room accordingly, passing through the study and smoothing back her hair from her temples as she went, as if she sought by this action to put away from her mind the recollection of all that had just taken place, in order to devote herself entirely, as was her habit, to the care of her father's person and interests.

"Who is it, Corvalan?" she said, meeting the aid-de-camp in the dark passage leading to the courtyard.

"Commandant Cuitiño, señorita."

Manuela, accompanied by Corvalan, returned to the dining room.

"Commandant Cuitiño," said Corvalan, as he entered the room.

"Who is with him?"

"An escort of cavalry."

"That is not what I am asking you. Do you suppose that I am so deaf as not to have heard the horses?"

"He is alone, your Excellency."

"Show him in."

Rosas remained sitting at the head of the table; Manuela took a seat at one side of it, to his right, with her back to the door through which Corvalan had just left the room; Viguá at the foot, opposite Rosas; and the servant, placing another bottle of wine on the table, at a sign from Rosas withdrew.

Cuitiño's spurs were soon heard clanking on the bare floor of the study and then of the bedroom of Rosas and this celebrated pillar of the Federation shortly afterward appeared at the dining room door, carrying in his hand his sombrero adorned with a red ribbon two inches in width, the official mourning which the Governor had ordered to be worn for his deceased wife, and wearing a blue cloth poncho which reached to the knees. His hair fell in tangled locks over his sunburned countenance giving a still more horrible expression to a round and fleshy face marked by all the lines with which nature traces criminal propensities on the human features.

"Come in, my friend," said Rosas, examining him with a swift and stealthy glance.

"Good evening. With your Excellency's permission."

"Come in. Manuela, place a chair for the Commandant. You may go, Corvalan."

Manuela placed a chair at the corner of the table, Cuitiño thus remaining between Rosas and his daughter.

"Will you have anything?"

"Many thanks, your Excellency."

"Manuela, give the Commandant some wine."

As Manuela extended her hand to take the bottle, Cuitiño stretched out his right arm and turning the end of his poncho up over his shoulder took a glass from the table and held it out to Manuela so that she might pour the wine into it; but as she looked at the glass she started violently, striking the bottle from which she was about to pour the wine against it, and spilling part of the liquid on the table—Cuitiño's hand and arm were red with blood. Rosas observed this at once and a gleam of joy lighted up his countenance, habitually veiled under the eternal and mysterious night of conscience. Manuela, who had turned deadly pale, with a mechanical movement drew away her chair from Cuitiño's when she had finished pouring out the wine.

"To the health of your Excellency and of Doña Manuelita!" said Cuitiño, with a profound bow, drinking the wine, while Viguá made frantic attempts to draw Manuelita's attention to the Commandant's hand.

"What have you been doing?" asked Rosas with studied composure, fixing his eyes on the table-cloth.

"As your Excellency told me to come back and see you after executing my commission—"

"What commission?"

"Well, as your Excellency desired me—"

"Ah! yes, to take a turn through the Bajo. True; Merlo told Victorica some story about some men who were going to join the army of the Unitarian savage Lavalle, and now I remember that I told you to be on the look-out; for though Victorica is a good Federal it is also true that he is a Galician, and at the most critical moment he is apt to be found napping."

"Just so."

"And you went down to the Bajo, eh?"

"I went there, after coming to an understanding with Merlo about what we were to do."

"And did you find them?"

"Yes; they went with Merlo, and at a signal which he gave me I attacked them."

"And did you capture them?"

"Did I capture them? Does not your Excellency remember what you told me?"

"Ah! true! As those savages keep me with my head like an oven—"

"Just so."

"I am tired of them now. I don't know any longer what to do with them. Up to this all I have done has been to arrest them and treat them as a father treats his unruly children. But they won't be warned; and I have told you already that it will be necessary for you good Federals to take charge of them; for after all it is you they will persecute if Lavalle should triumph."

"How could he triumph?"

"You would only be doing me a service by relieving me of the command; I retain it only because you force me to do so."

"Your Excellency is the Father of the Federation."

"And as I said, it is your place to help me. Do whatever you like with those savages, for imprisonment doesn't frighten them. They will shoot you all if they triumph!"

"How could they triumph, señor?"

"And I have already told you to say the same thing, as if it came from yourself, to the rest of our friends."

"As soon as we meet, your Excellency."

"And were there many of them?"

"Five."

"And do you think they will have any inclination to attempt to leave the country again?"

"They have been already taken in a cart to the police headquarters, as Merlo told me the Chief of Police had directed."

"That is what they expose themselves to. I am very sorry for it; but you are quite right; all you do is to protect yourselves, for if they were to triumph they would shoot you all."

"These won't, your Excellency," said Cuitiño, a smile of ferocious joy crossing his repulsive countenance.

"Did you wound any of them?"

"Yes, in the throat."

"And did you see if they had any papers about them?" asked Rosas, whose countenance, unable any longer to keep on the mask of hypocrisy, shone with the joy of gratified revenge now that he had artfully drawn out the horrible truth which it did not suit him to ask openly.

"None of the four had any papers," answered Cuitiño.

"Of the four? Why, did you not tell me there were five of them?"

"Yes, señor, but one escaped."

"Escaped!" exclaimed Rosas, with swelling breast, head thrown back and eyes from which flashed the magnetic rays of his dominating will, fascinating, as if by a divine—or infernal—power, the eyes and the mind of the ruffian before him.

"Escaped, your Excellency," he repeated, casting down his eyes, unable to support for more than an instant the gaze of Rosas.

"And what is the name of the man who escaped?"

"I don't know, your Excellency."

"Who knows then?"

"Merlo must know, señor."

"And where is Merlo?"

"I have not seen him since he gave me the signal."

"And how did it happen that the Unitarian escaped?"

"I don't know—I will tell your Excellency. When we made the charge one of them ran toward the barranca—a number of the soldiers followed him—they dismounted to capture him; but they say that he had a sword and that he killed three of them. Then, they say, someone came to his assistance; this was near the house of the English consul."

"Of the consul?"

"Down by the Residencia."

"Yes; well, and then?"

"Then, one of the soldiers came to tell me of the man's escape, and I sent in every direction in pursuit of him; but I knew nothing about it at the time."

"And why did you not know about it?" asked Rosas, in a voice of thunder, compelling Cuitiño, on whose countenance was depicted the abjectness of the wild beast in the presence of its tamer, to lower his eyes before the fire of his glance.

"I was despatching the others," he answered, without raising his eyes.

Viguá, who, during this dialogue had been gradually moving his chair farther and farther away from the table, as soon as he heard the last words moved it back so suddenly that he struck both the chair and his head against the wall. During all this time Manuela, pale and trembling, had made not the slightest movement, not even raising her eyes, lest they should encounter Cuitiño's hand or her father's terror-striking glance.

The noise made by Viguá's chair caused Rosas to turn his head in the direction whence it came, and this temporary distraction sufficed to give a new turn to his thoughts and a new mood to his spirit, by nature variable and capricious.

"I have asked you all this," he said, regaining his former composure, "because this Unitarian must be the man who has the communications for Lavalle and not because I am sorry that he was not killed."

"Ah! if I had only caught him!"

"If you had only caught him! One must be very alert to catch a Unitarian! I wager you won't be able to find the one who escaped."

"I shall find him, if I have to go to look for him in the depths of hell, begging your Excellency's and Doña Manuela's pardon."

"Impossible that you should find him!"

"I may find him, for all that."

"Yes; I wish you to find me this man because the communications he carries must be of importance."

"Have no fear, your Excellency; I will find him; you shall see that he will not escape me."

"Manuela, call Corvalan."

"Merlo must know his name. If your Excellency wishes—"

"Go see Merlo. Do you require anything?"

"For the present, nothing, señor. My life is at the service of your Excellency and I would sacrifice it for you at any moment if it should be necessary. You do too much for us all in protecting us against the Unitarians."

"Here, Cuitiño, take this for the family." And Rosas took from the pocket of his jacket a roll of bank-notes which he handed to Cuitiño, who had risen to his feet.

"I take them because your Excellency wishes me to do so."

"Serve the Federation, my friend."

"I serve your Excellency because your Excellency is the Federation; and your daughter Doña Manuelita also."

"There, go look for Merlo. Will you take some more wine?"

"I have had sufficient."

"Good-bye, then;" and he held out his hand to take Cuitiño's.

"It is dirty," said the ruffian, hesitating to give his bloodstained hand to Rosas.

"Give it here, friend; it is Unitarian blood." And as if he delighted in its contact Rosas held Cuitiño's hand in his for some seconds.

"I would sacrifice my life for your Excellency."

"Good-bye, Cuitiño."

And as the latter left the room Rosas measured with a keen and intelligent glance this human guillotine that moved in obedience to his terrible will; this man whose dagger, always raised to strike the virtuous and the learned, the old man and the child, the warrior and the virgin, yet fell at the Dictator's feet, under the spell of his magnetic glance. For the obscure and hireling myrmidons whom this man had raised up from the dregs of society to stifle with their pestiferous breath liberty and justice, virtue and genius, had early acquired that habit of unreasoning and blind obedience which the brute matter of humanity yields to physical strength and to superior intellect when these make it their study to flatter it on the one hand and dominate it on the other.

Diabolical science, whose first rudiments are taught by nature and which the propensities, self-interest and the study of mankind complete later. Sole and exclusive science of Rosas, whose power was based wholly on the exploitation of the evil passions of men whom he caused to persecute and destroy one another, solely by stimulating the instincts and flattering the ambitions of the populace—a populace ignorant because of their station, revengeful because of their blood, and passionate because of their climate.

VI

Victorica

G ood-night, Doña Manuelita," said Cuitiño to Rosas' daughter, meeting her at the door of her father's study, which she was about to enter accompanied by Corvalan, as he was leaving it.

"Good-night," returned the young girl, drawing closer to Corvalan's side, as if she shrank from contact with the sanguinary demon who was passing by her.

"Corvalan," said Rosas to his aid-de-camp, as the latter entered the room with Manuela, "go and call Victorica."

"He has just arrived and he is in the office. He asked me this moment if he could speak with your Excellency."

"Let him come here."

"I will go and call him."

"Listen to what I am going to say to you."

"Señor?"

"Mount your horse, ride to the house of the English Minister, ask for him and tell him that I desire to see him immediately."

"And what if he should be asleep?"

"Let him be wakened."

Corvalan bowed and left the room to execute his commissions, pulling up his red silk sash that had slipped over his abdomen, dragged down by the weight of his sword, whose point was now touching the ground.

"How terribly afraid your Reverence was of Cuitiño! Come nearer to the table and don't sit there flattening yourself against the wall like a spider. What was it that frightened you?"

"His hand," answered Viguá, drawing his chair closer to the table, with an air of relief at finding himself free from the presence of Cuitiño, who had caused him to pass so uncomfortable a quarter of an hour.

"Manuela, you did not behave well," said Rosas, turning to his daughter.

She was about to answer when the sound of footsteps outside the door was heard and Rosas, turning his head in that direction, said to a man who appeared in the doorway:

"Come in, Victorica."

Victorica was at this time a little over fifty years of age; he was of medium height and well-proportioned. His mottled complexion was somewhat bronzed; his black hair was beginning to turn gray; his forehead was broad, but protuberant over the heavy eyebrows; his eyes were small and dark, and his glance was sullen and piercing; two deep lines furrowed his face from the outer edge of the nostrils to the corners of the upper lip; and a harsh and repulsive expression was stamped upon his countenance, in which the ravages made by violent passions were more noticeable than those made by time; and it was said that on that countenance a smile was rarely to be seen. The Chief of Police of Rosas was attired in black trousers, a scarlet waistcoat and a jacket of blue cloth trimmed with black silk braid, from one of the buttonholes of which hung a Federal device twelve inches in length. From his right wrist hung a whip with a silver handle, and in his left hand he carried a broad-brimmed hat with the regulation scarlet mourning band.

After a bow, profound but without affectation, he seated himself at Rosas' invitation in the chair in which Cuitiño had been sitting.

"Do you come direct from your office?" said Rosas.

"Direct."

"Is there anything new?"

"They have brought in the bodies of the men who were going to cross the river tonight; that is to say, three bodies and a dying man."

"And he?"

"Is dead. I thought he ought to share the fate of his companions."

"Who was he?"

"Lynch."

"Have you the names of the others?"

"Yes, señor."

"And they are—"

"Besides Lynch, the bodies have been identified as those of one Oliden, of Juan Riglos, and of young Maisson."

"Papers?"

"None."

"Did you make Merlo sign the denunciation?"

"Yes, señor, the denunciations are always signed, as your Excellency has ordered."

"Have you brought it with you?"

"Here it is," answered the chief of police, taking from the outer pocket of his waistcoat a Russia-leather pocket-book containing a number of papers, from which he selected one which he spread out on the table.

"Read it," said Rosas.

"Victorica read as follows:

"'Juan Merlo, a native of Buenos Ayres, by occupation a butcher, a member of the Sociedad Popular Restauradora, serving in the commissariat department and absent from duty on temporary leave through the recommendation of his Excellency, the Illustrious Restorer of the Laws, appeared before the Chief of Police on the afternoon of the 2nd of the current month and declared: That having learned from a servant maid of the Unitarian savage Oliden, with whom he is intimately acquainted, that the latter was preparing to fly to Montevideo he presented himself on the following morning at the house of the aforesaid Unitarian savage Oliden, whom he had known for many years, saying that he had come to ask him for a loan of five hundred dollars, as he desired to desert and cross over to Montevideo, but that he could not do so without that amount to pay for his passage in the boat of an acquaintance of his who did a business in taking emigrants across the river. That thereupon Oliden questioned him closely and finally convincing himself that the deponent really desired to fly the country, told him that he himself and four of his friends also desired to emigrate, but that they knew none of the owners of the boats which carried emigrants; that the deponent then offered to make arrangements for the flight of all, in consideration of the sum of eight thousand dollars, to which the other at once agreed; that he pretended to make many journeys back and forth for this purpose, finally fixing ten o'clock on the night of the 4th as the time for their departure, it being agreed that he was to go to Oliden's at six o'clock on the evening of the said 4th to learn from him the place or the house at which they were all to meet at the hour mentioned. All which he made known to the police in order that they might communicate it to his Excellency, in faithful fulfillment of his duty as a defender of the sacred cause of the Federation; adding that throughout the whole of this affair he had taken care to consult with Don Juancito Rosas, his Excellency's son, and to act in accordance with his advice.

"'Signed in Buenos Ayres on May 3, 1840.

JUAN MERLO

"It was in virtue of this declaration that I received from your Excellency last night the orders which I gave Merlo to put himself in communication with Commandant Cuitiño."

"When did you next see Merlo?"

"This morning at eight o'clock."

"And did he tell you if he knew the names of any of Oliden's companions?"

"Up to this morning he had not learned the name of any of them."

"And was there anything of special importance in tonight's occurrence?"

"One of the Unitarians escaped, according to what I have been told by the men who escorted the cart."

"Yes, señor, one of them escaped and he must be found."

"I hope that we shall find him, your Excellency."

"Yes, señor, he must be found; for once the government lays its hand upon a Unitarian the Unitarian must not have it in his power to say that the hand of the government cannot hold what it has caught. In such cases the number of men matters little; a single man who defies my Government does it as much harm as two hundred or two thousand would."

"Your Excellency is quite right."

"Of course I am right. Besides, according to the account I have received the Unitarian who escaped resisted; more than that, he was aided by someone; neither of these things should happen; I will not have them happen. Do you know why the country has always been in a state of anarchy? Because everyone has drawn his sword to fight against the government the day he has taken it into his head to do so. Woe to you and woe to all the Federals if I should give the Unitarians the chance to fight against you, when you are carrying out my orders."

"It is a new case!" said Victorica, who in reality was well aware of the truth of Rosas' observations regarding the future importance of the event which had taken place that night.

"It is new, and it is for that reason that it is necessary to pay attention to it; for in the present state of things I will have no innovations but my own. It is new but before long it might become old if it were not promptly made an example of."

"But Merlo was to have gone with them and he must know the name of the man who escaped."

"That remains to be seen."

"I will send for him at once."

"It is not necessary. He has been sent for already."

"Very well, señor."

"Someone else has taken charge of Merlo and you will learn tomorrow whether he knows the name which I desire to know or not. In either case you will take the necessary measures."

"Without loss of time."

"Let us see; if Merlo does not know the name what will you do then?"

"I?"

"Yes, you, my Chief of Police."

"I will give orders to the commissaries and to the principal agents of the secret police to direct their subordinates to search for a man who—"

"To search for a man who is a Unitarian in Buenos Ayres!" said Rosas, interrupting Victorica with a sardonic and contemptuous smile which covered the poor man with confusion, for he had fancied he was unfolding a plan worthy of the Inquisition in search of a heretic.

"And you would have your trouble for your pains," continued Rosas. "Don't you know yet how many Unitarians there are in Buenos Ayres?"

"There must be—"

"Enough to hang you and every other Federal if I were not here to labor for you all, acting the part even of chief of police."

"Señor, I do all I can for your Excellency."

"You do all you can, perhaps, but you do not do all that it is necessary for you to do; and if you doubt the truth of what I say see the proof of it in this case: You want to search the city for a Unitarian; to look for a grain of wheat in a bushel of chaff, while you have in your pocket, if not the name of the Unitarian, the shortest way to its discovery."

"I!" exclaimed Victorica, growing every moment more disturbed, but by a strong effort of self-control maintaining a serene countenance.

"Yes, you, señor."

"I assure your Excellency that I do not understand you."

"And that is why I complain—because I have to teach you everything. From whom did Merlo learn of the contemplated flight of the Unitarian savage Oliden?"

"From a servant-maid."

"In what family was that negress, mulatto woman, or whatever else she may be, at service?"

"In the family of Oliden, according to the declaration."

"In the family of the Unitarian savage Oliden, Señor Don Bernardo Victorica."

"Pardon me, your Excellency."

"With whom was the man who escaped going to embark?"

"With the Unitarian savage Oliden, and the other savages who accompanied him."

"And do you suppose that Oliden went out into the street to gather together the first savages he chanced to meet to embark with them?"

"No, your Excellency."

"Those savages then were friends of Oliden?"

"Naturally," said Victorica, who began to understand the point to which Rosas was coming.

"If they were friends of his then they must have visited him?"

"Undoubtedly."

"And the servant who denounced Oliden must know who the persons were who visited him with most frequency."

"Assuredly."

"What persons were with him today, yesterday, and the day before yesterday?"

"Just so; she must know it."

"Such and such persons were with him; Maisson, Lynch and Riglos are dead; search among his other visitors, and if you don't find what you are looking for in that way, don't lose your time searching any further."

"Your Excellency's genius is unparalleled; I will do exactly as your Excellency has indicated to me."

"It would be better if you had done it without requiring it to be indicated to you. It is because I have no one to aid me that I have to do the work of all of you," answered Rosas.

Victorica cast down his eyes, transfixed by the imperious and at that moment contemptuous glance of Rosas, as by a fiery arrow.

"You know, then, what you have to do?"

JOSÉ MÁRMOL

"Yes, your Excellency. Has your Excellency any further orders to give me tonight?"

"None; you may retire."

"Tomorrow I will carry out your Excellency's orders with regard to the servant."

"I have given you no orders; I have taught you what you did not know."

"I thank your Excellency."

"There is no occasion."

And Victorica, bowing profoundly to father and daughter, left the room, after paying, like all who entered it, his due tribute of humiliation, fear and servility; uncertain whether he left Rosas pleased or displeased—a wearing and terrible uncertainty in which the Dictator, on principle, constantly kept the minds of those who served him; for fear might repel them and too much confidence might make them arrogant.

A long period of silence followed the departure of the Chief of Police; for while Rosas and his daughter remained silent, awake, each absorbed in thoughts of a very different nature, Viguá, who had eaten to repletion, remained silent wrapped in profound sleep, his folded arms resting on the table and his head buried in them.

"Go to bed," said Rosas at last to his daughter.

"I am not sleepy, señor."

"No matter; it is late."

"But you will be left alone."

"I am never alone. Mandeville is coming, and I do not wish him to waste time paying you compliments. Go."

"Very well, papa; call me if you should require anything."

And Manuela, approaching her father, kissed him on the forehead, and taking a candle from the table, she returned to the interior of the house.

Rosas then stood up and clasping his hands behind his back began to walk up and down the room from the door which led into his bedroom to that through which Manuela had gone out.

Ten minutes, during which Rosas seemed absorbed in thought, passed in this way, when the noise of horses' hoofs approaching the house was heard. Rosas paused to listen just beside Viguá's chair, and when he perceived that the horses had stopped at the street door he brought down his open palm so heavily upon the neck of the mulatto that if the forehead of the latter had at the time been resting not on his fleshy arms but on the table his nose would have infallibly been broken.

"Ay!" exclaimed the poor wretch, starting to his feet in terror.

"There is no need to be alarmed; wake up, your Reverence, for someone is coming, and listen to what I am going to say. Take care that you don't fall asleep again; sit down beside the man who is about to enter the room and when he rises to go give him an embrace."

The mulatto looked for a moment at Rosas and then nodded in assent, with unmistakable signs of repugnance.

Rosas resumed his seat at the table just as Corvalan entered the room.

VII

Sir John Henry Mandeville

D id the Englishman come with you?" said Rosas to his aid-de-camp, as the latter entered the room.

"He is outside, your Excellency."

"What was he doing when you arrived?"

"He was going to bed."

"Was the gringo surprised?"

"I think so."

"I think so! What the devil are your eyes for? Did he ask you anything?"

"Nothing. As soon as he heard your Excellency's message he ordered his horse to be saddled."

"Let him come in."

The personage whose acquaintance the reader is now about to make was one of those men who, so far as English statecraft is concerned, are to be met with frequently among British diplomatists in every country, but who, in respect to forgetfulness of his official position and of his dignity as a man, could be found only in a country whose government resembled that of Rosas; and, as there could be only one such country, it may consequently be said, who are to be found only in Buenos Ayres.

Sir John Henry Mandeville, the English Minister Plenipotentiary to the Argentine Government, had obtained from Rosas what the latter had refused to his predecessor, Mr. Hamilton; that is, the conclusion of a treaty regarding the abolition of the slave-trade. And from this triumph over Mr. Hamilton it was that the English Minister's personal sympathy for Rosas first sprang. He could not fail to perceive, however, that what had really impelled the Dictator to conclude the treaty of the 24th of May, 1839, was the necessity of seeking in the friendship and protection of Her Britannic Majesty's Government a support which had become necessary to him since the 23rd of September, 1838. But whatever its causes this treaty was a triumph for the minister which he owed to Rosas.

But men like Rosas neither desire friends nor are they the friends of any man; for them humanity is divided into enemies and slaves. In

Sir John Henry Mandeville he saw only his chief *cheval de bataille* in the French Question; and regard for historic truth compels us to say that if Rosas did not profit by his services as much as he had expected to do it was not through any fault of the minister's but only because of the nature of the question, which did not admit of the Cabinet of St. James acting in accordance with the insinuations of their Minister in Buenos Ayres, notwithstanding his communications regarding the preponderance which France was acquiring in the Plata and the injury which resulted to English commerce from the closing of the ports of the Republic by the French blockade.

The attention of all Europe was fixed upon a question then pending which affected the balance of power among her great nations; this was the Eastern Question. Russia, Prussia, Austria, England and France were all interested in this Question, their most sanguine expectations, however, being limited to the maintenance of the peace of Europe.

This Question was simply a hereditary quarrel between the Sultan and the Pacha of Egypt.

France insisted that the demands of Mehemet-Ali should be acceded to, while England opposed this view, consenting only that Syria, as far as Mount Carmel, should be added to the pachalik of Egypt. But Russia, meantime, declared herself the natural protector of Constantinople against any enemy who might advance upon her through Asia Minor. Let France and England unite against Mehemet-Ali and leave Russia to protect Constantinople, said the Emperor. But England, whose Cabinet was directed by Lord Palmerston, had sufficient political perspicacity to comprehend all the danger she ran in allowing the Tulip of the Bosphorus to remain under the paw of the Bear of the North. And veiling under the flowery phrases of the most refined diplomacy his rejection of the propositions of the Cabinet of St. Petersburg, Lord Palmerston endeavored, and with success, to convince it that the protection which Constantinople required should be given her by means of a Russian squadron in the Bosphorus and an Anglo-French squadron in the Dardanelles.

The state of the Eastern Question, then, at the beginning of the year 1840, was the following: Russia, England, Austria, and Prussia were agreed that Mehemet-Ali should be confined to his hereditary possession of Egypt; but France refused to consent to this solution of the question. All the powers, however, had agreed to unite in protecting Constantinople, without ceasing to watch one another, with that mistrust which is a characteristic of the international politics of Europe.

In such a state of things it is easy to comprehend that England was not disposed to give a great deal of attention to her markets of the Plata while she was obliged, through fear of Russia, to draw closer her alliance with France in presence of the gravest question of the times.

Sir John Henry Mandeville, however, was not for this reason discouraged. And strongly favoring the personal interests of Rosas, he labored as much as it was. possible for one in his position to do, to give a contrary direction to affairs in the Plata.

Rosas had absolute confidence in him; that is to say, he knew that the British Minister, like everyone else in the country, suffered from the malady of fear, and he relied upon his intelligence whenever he needed to concoct a political intrigue, as he relied upon the dagger of his Mashorqueros whenever a victim was to be sacrificed to his system.

Such was the personage who, after passing through the study and the bedroom of Rosas now entered the dining-room, where the latter was waiting for him. He was dressed entirely in black and seemed to be about sixty years of age. He was below rather than above the medium height; had a high, bald forehead; a distinguished cast of countenance; a fair complexion and blue eyes, small but shrewd and piercing, which were at this moment somewhat bloodshot, as his face was somewhat flushed. And this was natural, for it was past three o'clock in the morning, too late an hour for a man of his age, who had just been heating himself, with some of his friends over a steaming punch-bowl, to be out of his own house.

"Come in, Señor Mandeville," said Rosas, rising from his chair, but without advancing a single step to meet the English Minister as the latter entered the dining-room.

"I have the honor to place myself at your Excellency's orders," said the Minister, bowing gracefully and unaffectedly, and advancing toward Rosas with outstretched hand.

"I have disturbed you, Señor Mandeville," said Rosas, in suave and insinuating accents, politely motioning the Englishman to a chair at his right and sitting down himself.

"Disturbed me! Oh, no, General! Your Excellency gives me, on the contrary, a real pleasure when you do me the honor to call me to your presence. Señorita Manuelita is well?"

"Quite well."

"I regret not to have the pleasure of seeing her tonight."

"She will regret it also— But with your permission, we will now have done with compliments and talk of something more serious," said Rosas, throwing his arm over the back of his chair. "When do you intend to despatch the packet?"

"As far as the Legation is concerned it will be ready to sail tomorrow, but if your Excellency wishes it to delay a little longer—"

"That is precisely what I wish."

"Then I will give orders to detain it for whatever time your Excellency may require to finish your communications."

"Oh, my communications were finished yesterday."

"Then may I ask—"

"My communications are ready, but yours are not."

"I believe that I told your Excellency that they have been finished since yesterday; and I have now only a few private letters to write."

"I am not speaking of letters."

"If your Excellency would deign to explain to me—"

"I believe that it is your duty to inform her Majesty's Government, faithfully and in accordance with the facts, of the situation of affairs on the Plata at the time of the departure of the packet for Europe. Am I right?"

"Quite right, your Excellency."

"But this you have not yet been able to do, since you are not in possession of those facts."

"I inform my Government regarding general questions, public events, but I cannot inform it of facts which pertain to the internal policy of the Argentine Cabinet, since they are altogether unknown to me."

"That is very true; but do you know just how much the general questions you speak of are worth, Señor Mandeville?"

"How much they are worth?" said the Minister, repeating the phrase in order to gain time for reflection.

"How much they are worth, yes señor; how much they are worth to enlighten the Government to which such generalities are written."

"They are worth—"

"Nothing, Señor Minister."

"Oh!"

"Nothing. You Europeans abound in generalities whenever you wish to appear to know a thing thoroughly respecting which you are totally ignorant. But this system has exactly the opposite effect of that which you desire to produce, for you generalize on false data."

JOSÉ MÁRMOL

"Your Excellency means to say—"

"I mean to say, Señor Minister, that it is your habit to speak of matters which you do not understand—at least that is the case in regard to my country."

"But a Foreign Minister cannot know the private affairs of a Government in which he has no part."

"And it is for that reason that a Foreign Minister, if he wishes to give his own Government correct information, should go to the Chief of the Government whose affairs he is ignorant of, and hear and be grateful for his explanations."

"That is what I do."

"Not always."

"To my regret."

"That may be. Come, do you know what is the real condition of affairs at present? Speak frankly."

"I think that all the probabilities are in favor of the triumph of your Excellency."

"And is there any special ground on which you base that opinion?"

"Undoubtedly."

"And what is it, Señor Minister?"

"Your Excellency's strength."

"Bah! that is a very vague phrase in the case with which we are dealing."

"Vague, señor!"

"Certainly; for although I have in effect strength and resources, the anarchists have also strength and resources. Is not that true?"

"Oh, señor!"

"For example, do you know what Lavalle's situation in Entre-Rios is?"

"Yes, señor, he has been unable to move his troops since the battle of Don Cristóbal, in which the arms of the Confederation obtained so signal a triumph."

"But General Echagüe remains inactive for want of horses."

"But your Excellency, who is all-powerful, will see that the general has all the horses he requires."

"Do you know what the condition of Corrientes is?"

"I believe that if Lavalle were defeated the Province of Corrientes would return to the Federal League."

"Meanwhile Corrientes has taken up arms against my Government; and that makes two provinces already."

"True, that makes two provinces; but—"

"But what?"

"But the Confederation has fourteen."

"Oh! not so many."

"Your Excellency means—"

"That it has not now fourteen; for the provinces that have joined the Unitarians cannot be counted as Federal provinces."

"True, true, your Excellency; but the action of those provinces is of no importance—at least such is my opinion."

"Did I not tell you that your generalities were always based on false data?"

"Does your Excellency think so?"

"What I say I think, Señor Minister. Tucuman, Rioja, Catamarca and Jujuy are all provinces of the greatest importance, and the action of which you speak is nothing less than a real revolution with abundant resources in money and men."

"That would be deplorable."

"So it would. Tucuman, Salta and Jujuy threaten me on the north, as far as the frontier of Bolivia; Catamarca and Rioja, on the east, as far as the slope of the Cordillera; Corrientes and Entre-Rios on the coast; and who else, Señor Minister?"

"Who else?"

"Yes, señor, that is the question I have asked you; but I will answer it myself since you are afraid to name my enemies. In addition to those, Rivera threatens me."

"Bah!"

"He is not so insignificant as you suppose, for he has an army today on the other side of the Uruguay."

"Which it will not cross."

"Probably not; but we must reason on the supposition that it will, and there you have me surrounded on all sides by enemies encouraged, supported and protected by France."

"In truth the situation is serious," said the Minister, slowly, unable to comprehend the object of Rosas in thus disclosing himself the dangers that menaced him, a thing which the astute Dictator would assuredly not have done without some powerful ulterior motive.

"It is very serious!" repeated Rosas, with a composure which completed the perplexity of the diplomat. "And now that you know the dangers by which I am menaced, will you tell me on what grounds you base your conviction, in your communications to your Government, of my complete triumph over the Unitarians; for you do not doubt that I will obtain a complete triumph?"

"And what more grounds are necessary, your Excellency, than the military strength, the prestige, the popularity which are the sources of your Excellency's glory and fame?"

"Bah! bah! bah!" exclaimed Rosas, laughing frankly, as if in pity or contempt of his hearer's ignorance.

"I do not know, General," said the Minister, disconcerted at the unexpected result of his polite flattery, or rather of the expression of his belief, "which of the words that I have just had the honor of pronouncing is the unfortunate source of your Excellency's mirth?"

"All of them, Señor Diplomat," responded Rosas with undisguised irony.

"But Señor—"

"Listen to me, Señor Mandeville; all that you have just said would do very well to say to the people, but not at all to write to Lord Palmerston, whom the Unitarians of Montevideo call the *eminent* Minister."

"Will your Excellency do me the honor to explain to me why?"

"I am coming to that. I have told you in detail all the dangers which at present threaten my Government, that is to say, the order and the peace of the Argentine Confederation. Is not that true?"

"Quite true, your Excellency."

"And do you know why I have just enumerated all those dangers? Oh, you do not understand, you cannot perceive the cause of my frankness, which perplexes and confounds you! But I will tell it to you now. I have said all that I have said because I know very well that on this interview you will base a protocol which you will presently send to your Government; and that is precisely what I most desire."

"That is what your Excellency desires!" exclaimed the Minister, more astonished now than he had been perplexed before.

"I desire it, and the reason why I desire it is that it suits me that the English Government should learn these details from me myself before learning them from the organs of my enemies; or at least that it should learn them simultaneously from both. Do you understand my object now? What would I gain by concealing from the English Government a situation which it cannot fail to learn publicly and officially, through a thousand different channels? To conceal it would be to show fear, and I have no fear whatever of my present enemies."

"It is for that reason that I said to your Excellency that with your resources—"

"Still harping on my resources, Señor Mandeville!"

"But unless it be with your resources—if your Excellency has no resources—"

"I have resources, Señor Minister," interrupted Rosas brusquely, whereupon the Englishman abandoned his last hope of understanding Rosas that night, and not knowing very well what to say, uttered the words:

"Well then!—"

"Well then! well then! It is one thing to have resources and another thing to rely altogether upon those resources to free yourself from a bad situation. Do you suppose that Lord Palmerston does not know how to add and to subtract? Do you suppose that if he adds up the number of the enemies and the resources, backed by the powerful aid of France, that threaten the Government and the Federal system of the country, the *eminent* Minister will have a great deal of confidence in my triumph, even though you should show him that I have an equal amount of resources at my demand? And do you suppose that he would then exert himself greatly to support a Government whose situation offered no probability of its remaining in existence more than a few months, a few weeks, perhaps? Do you suppose—granting even that your Government desired to aid me against my enemies, supported by France—that the distance is less from London to Paris and from Paris to Buenos Ayres, than from Entre-Rios to the Retiro and from Tucuman to Santa Fé, and that Lord Palmerston does not know this? Bah, Señor Mandeville, I never expected a great deal from the English Government in my difficulty with France, but I expect less than ever now, since the accounts you send that Government are based on calculations of my strength."

"But, General," said the Englishman in despair, for he understood less and less every moment what Rosas was aiming at, "with what else but your military strength, your armies, the Federals, in short, does your Excellency expect to vanquish the Unitarians?"

"With themselves, Señor Mandeville," said Rosas, with German phlegm, fixing his scrutinizing gaze on the countenance of the Minister, to observe the impression caused him by the sudden raising of the curtain which concealed the mysterious stage of the Dictator's mind.

"Ah!" exclaimed the minister, opening wide his eyes, as if his imagination had suddenly expanded within the vast circle traced for it by those few words, in which he saw the explanation of all the reticences and paradoxes that a moment before he had been unable to comprehend, in spite of his diplomatic skill and experience which enabled him at times to divine the reservations of Rosas.

"With themselves," repeated the latter tranquilly. "And they are today my principal army, my strongest power, or rather the power most destructive to my enemies."

"In effect, your Excellency introduces me into a region of ideas where, frankly speaking, I had never before penetrated."

"I know it," answered Rosas, who never lost an opportunity of making others conscious of their mistakes or their ignorance. "The Unitarians," he continued, "have not had thus far, nor will they ever have, what they require in order to be strong and powerful, numerous and influential as they are. They have men of great ability, they have the best soldiers in the Republic, but they have not unity in action; they all command, and for that reason no one obeys. The point they all wish to reach is the same, but they proceed toward it by different roads and they will never arrive at it. So then, Señor Minister, when one has enemies like those the best way of destroying them is to give them time to destroy themselves; and that is what I am doing."

"Excellent! that is a magnificent plan!" said the Englishman enthusiastically.

"Allow me, I have not yet finished," said Rosas, with the same phlegm as before; "when one has enemies like those, I repeat, one does not estimate them by their numbers but by the value which each fraction, each circle, each man represents; and comparing these fractions with the opposite power, solid, organized, where only one commands and all the others obey, as the hand obeys the will, it may be assumed that the triumph of the latter is certain, infallible, even though, numerically considered, it may appear inferior to its enemies taken as a whole. Do you see now the way in which my situation and that of my enemies is to be regarded?"

"Ah! I understand, I understand, your Excellency," said the minister, rubbing his white hands together with that keen sense of satisfaction which one experiences who has just found himself relieved from a state of anxiety or doubt. "I will rewrite my communications, so that Lord Palmerston may, with full knowledge of the facts, give his attention to the situation of affairs, looking at it from the point of view which your Excellency has so ably and so clearly indicated."

"Do what you choose. All I desire is that you should write the truth," said Rosas, with a certain air of indifference, under which the minister, if he had been at this moment less enthusiastic, might have perceived that Rosas had now begun to act a part.

"It is as important to the English Cabinet to know the truth regarding the present situation, as it is to your Excellency that they should know it."

"To me?"

"Why! Would not your Excellency regard the aid of England as the greatest possible support?"

"In what sense?"

"For instance, if England should oblige France to end the question of the Plata, would not that be for your Excellency a triumph over one half of your enemies?"

"But this intervention of England—did you not promise it to me from the commencement of the blockade?"

"Very true, your Excellency."

"And from one packet to another has not the time passed without your receiving the instructions which you are always asking for, but which never arrive?"

"True, your Excellency; but now at the slightest hint from the English Government, the Government of his Majesty the King of the French will despatch a plenipotentiary to settle this unfortunate question with your Excellency. There can now be no doubt of that."

"And why not?"

"The French Government finds itself today in a most difficult position, your Excellency. In Algeria the war has burst forth with renewed violence. Abd-el-Kader now appears as a formidable enemy. In the Eastern Question France only has demands different from and opposed to those of the other four Great Powers that have interfered between the Sultan and the Pacha of Egypt; fifteen ships, four frigates and several smaller vessels have been sent by the French Government to the Dardanelles; and if that Government persists in its demands, or if Russia maintains her right to protect Constantinople, Louis Philippe will within a very short time be obliged to send all his squadrons to the Bosphorus and the Dardanelles. At home France is not any more tranquil or secure. The attempt of Strasburg has set all the Bonapartists in motion and the old parties are beginning to raise their parliamentary standard. The ministry of Soult, if it has not fallen already will soon fall, and the Opposition is working both openly and in secret to make some one of its eminent members President of the Council. In this situation France needs to strengthen more than ever her alliance with England; and for a question which concerns her as little as does that of the Plata, the French Cabinet will not put upon Lord Palmerston a slight which in the present circumstances might have very dangerous consequences."

"Whether it does so or not is to me a matter of indifference, Señor Minister. I am in no danger either in Constantinople or in Africa, and as far as the blockade is concerned, it is not I who suffer most by it, as you are aware."

"I know that, I know that, your Excellency; it is British commerce which suffers by this prolonged blockade."

"Do you know the amount of English capital shut up in Buenos Ayres because the French squadron will not allow it to leave the country?"

"Two million pounds sterling, in native products, which deteriorate every day."

"Do you know the amount spent monthly in taking care of those products?"

"Twenty thousand pounds sterling, your Excellency."

"Exactly."

"All this I have just communicated to my Government."

"Do you know the amount of British capital invested in manufactures, which has been stopped in its transit and deposited for the most part in Montevideo?"

"A million pounds sterling. This fact too I have communicated to my Government."

"I am glad that it should know of these losses, since it chooses to suffer them. You are the ones interested. As far as I am concerned I know how to protect myself against the blockade."

"I have often said that your Excellency can do all you desire to do," said the minister, with a smile polite and flattering, but at the same time perfectly sincere.

"Not all, Señor Mandeville," said Rosas, throwing himself back in his chair, and fixing his eyes, piercing as arrows, on the countenance of the man whose thoughts he was evidently about to probe to their depths; "not everything; when a Foreign Minister, for example, secretly opens his door to a Unitarian fleeing from justice I cannot rely upon his frankly coming to tell me of the fact and asking me a favor which I would have no hesitation in granting him."

"What! Has such a thing occurred? For my part, I do not know what minister your Excellency refers to."

"You do not know, Señor Mandeville?" asked Rosas, dwelling upon every word and riveting his eyes on Sir John Henry Mandeville's countenance.

"I give your Excellency my word—"

"Enough," interrupted Rosas, who before he had spoken was convinced that the minister was in truth ignorant of what he desired to know, and to learn which alone he had sent for him. "Enough," he repeated, rising and walking about the room lest he should betray in his countenance the rage which at that moment shook his soul.

The minister rose from his chair also.

"You are going then, Señor Mandeville?" said the Dictator, holding out his hand to Mandeville, who had already taken his hat—And without waiting for an answer he continued:

"When do you intend to despatch the packet?"

"The day after tomorrow, your Excellency."

"That is too late. Make your secretary work hard and let the packet sail tomorrow afternoon, or rather this afternoon, for it is already four o'clock."

"It shall sail at six this afternoon, your Excellency."

"Good-night, Señor Mandeville."

And the minister, after three or four profound bows, left the room.

"Señor! señor! what am I to do to the gringo?" asked Viguá, who had been maintaining a violent struggle with sleep during this long conversation, of which he had not understood a single word.

But Rosas, who had not even heard the question, threw himself into a chair and abandoned himself to profound and anxious thought.

VIII

An Angel and a Demon

At a few minutes past twelve o'clock on the day following the night on which the events occurred which we have just narrated, that is to say, on the 5th of May, a yellow carriage drawn by two handsome black horses entered the Calle de las Piedras and driving to the rear of San Juan stopped at a house whose door seemed to have come from the infernal regions, so brilliantly red was its color.

A moment afterward a footman opened the door of the carriage and a young girl, slender and graceful in figure, attired in a gown of hyacinth-colored silk and a white cashmere shawl with an orange border, alighted from it, allowing a glimpse to be caught, as she did so, of a diminutive foot encased in a violet satin boot. This young girl was between seventeen and eighteen years old, and was as beautiful as the dawn, if we may be allowed this ethereal comparison. Her golden curls fell from under the brim of a Leghorn straw hat down either side of a face that seemed to have stolen its color and its freshness from some newly-opened rose. A broad and intellectual forehead; eyes limpid and blue as the sky that lighted them, surmounted by finely penciled arched eyebrows of a darker hue than the hair, a delicately chiseled nose, with that almost imperceptible curve that is the distinctive mark of imagination and genius, and finally, a small rosy mouth whose lower lip gave it a resemblance to that of the princesses of the house of Austria from the charming defect of projecting slightly beyond the upper one, complete the description, in so far as it can be described, of this beautiful and distinguished countenance, whose every feature revealed refinement of soul, of organization, and of race, and to do full justice to which the pen would seek in vain.

Crossing the threshold of the door, the young girl was obliged to call to her assistance all her strength of will, as well as her perfumed handkerchief, to enable her to make her way through the crowd of negresses, mulatto women, servants, ducks, hens and other animals, including a number of men dressed in red from head to foot, and having every sign and appearance of being sooner or later destined to the gallows, that filled the hall and a part of the yard of the house of

Doña María Josefa Ezcurra, sister-in-law of Don Juan Manuel Rosas, in which she now found herself.

With no little difficulty she reached the parlor door and after tapping lightly on the glass, entered the room, thinking that she would find there someone from whom she might inquire for the mistress of the house. But the only persons she found in it were two mulatto women and three negresses who, comfortably seated, and staining with their muddy feet the black-and-white matting which covered the floor, were conversing familiarly with a soldier with a red *chiripá* and a face in which it was impossible to distinguish where the beast ended and the man began.

The six individuals looked with inquisitive and insolent eyes at the newcomer, on whose person they saw none of the devices of the Federation with which they themselves were profusely decorated but the ends of a small bow of pink ribbon peeping from under the left side of the brim of her hat.

"Is Señora Doña María at home?" said the young girl, after a moment's silence, without addressing directly any of the persons whom we have just described.

"She is; but she is busy," responded one of the mulatto women, without rising from her chair.

The girl hesitated for an instant, then, resolving to end the embarrassing situation in which she found herself she crossed over to one of the windows that looked out upon the street, opened it, and, calling to her footman desired him to come to her.

The footman at once obeyed, and as soon as he appeared at the parlor door the young girl said to him:

"Knock at the door opening into the inner yard of this house and ask if Señora Doña María Josefa will receive Señorita Florencia Dupasquier."

Florencia—in whom our readers will have already recognized the mischievous angel who played with Daniel's heart, remained standing while waiting for the answer to her message.

Before many minutes had elapsed, a respectably-dressed woman-servant made her appearance and asked the young girl to have the goodness to wait for a moment.

She then informed the five ladies of the Federation seated in the parlor that the Señora could not see them until the afternoon, adding that they must not fail to return then. They at once rose to go, but one of the negresses as she was leaving the room could not refrain from casting an angry glance at the girl who had been the cause of the slight which they had just received—a glance that failed to reach its destination, however, for Florencia, since she had entered the parlor had not once deigned to turn her eyes in the direction of those strange visitors of the sister-in-law of the Governor of Buenos Ayres.

The servant left the room but the soldier, who had not received orders to retire and who was there by previous appointment, thought himself fully authorized to sit down, at least outside the parlor door, and Florencia was at last left entirely alone.

Seating herself on the only sofa in the room she pressed her hands to her eyes and remained thus for a few moments, as if she desired to rest her mind and her vision after the disagreeable strain to which they had just been subjected.

Meanwhile Doña María Josefa was hurriedly dismissing, in a room adjoining the parlor, two women-servants to whom she continued to talk without ceasing while she placed one over another some twenty petitions which had been sent to her during the day, accompanied by their corresponding gifts of which the ducks and hens in the hall formed no small part, in order that she might transmit them to the Restorer, though the Restorer was very certain to be troubled by none of them. And she was in haste, as we have said, because Señorita Florencia Dupasquier, who had just been announced, belonged, on her mother's side, to one of the oldest and most distinguished families of Buenos Ayres, intimately acquainted for a long time past with the family of Rosas, although at the period of which we speak, availing themselves of the excuse of M. Dupasquier's absence, his wife and daughter appeared but rarely in society.

The door of the room adjoining the parlor at last opened and the hand of the elegant Florencia was clasped in the dirty hand of Doña María Josefa—a woman of short stature and spare frame, with a withered face, small eyes, and unkempt gray hair, over which floated the ends of a large bow of blood-colored ribbon, and in whose countenance the traces left by her fifty-eight years of life had been notably augmented by the action of violent passions.

"What a wonder to see you! And why did not Doña Matilde come with you?" she said, seating herself on the sofa at Florencia's right.

"Mamma is a little indisposed and not being able to present her respects to you in person she has sent me to do so in her stead."

"If I did not know Doña Matilde and her family as well as I do I should believe that she had turned Unitarian; for the Unitarians are to be known now by the seclusion in which they live. And do you know why it is that those idiots shut themselves up in their houses?"

"I? No, señora, how should I know?"

"Well, they keep in their houses so that they may not have to wear the badge, as is the law; or have it stuck to them with pitch, which is stupid; what ought to be done, I say, is to nail it to their heads so that they couldn't take it off even in their houses; and—but you don't wear it, either, Florencia, as it ought to be worn."

"But I wear it, señora."

"You wear it! You wear it! That is the same as if you wore nothing. The Unitarian women wear it in that way too; and although you are the daughter of a Frenchman you are not filthy and loathsome as all of them are. You wear it; but—"

"And that is all that is required, señora," said Florencia, interrupting her, desiring to take the initiative in the conversation in order to soften in some degree this fury with whom avarice was one of the cardinal virtues.

"I wear it," she continued; "and besides that I have brought you this small donation which mamma desires to make through you to the Woman's Hospital, whose resources, they say, are so nearly exhausted." And Florencia took from her pocket a small ivory pocket-book containing four bank-notes neatly folded, which she put into Doña María Josefa's hand and which were in reality her savings from the monthly allowance which her father had given her ever since her fourteenth birthday.

Doña María Josefa unfolded the notes and her eyes dilated when she saw that each note bore the number 100; and rolling them up and putting them inside the bosom of her black gown she said, with that air of gratified avarice so well painted by Molière:

"This is being a Federal! Tell your mamma that I will inform Juan Manuel of this act of humanity, which does her so much credit; and tomorrow I will send the money to Señor Don Carlos Rosado, one of the trustees of the Woman's Hospital"; and she pressed her hand upon the notes as if she was afraid that the lie she had just uttered might come true.

"Mamma would consider herself amply repaid if you would have the goodness to say nothing about this act which she regards as a duty. You know that the Señor Governor has not time to attend to everything. The war occupies every moment of his time, and if it were not for you and

Manuelita he would never be able to attend to all the responsibilities with which he is burdened."

"And well we help the poor man!" answered Doña María Josefa, settling herself comfortably on the sofa.

"I don't know how Manuelita manages to keep well. She sits up all night, they say, but that will finally make her ill," said Florencia, in the most sympathetic of tones.

"Of course it will make her ill. Last night, for example, she did not go to bed until four in the morning."

"Until four?"

"And after."

"But I believe that fortunately there are now no disturbances."

"Bah! how easy it is to see that you know nothing about politics. Now, more than ever."

"True, I cannot have a knowledge of secrets which only you and Manuelita are worthy of knowing; but I imagined that Entre-Rios, which is the theater of the war, being so far away, the Unitarians here would not give much trouble to the government."

"Poor child! All you know anything about is your bonnets and your gowns. And the Unitarians who want to leave the country?"

"Oh! they cannot be prevented from doing that! The coast is immense!"

"They cannot be prevented, you say?"

"So it seems to me."

"Bah! bah! bah!" and Doña María Josefa burst into a demoniac laugh, disclosing to view three small yellow teeth, the only ones that remained in her lower jaw. "Do you know how many they captured last night?" she asked.

"No, señora," answered Florencia, with an air of the most complete indifference.

"Four, child."

"Four?"

"Exactly."

"Those, at least, cannot go away, for I suppose they are by this time in prison."

"Oh! I will answer for it that they will not go away. Something better has been done with them than putting them in prison, however."

"Something better!" exclaimed Florencia, in feigned surprise, concealing the fact that she already knew the fate of those unfortunate men, for she had just come from the house of the Dictator's sister,

Señora de Mancilla, from whom she had learned the tragic events of the preceding night, although she had not heard a word regarding the man who had had the good fortune to escape.

"Better, of course. The good Federals have taken charge of them; they have—they have shot them."

"Ah! they have shot them!"

"And well done; it was a piece of good fortune, although accompanied by a trifling piece of ill-fortune."

"Oh! but only a trifling one, you say, and trifles trouble people like you very little."

"Sometimes they do. One succeeded in escaping."

"But there won't be much difficulty in finding him, for the police are very active, I believe."

"Not very."

"They say that in that department Señor Victorica is a genius," persisted the mischievous diplomatist, who desired to wound Doña María Josefa's vanity.

"Don't talk nonsense. I—I and no one else it is, who do everything."

"So I have always understood; and in the present instance I am almost sure that you will be of more use than the chief of police."

"You may swear that."

"Although on the other hand, your many occupations may perhaps prevent you—"

"Nothing, nothing shall prevent me. Sometimes I wonder how I can find time to do all I do. Two hours ago I left Juan Manuel's house, and I know more now about the fugitive than Victorica himself, whom they extol so greatly."

"Is it possible?"

"Just as you hear."

"But that is incredible—two hours—and you a woman!"

"Just as you hear," repeated Doña María Josefa, whose weaknesses were: to boast of her exploits, to criticize Victorica and to endeavor to win the admiration of all who heard her.

"I believe it because you say so, señora," continued Florencia, who was entering at a rapid pace the dark cavern in which this fanatic guarded her ill-kept secrets.

"Oh! you may take my word for it just as if you saw it."

"But you must have sent at least a hundred men in pursuit of the fugitive?"

JOSÉ MÁRMOL

"Not at all. Why! I sent for Merlo, who is the man who denounced them; he came, but the ass can neither tell the name nor give a description of the one who escaped. Then I sent for several of the soldiers who took part in the affair of last night; and sitting there on the door-step is the one who has given me the best information. And—you shall hear what a clue! Camilo!" she called, and the soldier entered the room and advanced toward her, hat in hand.

"Tell me, Camilo," she continued, "what signs can you give of the filthy, loathsome Unitarian savage who escaped last night?"

"That he must have a great many wounds on his body and that I know where one of them is," answered the soldier, with an expression of savage joy on his countenance.

"Where?" asked the old woman.

"On the left thigh."

"What kind of a wound is it?"

"A saber-cut—and a deep one."

"Are you certain of what you say?"

"I ought to be certain! It was I who gave him the wound, señora."

Florencia leaned back in a corner of the sofa.

"Very well; you may go now, Camilo."

"Now you have heard," continued the sister-in-law of Rosas, turning to Señorita Dupasquier, who had not lost a single word of what the ruffian had said, "now you have heard—wounded in the thigh. Oh! it is a discovery which is worth a few thousands! Don't you think so?"

"I? I do not comprehend, señora, of what importance it can be to you to know that the man who escaped has a wound in the left thigh."

"You do not comprehend?"

"Assuredly not, for I suppose that the wounded man is by this time in his own or some other person's house having his wounds dressed, and wounds cannot be seen through the walls of a house."

"Innocent child!" exclaimed Doña María Josefa, laughing and slapping Florencia on the knee with her lean and bony hand; "innocent child! that wound affords me three clues to the hiding-place of the fugitive."

"Three clues to his hiding-place?"

"Just so; hear what they are and learn something: the physicians who attend wounded men; the apothecaries who sell remedies for wounds; and the houses in which it is observed that there is a sudden case of sickness. What do you think of them?"

"If you think them good, señora, they must be so," said the young girl, who was now obliged to make a great effort of self-control, to be able to endure longer the presence of this woman whose breath, it seemed to her was infected by the venom of her soul.

"And if these should fail, I have another clue in reserve—the washerwoman who washes the wounded man's bloodstained linen. And that I know would not have occurred to Victorica in a year."

"I believe it."

"And still less to any of those fatuous and spendthrift Unitarians who think they know everything and can do everything."

"Of that I have not the slightest doubt," exclaimed Señorita Dupasquier, so promptly and in so joyful an accent that anyone but Doña María Josefa would have at once comprehended the satisfaction it gave the young girl to do this justice to the Unitarians—to that distinguished class to which she herself belonged by birth and education.

"Oh, Florencia! don't go and marry a Unitarian! Along with being filthy and loathsome, they are such fools that the most insignificant Federal could twist any of them around his finger. And apropos of marriage, what has Señor Don Daniel been doing with himself of late that he is to be seen nowhere?"

"He is very well, señora."

"I am glad to hear it. But take care; keep your eyes open. Mind, I am giving you good advice."

"Keep my eyes open! And to see what, señora?" asked Florencia, whose curiosity as a woman in love was a little piqued.

"To see what? Oh, you know what! Lovers divine those things."

"But what do you wish me to divine?"

"Why! Are you not in love with Bello?"

"Señora!"

"Don't try to hide from me what I know."

"If you know—"

"If I know, I ought to warn you that there are Moors on the coast; to take care that you are not being deceived, for I am as fond of you as if you were my own daughter."

"Deceived! By whom? I assure you, señora, that I do not understand you," replied Florencia, a little disturbed, but making an effort to hide her feelings, in order to draw from Doña María Josefa the secret which the latter hinted she possessed.

JOSÉ MÁRMOL

"Well, that is amusing! And whom should I allude to but Daniel himself?"

"Oh! that is impossible, señora. Daniel has never deceived me," answered Florencia, proudly.

"So I have wished to think, but I have facts."

"Facts?"

"Proofs. Don't you ever let your thoughts dwell on Barracas? Come, tell me the truth; no one can deceive me."

"I think sometimes about Barracas, but I don't see what Barracas can have to do with me."

"With you, indirectly; with Daniel, directly."

"You think so?"

"And a certain Amalia, a first cousin of a certain Daniel, an acquaintance, and something more, of a certain Florencia, thinks so too, and knows so even better than I do. Do you understand now, my innocent dove?" said the old woman, laughing and stroking with her dirty hand Florencia's polished and rosy shoulder.

"I comprehend in part what you wish to say to me but I believe there is some mistake in all this," answered the young girl, with feigned composure, for her heart had just received a blow for which it was not prepared, although she knew perfectly well the slander-loving disposition of the person with whom she was speaking.

"I am not mistaken. No, señorita. Whom does this Amalia, a widow, living a solitary and independent life, receive in her villa? Daniel only. How do you suppose that Daniel, who is young and handsome, and his cousin, who is young and beautiful and the mistress of her actions, spend their time when they are together? Not praying, I imagine. Why does Amalia lead the secluded life she does? Daniel must know, for he is the only one who visits her. What does Daniel do with himself of late, that he is to be seen nowhere? Daniel goes every afternoon to visit his cousin and in the evening he visits you. That is the way with the young men of the present day—they divide their time among as many women as they can. But what is the matter? You look pale."

"It is nothing, señora," said Florencia, who had, in fact, turned very pale, for all the blood in her body had rushed to her heart.

"Bah!" exclaimed Doña María Josefa, with a strident laugh; "bah! bah! bah! And I haven't told you everything, either. See what girls are!"

"Everything!" exclaimed Florencia.

"No, I don't want to do anyone an injury," and she continued to laugh boisterously, enjoying the tortures she was inflicting on the heart of her victim.

"Señora, I am going now," said Florencia, rising with trembling limbs.

"Poor child! Pull his ears well for him; don't allow yourself to be deceived," said Doña María Josefa, without rising, bursting again into a malicious laugh. And it seemed to be the laughter of a devil that alternately contracted and expanded the coarse, loose, blotched skin of the face of the woman who at this moment would have served as a perfect model for one of the witches of Spanish legend.

"Señora, I am going now," repeated Florencia, giving her hand to the woman who had just clouded the happiness reflected in the clear and shining mirror of her soul with the first shadow of a horrible suspicion of her lover's fidelity.

"Well, child, good-bye. Remember me to your mamma and tell her to get well quickly so that we may see each other soon. Good-bye, and keep your eyes open, eh!" and, still laughing, she rose and accompanied Señorita Dupasquier to the street door.

IX

ONE OF DANIEL'S AGENTS

At nine o'clock on the morning of the same day, to go back a little in our story, Daniel was tranquilly dressing, with the assistance of his faithful Fermin, who had already executed all the commissions with which he had been entrusted by his master.

"And now tell me who are outside," said the latter, after he had drawn from Fermin by innumerable questions, a minute description of the looks, the manner and the dress of the beautiful Florencia when he delivered to her the flowers and the letter which Daniel had sent her.

"The woman you sent me for and Don Cándido."

"Ah! my master in pot-hooks and hangers, the genius of adjectives and digressions! And what may be the object of his visit? Do you know, Fermin?"

"No, señor. He says that he desires urgently to speak to you; that he came this morning at six and found the door closed; and that he returned at seven and has been waiting ever since for you to rise."

"The devil! my former writing master has not lost his love of tormenting me, it seems; and he would have liked to make me get up at six o'clock in the morning! Show him into my study, but not until Doña Marcelina has gone. And you may send her in now," he added.

"Shall I show her in here?" asked Fermin hesitatingly.

"Here, my chaste Señor Don Fermin; I believe I am not speaking in Greek. Here, into my bedroom, and take care to close the door leading from the study into the parlor and the door of this room also when you have shown her in."

A few moments later the rustling of stiffly starched skirts announced to Daniel the approach of Doña Marcelina through the adjoining room.

A moment afterward she appeared, dressed in a claret-colored gown and a yellow merino shawl with a black border. A stiff white handkerchief, which she held by the middle, in order to display fully the cupid embroidered in pink wool on each of its corners, and a large knot of red ribbon set on the left side of her head, completed the visible part of the adornment of this woman, on whose plump, swarthy face, of which the best feature was a pair of large black eyes that must have been beautiful before they had lost their pristine brilliancy, forty-eight winters with their corresponding storms had left clearly defined traces—traces which two thick ringlets of coarse hair, of a hue between chocolate and weak coffee color, falling on either side down to her chin, tried in vain to disguise. Add to this a figure rather tall than short, rather stout than slender, with a bust of exuberant proportions, and the reader will have an approximate idea of Doña Marcelina, as Daniel greeted her without rising with that smile that has nothing of familiarity but that is yet distinctly encouraging, which is characteristic of persons of rank accustomed to deal with inferiors.

"I want you to do me a service, Doña Marcelina," he said, motioning her to a seat opposite to him.

"I am always at your orders, Señor Don Daniel," answered the newcomer, seating herself and spreading out her skirt, taking it at either side between the tips of the thumb and forefinger, as if she were preparing to dance the modest and stately minuet, causing the chair on which she sat to disappear under its voluminous folds.

"First of all, how do you do and how are all at home?" asked Daniel, who was a man who never set his foot down firmly on the ground without having first tested it, even though he had walked over it the day before.

"Full of troubles, señor. The life one leads in Buenos Ayres in these days is hard enough to expiate all the sins one has ever committed."

"You will have so much the less to settle for, when you pass to life eternal," responded Daniel, regarding his hands as if they engaged all his thoughts.

"There are some people who have more sins than I to answer for, who won't be kept out of heaven by them," returned Doña Marcelina with a nod.

"For instance?"

"For instance, those you know of."

"There are certain things that I forget with facility."

"Well, I don't, and if I were to live to be a hundred years old, I should never forget them, not even for a day."

"That is wrong; to forgive our enemies is a precept of our religion."

"Forgive them! After the mortification they made me suffer; after the danger they made me run and from which I was only saved by the influence of one of my friends, who took pity upon 'innocence oppressed by tyranny, which is the most inhuman thing there can be,' as

Rousseau says," emphatically exclaimed Doña Marcelina, whose weak point was a fondness for making quotations on every possible occasion.

"By-the-by, what are you reading now, Señora Doña Marcelina?"

"I am finishing *El Hijo del Carnavel* to read *Lucinda* afterwards, as soon as my niece Tomasita gets through with it."

"Excellent books! And who lends you this choice collection of works?" said Daniel, leaning his elbow on the arm of his chair and fixing his tranquil and penetrating gaze on the countenance of the scatter-brained woman opposite to him.

"They are not lent to me. His Reverence, Father Gaëte, brings them to my niece Andrea."

"And what would you do," said Daniel, gravely, "if the reverend curate of La Piedad should some day find in your house what I found there the day I entered it for the first time, introduced by Mr. Douglas?"

"Good Heavens! I should be ruined! But Father Gaëte will not be as inquisitive as Señor Don Daniel Bello was," said Doña Marcelina, with an air of friendly reproach.

"You are right, and I was right also. I went to your house to deliver to you a letter which you were to take to the address I should give you. I asked you for a pen and ink to direct the letter; at that moment there was a knock at the door; you told me to hide myself in the bedroom, saying that I would find a pen and ink on the table there; I looked, but could not find them; I opened the drawer, and—"

"You ought not to have read what was in it, you little rogue;" interrupted Doña Marcelina, her tone growing more affectionate every moment, as it always did when Daniel spoke to her on this subject—a thing which happened every time they met.

"And how could I resist the temptation? Montevidean newspapers!"

"Sent to me by my son, as I have already told you."

"Yes, but the letter!"

"Ah, yes, the letter! On account of that those barbarians would have shot me without compunction. How imprudent I was! And what have you done with the letter, my handsome youth? Do you still keep it?"

"Oh! to say that you would crop the hair of every woman belonging to the family of Rosas, when Lavalle should enter the city—that was very serious, Doña Marcelina!"

"What would you have! The heat of passion! The insults I had received! But I would not be capable of doing it! And the letter, do you still keep it, you rascal?" again asked Doña Marcelina, forcing a smile.

"I have already told you that I took that letter in order to save you from a danger."

"But you ought to have torn it up."

"That would have been an unheard-of piece of stupidity."

"But what are you keeping it for?"

"In order to have a document by means of which to turn your patriotism to account, if things should one day change. I desire that the services you are constantly rendering me shall be well rewarded later."

"Is that your only reason for keeping it?"

"You have thus far given me no cause to change it for any other," replied Daniel slowly, dwelling upon every word.

"Nor will I ever do so!" exclaimed the poor woman, relieving her breast by a deep drawn sigh of the weight that had oppressed it during the conversation about the letter that was her constant nightmare.

"I believe it. And now let us proceed to business. Have you seen Douglas?"

"I saw him three days ago. Last night he took five persons across, two of whom were sent to him by me."

"Very good. You must see him again today, and immediately."

"I will go at once."

Daniel went into his study, took from beneath the bronze inkstand the letter which he had placed there the night before, enclosed it in a second envelope, and taking a pen with him, returned to the bedroom.

"Write the address on this letter."

"I?"

"Yes, you; 'To Mr. Douglas.'"

"Nothing more?"

"Nothing more."

"It is done," she said, when she had written the address dictated by Daniel, using her massive knee as a table.

"Go to Mr. Douglas, ask to see him in private, and give him this letter from me."

"Very well."

"One thing more.—Remember that the slightest indiscretion on your part, without costing me a hair would cost you your head."

"My life has been in your hands for a long time past, Señor Daniel; but even if that were not the case I would die for the least of the Unitarians."

JOSÉ MÁRMOL

"We are not talking now of the Unitarians, nor have I ever told you that I am one—Are you sure that you remember all that I have said?"

"I don't know any other who has a memory to equal mine," answered Doña Marcelina, who was somewhat disturbed by the serious tone in which Daniel had just spoken.

"Good; we will now say good-bye, then."

And Daniel, going into his study, opened his desk and took from it a 500 dollar bank-note, which he put into Doña Marcelina's hand, saying:

"There is something to buy bon-bons for yourself and your nieces."

"You are a jewel!" cried Doña Marcelina, effusively. "Good-bye Don Daniel," and with a bow that was not without a certain air of good breeding, she left the room, moving like a Hamburg poleacre under full sail.

X

In which the Man with the Bamboo Cane Makes His Appearance

Doña Marcelina was no sooner outside the parlor door than Fermin introduced the schoolmaster into Daniel's room.

Holding his hat in his left hand and his bamboo cane in his right the schoolmaster entered with magisterial gait, and laying his hat and cane on a chair, advanced toward Daniel with outstretched hand.

"Good-morning, my dear and esteemed Daniel. Today, because I desire most particularly to see you, it seems that I have had greater difficulty in doing so than ever before. I, your first teacher! But I have obtained access to you at last, and, with your permission, I will take a seat."

"You know, señor, that I generally rise late."

"You always had that incorrigible habit, that ineradicable vice; more than once did I punish you severely for not being present at the improrogable hours of study."

"And with all your punishments you did not succeed in teaching me to write, which is the worst thing that could have happened to me, my dear Señor Don Cándido."

"For which I congratulate myself cordially."

"Indeed! A thousand thanks, señor."

"In the thirty-two years during which I exercised the noble, arduous, and delicate functions of the primary teacher, I invariably observed that dull-witted boys acquired with facility a beautiful, legible, free and neat handwriting, while boys of great and brilliant promise like yourself never learned to write even tolerably well."

"Thanks for the compliment, but I assure you that I should be very well satisfied to have less genius and a better hand."

"But that does not prevent you from entertaining an affectionate and sincere regard for me, does it?"

"Certainly not, señor; I respect you, as I respect all the persons who directed my early education."

"And you would do me a service the day I should ask you to do me one?"

"On the instant, if it were in my power to do so. Speak frankly."

"Yes?"

"At the present day, for instance, reverses in fortune are very general. Nothing is more common than pecuniary difficulties in times like these through which we are passing. Speak frankly," repeated Daniel, who, from a feeling of delicacy, wished to spare his former master the embarrassment of enlarging on the political situation in its bearing on private interests, in case it should have been a pecuniary matter that had brought Don Cándido to his house.

"No, it is not money that I need; fortunately, with my savings I have accumulated a small capital, on the interest of which I live passably well, comfortably, even. It is something of much greater importance that I desire from you. There are terrible epochs in life—epochs of calamity, of public disturbance, when revolutions put us all, the innocent and the guilty alike, in danger. For revolutions—"

"I beg your pardon, señor, but I think you have wandered from your subject," said Daniel, who knew by experience that the man to whom he was speaking was one of those whose digressions are interminable, if they are allowed to go on talking without interruption.

"I am coming to it."

"The best way in the world, señor, to arrive quickly at the point we wish to reach is to begin at the beginning and to go straight forward. To the matter in hand, then," insisted Daniel, who although he sometimes amused himself with the prolixities of his old writing-master had today neither the time nor the inclination for diversion.

"Well, then, I will speak to you as to a tender, affectionate, discreet and rational son."

"The last will suffice, señor. Proceed."

"I know that you are securely anchored," continued Don Cándido, of whose oratorical style circumlocution and a profuse use of adjectives were the distinguishing characteristics.

"I do not understand you."

"I mean that your exalted connections, your distinguished friends, the close and intimate ties—"

"For the love of Heaven, señor! Believe me, there are certain situations which it is not in my nature to endure for any length of time with patience. What is it you wish to say to me?"

"I was coming to that. You have many acquaintances?"

"A great many, señor."

"And one of them is the Chief of Police, Don Bernardo Victorica. Is it not so?"

"It is, señor."

"Then, Daniel, do me—"

"What?"

"Daniel, by the first copies you wrote, which I corrected with so much pleasure, I ask you to have me—are we alone?"

"Quite alone," answered Daniel, somewhat surprised to see that Don Cándido grew paler and paler as he went on speaking.

"Then, dear and esteemed Daniel, have me—"

"What? in the name of all the saints in heaven?"

"Have me put in prison, Daniel," said Don Cándido, placing his mouth close to the ear of his former pupil, who, turning round quickly, fixed his eyes intently on the ex-schoolmaster's face, to see if he could discover in it any signs of insanity.

"You are surprised?" continued Don Cándido. "Nevertheless I ask this service from you, as the most precious, the most important service which one human being could render another."

"And what is your object in wishing to be put in prison?" asked Daniel, who had been unable to come to any conclusion calculated to reassure him regarding the mental condition of his interlocutor.

"What is my object? To live in security, in tranquillity, in peace, until the frightful, horrisonant tempest which threatens us passes over."

"The tempest?"

"Yes, young man. You know nothing yet of the terrible and sanguinary revolutions of men, and above all of the fatal mistakes which may be made in them. In the year '20, that terrible year in which everyone in Buenos Ayres seemed to have gone mad, I was imprisoned twice by mistake and I tremble lest, in the year '40, when they all seem to have become demons, they should cut my head off—by mistake also. The hour has not yet come, but the hour is at hand—"

"And what makes you say that the hour is at hand?" asked Daniel who began to perceive that there might be something serious in Don Cándido's idea.

"Oh! that is the secret which I have carried in my breast like a wheel set with daggers, since four o'clock this morning."

"Señor, I declare to you frankly that if you do not speak to me clearly and without secrets in your breast, I shall not be able to understand a word of what you say, and I shall have the pain of telling you that I have some necessary business to attend to at this moment."

"No, you will not go. Listen to me."

JOSÉ MÁRMOL

"Well, I am listening."

Don Cándido rose, crossed over to the door which opened into the parlor, looked through the keyhole, and after convincing himself that no one was on the other side of the door, he turned to Daniel and whispered to him in mysterious accents:

"La-Madrid has declared against Rosas!"

Daniel bounded from his chair, a gleam of joy shone in his countenance, instantly quenched by his powerful will, long trained to repress every outward expression of emotion.

"You are raving, señor," he answered, quietly, sitting down again.

"It is true, Daniel, as true as that we are now conversing together and alone. Is it not true that we are alone?"

"So true that if you do not at once tell me all that you say you know, I shall believe that you think me still a child and that you are making sport of me." And Daniel fixed his keen and sparkling glance on the countenance of the man whose most secret thoughts he was about to probe.

"Don't get angry, my dear and esteemed Daniel. Listen to me, and you will be convinced of the truth of what I say. You know that when I gave up teaching writing, four years ago, I retired to my own house to live quietly on the interest of my small fortune. And to attend to the house and to my wardrobe I retained in my service an elderly woman—a white woman of the coast; an excellent woman, neat, careful to a fault, economical—"

"But señor, what has this woman to do with General La-Madrid?"

"You shall hear. This woman has a son who, ever since he was ten years old, has been at work in Tucuman—an excellent son; he never neglects to send a part of his earnings to his mother. Having told you this—. Have you comprehended it well?"

"Too well, señor."

"Let us proceed then to what relates to me. My house has a door opening into the street. Ah! I forgot to tell you that the son of the woman who serves me, came from Tucuman as the bearer of despatches, in the middle of last year—do you understand?"

"I understand."

"Good; my house, then, has a door opening into the street, and my servant's room a window, without bars, also opening on the street. During these last few months, in which everyone in Buenos Ayres has been living in constant terror, sleep has fled from my eyes and I pass the night in a sort of nightmare. I used to join a card party in the house of some old acquaintances, honest, worthy people, who never speak of the recondite politics of our adverse, unfortunate and calamitous times; but I do not go there now and when evening comes I shut myself up in my house."

"But, good Heavens! señor, what has the card party to do with—"

"I am coming to that."

"To what? to the card party?"

"No, to what I was going to tell you—"

"About La-Madrid?"

"Yes."

"Thank Heaven!"

"At four o'clock this morning I was lying awake as usual when suddenly I heard a horse stop outside the door, and the clanking of a scabbard told plainly that the man who was dismounting was an officer or a soldier. I am not a man of arms; I have a horror of bloodshed, and I will frankly confess to you that I began to tremble and a cold sweat covered me from head to foot; and no wonder, is it not so?"

"Proceed, señor."

"I will proceed. I sprang out of bed and noiselessly opened the shutter and then an inch of the window; the night was dark, but I saw that the horseman outside was knocking softly at the window of my servant Nicolasa's room; and that after they had exchanged a few words, which I did not catch, the window was opened and the man entered the room. My ideas became confused, my head was like an oven and believing myself betrayed, without losing an instant I went barefooted as I was into the yard and looked through the keyhole of Nicolasa's room. And what do you think I saw?"

"Tell me."

"Nicolasa's obedient son embracing his mother. I wished to reassure myself, and I listened attentively. Nicolasa offered to make him up a bed, but he said that he had to return immediately to the Governor, to whom he had brought letters from Tucuman, which he had just delivered."

"Go on and forget nothing," said Daniel, who was not now annoyed by the adjectives, the digressions, or the circumlocutions of Don Cándido.

"He told her that the letters were from some wealthy gentlemen of Tucuman, probably informing the Governor of the action of

General La-Madrid. Nicolasa, curious and inquisitive like all her sex, questioned him on the subject, and the son, conjuring her to observe the most profound secrecy, told her that on arriving in Tucuman La-Madrid had declared himself openly against Rosas; that the people had received him with rejoicings, and that the Government had appointed him General-in-Chief of all the troops of the line and the militia of the Province, and Colonel Don Lorenzo Lugones, Chief-of-Staff. Imagine, my son, my state of mind standing, undressed as I was, at Nicolasa's door!"

"Yes, yes, go on," said Daniel, without showing in his countenance the slightest mark of interest.

"Why proceed? What more do we need to know? The rest was all about feasts, rejoicings, and military movements in the provinces, almost all of them against Rosas."

"But he may have mentioned some name, some event."

"None. He was hardly ten minutes with his mother; he promised to return today, unless he should be sent back to Tucuman. Oh! I am going to tell you all about him—"

"How old is this man?"

"He is young, twenty-two or twenty-three, at the most; tall, fair, with an aquiline nose, good-looking, graceful, robust, manly."

"At twenty-two or twenty-three a man is rarely bad. A son good in absence must have a good heart. He could have had no interest in deceiving his mother; the news then must be true. Divine Providence!" said Daniel to himself, without giving any heed to Don Cándido's last adjectives.

"Well," he said aloud, "all that you tell me about General La-Madrid may be quite true, but I don't see how you are affected."

"Affected? Let me be frank; you can't be friendly to the Government; you can't desire disturbances and bloodshed. Am I right?"

"Señor, I am greatly honored in receiving your confidences. Be assured of my silence but I cannot make confidences regarding my political opinions."

"Well, well, that is prudent; but I know what I am talking about. This affair of General La-Madrid will enrage the Governor; his sanguinary fury will communicate itself to all those gentlemen whom neither you nor I have the honor of knowing and who, without doubt, are the emissaries of Satan. The threats of the *Gaceta* will be fulfilled: they will kill right and left. Although I am innocent, they may kill me, if only through mistake. And this is what must be prevented; this is what you, my dear and esteemed Daniel, must prevent."

"And how?"

"By having me put in prison on some civil charge. The prison will not be invaded, and even if it were there would be time enough for the alcalde to declare the cause of my imprisonment. I shall live as contentedly in prison as I should in my own house once my mind is at rest. The soldiers will not frighten me; on the contrary, they will be a guarantee against the assaults of the Sociedad Popular, and especially against all mistakes."

"What you say is sheer nonsense; but supposing it were sense, Don Cándido, how could I put you in prison? On what pretext?"

"Nothing easier. Go at once to Victorica and tell him that I have just insulted you grossly and that you demand my imprisonment; they will arrest me; I will make no protest; and there I am in prison, until I ask you to take me out of it."

"But, señor, it is not the custom in Buenos Ayres for a grown man to complain to the authorities when he receives a personal insult. However, your situation interests me," continued Daniel, perceiving that use might be made of this coward who would do whatever he was told for the assurance of protection from imaginary danger.

"Ah! I knew you would help me; you are the noblest, the best, the most feeling of all my pupils. You will save me?"

"I think so. Would you be satisfied with a situation under an undoubted Federalist?"

"The very height of my ambition! I have never been an employee, but I will become one; an employee without salary. I cede all my emoluments for whatever object my noble and distinguished patron may designate, and express for him my heart-felt, profound and loyal respect. You have saved me, Daniel."

And Don Cándido rose and embraced his pupil with an effusiveness which he himself would have called enthusiastic, ardent, spontaneous and sympathetic.

"Go home with an easy mind, Don Cándido, and be sure to return tomorrow."

"Without fail! without fail!"

"But not at six in the morning, you understand."

"No, I will come at seven."

"Nor at seven. Come at ten."

JOSÉ MÁRMOL

"Very well, I will come at ten; I will be exact and punctual at the rendezvous."

"One word more; observe the most profound silence with regard to the affair of General La-Madrid."

"I have resolved not to close my eyes tonight lest I should talk of it in my sleep. I swear it to you on the faith of an honorable and peaceable citizen."

"No oaths, señor; and good-bye until tomorrow," said Daniel, smiling and shaking hands with his master.

"Good-bye until tomorrow, my dear and esteemed Daniel, the best and most generous of all my pupils. Goodbye until tomorrow."

And Don Cándido Rodriguez left Daniel's house holding his bamboo cane under his arm and with a mind comparatively at rest; for before many hours were over he should be employed in the service of a great personage of the Federation.

"It is twelve o'clock, Fermin. Quick, a coat of some kind," said Daniel to Fermin, who at this moment entered.

"There is a messenger outside from Colonel Salomon," said Fermin.

"With a letter?"

"No, señor, Colonel Salomon sends to tell you that he does not write, but that the Society will meet today at four o'clock and that he will expect you at half-past three."

"Very well; help me to dress."

XI

Florencia and Daniel

It wanted but a few minutes to two by the great clock of the Town Hall, when Daniel Bello left the house of Don Felipe Arana, Minister of Foreign Affairs, in the Calle de Representantes.

Daniel had gained nothing by his visit to the minister, as far as his friend Eduardo was concerned, or rather he had gained a great deal in satisfaction, for he found that Minister Arana had learned little of the affray in the Bajo de la Residencia.

He should hear himself, then, from Florencia, to whose house in the Calle de la Reconquista he now bent his steps, the reports of Doña Agustina Rosas de Mancilla and Doña María Josefa Ezcurra, whose version would come directly from the house of Rosas. And how well—or how ill-informed were the Sociedad Popular and its president regarding the occurrences, he would hear later.

To his great relief Don Felipe Arana, who had much respect for the abilities of Daniel, had consented with characteristic simplicity to accept the young man's advice.

Arrived at Florencia's house Daniel entered it and proceeded unannounced to the salon.

Standing beside a table, her eyes fixed on the flowers contained in an exquisite porcelain vase, Florencia neither saw the flowers nor perceived their fragrance.

So complete was her abstraction that she became aware of the presence of someone else in the room only when a kiss pressed on her left hand startled her from her brooding melancholy.

"Daniel!" exclaimed the young girl, turning to him quickly and as quickly drawing back.

"Señor, mamma is not at home," she added, in calm and dignified tones.

"Mamma is not at home! señor!" repeated Daniel. "Florencia, I declare upon my honor I do not understand either your words or your manner."

"I mean that I am alone and that I expect you to treat me with all the respect due to a young lady."

Daniel reddened to the roots of his hair.

"Florencia, have I lost my senses?"

"Your senses, no, but you have lost something else."

"Something else?"

"Yes."

"And what is that, Florencia?"

"My esteem, señor."

"Your esteem, I?"

"But of what consequence to you is either my esteem or my affection."

"Florencia!" exclaimed Daniel, taking a step toward her.

"Stop, señor!" cried the young girl extending her hand with a gesture so full of dignity and resolution that Daniel remained motionless.

The lovers stood looking at each other in silence, each waiting an explanation from the other.

"I think," said Daniel, at last, "that if I have lost your esteem I have the right to ask you the cause of that misfortune."

"And I, señor, have the right to refuse to answer," responded Florencia, haughtily.

"Florencia!" exclaimed Daniel in an angry voice, "all this is horribly unjust, and I demand an explanation."

"Ah! now you demand? That is another question," said Florencia, measuring Daniel with a contemptuous glance from head to foot.

His self-esteem, his honor, his loyalty, protested.

"I demand, or I ask, as you choose, but, do you understand, señorita, I will have an explanation of this scene," he returned.

"Be calm, señor, be calm; you should not tire your voice by raising it so much. You are speaking to a woman."

Daniel trembled.

"My God! I am mad, I must be mad!" he exclaimed. "Florencia, your behavior is unjust, unparalleled; will you deny me an explanation?"

"An explanation! And of what, señor? Of my unjust behavior?"

"Yes."

"Bah! It is folly to ask that. In these times no one thinks of asking an explanation of injustice."

"In political matters, yes—that may be very true, but we are not discussing politics."

"You are mistaken."

"I am mistaken!"

"Yes, with me they are the only matters which it suits you to treat of; the only ones for which you have need of me."

Daniel understood that she was referring to the service he had asked of her.

"I supposed," he said, coldly, "that Señorita Florencia Dupasquier cared enough for Daniel Bello to take a little trouble on his account if the lives of his friends, his own life, perhaps, were threatened."

"Señorita Dupasquier knows perfectly well that if any danger threatens Señor Bello, he will not be without a safe and happy retreat in which he can conceal himself and escape it."

"I! a happy retreat in which I can conceal myself," repeated Daniel, more and more bewildered.

"That is what I have said, a happy retreat, a grotto of Armida, an island of Calypso, a fairy palace. Do you not know where it is, Señor Bello?"

"This is unendurable."

"On the contrary, it is delightful."

"In the name of Heaven, or of hell, where is this retreat?"

"In Barracas, for instance."

"In Barracas!" exclaimed Daniel taking a few hurried steps toward Florencia.

"Well, would you not be happy there?" said the young girl, facing Daniel. "Besides," she went on, with a nod and a disdainful smile, "you would take good care not to allow yourself to be wounded—especially in the thigh, with an enormous saber."

"My God! they are lost!" exclaimed Daniel, covering his face with his hands.

There was a moment's silence; then, without giving Florencia time to avoid him, Daniel threw himself at her feet and clasped his arms around her.

"In the name of Heaven, Florencia," he cried, raising an ashen face to hers, "in your own name, you, who are my heaven, my God, my all on earth, explain to me the meaning of your words. I love you. You are my first, my only love. There is not a woman on earth more dearly loved. But God knows it is not love that should occupy us now when death is impending over so many innocent heads, perhaps mine among them, soul of my soul! It is not even my own life that concerns me, no; I have risked that every hour, every minute of the day; it is the life of—. Listen,

Florencia, for your soul and mine are one, and I confide my secrets to you as I would to God; listen—it is Eduardo's life and the life of Amalia that are now in danger; but the dagger that pierces Eduardo's breast will pierce mine too."

"Daniel!" cried Florencia, bending over her lover. Sincerity, passion, truth, were reflected in his countenance and his words.

"Yes," he continued, still clasping Florencia's waist, "Eduardo was marked for assassination last night; I saved him, but dying, I feared. I had to conceal him, for the assassins were Rosas' men. But neither his house nor mine was safe."

"Eduardo assassinated! My God! But he will not die, say he will not die!"

"No, he is saved. I took him to the house of Amalia—Amalia, who is the only member of my mother's family left me. Amalia, the woman whom, next to you, I love best in the world, as one loves a sister. Great God! I may have precipitated her ruin, Amalia's, who was so tranquil and happy."

"Her ruin! But why, Daniel? Why?"

She shook him by the shoulders for his pallor filled her heart with terror.

"Because to Rosas mercy is a crime. Eduardo is in Barracas, and you mentioned Barracas; Eduardo is wounded in the left thigh, and—"

"They know nothing, they know nothing!" cried Florencia; "they know nothing, but they may learn everything. Listen!"

She made her lover rise, and drawing him to a chair repeated briefly her conversation with Doña María Josefa.

Daniel heard her to the end without interruption.

"Wretches!" he exclaimed when she paused. "It is a brood of demons. Venom, not blood, flows in their veins, and when the dagger fails they slay honor with their breath! Vile woman! to take pleasure in torturing the heart of a child. Florencia, it would be an insult to you to suppose that you could believe her instead of me. She tortured you with calumny. Do you doubt me now, Florencia?"

"No, but I wish to see Amalia with my own eyes."

"You shall."

"I wish to see her often."

"Very well."

"At once—"

"Very well; is there anything more you wish?" asked Daniel gravely.

"Nothing more," answered Florencia, holding out her hand to Daniel, who took it in both of his. "Go, and take care of Eduardo; that is all I have to say to you now."

XII

PRESIDENT SALOMON

Facing the side wall of the little church of San Nicolás, at the intersection of the Calle de Corrientes and the Calle del Cerrito, there stood, at the time of our story, an old house, with small, projecting windows and a street door with a wooden threshold a foot and a half above the level of the ground. The street outside this house, which was that of Don Julian Gonzalez Salomon, President of the Sociedad Popular Restauradora, Colonel of Militia, and grocer by occupation, was obstructed for the length of the block, at four o'clock on the afternoon of the same day on which the events already related took place, by horses wearing the Federal colors; bright red saddle-cloths, headpieces of pink feathers or wool, and cruppers with tassels of the same color, while their headstalls, reins and bridles glittered with silver.

The parlor of Colonel Salomon's house was crowded with the riders of these horses, all of them dressed alike in the principal parts of their attire, that is to say, all wearing a black hat adorned with a red band four inches in width, a dark blue jacket with its corresponding badge half a yard in length, a red waistcoat, and an enormous dagger at the waist. And, like their dress, the faces of these men seemed to be in uniform—a heavy mustache, whiskers ending at the chin, and an expression such as is to be met with only in the calamitous times of popular revolutions, and which one does not remember ever having seen at any other time in any part of the world.

Sitting, some on the wooden and cane chairs that stood in disorder around the room, others in the window seats and others on the pine table covered with a red baize cloth, on which President Salomon was accustomed to write his signature, previously sending to the grocery contiguous to his house, for a pomade pot which there served as an inkstand, each of these gentlemen was a tobacco censer sending forth dense clouds of smoke through which could be discerned their sunburned and repulsive faces. But their illustrious president was not among them. He was in the room adjoining the parlor, seated at the foot of a large cot which served him as a bed, learning by heart a short address which a man who was his complete antithesis in mind and person was repeating to him for the twentieth time. This man was Daniel, and their conversation was as follows:

"Do you think I know it now?"

"Perfectly, Colonel. You have a prodigious memory."

"But see—do me the favor to sit beside me and if I should forget the words whisper them to me softly."

"I was just going to suggest that very thing. But remember on your side, Colonel, that you are to present me to our friends and to tell them what I have told you."

"I will take care of that. Let us go in now."

"Wait a moment. As soon as you take your seat, have the secretary read the list of those present; for it is necessary, Colonel, that we should proceed with the same order in our Federal Society as they do in the Chamber of Representatives."

"I have already told Boneo to do so, but he is a lazy fellow who can do nothing but talk."

"No matter; tell him again, and he will do it."

"Very well; let us go in now."

And President Salomon and Daniel Bello, the latter attired in a black coat and wearing a long Federal badge, entered the assembly-room.

"Good-afternoon, gentlemen," said Salomon, in the most serious and dignified tone imaginable, walking toward the chair that stood before the pine table.

"Good afternoon, President, Colonel, gossip, etc.," answered each of those present, according to the title which he was accustomed to give Don Julian Salomon, all at the same time glancing keenly at the man who accompanied the president, from whose dress they missed the principal Federal attributes and whose face and hands they thought, besides, too refined in appearance.

"Gentlemen," said Salomon, "this gentleman is Don Daniel Bello, son of Don Antonio Bello, the planter, a Federal patriot to whom I am indebted for many favors. The gentleman, who is as good a Federal as his father, desires to join our society and is only waiting for the arrival of his father in the city to do so, but meantime, he wishes to come occasionally to participate in our Federal enthusiasm. Long live the Federation! Long live the Illustrious Restorer of the Laws! Death to the filthy and loathsome French! Death to the swineherd Louis Philippe! Death to the filthy Unitarian savages bought by filthy French gold! Death to the turncoat Rivera!"

And these exclamations, uttered in a voice of thunder by President Salomon, were repeated in chorus by all present who, while they shouted, brandished above their heads the daggers which they had unsheathed at the first cry of their president.

When the storm had subsided, Salomon sat down, his secretary Boneo on his left hand, and Daniel on his right.

"Señor Secretary," Salomon then said, throwing himself back in his chair, "read the list of those present."

Boneo took from some papers that were lying on the table the one nearest to him, and read aloud the following names which he had just written down in pencil:

"Present: the Señor President, Señores Cuitiño, Parra, Parra, jr., Maestre, Alen, Alvarado, Moreno, Gaetano, Larrazabál, Merlo, Moreira, Diaz, Amoroso, Viera, Amores, Maciel, Romero, Boneo."

"Are those all?" asked Salomon.

"Those are all the members present."

"Read the list of the absent members."

"Of the whole Society?"

"Yes, certainly. Are we of less consequence than the representatives? We are as good Federals as they are and we ought to know who are present and who are absent, as they do in the Chamber of Representatives. Read the list."

"Absent members," began Boneo; and he proceeded to read the names of the remaining members of the Sociedad Popular Restauradora, which consisted of 175 individuals of all classes of society.

"Bravo! Now we all know one another; although some of the names in that list may be there through compulsion," said Daniel to himself, when the secretary had finished reading the names of the members; and he gave Salomon's wide trousers a gentle pull.

"Gentlemen," then said the President of the Sociedad Popular, "the Illustrious Restorer of the Laws is the Federation; we ought therefore to be ready to sacrifice our lives for our Illustrious Restorer, for we are the pillars of the holy cause of the Federation."

"Long live the Illustrious Restorer of the Laws!" cried one of the members whose words all the others echoed in chorus.

"Long live his illustrious daughter, Señorita Manuelita de Rosas y Ezcurra!"

"Long live the Hero of the Desert, the Restorer of the Laws, our Father and the Father of the Federation."

"Death to the filthy French and the swineherd King!"

"Gentlemen," continued the president, "in order that our Illustrious Restorer may be able to save the Federation from—may be able to save the Federation from—in order that our Illustrious Restorer may be able to save the Federation from—"

"From the imminent danger," whispered Daniel, almost in his ear.

"From the imminent danger which threatens it, we must pursue the Unitarians to the death, so that every Unitarian must be pursued by us to the death."

"Death to the filthy, disgusting Unitarian savages!" shouted another member of the Society, named Juan Manuel Larrazabál, whose words were repeated in chorus by all the other members, dagger in hand.

"Gentlemen, we must pursue them all without pity."

"Both men and women," shouted Juan Manuel Larrazabál, who appeared to be the most enthusiastic of the assembled members.

"Our Illustrious Restorer is not satisfied with us, because we do not serve him as we ought," continued Salomon.

"Now comes in the occurrence of last night," whispered Daniel to the president behind his handkerchief, with which he pretended to be wiping his face.

"Now comes in the occurrence of last night," repeated Salomon as if this reminder were a part of his discourse.

Daniel gave the president's trousers a vigorous pull.

"Gentlemen," continued Salomon, "we are all aware that a number of Unitarian savages attempted to fly the country last night and that they did not all succeed in doing so because Commandant Cuitiño behaved like a good Federal. One however, escaped and is now in hiding; and the same thing must continue to happen every day unless we act like defenders of the sacred cause of the Federation. I have called you together in order that we may once more swear to pursue the filthy Unitarian savages who attempt to escape to Montevideo to join the turncoat Rivera and sell themselves for filthy French gold. This is what our Illustrious Restorer of the Laws desires! I have ended, and long live the Illustrious Restorer of the Laws and death to all the enemies of the holy cause of the Federation!"

"Death by the dagger to the filthy Unitarian savages!" cried another enthusiastic Federal, and this cry and all the usual ones were repeated for fully ten minutes, not only in the parlor but also in the street, where a crowd as enthusiastic and respectable as that which was shouting and yelling in Colonel Salomon's house had gathered around the windows.

The storm of cries and yells having at last subsided Daniel asked the president with the most self-possessed air in the world for permission to speak, which being granted, he said:

"Gentlemen: I have not yet the honor of belonging to this illustrious and patriotic Society, although I hope shortly to join it; but my opinions and my associations are known to everyone, and I hope in time to be able to lend the Federation and the Illustrious Restorer of the Laws services as important as those rendered them by the members of the Sociedad Popular Restauradora, which is now famous not only in the Republic but throughout America."

Fresh applause and fresh cries greeted this flattering exordium.

"But, gentlemen," continued Daniel, "it is to the members now present that I must offer the congratulations which every good Federal owes them; for while I do not wish to deny the zeal of the other members for our holy cause I see that it is you who come forward to support the Illustrious Restorer of the Laws, while the others absent themselves from the Federal meetings. The Federation recognizes no privileged class. Lawyers, merchants, employees, we are all equal here, and whenever a meeting is held, whenever there is anything to be done for the advantage of his Excellency or wherever danger threatens, all should assemble at the call of the president, instead of leaving the labor and the risk to a few. They may all be very good Federals, but it seems to me that those who are here this afternoon are not Unitarians, that the others should disdain to assemble with them. I say this because I think such must be the opinion of his Excellency the Illustrious Restorer, which we should cause to be more respected for the future."

Daniel did not fail in his purpose. The enthusiasm produced by this discourse surpassed his utmost expectations. All the members of the Society who were present shouted, swore and blasphemed against those who had absented themselves from the meeting and whose names the secretary, Boneo, had read. Names of absent members began to circulate, not now as such, but as Unitarians in disguise; and Daniel nodded a malicious approval of these demonstrations, saying to himself:

"So, so; I will set you against one another still more in the future, my bloodhounds, so that you may yourselves destroy one another."

President Salomon again addressed the meeting, urging all to watch the Unitarians closely, and especially to watch those points on the coast at which it was probable they would attempt to embark; and after fresh manifestations of enthusiasm and fresh cries, he declared the session closed at half-past five o'clock.

Daniel left the house of President Salomon well pleased—they knew nothing about Eduardo. At the corner of the Calle de Cuyo he found Fermin waiting for him, holding his horse by the bridle. The street was full of people and without looking at his servant Daniel said to him as he mounted:

"At nine."

"At the appointed place?"

"Yes."

"And turning his horse's head in the direction of Barracas, Daniel rode at a quick pace across the Plaza de las Artes, and down the Calle del Buen Order, reaching the Barranca de Balcarce as the last rays of the setting sun were fading in the sky. As he was about to descend the barranca he heard a voice behind him calling him by name; and turning his horse around he saw, twenty paces away, running after him, visibly exhausted and panting for breath, his worthy writing master, holding his bamboo cane in one hand and his hat in the other. Coming up with Daniel, he caught hold of his pupil by the thigh, to which he clung in silence for two or three minutes, unable to recover his breath sufficiently to speak.

"What is the matter, what has happened, Señor Don Cándido?" asked Daniel at last, alarmed at the ex-school-master's pallor.

"Something horrible, barbarous, atrocious, unparalleled in the annals of crime."

"We are in a public road, señor; say what you have to say, but let it be without delay."

"Do you remember my old and industrious servant's noble and generous son?"

"Yes."

"Do you remember that he came to my house last night and—"

"Yes, yes, what has happened to him?"

"They have shot him, my dear and esteemed Daniel, they have shot him."

"When did they shoot him?"

"At seven o'clock this morning; they were on the watch for him when he left the Governor's house last night. They were doubtless afraid—"

"That he would reveal or that he had already revealed what he knew; I will spare you the words."

"But I am lost, doomed. What shall I do, my dear Daniel, what shall I do?"

"Get your pens ready to enter tomorrow upon your duties as private amanuensis of the Minister of Foreign Affairs."

"I, Daniel?" And in an ecstasy of joy Don Cándido covered his pupil's hand with kisses.

"Now take any other road but the one you came by and return home."

"I will. I arrived at your house just as Fermin was leaving it with your horse: I followed him; then I followed you, and—"

"Very well; one thing more—have you any intimate friend, man or woman, at whose house you occasionally spend the night?"

"Yes."

"Go at once, then, and settle it with that person that you spent last night in his company, so as to be prepared for anything that may happen. Good-bye, señor."

And Daniel put spurs to his horse, and at the risk of a dangerous fall, galloped down the Barranca de Balcarce and entered the Calle Larga, dark already from the shadows cast by the houses and the trees, on whose tops the last gleams of the setting sun were fading.

This was the same road which he had traversed eighteen hours before, carrying the almost lifeless body of his friend, and it was to Amalia's house, in which Eduardo had received hospitality and been restored to life, that Daniel was now directing his course.

XIII

The White Rose

We will now ask the reader to accompany us to the villa at Barracas, where, on the morning of the 24th of May, twenty days after the day on which we first entered it, Amalia and Eduardo are sitting side by side upon a sofa in the salon conversing together, the former with heightened color, her eyes fixed on a beautiful white rose which she holds in her hand, the latter, pale as marble, with purple shadows under his large melancholy black eyes—his eyes, his hair and his beard seeming blacker from the contrast which they present to the pallor of his countenance.

But before following them in their conversation we will acquaint the reader in a few words with the chief facts of Amalia's history, up to the period at which our story opens.

Born in the province of Tucuman she had lost her father at the age of six, and at seventeen, in accordance with the wishes of her mother, who desired to give her a protector, she had married Señor Olabarrieta, an old friend of the family, who left her a widow within a year after their marriage. Three months afterward her mother died. Left alone in her native place, where everything served to remind her of her losses, she resolved to abandon it forever and established herself permanently in the city of Buenos Ayres, to which her mother's family had belonged; and here she had been living for eight months, tranquil, if not happy, when the events of the night of the 4th of May made us acquainted with her.

"Well, señora?" Eduardo was saying.

"Well, señor, you do not know me, you confound me with the generality of my sex, if you think that my lips could utter what my heart did not feel, or rather, for we are not now speaking of the heart, what I did not really mean."

"But, señora, I ought not—"

"I am not speaking of what you ought not to do," interrupted Amalia, with an enchanting smile, "I am speaking of what I ought to do. I have fulfilled toward you a sacred obligation, imposed upon me by humanity, and rendered easy to me by my character and disposition. You sought an asylum, and I opened my doors to you. You entered them dying, and I succored you. You needed care and consolation and I lavished them upon you."

"For which I thank you, señora—"

"Allow me; I have not yet finished. In all this I have done nothing but fulfill a duty imposed upon me by religion and humanity. But I should only partially fulfill that duty if I consented to your leaving my house now. Should you do so your wounds would reopen, and with fatal consequences, for the hand that made them will strike again the moment the secret is discovered which chance and the vigilance of Daniel have thus far kept concealed."

"You know, Amalia, that they have been unable to obtain any clue to the identity of the fugitive of that fatal night."

"But they will obtain it. You must not leave my house until you are entirely well. Perhaps it may even be necessary for you to emigrate," added Amalia, lowering her eyes as she uttered the last words. "Well," she resumed, looking up again, after a moment's silence, "I am independent, entirely independent; there is no one to whom I am obliged to render an account of my actions; I know that I am fulfilling a duty dictated to me by my conscience and, without attempting to impose my will upon you, for this I have not the right to do, I repeat that it will be altogether against my wishes if you leave my house, as you desire to do, before you are entirely well and can do so with safety."

"As I desire to do! Oh, no, Amalia, not that!" exclaimed Eduardo, drawing nearer to the adorable woman who thus sought to detain him; "no, I could spend a lifetime, an eternity, in this house. In the twenty-seven years of my existence, I have lived truly only when I thought I was dying; my heart has experienced joy only when my body was racked with pain; in short, I have been happy only when I was surrounded on all sides by misfortune. I love the air, the light, the very dust of this house, but I tremble at the danger you incur. Though Providence has thus far watched over me the sanguinary demon who persecutes us all may at last discover my hiding-place and then—Oh! Amalia, I wish to purchase your tranquillity at the sacrifice of my happiness as I would purchase your peace of mind at the price of my blood!"

"And what would there be great or noble in the soul of the woman who, on her side, would not brave a danger to save the man whom—whom she has called her friend?"

"Amalia!" exclaimed Eduardo, rapturously, seizing her hand.

"Do you think, Eduardo, that under the sky which covers us there are not women also who would identify their lives and their destinies with the lives and the destinies of their countrymen? If I had a brother, a husband, a lover, and he were obliged to fly his country, I would accompany him into exile; if he were in danger in it, I would interpose my breast between his breast and the dagger of the assassin; and if it were necessary that he should mount the scaffold for liberty's sake in the land which saw its birth in America, I would still accompany my husband, my brother, or my lover; I would mount the scaffold with him."

"Amalia! Amalia! I shall become a blasphemer—I will bless the misfortunes of our country since they inspire words like those you have just uttered," exclaimed Eduardo, pressing Amalia's hands between both of his. "Forgive me, I have deceived you; a thousand times, forgive me. I had divined the nobility and the generosity of your heart; I knew that no vulgar fear could find a place in it. But my departure is dictated by another motive, by honor. Amalia, do you guess nothing of what is passing in the heart of the man on whom you have bestowed life to maintain it in a celestial delirium which he had never felt before?"

"Never?"

"Never! never!"

"Oh! say that again, Eduardo," exclaimed Amalia, pressing, in her turn, Belgrano's hand between her hands while her eyes exchanged with his those indescribable magnetic glances in which two congenial souls, tempered in the same divine fire, mingle their being.

"It is true, Amalia, it is true. I had never before lived the life of the heart, and now—"

"And now?" repeated Amalia, pressing Eduardo's hand again between hers with an agitation which she could not conceal.

"Now, I live in it; now I love, Amalia." And Eduardo, pale and tremulous with blissful emotion, raised to his lips the beautiful hand of the woman in whose heart he had just planted, with its first love, the first hope of happiness that had stirred her existence; and during this hurried action, the white rose dropped from Amalia's hands and fell at Eduardo's feet. Lifting to his her eyes full of tenderness, while a fugitive smile curved her rosy lips, Amalia pointed silently to the rose lying on the floor.

"Ah!" Eduardo cried, taking up the rose and pressing it to his lips, "I will treasure forever this rose, the divine bond of my happiness on earth, as I shall treasure in my heart the image of her I love."

"Not yet," said Amalia, taking the rose hastily from Eduardo's hand. "Today I have need of this flower; tomorrow it shall be yours."

"But that flower is my life, Amalia; why do you take it from me?"

"Your life, Eduardo? Enough, not another word, for God's sake," cried Amalia, drawing away from the young man's side. "I am unhappy," she continued; "this flower, fallen at the moment in which you spoke to me of love, has been interpreted. And it has been truly interpreted; but a horrible thought has just crossed my foreboding mind. Enough, enough now."

"And what could now prevent our happiness in this world—"

"Any foolish act, a thing very easy for certain persons to commit in certain situations in life, in this world, the best of all possible worlds, as somebody has called it," said Daniel Bello, who at this moment entered the salon from the inner rooms, through which he had passed unheard.

"There is no need to disturb yourselves," he continued, observing the movement which Eduardo made to draw away from the place which he had occupied on the sofa beside Amalia. "But since you have made room for me I will sit down between you."

And Daniel, seating himself on the sofa between his cousin and his friend, and taking a hand of each, continued:

"I will begin by confessing to you that I heard nothing but Eduardo's last words, which I might just as well not have heard, for I have been imagining them for many days past. I have finished." And he bowed with ironical gravity to his cousin, whose face was suffused with blushes, and to Eduardo, who was frowning.

"Ah! since neither of you wishes to answer me," continued Daniel, "I must carry on the conversation alone. Which do you prefer, cousin? Shall Señora Dupasquier's carriage come for you here, or will you go in yours to Señora Dupasquier's house?"

"I will go there," said Amalia, forcing a smile.

"Thank Heaven that I see a smile! Ah! and you too, Señor Don Eduardo? Praised be Bacchus, god of joy! I was beginning to think that you were both really angry, because I had overheard a little of the much that you must naturally have to say to each other in this solitary, enchanted palace, which I must one day, although it may not be before a year from now, come to live in with my Florencia. Will you give me your promise to lend it to me, Amalia?"

"You have it."

"A thousand thanks! Now, then, about tonight; let us fix an hour, like the English, who are never unpunctual except in America—ten, will that hour suit you?"

"I should prefer to go later?"

"Eleven?"

"Later still," answered Amalia.

"Twelve?"

"Very well, twelve."

"Good. At twelve o'clock tonight, then, you will be at Florencia's house, to accompany her to the ball; since on that condition only will Señora Dupasquier consent to her daughter's going."

"Yes."

"Who will be your escort?"

"I," said Eduardo, hastily.

"Gently, gently, my friend. You will take good care not to be anybody's escort at twelve o'clock tonight."

"But how is she to go alone?"

"But how are you to go with her, on the night of the twenty-fourth of May," answered Daniel, looking fixedly at Eduardo, and accentuating the words *twenty-fourth*.

Eduardo lowered his eyes; but Amalia, who, with the instinct of affection had comprehended that these words concealed some mystery, turned to her cousin quickly and said:

"May I know how the night of the twenty-fourth of May differs from any other night, that this gentleman should not do me the honor to accompany me?"

"Your question is very just, my dear Amalia, but there are certain things that we are compelled to keep from the ladies."

"Then there is something political in this, is there not?"

"Perhaps."

"I have no right to demand from this gentleman that he shall accompany me, but I think that I have at least the right over both of you to recommend you to be a little prudent."

"I will answer to you for Eduardo."

"For both of you," Amalia hastened to say.

"Very well, for both of us. It is agreed, then, that you will be at Florencia's at twelve. Pedro will drive you and Eduardo's servant will be your footman. At Madame Dupasquier's you will take her carriage and go with Florencia to the ball; your own will return for you at four in the morning."

"Oh, that is too much! Four hours! One is enough."

"One is too little."

"I think, considering the sacrifice I make, that it is too much."

"I know that, Amalia; but it is a sacrifice you make for the security of your house, and consequently, for Eduardo's undisturbed continuance in it. I have told you a dozen times over that to absent yourself from this ball given to Manuela for which she has sent you an invitation at Agustina's request would be to run the risk of giving offense; and then we should be badly off. To go to this ball and to leave it before any other lady, would be to draw upon yourself the unfavorable notice of everybody."

"And what do those people matter to me?" said Amalia, in a tone of marked contempt.

"Very true; this lady should care nothing for the resentment of those people; nor have I ever thought with you, Daniel, that she should do them the honor to attend their ball," observed Eduardo.

"Bravo! Excellent!" cried Daniel, bowing first to Amalia and then to Eduardo. "You talk like a pair of sages," he continued, "and you have convinced me that it is a piece of folly for my dear cousin to go to the ball. Let her not go, then. But in that case she would do well to begin at once to burn her blue hangings so that they may not offend the sensitive eyes of the Mashorca,* when she has the honor of receiving a visit from them within a few days."

"That *canaille* in my house!" exclaimed Amalia, her eyes flashing haughtily as she lifted up her queenly head. "Well, then," she continued, "my servants will treat them as they would dogs—they will turn them into the street."

"Excellent! Magnificent!" exclaimed Daniel, rubbing his hands together; then, leaning his head against the back of the sofa and looking up at the ceiling he asked with freezing calmness:

"And how are your wounds today, Eduardo?"

A sudden thrill, as if she had received an electric shock, ran through Amalia's frame. Eduardo did not answer. They had both comprehended on the instant all the horrible recollections which Daniel meant to

---

* Mas-horca (more gallows) pronounced like mazorca, an ear of corn, the emblem of the Sociedad Popular Restauradora.—*Translator's note*.

bring to their minds by his question and at the same time the warning which he intended to convey to them by it.

"I will go to the ball, Daniel," said Amalia, while tears of wounded pride started to her eyes.

"But it is terrible that I should be the cause of your having to do so!" cried Eduardo, rising and walking hastily up and down the room, unmindful of the exquisite pain which his agitated steps caused in the wounded limb, on which he could hardly yet stand without support.

"Come! for the love of Heaven!" said Daniel, rising, taking Eduardo by the arm, and leading him back to the sofa; "come, I must treat you as if you were a pair of children. Can I have any other object in all I do than your own safety? Have I not done the same, have I not made the same efforts to persuade Madame Dupasquier to attend this ball with my Florencia? And why, Amalia? Why, Eduardo? To keep the future of all of us free, in some degree, from the prejudices, the suspicions which are now forging the thunderbolt for the head over which they gather. Death hovers over the heads of all of us; the sword and the thunderbolt are in the air; and all must be saved. In exchange for these small sacrifices I procure for all the only guarantee possible; and in their security I have the guarantee of my own security also, I, who today need the confidence, the protection, the esteem, I may say, of those people in order later to be able, at the moment least expected, to tear the mask from my face and—. But it is agreed, is it not?" said Daniel, interrupting himself, and by an admirable effort of self-control forcing a smile to his countenance, a moment before troubled and serious, in order to reveal to his cousin no more than he had already done of the mysteries of his political life.

"It is agreed, yes," said Amalia. "At twelve I will be at the house of Madame Dupasquier—of those new friends whom you have given me and to whom you seem determined that I shall so soon become troublesome."

"Bah! Señora Dupasquier is a saint and Florencia thinks you charming, now that she knows you are not her rival—"

"And Agustina, Agustina, what motive, what interest has she in wishing to know me. Is it jealousy, also?"

"Also."

"Of you?"

"Unfortunately no."

"Of whom, then?"

"Of you."

"Of me?"

"Yes, of you; she has heard your beauty, your exquisite furniture and your gowns talked about, and the Queen of Beauty and Fashion wishes to know her rival in them; that is all."

"Bah. But Eduardo, how about him?"

"I will take him with me."

"You will take him with you?"

"Yes. Was it not agreed that you were to lend him to me for today?"

"But to go out in the daytime! You spoke of taking him to your house for a few hours tonight."

"True, but I cannot return here until tomorrow."

"But he will be seen."

"No, señora, he will not be seen; my carriage is at the door."

"Ah! I did not hear it stop," said Amalia.

"I knew that already."

"But it is still early," said Eduardo.

"No señor, on the contrary, it is late."

"He is irresistible, señora," said Eduardo, rising and taking the hand which Amalia extended to him.

"Oh, that is a characteristic of my family," said Daniel, crossing over to one of the windows, while Eduardo and Amalia took leave of each other with a lingering handclasp.

"My Amalia," said Daniel, when Eduardo had left the room, "no one in the world could watch over Eduardo more faithfully than I will. Nor is there anyone in the world who desires your happiness more earnestly than I do. I guess everything and I approve of everything. Leave me to act as I think best. Are you content?"

"Yes," answered Amalia, her eyes filling with tears.

XIV

SCENES IN A BALLROOM

The sun of the 24th of May, 1840, had just set, precipitating into eternity the day remembered in Buenos Ayres as the eve of the anniversary of her great revolution. On that day, thirty years before, when it set it had seen disappear forever the regal authority of the last of our Viceroys, whom on the same day in 1810, the Town Council had constituted President of a Board of Administration, and whose authority declined still further a few hours later, against the will of the Council, but by the will of the people.

Night had thrown her starry mantle over the sky, and from the Palace of the ancient Delegates of the King of Spain streamed a flood of light which surprised the eyes of the people of Buenos Ayres, accustomed as they had been for some years past to see dark and gloomy the fortress of their good city, the residence of her former governors both before and after the revolution, but which had been converted into barracks and stables at the accession to power of Don Juan Manuel Rosas.

The vast salons in which the Marchioness of Sobre-Monte had given her splendid balls and card-parties, magnificently luxurious in the time of the Presidency, and the scenes of amorous intrigues and domestic dissensions in the time of Governor Dorrego, ruined and sacked in the time of the Restorer of the Laws, had been swept, carpeted with the carpets of San Francisco and furnished with chairs lent by good Federals for the ball to be given for the Governor's daughter by his infantry guard, but which his Excellency could not attend, as on this day he honored with his presence the table of the English Minister, who was celebrating in his house his Sovereign's birthday. And his Excellency's health might suffer by going incautiously from a banquet to a ball, for which reason it had been decided that the Señorita his daughter should represent him at the entertainment.

The lanterns in the Plaza de la Victoria, the illumination of the interior of the palace, from whose long glazed galleries streamed a flood of light that extended as far as the Plaza of the 25th of May, the public raffle, the merry-go-rounds, and above all the approach of that 25th of May which never fails to exercise its magic influence over the spirits of her sons, drew the people of Buenos Ayres, ever ready to pass from tears to laughter, from grave to gay, from the great to the little, to the two great plazas.

Meanwhile the invited guests had begun to arrive at the palace, and by eleven o'clock the salons were filled and the first quadrille had ended.

The grand salon was resplendent. The gold of the military uniforms and the diamonds of the ladies glittered in the light of hundreds of candles, very badly arranged, but which nevertheless shed an abundance of light.

There was something there, however, foreign both to the place in which the entertainment was given and to the entertainment itself; that is to say, there was a preponderance of new faces, of those men, rude, stiff and silent, who show plainly that they are out of their element when they find themselves in a social circle to which they do not belong, and those women who do nothing but fan themselves, keep their mouths shut, hold their heads erect and look very serious, wishing to give it to be understood that they are quite accustomed to mingle in high society but feeling the contrary of what they wish to show.

The dancing proceeded in silence.

The soldiers of the new epoch, suffocating in their tightly buttoned uniforms, their hands cramped by their gloves, and perspiring with the pain caused by their lately adopted boots, could not imagine that anyone could be anything else than very stiff and very serious at a ball.

The ladies, some because they had come at the urgent request of their husbands—and these were the Unitarian ladies; others, because they were angry at not finding themselves among persons of their own class exclusively, and these were the Federal ladies, were all in a very bad humor—the former disdainful, the latter jealous.

The daughter of the Governor had just arrived, and the noisy applause of the Federals accompanied her as she passed through the galleries and salons.

Attired in a gown of white tulle over a pink slip, she was not magnificent as many of the other women were, but she was elegant and graceful.

A few minutes after Manuela's arrival Señora Doña Agustina Rosas de Mancilla made her appearance and every eye was turned toward her. Here it was neither fear nor adulation, it was the frank admiration of beauty which inspired the enthusiasm of the men and the praises of the women.

At the period of which we write the younger sister of Rosas, wife of General Don Lucio Mancilla, was not of the slightest political importance, nor did she concern herself in the least about either Unitarians or Federals. Nor had her intellect at this period, whether from want of opportunity or because of a tardy development, manifested that activity and scope for which it was afterward remarkable.

The importance of this woman in 1840 was derived neither from her husband, her brother, nor any other human being; it had been conferred upon her by God.

In 1840 she was barely twenty-five years of age. Prodigal nature, in love with her own handiwork, had lavished upon her all her richest gifts, and under her influence the flower of youth had bloomed into radiant beauty—a beauty which might have served as a model for the sculptor or the painter but to which neither could do full justice. The chisel would strive in vain to give the statue the pure outlines of her shoulders and throat; and the brush to combine in its hues the indescribable color of her eyes, at times of a brilliant and velvety black, at times softly veiled by dusky shadows; the carmine of her lips, the pearly whiteness of her teeth, the milk and roses of her skin. Overflowing with life and health, and gloriously beautiful, this Flower of the Plata was now in the splendor of her first youth and was, as she had a right to be, the delight of the eyes of the men and even of the women who, with their keen, and in this instance, prejudiced sight, could discover no other defects in Agustina than that her arms were a trifle too plump and her waist not perfectly rounded.

But the beauty of Agustina, who would have served the sculptor as a model for a magnificent Diana, the painter as a model for a splendid Rebecca, was yet not in harmony with the poetic beau ideal of the XIXth century; there was too much boldness, it may be said, in the outlines of her form, and there were too few of those sentimental lines, those indefinable contours, that vague, sweet, tender and spiritual expression which constitutes the type of beauty peculiar to our century, in which mind and feeling have so large a part in taste and art: such was Doña Agustina Rosas de Mancilla in 1840, as she entered the ballroom we have described, radiantly beautiful and magnificently attired. Her arms, her neck, and her head were covered with diamonds, and the compression of her waist lent the rosy hue of her cheeks a brightness which appeared too vivid only to the Unitarians of her own sex. But accustomed as were most of those present, especially the men, to regard Agustina as the queen of the beauties of Buenos Ayres they thought that tonight she had won this title to retain it undisputed forever.

Her dress was of white lace over satin of the same color, and her Greek coiffure showed to advantage, not the rounded contours of her beautiful head, but a diamond knot which confined her Federal coil.

The enchantress walked through the salons, before seating herself, leaning on the arm of her husband, General Mancilla, who seemed to have recovered something of his lost youth, together with the well-bred and graceful bearing which this gentleman of a former epoch had acquired and displayed in the cultured society which he frequented when he belonged, heart and soul, to the Unitarian party.

Every eye followed Agustina with eager admiration. But suddenly a low murmur arose at once from every corner of the ballroom. All eyes were now turned toward the door, and Agustina herself, moved by the general impulse, directed her beautiful eyes toward the center of universal observation. Two young women had just entered the ballroom arm in arm—Señora Amalia Saenz de Olabarrieta and Señorita Florencia Dupasquier.

The former, observing the rigorous etiquette of widowhood, wore a gown of pale lilac satin, under another of black lace, shorter than the first. Her waist, round and delicate as that of a Greek statue, was encircled by a ribbon of the same color as the under dress, whose ends fell to the bottom of the black skirt. Her tucker was also of lace, and a small bow of ribbon, of the same color as the ribbon which encircled her waist, set in the front of the corsage, completed the adornment of her simple and elegant costume. On either side of her face her hair fell in glossy curls down to her alabaster neck and among them, above the right temple was placed a beautiful white rose. The rest of her luxuriant chestnut hair was wound around her head in a double braid that seemed to be fastened only by a gold pin, of which the head was a magnificent pearl; and under the braid, on the left side of the head, peeped out the end of a red ribbon, the official adornment imposed, under terrible penalties, by the Restorer of Argentine liberty.

Florencia wore a gown of white crape with a tucked skirt adorned with two garlands of rosebuds, which, descending from the waist in the form of an apron to the top of the lowest tuck, passed around the bottom of the skirt. The sleeves were very short and a tucker of the finest lace was fastened in front by a red rose.

Her hair, parted in the middle, fell, like Amalia's, in silky curls down either side of her face, a triple braid, intertwined with strings of pearls, crowning her head; while two rows of pearls, escaping from the braid, adorned the white and chaste forehead of the young girl. A bunch of rosebuds, similar to those on the dress, was set gracefully and artfully on the left side of the head, so that nature's lovely adornment might serve as the repulsive symbol of the Federation.

Agustina's reign was over. She had just been deposed from her throne by a revolution effected in the universal admiration by the beauty of Amalia.

Señorita Dupasquier was enchanting, but hers was a beauty already known while this was the first time that Amalia had appeared in public. And novelty, that despotic sovereign of society, allied itself with the radiant beauty of Amalia to captivate the glances and the admiration of everyone.

Agustina herself could not refrain from allowing her admiring gaze to dwell upon her for a long time.

Several young men hastened to offer their arms to the newcomers to conduct them to their seats, for in this ball no lady received the guests.

But whether from chance, or led by that instinct, seldom at fault, by which people recognize their social equals without knowing who they are, Amalia and Florencia crossed the ballroom and seated themselves in a corner where the Unitarian ladies were sitting together.

Florencia was at once invited by a young friend of Daniel's for the quadrilles which were forming, but Amalia, who knew no one, remained sitting at the side of an old lady, who had all the air of an old marchioness of the time of Louis XIII in France, or of the Viceroy Pezuela in the city of the Incas.

"You have come very late, señorita," said the old lady to Amalia, with an almost imperceptible but graceful inclination of the head.

"True, but it was not possible for me to come earlier," answered Amalia, returning the salutation of her neighbor whom, from her countenance and dress, she at once recognized to be a person of distinction, as she at the same time recognized how slight was her enthusiasm for the Federal cause by the small knot which she wore, almost hidden among the lace of her black headdress, for at this period one's Federalism was estimated by the size of the badge worn, and two persons meeting knew perfectly well each other's political opinions merely by looking at the button-hole of the coat, if they were men, or at the head, if they were women.

"I believe this is the first time I have had the honor of meeting you. Perhaps you have come from Montevideo?"

"No, señora, I have been living in Buenos Ayres for several months past. My name is Amalia Saenz de Olabarrieta," responded Amalia, hastening to satisfy the curiosity of her companion, whom she had already discovered to be of a talkative and inquisitive disposition.

"Ah! you are the widowed Señora de Olabarrieta? I am very glad to know you. I have often heard you spoken of, and certainly there was no exaggeration in what I heard."

"May I know, señora, if it is not indiscreet to ask, to whom I have the honor of speaking?"

"I am Señora de N—"

"Ah, I congratulate myself on having this opportunity of paying my respects to Señora de N—. For myself, I am as much a stranger here as I would be in Constantinople."

In the conversation which followed, in which Señora de N— bore the principal part, the latter related to Amalia in satirical and incisive phrases the histories of most of the personages present.

"And can you tell me," said Amalia, after an interval of silence, "who that gentleman is who is twirling a white kid glove, and who is noticeable for the exaggerated size of his red badge."

"What! Don't you read the *Gaceta?*"

"The *Gaceta?*"

"Yes, the *Gaceta Mercantil.*"

"I never read it, but even if I did—"

"If you did you would have known that that gentleman could be no one but the editor of the *Gaceta*. His name is Nicolas Mariño. It is he who preaches the slaughter of the Unitarians. What eyes! Have you noticed his eyes?"

"Yes, señora," answered Amalia, laughing.

"And do you know one thing?" continued Señora de N—."

"What is that, señora?"

"That I observe that Nicolas Mariño is looking at you a great deal more than he ought to do with those eyes of his, which is the very worst thing that could happen to a girl of your beauty."

"Thanks, señora."

"And above all of your principles; for you would not do that man the honor to receive him in your house, is it not so?"

"I have already formed my circle of acquaintances, and it would be difficult for me to add new ones to it," responded Amalia, avoiding a direct answer.

"And especially a man like that," continued Señora de N—. "And he is looking at you, he is looking at you; there is not a doubt of it. Oh, and that is an honor! The editor of the *Gaceta!* The Commandant of the illustrious body of night-watchmen! But there! at last his wife is diverting him from his melancholy contemplation."

"That lady with the red satin gown trimmed with yellow and black, and a headdress of gold fringe, is the wife of Señor Mariño?"

"Yes."

"Ah! Do you know, señora," resumed Amalia, after a moment's silence, "that, without denying that the biographical sketches you have given me are interesting, it would interest me even more to know which of those ladies is Manuelita and which Agustina?"

"They are both at this moment dancing in the next room. You may have heard that Agustina is a beauty?"

"Certainly, that is the universal opinion. Is it not your opinion, also?"

"Assuredly it is; she is a beautiful country girl, but still a country girl; that is to say, her complexion is too red; her hands and arms are too large; she is too rustic for polished, and too frivolous for intellectual society."

"It would be unfortunate for you, señora," said Amalia, "if Agustina were to know in what terms you speak of her beauty; for, in general, persons of our sex do not readily forgive a slight of that kind."

"Bah! do you suppose she does not know it? Do you suppose that all those people do not know how we regard them?"

"We?"

"Yes, we. They know that if we come to their entertainments it is only for the sake of our sons or our husbands."

"It is dangerous, however."

"That is our only revenge—let them know it; let them understand the difference there is between them and us. For the rest, the risk is not great, for what can they do to us? Besides, we talk only among ourselves."

"Always?" asked Amalia, with the most malicious smile imaginable.

"Always, as now, for instance," answered Señora de N— with perfect composure.

"I beg your pardon, señora, I have not had the honor of telling you what my opinions are."

"What an idea! The moment you sat down beside me you told them to me?"

"I?"

"Yes, you, señora; you. Faces like yours, manners like yours, language like yours, dresses like yours, the ladies of the present Federation neither have, nor use, nor wear. You are one of us, even if you did not wish to be so."

"Thanks, señora, thanks," said Amalia, with her habitual smile.

XV

Daniel Bello

Daniel entered the ballroom at half-past twelve; but before following him in it let us go back three hours, in our story, and enter with him a house in the Calle de Cochebamba, into which, for half-an-hour previously, men muffled in their cloaks had been entering in twos and threes, none of them knocking at the door to ask admittance, but one of the party, in each case, putting his mouth to the keyhole and pronouncing the word "Twenty-four," the door opening instantly at this password and closing instantly after admitting the party giving it.

The house is Doña Marcelina's and the parlor, whose windows look out upon the street, had been converted on this night into a general encampment. The double bed and the canvas cots of her distinguished nieces had been transferred to it from the bedroom, around which all the parlor chairs, those of the dining-room, three trunks and a bench had been ranged, the bedroom having been converted hastily into an assembly-room for this evening, a pine table on which stood two tallow candles, in candlesticks, being placed at one end of the apartment, with a chair in front of it, which was evidently the presidential chair.

Some standing, others sitting, others reclining comfortably on the cots and the bed, a numerous party of men occupied Doña Marcelina's parlor, which was dark save for the faint light of the stars that entered through the small, dim window panes.

Conversation was carried on in whispers, and from time to time some member of the party would approach one of the windows and look cautiously up and down the dark and deserted Calle de Cochebamba.

The metallic vibrations of the clock of the Town Hall, striking the hour, reached this mysterious meeting.

"It is half-past nine, gentlemen, and no one could make a mistake of an hour when an important appointment is in question. Those who have not come now will not come at all. Let us call the meeting to order."

At the conclusion of this address, pronounced by a voice well known to us, the shutters of the windows were closed and the door of the room adjoining the bedroom was partly opened, allowing the light to enter from it.

A moment later Daniel Bello seated himself in the chair standing in front of the pine table, Eduardo Belgrano sitting at his right, the remaining seats being occupied by twenty-one men, the eldest of whom could not be more than twenty-five or twenty-six years of age, and whose features and dress showed that they belonged to the cultured and intelligent class.

"My friends," said Daniel, looking around the assemblage, "thirty-four men were to have met here tonight, yet there are only twenty-three of us present. But whatever may be the causes for which our friends have deserted us let us not insult any of them by thinking him a traitor or entertain the slightest suspicion regarding his secret. Thirty-two men were selected by me; each received timely notice to be here tonight, and I know well, gentlemen, who are the men in Buenos Ayres whose honor is to be relied upon. Now, a few words to inspire you with perfect confidence in this house. Should we be surprised in it by the tyrant's assassins our doom would be instantly sealed. But if he has power I have understanding and prevision. This house overlooks the barranca on the coast. The water is within less than two hundred yards from it, and there are at this moment two boats at the river's edge waiting to take us on board. Should we be surprised, we can escape to the barranca through the window of a room in the rear, which looks out upon it; and even should we be attacked there, I think that twenty-three men, more or less well armed, might without any difficulty make their way to the shore. Once in the boats, those of us who desire to return to the city will have several leagues of coast from which to choose a landing place; and those who wish to leave the country have the eastern bank within a few hours' sail. Guarding the street door is my faithful Fermin. At the window overlooking the barranca is Belgrano's servant, of whose fidelity we have had repeated proofs; and, finally, on the roof is a person in whom I have every confidence and whose want of courage is our best guarantee; for if fear should prevent him from calling out to warn us it will not prevent him from making the roof over this room tremble under his steps when he is running away; he is a former teacher of most of us; he does not know who are here tonight, but he knows that I am here; and that is sufficient for him. Are you satisfied?"

"The exordium has been somewhat lengthy, but now that it is ended, I do not believe there is anyone here who after having heard it does not think himself as safe as if he were in Paris," said a young man with black eyes and a cheerful and open cast of countenance who, during Daniel's discourse, had occupied himself in playing with his watch chain.

"I know the ground I am plowing, my dear friends; I know that you are all uneasy, and I know, besides, that I am responsible for whatever may happen to you. Now, let us proceed to the object of our meeting.

"Here, gentlemen," continued Daniel, producing a pocketbook filled with papers, from which he selected one, "is the first document concerning which I wish to speak to you; it is a list of the persons who, during the month of April and the first half of the present month of May have emigrated to the Oriental Republic. They number one hundred and sixty men, all young, patriotic and enthusiastic. I have reasons for assuring you that those engaged in the business of taking emigrants to the Banda Oriental have had applications for more than three hundred passages, and this since the assassinations of the 4th of May.

"Now, hear what is the condition of the Liberating Army and of the interior provinces in order that you may the better understand the significance of the fact I have just stated.

"Since the action of Don Cristóbal, in which the battle was won and the victory lost, the Liberating Army has been encamped on the heights of Arroyo Grande besieging the troops of Echagüe, shut up in Las Piedras, and all this at a few leagues' distance from the Bajada; and all the probabilities seem to be in favor of General Lavalle in case of another battle. If he gains it, the passage of the Paraná will be the immediate result, and the campaign will then begin by an attack on Buenos Ayres. If he is defeated, the remnant of his army will reörganize on the north of our province, since they have the blockading vessels in which to cross the river; you see then that in either case the Province of Buenos Ayres is waiting for General Lavalle.

"In the provinces the league has spread like a conflagration. Tucuman and Salta, La Rioja, Catamarca and Jujuy no longer belong to the tyrant; they have declared against him and they are preparing their armies. The friar Aldao is not strong enough to put down the revolution, and Córdova will submit to the first invader. Rosas has fixed his hopes on La-Madrid; La-Madrid has deserted him."

"What!" cried his hearers in chorus, all rising to their feet with the exception of Eduardo, who seemed absorbed in tender meditation.

"It is true, General La-Madrid, commissioned by Rosas to seize the park of artillery at Tucuman, has allowed the revolution to seize him;

and on the 7th of April he put upon his breast the blue-and-white ribbon of Liberty and trampled under his foot the shameful symbol of the Federatoin of Rosas."

"Bravo! Bravo!"

"Silence, silence, gentlemen; here is another document; hear it."

"LIBERTY OR DEATH.
"General Order of April 9, 1840.

"By order of the Government General Gregorio Araoz de La-Madrid has been appointed General-in-Chief of all the troops of the line and the militia of the Province; Colonel Lorenzo Lugones, Chief of Staff, and Colonel Mariano Acha, Chief of Cuirassiers."

A spontaneous burst of emotion followed these words. There were no shouts, no huzzas, but every face was eloquent, and embraces and hand-clasps pronounced discourses and registered vows. Daniel surveyed the scene with his eagle glance; he manifested no enthusiasm; he was studying the complex book of human nature.

"You see, gentlemen," he continued with his usual imperturbable calmness, "that on all sides the revolution rises gigantic, but the revolution is aimed at an object. Why should we not believe that the revolution will be logical and that it will seek that object in the place in which it hides itself? That object is a head and that head is in Buenos Ayres. If the efforts of all are to be directed to this point, is it not true, gentlemen, that we too ought to contribute to the triumph that is approaching?"

"Yes, yes," cried his hearers in chorus.

"Now, count the patriots who have left Buenos Ayres; calculate the number that will leave it in the future unless we can succeed in stemming this torrent of emigration, and then tell me if the same number of men would not be sufficient to coöperate effectually in the city with the revolution which the arms of General Lavalle, or the arms of the Coalition of Cuyo will effect in the province.

"Emigration leaves Buenos Ayres, that is to say, gentlemen, the center whence radiates the power of Rosas, in the possession of women, cowards and the Mashorqueros.

"Would three or four hundred men who should enroll themselves in the ranks of his army assure the triumph of General Lavalle? Well, gentlemen, three or four hundred brave men will be sufficient to raise the city in revolt and hang Rosas and his Mashorca from the lamp posts in the streets the day on which they are surprised by the news of the approach of any one of the armies of freedom.

"Is there danger in remaining in Buenos Ayres? Will there be danger and bloodshed the day on which we give the first cry of freedom? But gentlemen, are there not danger and bloodshed in the field? Are there not misery and humiliation in exile?

"Believe me, my friends; I am nearer to Rosas than any of you; I risk more than my life, for I expose my honor to the suspicion of my compatriots. Believe me, then, that the worst course the youth of Buenos Ayres could pursue in the desire which animates them to free their country would be to absent themselves from it."

"That is my opinion; that is my belief," said one of the young men present. "I would die by the dagger of the Mashorca rather than quit the city. Rosas is in it, and it is Rosas whom we must seek on the day in which one of our armies enters the province. Rosas dead, we should look around us in vain to find a single enemy."

"Are you of that opinion, also, my friends?" asked Daniel.

"Yes, yes, we must remain," responded all enthusiastically.

"Gentlemen," said Eduardo Belgrano, when silence was restored, "there is not a word which Señor Bello has uttered that is not entirely in accordance with my opinions; and yet I was one of those who had resolved to emigrate from the country and I do not know yet but that I may at any moment again resolve to do so. There is, then, an apparent contradiction between my opinions and my conduct, and consequently I owe you an explanation, which I am now going to give you.

"Señor Bello has said that three or four hundred men would be sufficient to destroy the power of Rosas in the city and I would willingly believe this to be the case. But suppose there were even three or four thousand of us hostile to Rosas, do you know, gentlemen, what that number represents in Buenos Ayres? It represents one man.

"A party is not powerful through numbers, but through union. A million unassociated men are worth no more than two or three men united in their ideas, in their will and in their acts.

"Let us study carefully the political system of Rosas and we shall find the secret of his power to lie in the disassociation of the citizens. Rosas is not the Dictator of a people; that would be too vulgar a tyranny for men like us to submit to. Rosas tyrannizes over every family in its house, every individual in his room; and to effect this miracle he only needs, in fact, a few dozen assassins.

　　　　　　　　　　　　　　　　　　　　　　JOSÉ MÁRMOL

"Small states without social distinctions or a titled class, in which neither virtue, knowledge nor patriotism confers prestige on its possessor, at once ignorant and vain, sensitive and jealous, the countries of South America have as their only elements of union with one another and within themselves, Catholicism and political independence.

"Without comprehending yet the advantages of association of any kind it is in political parties that it exists least.

"A spirit of constitutional indolence, natural to the race, serves to complete the work of our moral disorganization and we meet, we talk, we agree today, and tomorrow we separate, we betray each other, or at least we neglect to meet together again.

"Without association, without the spirit of association, without the hope of being able to improvise that lever of European power and European progress called association, on what can we count for the work we propose to accomplish? On public opinion? Ah, gentlemen, that opinion has existed for many years in our country, and yet the Mashorca, that is to say, a hundred ruffians, take us one by one, and do with us whatever they wish. This is the simple fact, and I prefer to die on the field of battle to dying in my house, waiting for a revolution which all the people of our city together could never effect, for all together we represent only the value of one man.

"Meanwhile, what my friend has said is an indisputable truth; that is to say, it would be more opportune and efficacious to exterminate tyranny in the single person of Rosas. Tell me if it be possible to establish association and I will be the first to cast aside all idea of abandoning the country."

A general silence followed this discourse.

All the young men kept their eyes fixed upon the ground. Daniel alone held his head erect, while his looks studied their countenances one by one.

"Gentlemen," he said at last, "my friend Belgrano has expressed my sentiments, in so far as the spirit of individualism which, to the misfortune of our country, has always characterized the Argentines, is concerned. But the evils resulting from this defect of our education in the past are the best hope we have that we will correct ourselves of it; and to urge upon you the benefits of association after persuading you of the necessity of remaining in Buenos Ayres was the second part of the purpose that brought me here tonight. You have agreed with me that we should await events in Buenos Ayres; you must agree with me also, that if those events find us disunited we shall profit but little by them."

"United, our defense systematized, all banded together to avenge the first who falls, we shall either stay the hand of the assassin; or provoke the revolution; or we may emigrate in a body, when all hope of exterminating tyranny is at an end; or, finally, we can die in the streets of our city, leaving behind us an honorable example to future generations.

"I, who purchase at the price of my peace and my reputation the secrets of our enemies; I, who, with my heart throbbing with rage, take in my hand the bloody hands of the assassins of our country, will incite their envenomed hearts to crime by my words whenever I believe that that crime will arouse against them the vengeance of the oppressed. For the moment in which the hand of a brave man, in the light of day, plunges a dagger in the breast of one of the assassins, that moment, gentlemen, will be the last of the tyrant; for oppressed peoples need only a man, a battle cry, an instant's time, to pass amid the din of arms from slavery to liberty, from paralysis to action."

Daniel's countenance glowed, his eyes flashed fire. The glances of all were fixed upon him. Eduardo alone, who was of a contemplative and philosophic cast of mind, and of a haughty, frank and courageous temper, remained with his elbow resting on the table and his forehead leaning on the palm of his hand.

"Yes, association," cried one of the young men; "association today, to defend ourselves against the Mashorca, to await the revolution, to hang Rosas."

"Association tomorrow," said Daniel, raising his voice for the first time and throwing back his haughty, beautiful and intellectual head, "association tomorrow, to organize the society of our country."

"Association in politics to give her liberty and laws.

"Association in commerce, in industry, in literature and in science to give her learning and progress.

"Association in religion to cultivate the morality and the virtues which we lack.

"Would you have a country, would you have liberty, would you have free institutions, unite together against the enemy of our social reformation—ignorance! against the instigator of our savage passions—political fanaticism! against the propagator of our disunion, of our vices, of our rancorous passions, of our vain and stubborn spirit—religious skepticism. For believe me—we have neither religion, virtue nor knowledge; and we have nothing of civilization but its vices."

"Yes, yes, we will unite together," cried several voices in chorus.

"Yes, my friends, we will unite together," continued Daniel; "and while we are still filled with the enthusiasm inspired by this thought we should separate. I will draw up our constitution. It will be simple, the expression of a very simple requirement—that of being able to assemble together in a quarter of an hour whenever it may be necessary to do so for the support or the initiation of the revolution that is to overthrow the tyrant."

"Today is the 24th of May. On the 24th of June we will meet again in this house at the same hour as tonight."

"One word more; let each one of you use all his influence to prevent our friends from emigrating; but if they desire positively to do so, let them come to me; I will answer for their safe embarkation. But seek me only in that case. Otherwise shun me; censure my conduct among the indifferent; tarnish my name with your censure, for the time will come when I will purify it in the crucible of our country's liberty. Are you satisfied? Have you complete confidence in me?"

The young men all crowded around Daniel, and a hearty embrace was the answer he received from each.

Then the door leading into the parlor was opened, after that the street door; and ten minutes later the meeting had dispersed.

XVI

SCENES IN A BALLROOM—CONTINUED

Daniel entered the ballroom, as we saw at the beginning of Chapter XIV, at half-past twelve o'clock.

As Florencia was promenading through the room he crossed over to his cousin, who was sitting beside the uncompromising lady who seemed to know by heart the history of everyone present.

Señora de N— responded to Daniel's salutation somewhat coldly, and the latter, giving Amalia his arm, said to her as they walked through the room:

"Have you been talking much to that lady?"

"No; but she has been talking a great deal to me."

"Do you know who she is?"

"Señora de N—."

"The most uncompromising Unitarian in Buenos Ayres. But there is Manuela; I am going to present you to her."

"Tell me, must I cry, Long live the Federation! when I salute her?" said Amalia, with an ironical smile.

"Manuela is the only good one of the whole Rosas family; they may succeed in perverting her in the end, but nature made her excellent," said Daniel, almost in a whisper, for they were now within a few steps of the daughter of the Argentine Dictator.

"My cousin, Señora Amalia Saenz de Olabarrieta, desires to have the pleasure of paying her respects to you," said Daniel to Manuela, offering her his hand with a graceful bow.

Manuela rose from her seat, exchanged the customary compliments with Amalia in the most well-bred manner possible, and offered her a seat beside her.

Daniel, asking Amalia's permission to leave her for a moment, then went to look for Florencia, who had disappeared among the innumerable couples that crowded the salons.

However prejudiced Amalia's mind might be against the name of the young girl at her side, Manuela's amiability and simplicity produced their natural effect on her good and generous heart. Manuela, on her side, impressed by the beauty of Amalia, by the softness of her voice, and by her high-bred ease of manner, allowed herself to be drawn unresistingly by her sympathies toward the beautiful cousin of Daniel, who had managed to win for himself the good will of everyone around Rosas, the women regarding him as merely frivolous and susceptible, points of great importance with them, and the men as a young man who was cultivating his intelligence to be useful one day to the holy cause of the Federation.

Both girls, then, were engaged in an animated if not friendly conversation when Daniel approached his cousin, and Colonel Don Mariano Maza, Señorita Manuela, while, at the same time, Don Nicolas Mariño, Editor of the *Gaceta* and Commandant of the Night-Watchmen, stopped in front of the young girls.

A waltz was just beginning.

Colonel Maza offered his hand to the daughter of his Governor, who took it and rose from her seat; she was engaged to him for this waltz.

The editor of the *Gaceta* wished to imitate the pantomime of Maza; he held out his hand to Amalia, stammering a few unintelligible words.

Daniel, without a word, gave his cousin his hand for the dance, and turning to Mariño, as she rose said, with the politest smile possible:

"She is engaged for this dance, Señor Mariño."

And as this announcement admitted of no reply, the editor remained standing where he was, while the cousins took their places among the dancers.

When the dance was over Amalia and Florencia sat down together in a corner of the ballroom, and a few moments afterward Manuela, arm-in-arm with Agustina, approached them.

Daniel remained standing in front of Florencia and his cousin.

Manuela presented Agustina, who with her lips addressed Amalia, while her eyes were fixed on the beautiful pearl of the pin which fastened the magnificent hair of the young widow.

The four girls sat down together and while Manuela conversed with Florencia, Agustina occupied herself in putting question after question to Amalia about her dress, her ribbons, laces, etc.

Amalia was astounded at the frankness of the beautiful Agustina, and from time to time questioned Daniel with her eyes as to what manner of woman this was. Agustina, however, observed none of these glances. Hers were examining even to the stitches of Amalia's gown.

"I hope that we shall be very good friends," said Agustina to Amalia, after asking her if she knew where she could find a pearl like the one in her hair, in order that she might buy it.

"It will be a great honor for me, señora, to enjoy your friendship," answered Amalia.

"I have long desired this opportunity," continued Agustina; "and I had already thought of going to your house, without waiting for an introduction to you; for I am like that—I am very frank with my friends. And you will show me all your things, will you not?"

"With the greatest pleasure."

At this moment a short, thickset man with a dark complexion, and a tall, fair, stout lady, who were no other than Señor Rivera, doctor of medicine and surgery, and his wife, Doña Mercedes Rosas, also a sister of his Excellency the Governor, joined the group.

More noticeable even than this lady's gown of blood-colored satin, trimmed with black velvet, her large topaz earrings, or the strings of coral which encircled her neck, were several red moles on her face that contrasted vividly with the extreme fairness of her skin and that were especially exuberant on her round, full chin.

"I have been looking for you everywhere," she said to her sister Agustina.

"Well, now that you have found me, what do you want with me?"

"I am dripping with perspiration, child; let us go and eat something."

"Already?"

"Yes, already. How are you, Señor Bello?"

"Señora, I am at your service."

"And what have you been doing with yourself of late that you are to be seen nowhere? Making love to all the women? Is this your cousin?"

"Yes, señora; Señora Amalia Saenz de Olabarrieta, whom I have the honor to present to you."

"I am very glad to know you," said Doña Mercedes, giving her hand to Amalia, who had risen from her seat at Daniel's introduction. "I hope we shall be very good friends," she continued. "Don't wait for Bello to take you to my house; come and dine with me whenever you please. If you wish, my husband will go for you, for I am not as jealous as he is; this is my husband, Rivera, Dr. Rivera. Have you not met him before?"

"I have not had that honor, señora."

"Yes, a great honor. If you only knew what he is! He doesn't give me a chance to breathe; I say it to his face so that he may be ashamed of himself. Do you hear?"

"I hear, Mercedes; but you are only joking."

"Shameless fellow! Well, now you know; whenever you please he will go for you."

Amalia did not know what to answer. Fortunately, Commandant Maza, who seemed to be Manuela's escort tonight, now presented himself to take the latter to supper and a diversion was thus effected.

The moment Manuela stood up everyone else stood also.

The Federal ladies made haste to follow, like satellites, the radiant star of the Federation of 1840. Each one endeavored to get as near to her as possible in order to sit beside her at table.

The Unitarian ladies, on the contrary, either remained in their seats or withdrew as far as possible from the others; exchanging with one another at the same time eloquent and significant glances.

The moment Manuela and Agustina stood up Daniel made a sign to one of his friends, who, in response to a few whispered words from him offered his arm to Amalia, while Florencia took that of Daniel.

They were proceeding in this order to the grand dining-room of the palace through salons and galleries, when Señora de N—accompanied by a young man, approached Amalia and whispered to her:

"I congratulate you on your new friends."

Amalia responded with a smile.

"I understand that smile. We are of the same mind. But I have something serious to tell you."

"Something serious?" said Amalia, stopping with a sudden throb of the heart, for everything here, if it did not alarm her, made her uneasy.

"Yes."

"And what is it?"

"It concerns Mariño."

"The man with the eyes?"

"The man with the eyes."

"Well, and what is it?"

"That he follows you everywhere with his gaze, that he devours you with his eyes, and that he has just said to a friend of mine that the devil may take him if he does not win your favor."

"Ah! then let us congratulate ourselves, señora, and let us go to supper," said Amalia, taking her companion's arm again.

"No, no, softly;" said Señora de N—, "you do not know that man, my dear."

"That man! That man is a madman and nothing more, señora," answered Amalia, shrugging her shoulders slightly and taking leave of Señora de N— with an enchanting smile.

XVII

After the Ball

A few minutes after Amalia, Florencia and Daniel had left the palace, the carriage stopped at Madame Dupasquier's house in the Calle de la Reconquista, and after leaving Florencia there drove on some fifty paces further in the same direction and then stopped again beside another carriage which had been waiting for it, apparently, and from which Eduardo Belgrano alighted at the same moment in which Daniel alighted from Amalia's carriage. The young men exchanged a few words and Daniel then entered the carriage which Eduardo had just left, and which was his own carriage, and the latter took his friend's place at Amalia's side.

Amalia's carriage, with old Pedro as coachman and Belgrano's servant as footman, then drove rapidly down the Calle de la Reconquista in the direction of Barracas.

As the carriage was approaching the chapel of Santa Lucía, before turning into the Calle Larga, and while Amalia was relating to Eduardo the events of the ball, it was overtaken by three horsemen who at a gallop had descended the Barranca of General Brown and followed the carriage.

The intention of these men very soon became apparent; two of them placed themselves one on either side of the horses of the carriage, passing so suddenly in front of these that Pedro was obliged to pull them up.

The third horseman approached the carriage door and in a voice bland, but somewhat tremulous from the haste with which he had ridden, said:

"We are friends, señora; I know that you have an excellent escort in Señor Bello, but the roads are lonely and I have hastened after your carriage to offer you my company as far as your house."

The carriage had now stopped.

Pedro leaned forward as far as he could from his seat on the box to take a good aim at the head of one of the two men who rode beside the carriage horses, in order to send into it an ounce of lead, in the shape of a bullet, which he carried in the barrel of a cavalry pistol that had played its part meritoriously in half-a-dozen dramas represented twenty years before.

Eduardo's servant was preparing to jump down from the back of the carriage to take the measure of the first who should come within his reach with a thick stick, which he had prudently placed between the straps of the foot-board of the carriage and which he had taken from them the moment the carriage had stopped.

Eduardo had no other weapon than the small sword in his cane.

The individual who had spoken was wrapped in a dark poncho, and as he sat facing the carriage lamps his face remained in the shadow.

Neither Amalia nor Eduardo recognized the voice of the man who had spoken. But women have a wonderful faculty of divination that enables them to tell among a hundred men which is the one on whom their beauty has made an impression; and in the most difficult and the most unfamiliar circumstances a woman can at once divine whether she has any part in, and where to seek the clue to, what for everyone else is a profound mystery.

So that the unknown had scarcely finished speaking when Amalia, leaning toward Eduardo, whispered:

"It is Mariño."

"Mariño!" exclaimed Eduardo.

"Yes, Mariño; he is a madman."

"No, he is a scoundrel. Señor," continued Eduardo, raising his voice, "this lady has already a sufficient escort, and I request that you will have the goodness to retire and to order the men who have stopped our horses to do the same."

"It was not to you I addressed myself, Señor Bello."

"There is no one here of that name; there is no one here—"

"Silence, for Heaven's sake!—Señor," continued Amalia, addressing Mariño, "I thank you for your attention, but I repeat what this gentleman has said and I request that you will have the goodness to retire."

"This is too much. The word request has been used twice already," said Eduardo, putting his hand through the window to open the carriage door; but Amalia caught him by the arm, and by a superhuman effort drew him back to his seat.

"It appears to me that that individual is little accustomed to deal with gentlemen," said Mariño.

"Gentlemen who stop carriages at midnight may very justly be dealt with like highwaymen. Drive on, Pedro," cried Eduardo, in so stern and so resolute a voice that the two men who were beside the horses did not dare to stop them without an order to do so from the man who seemed to be their leader when Pedro gave the animals a cut with his whip, ready to use his pistol if anyone should still attempt to oppose the progress of his mistress's carriage.

Commandant Mariño, for it was no other than he, put spurs to his horse as the carriage started, and riding beside it said to Amalia:

"Know, señora, that it was not my intention to do you any injury, but I have been vilely treated; and the man who has received such an insult does not easily forget it."

Having spoken thus, Mariño, wheeling his horse around, rode back to the city, by way of the Barranca of Balcarce; while Amalia, five minutes later, entered her parlor, leaning on Eduardo's arm, looking a little paler than usual and somewhat disturbed by the scene which had just taken place.

XVIII

Doña María Josefa Ezcurra

We will now ask the reader to accompany us to a house which he has once before entered with us in the Calle del Restaurador.

The sister-in-law of his Excellency the Restorer of the Laws is giving audience in her bedroom, and the parlor adjoining, with its handsome black-and-white matting, which serves as a reception room, is crowded with the petitioners of the day.

An old mulatto woman is acting as aid-de-camp, mistress of ceremonies and usher.

Standing in front of the door opening into the bedroom she holds the latch with one hand as a sign that no one may pass through it without her permission, while with the other she takes the coppers or the bank-notes given to her, according to their station, by those who approach her to solicit the preference in obtaining early admittance to the presence of Señora Doña María Josefa Ezcurra. And never was audience composed of a greater variety of shades in class, color and race, than the audience here assembled. Mingled together indiscriminately are negroes and mulattos, Indians and whites, the lowest class and the middle class, the good and the bad—differing also in their passions, their habits, their prejudices and their hopes.

The latch is moved from the inside and the old mulatto woman opens the door to give exit to a young negress of from sixteen to eighteen years of age, who crosses the parlor holding her head as high as a court lady might do who has just been favored for the first time by the smiles of her Queen in the privacy of the Royal dressing-room.

Immediately the mulatto woman beckons to a white man, dressed in a blue jacket and blue trousers and a red waistcoat, who is standing beside one of the windows of the parlor holding his cloth cap in his hand.

The man makes his way slowly through the crowd to the mulatto woman, exchanges a few words with her and then enters the bedroom, the door of which is immediately closed behind him.

Doña María Josefa, wrapped in a large white merino shawl with a red border, was seated on a small bamboo sofa standing at the head of her bed, drinking a maté of milk which a young negro girl had just brought to her from an inner room.

"Come in, countryman; sit down;" she said to the man with the cloth cap, who seated himself, greatly embarrassed, in one of the wooden chairs standing in front of the sofa.

"Will you have bitter or sweet maté?"

"Whichever your Ladyship wishes," answered the man, who sat on the edge of the chair, turning his cap around between his hands.

"Don't call me your Ladyship. Address me as you would anyone else. Now we are all equal. The times of the Unitarian savages are over when the poor man had to go about giving titles to the man who wore a frock-coat or a new hat. Now we are all equal because we are all Federals. Are you in the army now, countryman?"

"No, señora. Five years ago General Pinedo gave me my discharge, on account of sickness, and after I got well I worked as a coachman."

"You served under Pinedo?"

"Yes, señora; I was wounded in action and they gave me my discharge."

"Well, Juan Manuel is going to call everyone to the service now."

"Yes, señora, so I have heard."

"They say Lavalle is going to invade the country and every one must defend the Federation because we are all its children. Juan Manuel will be the first to mount his horse, because he is the father of all the good defenders of the Federation. But exceptions will be made in the service, for it is not just that those should go to suffer the hardships of war who can serve the cause in other ways."

"No, indeed!"

"I have a list of more than fifty to whom I am going to have exemption papers given on account of the services they are rendering. For you must know, countryman, that the true servants of the cause are those who disclose the intrigues and the maneuvers of the Unitarian savages here in the city, who are the worst of all; isn't that so?"

"So they say, señora," answered the ex-soldier, returning the maté to the negro girl who had brought it to him.

"They are the worst of all; depend upon it. On their account it is, on account of their intrigues it is, that we have no peace and that men cannot work and stay at home with their families, which is what Juan Manuel desires. Don't you think that is the true Federation?"

"Of course, señora."

"To live without anyone troubling them about the service."

"Just so."

"And to be all equal, poor and rich, that is Federation, isn't it?"

"Yes, señora."

"Well, that is what the Unitarian savages don't want; and for that reason everyone who discovers their maneuvers is a true Federal and always has Juan Manuel's house and mine open to him to come in and ask whatever he wants; for Juan Manuel denies nothing to those who serve the country, which is the Federation; do you understand, countryman?"

"Yes, señora, and I have always been a Federal."

"I know it, and Juan Manuel knows it too; and that is why I have sent for you, certain that you would not conceal the truth from me, if you knew anything that might be useful to the cause."

"And what should I know, señora, when I live among Federals only?"

"Who can tell! You honest men allow yourselves to be easily imposed upon. Tell me, where have you been serving lately?"

"I am at present employed in the livery-stable of the Englishman."

"I know that, but before going there where did you serve?"

"In Barracas, in the house of a widow-lady."

"Who is called Doña Amalia, no?"

"Yes, señora."

"Oh, we know everything here, countryman! Woe to anyone who tries to deceive Juan Manuel or me!" said Doña María Josefa, fixing her small viper-like eyes on the face of the poor man, who was on thorns, not knowing what he was going to be asked.

"Of course," he answered.

"When did you enter the lady's service?"

"In November of last year."

"And you left it?"

"In May, of the present year, señora."

"On what day, do you remember?"

"Yes, señora, I left it on the 5th of May."

"The 5th of May, eh?" said the old woman, emphasizing each word with a nod. "And why did you leave that place?"

"The mistress told me that she wished to reduce her expenses a little and that for that reason she was going to discharge me as well as the cook, a young Spaniard. But before leaving, she gave each of us an ounce in gold, saying that perhaps she would send for us again and that we were to go to her if we should ever find ourselves in need."

"What a kind lady! She wanted to economize and she made presents of gold ounces!" said Doña María Josefa, sarcastically.

"Yes, señora, Doña Amalia is the best lady I know, present company excepted."

Doña María Josefa did not hear these words; her spirit was holding close converse with the devil.

"Tell me, countryman," she said, suddenly, "at what hour did Doña Amalia discharge you?"

"Between seven and eight in the morning."

"And she was always up at that hour?"

"No, señora, she usually rose very late."

"And did you notice anything strange going on in the house?"

"No, señora, nothing."

"Which of the servants remained with her when you and the cook left?"

"Don Pedro."

"Who is he?"

"He is an old soldier who served in the former wars and who has known the mistress ever since she was born."

"Who else?"

"A servant maid whom the mistress brought from Tucuman—a young girl; and two old negroes who take care of the villa."

"Very good; in all that you have told me you have spoken the truth; but, take care; now I am going to ask you something of great importance to the Federation and to Juan Manuel; do you hear?"

"I always speak the truth, señora," answered the man, lowering his eyes before the threatening look with which Doña María Josefa accompanied her words.

"And tell me, during the five months you remained in Doña Amalia's house, what men were in the habit of visiting her in the evenings."

"No one visited her in the evenings, señora."

"How, no one?"

"No one, señora. In all the time I was in her house I never saw anyone come to visit her in the evening."

"She spent the time praying, perhaps?"

"I don't know, señora, but no one came to the house," answered Amalia's former coachman who, in spite of his devotion to the sacred cause, was beginning to comprehend that the honor or the safety of Amalia was here concerned and he was annoyed that he should be thought capable of compromising her, when he was persuaded that there was not in the world a better or a more generous woman than she.

Doña María Josefa reflected for a moment.

"This upsets all my calculations," she said to herself.

"And tell me, did no one enter the house by day, either?" she said aloud.

"Some ladies went there occasionally."

"No, men, I am asking you."

"Señor Don Daniel, a cousin of the mistress, used to go there."

"Every day?"

"No, señora, once or twice a week."

"And since you left the house, have you seen the lady again?"

"I have gone there three or four times."

"And tell me, when you went there whom did you see besides your mistress?"

"No one."

"Was there no one sick in the house?"

"No, señora, they were all well."

"Very good, countryman," said Doña María Josefa, after a moment's reflection; "Juan Manuel had some information about that house, but I will tell him what you have said and if it is true you will have done a service to your mistress but if you have concealed anything from me you know what Juan Manuel is with those who don't serve the Federation."

"I am a Federal, señora, I always speak the truth."

"I believe it; you may retire now."

The moment Amalia's ex-coachman had left the room Doña María Josefa called the mulatto woman who guarded the door and said to her:

"Is the girl who came from Barracas yesterday there?"

"She is, señora."

"Let her come in."

A moment later a young negress, about twenty years of age, entered the room.

Doña María Josefa looked at her in silence for a moment and then said:

"You have not told me the truth; there is no man living in the house of the lady you have denounced, and no one has been sick there."

"Yes, señora, I swear to your Ladyship that I have told you the truth. I am employed in a grocery near the house of that Unitarian; and from the rear of the house I have several times seen a young man, who never wears a badge, walking in the Unitarian's garden, in the morning, cutting flowers. Then, I often see them both walking arm-in-arm in the garden; and in the afternoons they generally sit under a large willow, which is in it, and take their coffee there."

"And from where do you see that, you say?"

"The rear of the house I am in looks on the rear of the villa of the Unitarian, and I watch them from behind the fence because I hate them."

"Why do you hate them?"

"Because they are Unitarians."

"How do you know that?"

"Because Doña Amalia never salutes either the master or the mistress or me when she passes the shop; because her servants never come to the grocery to buy anything, when they know that the master and all of us are Federals; and because I have often seen her walking in the garden of the villa with a blue gown on. And when I saw Señor Marino's orderly and two other men watching the house these past few nights, and making inquiries at the grocery. I came to tell your Ladyship what I knew, because I am a good Federal. She is a Unitarian; yes, señora."

"And what more did you see in that house?"

"I told your Ladyship yesterday all I saw. A young man, who they say is the Unitarian woman's cousin, is there almost all the time, and lately Dr. Alcorta has gone there almost every day; and that is why I said to your Ladyship that there must be someone sick in the house."

"And do you remember anything else you said to me?"

"Ah, yes, señora; I said to your Ladyship that the sick person must be the young man who cuts the flowers, because in the beginning I saw that he limped badly."

"And when was in the beginning? How many months ago is that?"

"About two months ago, señora; he hasn't limped since that time; and the doctor doesn't go there now. Now he walks for hours at a time with Doña Amalia, without limping."

"Very good; you must keep a close watch on all that goes on in that house and tell me of it, for in that way you do a great service to the cause, which is the cause of the poor, because in the Federation there are neither blacks nor whites; we are all equal; do you understand?"

"Yes, señora; and for that reason I am a Federal; and all I find out I will come and tell your Ladyship."

"Very well, you may go now."

And the negress left the room very well pleased at having done a service to the sacred cause of the blacks and the whites, and at having spoken to the sister-in-law of his Excellency, the Father of the Federation.

XIX

Two of a Kind

Doña María Josefa Ezcurra was just about to leave her house to pay her dear Juan Manuel the second of the three visits which she made him daily, when Commandant Mariño, editor of the *Gaceta Mercantil,* entered it very familiarly.

Doña María Josefa did not keep her worthy visitor waiting long but went at once to the parlor to receive him, saying, as she entered the room:

"You are the only person I would have seen, for I was just going to Juan Manuel's; and I will tell you in the beginning that I am very angry."

"And so am I," answered Mariño, seating himself beside her on the sofa.

"Yes, but you have not as good reason to be angry as I have."

"I think I have; begin with your reason and I will tell you mine afterwards;" answered the editor, a man on whom nature had had the caprice to bestow a soul darkened by the blackest passions of which humanity is capable but in which shone at the same time some sparks of imagination and genius.

"Well, then, I have reason to complain of you because you are only serving us by halves."

"Serving us? Serving whom, Señora Doña María Josefa?"

"Whom? Juan Manuel, the cause, me, all of us."

"Ah!"

"Just so! And that cannot be pleasing to Juan Manuel."

"With respect to that, I will settle with the Governor myself," answered Mariño, looking straight at the old woman, although no one would have thought so; for his eyes always looked obliquely. "But tell me, how is it that I serve only by halves?"

"In this way; that while you preach in the *Gaceta* the slaughter of the Unitarian men you forget the Unitarian women, who are worse than the men."

"But it is necessary to begin with the men."

"It is necessary to begin and to end with them all, men and women alike; and I would begin with the women, who are the worst."

"Well, we shall deal with the Unitarian women when the time comes; but now I want to tell you that there are some ladies also who are not loyal friends."

"No? Well, as far as I am concerned—"

"It is precisely to you that I refer."

"Come! You are joking."

"No, señora; I am in earnest; I confided a secret to you a couple of weeks ago—do you remember?"

"About Barracas?"

"Yes, about Barracas; and you have gone and told every word of it to my wife."

"Why! I was only joking with her."

"Well, it was a joke that has cost me dear, for my wife is ready to tear my eyes out."

"Bah!"

"There is no bah about it; the matter is serious."

"What!"

"Very serious."

"Don't say that."

"Yes, I do say it; very serious. And there was no reason why you should make this trouble between my wife and me."

"Why, what an idea, Mariño! As she would have heard it through some other channel I told her that you thought the widow of Barracas very handsome, but nothing more. What an idea! How can you think I would want to sow discord between your wife and you?"

"Well, the harm is done now and let us forget it," said Mariño, looking away, determining to turn to his profit the treachery of this woman, for whom there were in truth neither Unitarian men nor Unitarian women, but only men and women whom she desired to injure.

"Well, suppose the harm is done, Mariño, you must know that some good has been done, also."

"How so?"

"Why! What did you tell me?"

"I told you that I should like to learn something about a certain lady who lived in Barracas; the sort of life she led; who visited her; who a man was who lived with her, and who appeared to be in hiding, as he never left the house or even appeared at any of the windows; and I also told you that in all this I had only a political interest; that is to say, the interest of our cause."

"Just so, a political interest!"

"Why, do you doubt it? You smile ironically."

"Why, that is my way."

"Yes, señora, I know that is your way."

"You see, I am as I am."

"I know what you are."

"And I, what you are."

"That is to say that we know each other."

"Well, go on, Mariño."

"That was all I told you, thinking you would not refuse me that service; you who know everything and can do everything."

"Well, then; you shall now hear all I have done and you will see whether I am your friend or not. I have known for a long time past that that woman at Barracas leads a very retired life, and that consequently she must be a Unitarian."

"Oh, perhaps not!"

"Yes, a Unitarian without a doubt."

"Well, go on."

"You told me you thought there was a man in hiding there."

"I only suspected it."

"No; plainly, in hiding; I know what I am saying."

"Go on."

"I sent one of my servants to make inquiries in the neighborhood. Near the house there is a grocery, and in the grocery there is a young negro girl; my emissary talked with her; told her that the widow's house was suspected; to observe, and she would see that the house was watched at night."

"And how did your emissary know that?"

"Because I told him so."

"But how did you know it?"

"Bah! Because I know you; and since I saw that you had a political interest in this business," said Doña María Josefa, ironically emphasizing the last words, "I supposed that you would not let the matter rest."

"Go on," said Mariño, secretly admiring the astuteness of this woman.

"My emissary told the young negress, then, that the house was suspected; that it was watched, and that if she was wise she would ingratiate herself with me by coming to tell me of it; which would enable her to say afterward that she was a better Federal than many whites are who try to humiliate the poor colored people without rendering any service to the Federation. The negress did not keep me waiting; she came at once to see me; and as if the idea had originated with herself she told me all she knew."

"And what does she know?"

"That there is a young and handsome man there," answered Doña María Josefa, adding these qualities on her own account in order not to lose the opportunity of mortifying a fellow creature.

"Well?"

"That he is very handsome and that he walks about the garden with his arm around the widow's waist."

"With his arm around her waist, or arm-in-arm with her?"

"With his arm around her waist or arm-in-arm with her, I don't remember which it was the negress said. That they take coffee together under a willow tree; that he holds the cup for her while she is drinking, and that there they remain until night falls, and then—"

"And then, what?" said Mariño, his blood on fire and his squinting eyes bloodshot.

"And then she sees them no more," said Doña María Josefa, with an indescribable expression of satisfaction.

"Well, but," said Mariño, "so far there is nothing certain in all this but that there is a man in that house, which is what I told you two weeks ago."

"What you say about there being nothing certain in it is not altogether true. Two weeks ago you desired to learn something about that house and who that man was; you were the only person interested in the matter then; but since yesterday the affair concerns us both equally."

"Since yesterday? And why?"

"Because since yesterday I have been making inquiries, and I have got an idea into my head; I don't know why it is but I fancy I am going to discover a certain person. In short, this is my affair and by myself, by myself alone, I will settle it; and that before long."

"But it interests me even more to learn what relations this man has with the widow than who he is; and this is the service I expect from you; for you must know that that house is a convent; neither the doors nor the windows are ever seen open; and, to add to the mystery the servants all seem to be dumb. In three weeks the only persons who have entered it are Señorita Dupasquier, three times; Bello, the widow's cousin, almost every afternoon; and Agustina four times."

"And why have you not made friends with Bello?"

"He is a good Federal, but he is very overbearing. I don't like him."

"And why have you not asked Agustina to take you to the house?"

"I don't wish to give so much publicity to the matter. It is a political advantage that I wish to gain with your help alone."

"Political, eh? Ah, rascal! But go on."

"My friend," said Mariño, in a tone full of amiability, "all I wanted from you was that with your powerful influence and with your unrivaled ability, you should make yourself necessary to that lady, and it seems that you have divined my wishes. Today for me, tomorrow for thee, as the saying is."

"No; look you, Mariño, in this matter I think I am going to do less for you than for myself; if what I suspect proves true, I think I am going to give a death-blow to Victorica in the estimation of Juan Manuel."

"So there is something serious, then?" said Mariño, a little perplexed.

"Perhaps; but have no fear for the little widow; we shall get her out of the business triumphant."

"One thing more; do me the favor, señora, not to say a word about these matters to my wife."

"Don't be a child! It was only a joke of mine," and the old woman burst into a demoniac laugh of satisfaction in the mischief she was making.

"Well, joke or no joke, it is better to say nothing about them; I entreat you not to do so," said Mariño, who, although he stood high in the favor of the Dictator, thought it very advisable to *entreat* this woman, whose weapons, he knew, were generally irresistible.

"Don't be afraid. Well, then, if I discover a certain thing which Victorica has not been able to discover, I will send it to your barracks. And you will take charge of it, do you understand?"

"I understand," answered Mariño, with an undefinable smile, comprehending that some victim was in question; for the man who once entered the barracks of the Night-Watchmen, left it only for eternity.

"Didn't I say so? We are going to be great friends, Mariño."

"We have been so for a long time past," answered the latter rising.

"Yes, cordial friends. So you are going? Good-bye, then; remember me to your wife; and pay no attention to any nonsense she may tell you."

"Good-bye, señora," returned the editor, surprised, almost, to hear issue from those lips only words steeped each in venom of a different kind.

XX

Prologue of a Drama

It was five o'clock on a cold and foggy afternoon and Eduardo was sitting before the fire on a stool at Amalia's feet in the parlor of the villa at Barracas, when suddenly a carriage was heard to stop at the door of the villa and a moment later Madame Dupasquier, her daughter and Daniel entered the room.

Amalia and Eduardo had recognized the carriage through the blinds; and as they had no secrets from those who were coming Eduardo remained in the room, a thing which he had not done on the occasion of any of Agustina's visits.

"Coffee, cousin, coffee, for we are perishing with cold," cried Daniel; "we left the table to come and take it with you but the idea was mine; you have neither the mother nor the daughter to thank for this visit; only me."

"Don't believe him, Amalia; it was I who suggested the visit; the lazy fellow would have stayed by the fire till morning," said Madame Dupasquier, a lady of some forty years of age, with high-bred features and a distinguished bearing, but on whose countenance there was an expression of morbid melancholy, an expression very generally to be seen during that reign of terror on the faces of ladies of distinction, whose health was perceptibly affected by the almost absolute seclusion in which they lived, as well as by their unceasing anxiety about the fate of their families or their friends.

"Very well; Madame Dupasquier may be right and I wrong; but there is no human logic that can deduce from that that I ought not to take coffee on a Friday."

"Yes, Amalia; give him coffee; give him anything he asks, to see if it will make him stop talking; for he is insufferable today," said Florencia.

Amalia had meanwhile pulled the bell-rope and given orders to Eduardo's servant to bring coffee; which was quickly served in the library, which adjoined the parlor, into which they passed.

The servant after bringing the coffee had placed a lamp on the round table in the library and closed the blinds of the windows that looked out on the Calle Larga, for it was now beginning to grow dark.

After a time the conversation turned to the tragic event which had caused Daniel to seek Amalia's hospitality for his friend.

"It has always been a mystery to us," said Amalia to Daniel, "how it was that you happened to appear so opportunely beside your friend on that terrible night."

"Well, I am in a good humor today, and I will tell you, my child. It was very simple."

Everyone assumed a listening attitude and Daniel continued:

"On the 4th day of May, at five o'clock in the afternoon, I received a letter from this gentleman," indicating Eduardo, "in which he informed me that he was going to leave Buenos Ayres that night. He is following the fashion, I said to myself; but as I am something of a prophet I began to fear some misfortune. I went to his house hoping to find him; in vain; it was shut up; I went to the houses of ten or twelve of our friends, one after another; in vain, also. At half-past nine I found it impossible to remain longer in this lady's house," indicating Mme. Dupasquier, "the first time in my life in which I have sinned in that way against good taste. I left it, then, exposing myself—exposing myself—this young lady here," indicating Florencia, "will finish the sentence. I left it, then, and directed my steps to the barrancas of the Residencia, where a certain Scotchman, a friend of mine, lives, who seems to have entered into a partnership with Rosas to leave us without men in Buenos Ayres—he taking some to Montevideo and Rosas sending others somewhere else. But my Scotchman was sleeping as profoundly as if he were on his native mountains waiting for Walter Scott to come back to earth to describe him. What was to be done? I called logic to my aid; no one embarks in a boat except at the river; Eduardo is going to embark in a boat, consequently he is to be found down by the river; and after constructing this syllogism I descended the barranca and began to walk along the shore."

"And alone!" exclaimed Florencia, turning pale.

"There! I will say no more, then."

"No, no; go on," said the young girl, making an effort to smile.

"Well, then, I began to walk toward the Retiro, and after I had walked a few hundred yards, when the silence and the solitude were beginning to make me grow desperate, I heard, first, a clashing of weapons and, proceeding in the direction whence the sound came, I heard and recognized the voice of the man I was seeking. After that— after that there is no more to tell," said Daniel, seeing that both Amalia and Florencia had become excessively pale.

Eduardo was thinking of something to say to give another turn to the conversation when a noise at the door of the parlor caused everyone to look in that direction; and through the glazed partition which separated it from the library they saw entering the room, Doña Agustina Rosas de Mancilla and Doña María Josefa Ezcurra, the sound of whose carriage wheels, rolling over the gravel walk, they had not heard, absorbed as they had been in Daniel's narration.

Eduardo therefore had not had time to retire to the interior of the house, as he was in the habit of doing on the arrival of any visitor who was not one of those now present.

Of all who were there Amalia was the only one who was not acquainted with Doña María Josefa Ezcurra; but when, going into the parlor she observed the narrow, shriveled and repulsive countenance of the woman, the low forehead, on the tangled hair above which was set an immense red bow, in diabolical harmony with the color of almost all of her attire, she could not avoid feeling a vague disquiet, a certain mistrust and fear which made her give only the tips of her fingers to the old woman when the latter held out her hand. But when Agustina said to her:

"I have the pleasure of presenting to you Señora Doña María Josefa Ezcurra," a nervous shudder passed like an electric shock through Amalia's frame and without knowing why her eyes sought those of Eduardo.

"You did not expect me in this bad weather, I suppose," continued Agustina, addressing Amalia, while they all seated themselves around the fire.

But whether by chance or intentionally Doña María Josefa took a seat at the left of Eduardo, whom Amalia took good care not to present. All the others had long been acquainted with her visitors.

"Your visit is indeed a pleasant surprise," answered Amalia.

"Misía María Josefa was determined upon our going out, and as she knows what pleasure it gives me to be in this house, she herself ordered the coachman to drive us here."

Daniel began to scratch the tip of his ear, looking at the fire as if all his attention was engrossed by it.

"But I see," continued Agustina, "that we are not the only ones who think of you; here is Madame Dupasquier who has not been to see me for more than a year; here is Florencia, who behaves like an ingrate toward me, and consequently here is Señor Bello. Besides which, I have the pleasure of seeing Señor Belgrano here, also, whom no one has seen anywhere for an age," added Agustina, who was acquainted with all the young men of Buenos Ayres.

Doña María Josefa eyed Eduardo from head to foot.

"It is by chance; my friends come to see me very seldom," responded Amalia.

"And if I do not go to see you, Agustina, you cannot deny that my daughter goes very often in my stead," said Madame Dupasquier.

"I have only seen her twice since the ball."

"But you live here so comfortably that your solitude is almost enviable," said Doña María Josefa to Amalia.

"I am tolerably comfortable, señora."

"Oh, Barracas is a delightful place!" continued the old woman, "especially for the health;" and indicating Eduardo by a gesture, she said to Amalia:

"This gentleman is convalescing from some illness, is he not?"

Amalia turned scarlet.

"Señora, I am perfectly well," answered Eduardo.

"Ah! excuse me. You look so pale."

"That is my natural color."

"Besides, as I saw you without any badge and with that necktie with a single fold, on a day so cold as this, I thought that you lived in this house."

"You see, señora," said Daniel hastily, desiring to prevent an answer that of necessity must be either a falsehood or too frank a declaration, both of which it was advisable to avoid, "in the matter of cold it is very much as one accustoms one's self; the Scotch live in a freezing climate and they go with their legs bare half way up the thigh."

"That may do for gringos; but as we are in Buenos Ayres here—" replied Doña María Josefa.

"And in Buenos Ayres, where the winters are so severe," added Madame Dupasquier.

"Have you had a fireplace made in your house, Misía María Josefa?" asked Florencia, who, like all the others, seemed bent upon diverting the old woman's attention from Eduardo, and whose suspicions concerning him they all seemed to divine.

"I have too much to do, child, to occupy myself with those things; when there are no longer any Unitarians to give us all the trouble they are giving us, we can think a little of our comfort."

"Well, I have not had a fireplace made in every room in my house only because Mancilla takes cold when he leaves the fireside," said Agustina.

"Mancilla must be hot enough today," returned Doña María Josefa.

"Why! is the General ill?" asked Amalia.

"He is never very well," returned Agustina, "but I have not heard him complain today."

"No, he is not hot from sickness," responded the old woman, "but from enthusiasm. Don't you know that for the past three days they have been celebrating the defeat of the filthy Unitarians in Entre Rios? There is not a single Federal who does not know that."

"That is precisely what we were talking about when you entered," said Daniel. "It was a terrible battle."

"In which they got what they well deserved!"

"Oh, I will answer for that!" said Daniel.

"And I also," added Eduardo; "and if it had not been that the night—"

"How, the night? Why, the battle took place in the daytime, Señor Belgrano," interrupted Doña María Josefa.

"Just so; it was in the daytime; but my friend wishes to say that if it had not been that the night came on and put an end to the combat not a single Unitarian would have escaped."

"Ah! of course not. And did you assist at any of the celebrations, Señor Belgrano?"

"We spent three days walking through the streets, admiring the decorations," answered Daniel, who trembled lest Edurado should speak.

"And how beautiful the banners are! Where do they get so many of them, señora?" said the artful Florencia, addressing Doña María Josefa.

"They buy them, child, or the good Federal women make them."

"Yes; well, I am a good Federal, and I shall take good care not to put my hands to that use," said Agustina. "When Mancilla asked me to make some last year I sent and borrowed Señor Mandeville's and I have kept them ever since and they are the ones I am using now and I shall never return them. And have you put out any, Amalia?"

"No, Agustina, this house is so retired!"

"And very right! Those detestable banners make such a noise! And then, the children! Eduardita almost fell from the roof today, reaching out to catch one."

"Oh! this house is not so far away!" said Doña María Josefa.

"But the most beautiful banners are those in the theater; have you been to the theater, Doña María Josefa?"

"No, Florencia, I never go to the theater. But I have heard that there has been a great deal of enthusiasm there. Have you been to the theater, Señor Belgrano?"

"Well, then," interposed Florencia, "the day on which I go I will call for you and we will go together, shall we not?"

"Don't trouble yourself, child; I never go to the theater," answered the old woman with a gesture of vexation seeing that no one, and especially Florencia, wanted to allow her to talk to Eduardo.

"The theater is the most appropriate place for the expression of a people's enthusiasm," said Daniel.

"Yes, but with so much shouting they prevent one from hearing the music," responded Agustina.

"Those shouts are the finest music of our sacred cause," said Daniel, with the most serious face in the world.

"Right; that is the way to talk," said the old woman.

"Florencia, why don't you play us something?"

"A good idea, Amalia. Florencia, go play something," said Madame Dupasquier.

"Very well, mamma. What shall I play, Doña Josefa?"

"Anything you like."

"Very well; come with me to the piano. I sing very badly, but to please you, I will sing for you my favorite song, 'The Birthday of the Restorer.' Come with me," and Florencia went over to Doña María Josefa, to give greater weight to her invitation.

"But, child, it costs me such an effort to rise when once I am seated!"

"Nonsense. I know that isn't so. Come."

"What a girl," said the old woman, with a Satanic smile. "Well, then, come. Excuse me, Señor Belgrano," and with these words the old woman, pretending to seek a support in rising, placed her thin and bony hand on Eduardo's left thigh, leaning so heavily upon it, that the young man, transfixed with pain, for the hand pressed precisely on the most sensitive part of the wound, leaned back in his chair and involuntarily exclaimed: "Oh, señora!" becoming at the same time almost unconscious and as pale as death.

Daniel covered his eyes with his hand.

Everyone, with the exception of Agustina, comprehended on the instant that in Doña María Josefa's action there had probably been something of sinister premeditation, and they all remained irresolute and perplexed.

"Have I hurt you? Excuse me, señor. If I had known that your thigh was so sensitive I should have asked you to give me your arm to help me to rise. See what it is to be an old woman! If it had been a girl, now, your thigh would not have hurt you so much. Excuse me, my handsome youth," she ended, and regarding Eduardo with an expression of satisfaction impossible to describe, she crossed the room and sat down beside the piano at which Florencia was already seated.

By a reaction natural in one of her haughty temper, Amalia on the instant cast aside all fear, all thought of temporizing with the epoch, or with those of the family of Rosas who were present; she rose, wet her handkerchief with Cologne-water and handed it to Eduardo, who was beginning to recover from the faintness that had for a moment overcome him; and, drawing away brusquely the chair in which Doña María Josefa had been sitting, she took another and sat down in the place which the former had occupied at her lover's side, regardless of the fact that she thus turned her back on the sister-in-law and friend of the tyrant.

Agustina, who had observed nothing, continued conversing with Madame Dupasquier about the indifferent and puerile matters which usually formed the subjects of her conversation.

Florencia sang and played, without knowing what she was doing.

Doña María Josefa looked alternately at Eduardo and at Amalia and smiled and nodded.

Daniel stood with his back to the fire, all the faculties of his soul in action.

"It is nothing; it is past; it is nothing," whispered Eduardo to Amalia, when he had in some degree recovered himself.

"But that woman is a demon! From the moment she came into the room she has done nothing but make us suffer," returned Amalia, while her eyes rested tenderly on Eduardo's countenance.

"The fire is very pleasant," said Daniel aloud, glancing with something of severity at Amalia.

"Very," assented Madame Dupasquier, "but—"

"But, you would say, señora, we shall be able to enjoy it only an hour or two longer," interrupted Daniel, comprehending that Madame Dupasquier was about to speak of retiring, at the same time giving her a glance which she had no difficulty in interpreting.

"Precisely; that is what I was going to observe," she responded; "we must enjoy the pleasure of our visit as long as possible, since it is one we so seldom give ourselves."

"Thanks, señora," said Amalia.

"You are right," said Agustina; "and I would stay too, if I were not obliged to go somewhere else."

"You are perfectly excusable," said Amalia, exchanging a glance of intelligence with Madame Dupasquier at the somewhat impertinent excuse given by Agustina.

"Well, how was the song? Did I sing it well?" said Florencia to Doña María Josefa, rising from the piano.

"Oh, very well! Is the pain gone, Señor Belgrano?"

"Yes, señora, it is gone now," answered Amalia, promptly, without turning her head to look at Doña María Josefa.

"You won't bear me any ill-will, eh?"

"Oh, there is no cause for that, señora," responded Eduardo, speaking to her with an effort.

"What I promise you is that I will tell no one that your left thigh is so sensitive—at least none of the girls, for if they were to know it they would all want to pinch you there to see you turn faint."

"Will you be seated, señora," said Amalia, turning her head toward Doña María Josefa, but without raising her eyes, and pointing to a chair at one end of the semicircle which they formed around the fire.

"No, no;" said Agustina, "we are going now; I have another visit to make yet, and I must be home before nine."

And General Mancilla's beautiful wife rose from her seat, arranging the strings of her black velvet bonnet which set off admirably the fair beauty of her face.

In vain Amalia tried to divest her mind of the prejudice against Doña María Josefa Ezcurra that had taken possession of it; she did not yet comprehend the evil intention which had prompted her actions, but their unmistakable rudeness was sufficient to render her presence repugnant to her; and never was a more frigid leave taken of this woman, all-powerful at that time, than was now taken of her by Amalia. She gave her barely the tips of her fingers and neither thanked her for her visit nor asked her to repeat it.

Agustina perceived nothing of all this, occupied as she was in taking leave of the others and in looking at herself furtively in the large mirror over the chimney-piece. Her adieus made, she took the arm of Daniel, who conducted her and Doña María Josefa to their carriage. But even at the parlor door the latter turned round and said to Eduardo:

"Don't bear me any ill-will, eh? But don't go and put Cologne-water on your thigh for that would make it smart."

The silence which followed the departure of Agustina and her companion continued for some minutes after their carriage had driven away.

Amalia was the first to break it, saying, as she looked at the others with genuine astonishment:

"But what sort of a woman is that?"

"She is a woman who resembles no one but herself," said Madame Dupasquier.

"But what have we ever done to her?" asked Amalia. "What could have made her come to this house when all she did while she was here was to mortify everyone in it; and that, when she knew neither me nor Eduardo?"

"Ah, cousin! all our labor has been in vain; that woman came with a purpose to your house; she must have received some information; she must have had some suspicion regarding Eduardo, and unhappily she has just discovered everything!"

"But what has she discovered?"

"Everything, Amalia. Do you suppose that her leaning her hand on Eduardo's left thigh was accidental?"

"Ah!" exclaimed Florencia; "yes, yes; she knew something about a wound in the left thigh!"

The ladies and Eduardo looked at one another in amazement.

Daniel continued calmly and with the same seriousness as before:

"True; that was the only sign she had of the man who escaped from the assassins on the night of the 4th of May. She cannot have come to this house without some sinister purpose. The moment she arrived she eyed Eduardo from head to foot; she addressed no one but him; and when she saw that we all tried to prevent her from conversing with him she sought by a single coup to discover the truth and she leaned on the wounded limb in order to read in Eduardo's countenance the result of the pressure of her hand. Only the devil himself could have suggested such a thought to her and she has gone away perfectly convinced that nothing but pressure on a freshly healed wound would have caused Eduardo the pain which she saw she caused him, and which she observed with delight."

"But who could have told her of it?"

"Let us not talk of that now, my poor Amalia. I am perfectly convinced of the truth of what I say, and I know that we are all standing now on the brink of a precipice. Meanwhile, there is one thing that must be done immediately."

"What is that?" exclaimed the ladies, who were hanging on Daniel's words.

"Eduardo must leave this house at once and come with me."

"Oh, no," exclaimed Eduardo, rising to his feet, his eyes flashing haughtily, and placing himself at his friend's side by the chimney-piece.

"No," he continued. "Now I comprehend all the malignity of that woman's actions; but it is for the very reason that I believe that I have been discovered that I think I ought to remain in this house."

"Not one minute longer," answered Daniel, with the calmness which was habitual with him in difficult circumstances.

"And she, Daniel?" replied Eduardo, nervously.

"She cannot save you."

"No; but I may be able to save her from some insult."

"And so saving her, ruin you both."

"No; I will ruin myself only."

"I will take care of her."

"But will they come here?" asked Amalia looking anxiously at Daniel.

"Within a couple of hours, within an hour, perhaps."

"Ah, my God! Yes, Eduardo, go away instantly; I entreat you to do so," cried Amalia, rising and approaching the young man; an action instinctively imitated by Florencia.

"Yes, with us, you will come with us, Eduardo," said the beautiful and generous-hearted girl.

"My house is yours, Eduardo, my daughter has spoken for me," added Madame Dupasquier.

"In Heaven's name, señora, no, no. If only for the sake of my honor. Honor commands me to remain at Amalia's side."

"I cannot say with certainty that anything will happen tonight," said Daniel, "but I fear it; and should that be the case Amalia will not be alone; for within an hour I will return here to remain with her."

"But Amalia can come with us," said Florencia.

"No, she must remain here and I with her," answered Daniel. "If the night passes without incident tomorrow I will work hard, since Señora Doña María Josefa has worked so hard today. At all events let us lose no time. Get your hat and cloak, Eduardo, and come with us."

"No."

"Eduardo! This is the first favor I have ever asked from you. Allow yourself to be guided by Daniel tonight, and tomorrow—tomorrow we shall see each other again, whatever may be the fate that Heaven has in store for us."

As she uttered these words there was in Amalia's eyes, humid with sensibility, so tender, so melancholy an expression of entreaty that Eduardo's resolution gave way before it and his lips could only frame the words:

"Very well, I will go."

Florencia clapped her hands joyfully and ran into the adjoining room to get her hat and shawl, saying, as she returned:

"Home, home, Eduardo."

Daniel gazed at her, enchanted by her generosity of spirit, and with a smile full of affection and sweetness, he said:

"No, angel of goodness, neither to your house nor to his own. In either of them he might be sought. He will go somewhere else; that shall be my affair."

"But within an hour you will be with Amalia again?" asked Eduardo.

"Yes, within an hour."

"Amalia, this is the first sacrifice I have ever made for you but I ask you to believe, by the memory of my mother, that it is the greatest I could ever make."

"Thanks, thanks, Eduardo! Who could ever believe that fear could find a place in your heart? Besides, if I should need an arm to defend me you cannot doubt that Daniel would take your place."

Happily Florencia did not hear these words, as she had gone into the adjoining room for her mother's cloak.

A few minutes later the hall door of Amalia's house had been securely fastened, and old Pedro, to whom Daniel had given some instructions before leaving the house, was pacing back and forth between the hall and the courtyard against one of the walls of which rested Eduardo's double-barreled gun and a cavalry carbine, while from the belt of the veteran of the War of Independence hung a handsome dagger.

Eduardo's servant, meantime, was seated on the threshold of one of the doors opening into the yard, awaiting the orders of the soldier who, in accordance with Daniel's instructions, was not to open the hall door to anyone until his return.

XXI

A Restless Night

In spite of all Daniel's efforts, he found it impossible to return to Barracas within an hour, having had to accompany Madame Dupasquier and her daughter home in their carriage; to take Eduardo to a considerable distance from the Calle de la Reconquista, and on foot, in order not to betray to the coachman the secret of his place of hiding; to go back to his own house, give some orders to his servant, and have his horse saddled, before returning.

So that it was half-past nine, that is to say, an hour and a half after he had left his cousin's house, when he descended the Barranca of Balcarce, absorbed in thought, and almost convinced that Doña María Josefa's visit had been the result of information received by her regarding the secret they had so long succeeded in keeping unsuspected, and that the old woman, the spy of her brother-in-law, had now acquired the certainty of the truth of the information she had received.

"How avert the storm, my God!" said Daniel to himself, anxious and afraid, for the first time in his life, at the thought of the dangers that menaced the beings dearest to his heart.

As he reached the road leading from the Boca to Santa Lucía, he saw a party of six men on horseback turn into the Calle Larga and gallop rapidly up the street.

A secret presentiment seemed to warn him that these men were in some way connected with his affairs; and, acting on a sudden impulse, he reined in his horse just as they came up with him, and waited until they had passed him. But when they were some fifty paces in advance he again put spurs to his horse, and followed them at a gallop, always keeping the same distance behind them.

"Ah! I was not mistaken," he cried, as he saw the six horsemen ride up to Amalia's door, dismount and knock loudly on it, first with the knocker and then with the handles of their whips.

Before they had time to repeat the knocks Daniel had pushed his horse among the group and in a firm and resolute voice asked:

"What is the matter, gentlemen?"

"What is the matter? And who are you?"

"It is I who have the right to ask you that question. You are here with a warrant, are you not?"

"Yes, señor, with a warrant," said one of the men, approaching Daniel and eyeing him from head to foot, as the young man dismounted with a resolute air from his horse and called out in an imperious voice:

"Open, Pedro."

The six men had gathered around Daniel, not knowing what to do, each waiting for one of the others to take the initiative.

The door was opened on the instant and Daniel, thrusting aside the two men who were in front of it, entered resolutely, saying:

"Come in, gentlemen."

They all followed him quickly into the house.

Daniel then opened the door of the parlor and entered it.

The six men followed him into the room, dragging their sabers over the rich carpet, in which the rowels of their spurs made furrows.

Amalia, who was standing with a pale face beside the round table when the door opened, turned suddenly crimson when she saw the men who followed Daniel approach her with their hats on and the repulsive stamp of plebeian insolence on their countenances. But a swift glance from her cousin made her comprehend that she must maintain absolute silence.

The young man took off his poncho and threw it on a chair, displaying ostentatiously the red waistcoat which at this time began to be used by the most enthusiastic among the Federals, and the large badge which he wore on his breast, and turning to the six men, who had not yet been able to form a clear idea of what they were to do, said:

"Who is the leader of this party?"

"I am," said one of them, approaching Daniel.

"You are an officer?"

"An orderly of Commandant Cuitiño's."

"You have come to arrest a man in this house?"

"Yes, señor, we have come to search the house and to take him away with us."

"Very well; read that," said Daniel to Cuitiño's orderly, handing him a paper which he had taken from his pocket.

The soldier unfolded the paper, looked at it, examined on all sides a seal which was affixed to it, and handing it to another of the soldiers, said to him:

"Read it, you who know how."

The soldier approached the lamp and spelling out the words, syllable by syllable, at last read:

"Long live the Federation!

"Long live the Illustrious Restorer of the Laws!

"Death to the filthy, loathsome Unitarians!

"Death to the turncoat Rivera and the filthy French!

"Sociedad Popular Restauradora.

"The bearer, Daniel Bello, is in the service of the Sociedad Popular Restauradora; and whatever he does must be to the advantage of the Sacred Cause of the Federation, because he is one of its best servants.

Julian Gonzalez Salomon, *President*

Boneo, *Secretary*

"Buenos Ayres, June 10, 1840."

"Now then," said Daniel, looking at Cuitiño's soldiers, who were now in a state of the greatest perplexity, "who is the man you are seeking in this house, which is the same as if it were my own house, and in which Unitarian savages have never been concealed?"

Cuitiño's orderly was about to answer when suddenly all eyes were turned toward the door at the noise made by the hoofs of five or six horses entering the tiled hall and by the clanking of the sabers and spurs of their riders, as they dismounted and entered the parlor tumultuously.

Mechanically Amalia placed herself at Daniel's side, while her little maid Luisa, who was standing beside her, clung to the arm of her mistress.

"Dead or alive!" cried their leader, entering the parlor.

"Neither dead nor alive, Commandant Cuitiño," said Daniel.

"Has he fled?"

"No, those who flee, Señor Commandant," answered Daniel, "are the Unitarians who not being able to meet us face to face are working in secret to mislead us and to sow discord among us. With their tricks and the maneuvers they are learning from the gringos, the house of a Federal is no longer safe; and at the rate at which we are going, tomorrow they will inform the Restorer that in the house of Commandant Cuitiño, the best sword of the Federation, some Unitarian savage is concealed also. This is my house, Commandant, and this lady is my cousin. I live here most of the time, and I have no need to declare it upon oath, to be believed, when I say that where I am no Unitarian can be hidden. Pedro, take these gentlemen through the house, and let them search wherever they choose."

"Let no one stir from here," cried Cuitiño to the soldiers, who were preparing to follow Pedro. "The house of a Federal must not be searched," he continued; "you are as good a Federal as I am, Señor Don Daniel. But tell me how it is that Doña María Josefa has deceived me?"

"Doña María Josefa?" said Daniel, with well-feigned surprise.

"Yes, Doña María Josefa."

"But what has she told you, Commandant?"

"She has just told me that the Unitarian who escaped from us that night was hidden here; that she herself saw him this evening, and that his name is Belgrano."

"Belgrano!"

"Yes, Eduardo Belgrano."

"It is true that Eduardo Belgrano was here this evening; he came to pay a visit to my cousin, as he occasionally does. But I have seen that young man, whom I know very well, all this time in the city, whole and sound; and the man who escaped that night cannot be in a condition to go about amusing himself," said Daniel, looking with a significant smile at Cuitiño.

"What the devil does this mean, then? Am I the sort of man to be trifled with in this way?"

"It is the Unitarians, Commandant, who want to sow discord among the Federals; they must have told some story to Doña María Josefa, for the women do not know them as well as we do who have to be fighting with them every day. But no matter; search for that young man, who lives in the Calle del Cabildo, and if he is the Unitarian who escaped that night you will have no difficulty in recognizing him. Meanwhile, I am going to see Doña María Josefa and Don Juan Manuel himself, to know if we are to go about now searching one another's houses."

"No, Don Daniel, take no step in the matter. It is the Unitarians, as you say," answered Cuitiño, who believed Daniel to have great influence with the Rosas family.

"What will you take, Commandant?"

"Nothing, Don Daniel; all I want is that this lady should not be angry with me; but we didn't know whose house this was."

Amalia acknowledged the apology only by a slight movement of the head; for she was completely confounded, less by the presence of Cuitiño than by Daniel's extraordinary audacity.

JOSÉ MÁRMOL

"You are going then, Commandant?"

"Yes, Don Daniel, and I won't even take back any answer to Doña María Josefa."

"You are right; those are women's notions; nothing more."

"Good-night, señora," said Cuitiño, bowing to Amalia and leaving the room, followed by his whole party and accompanied by Daniel, to mount horse again.

XXII

Continuation of the Preceding

Amalia was still standing beside the table when Daniel, after Cuitiño's departure, returned to the parlor, laughing like a boy, and going up to his cousin, embraced her with the affection of a brother.

"Forgive me, Amalia," he said; "these are acts of moral and political heresy which I am obliged to commit at every step in this time of universal acting, in which I play one of the most extraordinary rôles. Poor creatures! They have the strength of the brute but I have the intelligence of the man. Now they are thrown off the scent, my Amalia; and above all, now they are in a state of anarchy. Cuitiño will now pay no attention to what Doña María Josefa may say about this matter; and the old woman will be enraged with Cuitiño."

"But where is Eduardo?"

"In a perfectly safe place."

"But will they go to his house?"

"Of course they will go to his house."

"Has he any papers?"

"None."

"And you and I, how do we stand?"

"Badly."

"Badly?"

"Badly; we have been in a very bad position ever since this evening. But there is nothing to be done but to let events take their course, and try to find in them the means of protecting ourselves against whatever dangers may threaten us."

"Well, but when shall I see Eduardo?"

"Within a few days."

"A few days! But was it not agreed that we were to see each other tomorrow?"

"Yes, but it was not agreed that Cuitiño was to visit us tonight."

"No matter; if he does not come here I will go to him."

"Softly. I can neither promise nor deny you anything. Everything will depend on the results of the visit of the demon we had here this evening. Don't imagine that the old woman will be satisfied to let matters stand as Cuitiño has left them; on the contrary, she will be more enraged now than ever, and will give us all trouble. There is one thing, however, which tranquilizes me."

"What is that, Daniel?"

"That Rosas and his friends Lave a great deal to think about just now."

"What has happened? Finish for Heaven's sake!"

"Nothing; a trifle, my dear Amalia," said Daniel, smoothing the hair over the forehead of his cousin, who was sitting beside him by the fire.

"But what is it? You are insufferable."

"Thanks."

"It is true; you are laughing."

"That is because I am happy."

"Happy?"

"Yes."

"And you have the courage to tell me so?"

"Yes."

"But why are you happy? Because we are all standing over a volcano?"

"No; I am happy—listen well to what I am going to say to you."

"I am listening."

"Very well; but first, Luisa, tell Eduardo's servant that as his master is not here I will take a cup of tea in his place."

"I repeat it, you are insufferable," said Amalia, when Luisa had left the room.

"I know it, but I told you that I was happy and that I would tell you why. Did I not?"

"I don't know," said Amalia, with a pout.

"Well, then, I am happy, in the first place because Eduardo is concealed in a safe house; and in the second because Lavalle is, with the knowledge and consent of everybody, in the good city of San Pedro."

"Already!" exclaimed Amalia, her eyes radiant with joy, taking her cousin's hand in hers.

"Yes, already. The army of the Liberators has already entered the Province of Buenos Ayres. It is only thirty leagues distant from the tyrant, and it seems to me that that is too important a matter not to engage the attention of our Restorer."

"Oh! but if that is the case we shall be free!" exclaimed Amalia, pressing her cousin's hand.

"Who knows, child, who knows! That will depend upon the manner in which operations are conducted."

"Oh, my God! To think that within a few days Eduardo will be free from danger. Can it be true, Daniel, that in three days Lavalle may be in the city of Buenos Ayres?"

"No, not so soon. But he may be here in a week or even in six days. But he may also never be here, Amalia."

"Oh, do not say that, for Heaven's sake!"

"Yes, Amalia, yes. If they take advantage of the popular feeling at the present moment and invade the city at any point Rosas will not take the field at the head of the insignificant forces which support him. No; if the city is attacked Rosas will go on board one of the vessels in the harbor and fly the country. But if General Lavalle delays to fight in the province then fortune may prove adverse to him. In this paper, which is a copy of the order of the army," continued Daniel, taking a paper from his pocketbook, "Lavalle declares that within a very few days the fate of the republic will be decided."

"And tell me, imprudent boy, how is it that you come to have that paper in your pocket?" cried Amalia.

"I have just received it in the house where I left Eduardo."

"And what house is that?"

"Oh, nothing less than the house of a Government official."

"Good Heavens! You have placed Eduardo in the house of an employee of Rosas?"

"No, señora, in the house of an employee of mine."

"Of yours?"

"Yes—but silence—a horse has just stopped at the door—Pedro!" cried Daniel, going out into the hall.

"Señor?" answered the faithful veteran of the War of Independence.

"There is someone at the door."

"Shall I open, señor?"

"Yes; they are knocking now; open," and Daniel seated himself again beside his cousin.

Amalia had grown very pale.

Daniel awaited, tranquil and self-reliant as usual, the new event which seemed to have come to complicate the situation of his friends and his own; for at this hour, near twelve o'clock at night, no one would come to this solitary house, except in connection with the events which preoccupied him.

Pedro entered the parlor with a letter in his hand.

"A soldier has brought this letter for the señora," he said.

　　　　　　　　　　　　　　　　　　JOSÉ MÁRMOL

"Is he alone?" asked Daniel.

"Yes, señor."

"Did you look up and down the street to see if anyone was in sight?"

"There is no one in sight."

"Very well; go back and be on the watch."

"Open it," said Amalia, handing the letter to her cousin.

"Ah!" exclaimed Daniel, when he had opened the letter. "Look at this signature; it is that of a great personage, an acquaintance of yours."

"Mariño!" exclaimed Amalia, turning crimson.

"Yes, Mariño. Am I still to read it?"

"Read it; read it."

Daniel read as follows:

"Señora:

"I have just learned that you have become involved in a very disagreeable affair, and one in some degree dangerous to your tranquillity. The authorities have received information that you had, concealed in your house for a long time, an enemy of the Government, a fugitive from justice.

"It is known that this person is no longer in your house; but as it is to be supposed that you are aware of his hiding-place I do not doubt but that you will be subjected to a rigorous examination by the authorities.

"In so difficult a situation I do not doubt but that you will need a friend; and as, owing to my position, I have some influence, I hasten to offer you my services in the entire confidence that should you accept them you will thenceforward be free from every danger.

"To obtain this result it will only be necessary for you to place your confidence in me, deigning to inform me at what hour tomorrow you will grant me the honor of an interview in order that we may agree upon the course to be taken in the present emergency. Advising you that your letter as well as my visit and the visits which I may in the future make you will be enveloped in the most profound secrecy—"

"Oh! enough, enough!" exclaimed Amalia, making a movement as if to snatch the letter from her cousin's hands.

"No, no, wait. There is something more."

Daniel continued:

"For some time past powerful motives, which perhaps with
your intelligence you will have already divined, have made me
seek, but in vain, the opportunity which now presents itself
to me, of being able to offer you my services with the most
profound submission and respect and with the friendship
with which your obedient servant salutes you.

NICOLAS MARIÑO

"That is all," said Daniel, looking at his cousin with the most quizzical expression that it would be possible for the human countenance to wear.

"But it is more than enough to show that that man is an insolent scoundrel!"

"That may be so. But as every letter requires an answer, it will be well to know what answer the letter of this man is to receive."

"What answer? Here, give me the letter."

"No."

"Oh, give it to me!"

"And what for?"

"To answer it with its fragments."

"Bah!"

"Oh, my God! To be insulted too! To ask letters and secret interviews from me!" exclaimed Amalia, covering her face with her hands.

Daniel rose, went into the library, and a few minutes later returned to Amalia, saying:

"This is the answer we are to give him. Listen:

Señor
"Authorized by my cousin, Señora Doña Amalia Saenz
de Olabarrieta, to answer your letter, it gives me pleasure
to inform you that you need no longer allow your fears
regarding my cousin's safety to disturb you, as she is
entirely ignorant of everything that is attributed to her and
perfectly tranquil in regard to the justice of his Excellency
the Governor, whom I shall have the honor of acquainting
tomorrow with all that has taken place tonight, concealing

nothing from him, in case this disagreeable affair should proceed any further.

"With which I remain yours respectfully,

"ETC. ETC."

"But that letter—"

"This letter will keep him awake for the rest of the night, trembling lest tomorrow it should fall into the hands of Rosas, to avoid which he will do all in his power tomorrow to have this matter dropped. And thus it is that I convert our enemies into our servants."

"Oh, yes, send that letter."

Daniel folded the letter and sent it to the soldier who was waiting at the street door.

Half an hour later Daniel was lying down, without having undressed, in Eduardo's bedroom, and Amalia was kneeling before her gold-inlaid ebony crucifix, praying for the safety of those she loved and for her country's freedom.

XXIII

Of How Things are Read that are not Written

O n the morning of the day following the night on which the events that we have just related took place, that is to say, on the morning of the 6th of August, the Dictator's house was besieged by innumerable messengers from the field, who succeeded one another without intermission.

None of them was detained in the office, General Corvalan having received orders to conduct them at once to the study of Rosas. And his Excellency's aid-de-camp, with his sash falling over his abdomen, his epaulets hanging down his back and his sword dangling between his legs, went ceaselessly back and forth through the courtyard, ready to drop with sleep and fatigue.

The countenance of the Dictator reflected the gloom that was in his soul. He read the dispatches of his chiefs in the field, informing him of General Lavalle's disembarkation and of his enthusiastic reception by the planters, and he gave the orders which he deemed expedient, for the campaign, for the general encampment at Santos Lugares, and for the city. But suspicion, that viper that unceasingly gnaws the heart of the tyrant, infused doubt and fear into all his arrangements, into every hour and moment of the day and night.

He despatched an order to General Pacheco to retreat toward the south, and half an hour later he sent after the messenger in hot haste to countermand the order.

He ordered Maza to march with his battalion to reinforce Pacheco, and ten minutes later he ordered Maza to prepare to march with all the artillery to Santos Lugares.

He appointed officers of the day for the command of the city troops, and each appointment was revoked and another substituted for it twenty times in the course of the day; and so it was with everything.

His poor daughter who had passed the whole night in vigil would put her head in at the door of her father's study from time to time, to see if she could divine in his countenance some anticipated success that might chase away the gloom that had shadowed it for so many hours past.

Viguá had twice put his deformed head in at the study door, but his Excellency's buffoon had seen in the countenances of the clerks that this was not a day for jesting with the master; and he contented himself with sitting down in the hall and eating the grains of Indian corn that from time to time fell around him from the great mortar in which the Dictator's mulatto cook was grinding the corn for her master's breakfast.

Rosas was engaged in writing a letter, and the clerks were writing others when Corvalan entered and said:

"Will your Excellency receive Señor Mandeville?"

"Yes, let him come in."

A moment later her Britannic Majesty's Minister entered, bowing profoundly to the Dictator of Buenos Ayres, who, without taking the trouble to return his salutation, rose and passing from the study into his bedroom, said:

"Come this way."

Rosas sat down on his bed and the minister took a chair to his left.

"Your Excellency is in good health?" asked the minister.

"I am in no mood to talk of health, Señor Mandeville."

"Yet that is what is of most importance," answered the diplomat, smoothing the nap of his hat.

"No, Señor Mandeville; what is of most importance is that Governments and their Ministers should fulfill their promises."

"Doubtless."

"Doubtless? Well, your Government and you, or you and your Government, have done nothing but lie to me and compromise my cause."

"Oh, your Excellency, that is very strong language!"

"It is what you deserve, Señor Mandeville."

"I?"

"Yes, señor, you. You have been promising me for a year and a half past, in the name of your Government, to mediate or intervene in this cursed French Question. And which is it you or your Government that has deceived me?"

"Your Excellency, I have shown you the original letters which I have received from my Government."

"Then it is your Government that has lied. The fact of the matter is that devil a thing either of you has done for my cause, and that, owing to the French, Lavalle is today within twenty leagues of the city, and the whole republic is in arms against my Government."

"Oh! the conduct of the French is unparalleled!"

"Don't be a fool. The French do as they ought to do, because they are at war with me. It is you English who have behaved with treachery toward me. What are you the enemies of the French for? What have you so many ships and so much money for, if when the occasion arrives to help a friend, you are afraid of them?"

"Afraid, no, your Excellency. But the peace of Europe, the balance of power on the Continent—"

"The balance of power be damned! You and your countrymen destroy the balance of power often enough and no one says anything to you about it. Treachery, and nothing but treachery; because you are all alike. Or perhaps you and your countrymen are Unitarians also, like the French?"

"Not that, not that, your Excellency. I am a loyal friend to your Excellency and to your cause. And your Excellency has the proof of it in my conduct."

"In your conduct when, Señor Mandeville?"

"In my conduct now."

"And what is your conduct now?"

"I am here now to offer your Excellency my personal services, in whatever you may wish to command me."

"And what would you do for me if my cause should chance to be lost?"

"I would have troops disembark from her Majesty's ships to protect the persons of your Excellency and of your Excellency's family."

"Bah! and do you suppose that the thirty or forty Englishmen who should land would be respected by the people, if they were to rise against me?"

"But if the troops were not respected by the people the consequences would be terrible for them."

"Yes. And a great deal of good it would do me for the English to bombard the city after I had been shot! That is not the way to help a friend, Señor Mandeville."

"Nevertheless—"

"Nevertheless, if I were the English Minister, if I were Mandeville, and you Juan Manuel Rosas, what I would do would be to have a boat lying ready at the foot of the barranca on which I lived, so that when my friend Rosas came to my house I could easily put him on board a vessel."

"Oh, very good, very good; I will do so."

"No, I am not telling you to do so. I have no need whatever of you. I only say what I would do if I were in your place."

"Very well, your Excellency. Your Excellency's friends will guard your safety while your Excellency's genius and valor guard the destinies of this beautiful land and the righteous cause which you support. Has your Excellency had news from the provinces of the interior?"

"And what do the provinces matter to me, Señor Mandeville?"

"The events taking place in them, however—"

"The events taking place in them do not matter to me a damn. Do you suppose if I conquer Lavalle and force him to retire to the provinces that I have a great deal to fear from the Unitarians who have risen against me there?"

"To fear, no; but the prolongation of the war!—"

"That is what would assure my victory, Señor Mandeville; the only dangers that threaten my Government are those close beside me; the dangers that are at a distance and are of long continuance far from doing me harm, are of advantage to me."

"Your Excellency is a genius."

"At least I have more understanding than the diplomats of Europe. A pity for the Federation if it had to be defended by men like you! Do you know why the Unitarians went to the devil?"

"I think so, your Excellency."

"No, señor, you do not know."

"Perhaps I may be mistaken."

"Yes, señor, you are mistaken. They went to the devil because they had become Frenchmen and Englishmen."

"Oh! the internecine wars!"

"Our wars, say."

"Well, then, the American wars."

"No, the Argentine wars."

"The Argentine wars, then."

"Those require men like me."

"Undoubtedly."

"If I triumph over Lavalle here, I can afford to laugh at the rest of the republic."

"Your Excellency knows that General Paz has marched against Corrientes?"

"You see! You see what fools the Unitarians are!"

"True; General Paz will be able to do nothing."

"No; it is not that he will be able to do nothing. He will be able to do a great deal. It is for another reason that they are fools. They are fools because one goes in one direction and another in another; and they quarrel and disagree among themselves, instead of all uniting together and coming down upon me, as Lavalle has done."

"Providence, your Excellency."

"Or the devil. But you were going to say something about the provinces."

"True, your Excellency."

"And what is it?"

"Has your Excellency had any news of La-Madrid or of Brizuela?"

"None of recent date."

"I have received some news of a late date from Montevideo."

"When?"

"Last night."

"And you come at twelve o'clock today to tell me of it?"

"No, señor. It is ten."

"Well, then, at ten."

"I am always tardy where your Excellency's welfare is not concerned."

"Your news is bad, then?"

"Exaggerations of the Unitarians."

"And what is it? Finish," said Rosas with ill-concealed uneasiness.

"One of my private letters contains this passage," said the minister, taking some papers from his pocket and selecting one which he prepared to read—"But first, does your Excellency wish me to read it?"

"Read, read."

"'At the beginning of July General La-Madrid entered Córdoba at the head of three thousand five hundred men and ten pieces of artillery. Santa Catalina and Rio Seco are in arms and the Governor and Captain General of Rioja has issued a proclamation to his compatriots inciting them to fight like heroes in defense of Argentine liberty.'"

"Have you heard anything else?"

"The dissensions between Rivera and the Argentine emigrants, between Rivera and Lavalle; between the friends of the Deputy Governor and Rivera, and between everyone in general continue to produce prodigious results in the neighboring republic."

"I know it. And from Europe?"

"From Europe?"

"Yes; I am not talking Greek."

"I believe, your Excellency, that the Eastern Question has become more complicated than ever and that the efforts of my Sovereign's Government will soon bring about a satisfactory termination to the unjust quarrel provoked by the French with your Excellency's Government."

"That is just what you told me a year ago."

"But now I have positive facts."

"The same as always."

"The Eastern Question—"

"Don't talk to me any more about the Eastern Question, Señor Mandeville."

"Very well, your Excellency."

"That the devil may take them all is what I wish."

"Affairs are very gravely complicated."

"Are they? Very good; and have you heard anything else?"

"For the present, nothing else, your Excellency. I am expecting the packet daily."

"Then you will excuse me, for I have something to do," said Rosas rising.

"I would not have your Excellency lose a moment of your precious time."

"Yes, Señor Mandeville, I have a great deal to do, for my friends don't know how to help me in anything."

And Rosas left the room, followed by the minister.

Rather from absent-mindedness than civility Rosas accompanied the minister to the door of the antechamber which opened into the hall where they found Manuela giving some orders to the mulatto woman who was still busy at her task of pounding the corn.

At this moment Doña María Josefa appeared upon the scene.

"Manuela," said Rosas, after salutations had been exchanged, "accompany Señor Mandeville to the door; or take him to the salon if he wishes. Good-bye, then, for the present, my friend. I am very busy, as you know, but I am always your friend."

"I am greatly honored in believing so, your Excellency; and I will not forget what your Excellency would do if you were in my place, and I in your Excellency's," said the minister, emphasizing the last words to show Rosas that he bore in mind his project about the boat.

"Do as you like. Good day."

And Rosas returned to his study accompanied by his sister-in-law, while the minister gave his arm to Manuela and proceeded with her to the salon.

"Good news," said Doña María Josefa to Rosas as they entered the room.

"About what?"

"About the man who escaped us on the 4th of May."

"Have they caught him?" asked Rosas with flashing eyes.

"No."

"No?"

"But we shall catch him; Cuitiño is an ass."

"But where is he?"

"Let us go and sit down first," said the old woman, passing with Rosas from the study into the bedroom.

XXIV

How We Discover that Don Candido
Rodriguez Resembles Don Juan
Manuel Rosas

On the same morning on which the events recorded in our last chapter took place, our old friend Don Cándido Rodriguez was walking up and down the hall of his house near the Plaza Nueva enveloped in a raisin-colored great coat which had been his companion in his frights of the year 1820; with a cotton cap pulled down over his ears; two large orange leaves stuck to his temples with tallow; a pair of old cloth shoes, which served him as slippers, on his feet; and his hands thrust into the pockets of his great coat.

The irregularity of his steps, the dark rings around his eyes, and the swift changes of his countenance gave evidence that he had spent a sleepless night and that he was just now carrying on an animated dialogue with himself.

A double knock at the door caused him to stop suddenly in his walk.

He approached the door, looked through the keyhole before inquiring who had knocked, and seeing only the torso of a man he ventured to ask in a perceptibly tremulous voice:

"Who is there?"

"I, my dear master."

"Daniel?"

"Yes, Daniel; open."

"Open?"

"Yes, in the name of all the saints; that is what I have said."

"Is it indeed you, Daniel?"

"I think so; do me the favor to open and you will see me."

"Listen; place your face in a direct line with the keyhole; but at the distance of a foot or two from it, so that I may be able to look at you and recognize you."

Daniel thought for an instant of giving the door a kick, and breaking open the lock, but for an instant, only, and did as his uncompromising master directed.

"Ah! it is indeed you!" said Don Cándido, and he opened the door.

"Yes, señor; it is I; I who have a great deal too much patience with you."

"Wait, stop, Daniel; go no further," exclaimed Don Cándido, taking his pupil by the hand.

"What the devil does this mean, Señor Don Cándido? Why must I go no further?"

"Because I have something very serious to say to you, Daniel. Who is this man whom you have introduced into my house?"

"Is that what you are going to talk about now! Don't you know him already?"

"I knew him when he was a boy, as I knew you and so many others; when he was a child, tender and innocent, like every child. But how do I know what his present life is; what his opinions, what his associations are? Can I believe that he is an innocent man when you bring him here to my house, in the silence and darkness of the night, and order me to allow no one to see him and to speak to no one about him? Can I believe that he is a friend of the Government when I see him without a single Federal badge and wearing a blue and white cravat? Ought I not to deduce conclusively from all this that there is here some political intrigue, some conspiracy, some plot, in which I am taking part without knowing it and without desiring it; I, a quiet, tranquil and peaceable man; I, who on account of my present important and delicate position as secretary of his Excellency, Minister Arana, a most excellent person, as are his lady and every one of his respectable family and even of his servants, ought, perforce, of necessity, to be circumspect and faithful to my official duties. Do you think—"

"I think you have lost your senses, Señor Don Cándido; and as I do not wish to lose mine, or to lose any more of my time, we will now consider our conference at an end and you will permit me to go see Eduardo."

"But how long is he to be in my house?"

"As long as God wills."

"But that cannot be."

"It will be, however."

"Daniel!"

"Señor Don Cándido, my distinguished master, let us state, in a few words, the position of everyone."

"Yes, let us do so."

"Listen to me. To shield you from the dangers to which you might be exposed from the Federation in these days, I obtained for you the position of private secretary to Señor Arana; is not that true?"

"Perfectly true."

"Very well, then; it is very probable that Señor Arana, together with all his secretaries, will some day or other be hanged, not by order of the authorities, but by order of the people, who may rise in rebellion against Rosas at any moment."

"Oh!" exclaimed Don Cándido, opening wide his eyes.

"Hanged, yes, señor," repeated Daniel.

"The secretaries also?"

"The secretaries also."

"That would be frightful."

"The secretaries and the minister, all together."

"So that if I resign my position as secretary, the Mashorca will assassinate me; and if I do not resign it, the people will hang me; and in addition to that, in either case, a misfortune may happen to me by mistake."

"Exactly; that is sound logic."

"Diabolical logic, Daniel; logic that will cost me my life on your account!"

"No, señor, it will cost you nothing if you will do what I tell you."

"And what am I to do? Speak."

"I am going to state the question in another way. We have now arrived at the critical moment of the war, in which Rosas must conquer Lavalle or Lavalle must conquer Rosas; is not that true?"

"Certainly, that is true."

"Well, then, in the former case you have in Don Felipe Arana a support that will enable you to continue in your present state of prosperity; and in the latter, you have in Eduardo the best shears with which to cut the rope of the people."

"In Eduardo?"

"Yes, and there is no need to say any more about the matter now, nor to return to it again."

"So that—"

"So that you must keep Eduardo in your house until I determine otherwise."

"But—"

"A less generous man than I would purchase your secrecy saying to you, Señor Don Cándido, the order of the army of Lavalle, which you gave me last night, copied in your own handwriting, was most important; and at the slightest indiscretion you commit this document will pass into the hands of Rosas, Señor Don Cándido—"

"Enough, enough, Daniel!"

"Very good, enough. We are agreed, then?"

"Agreed. But do you think I run any risk at present, Daniel?"

"None whatever."

"Will Eduardo be here much longer?"

"Have you entire confidence in Nicolasa?"

"As much as in myself. She hates all those people because they killed her son, her good, loyal, affectionate son; and since she has begun to suspect that Eduardo is in hiding she waits on him with more care, more zeal, more punctuality, more—"

"Let us go to Eduardo's room, Señor Don Cándido."

"Let us go, my dear and esteemed Daniel; he is in my study."

XXV

The Two Friends

L et us go, but leave me at the door," said Daniel, "I wish to speak with Eduardo alone."

"Ah, Daniel."

"What is the matter, señor?"

"Nothing; enter; go in; I will go to the parlor," said Don Cándido, turning back as Daniel entered the room which the schoolmaster called his study.

"Good day, my dear Eduardo," said Daniel to his friend, who was sitting in Don Cándido's old armchair, writing.

"And Amalia?" cried Eduardo.

"Amalia is well, thank Heaven."

"Daniel, I must return at once to Barracas."

"I understand that you should desire to do so, but I must warn you that if you do you will find yourself alone in the house when you arrive there, for my cousin will not be in it."

"For Heaven's sake, Daniel, for Heaven's sake don't make my situation harder to bear than it is! You do not know the tortures I am suffering on her account."

"Listen to what I have to tell you, Eduardo, and after you have heard it you will be able to take a more rational view of the situation."

And Daniel proceeded to inform Eduardo in a few words of the events of the preceding night, as well as of General Lavalle's intended invasion.

"You are right, you are right. I could not return to Barracas without compromising her," said Eduardo, when Daniel had ended, leaning his elbow on the table and resting his forehead on the palm of his hand.

"That is talking sensibly, Eduardo. There is now no other way of saving Amalia than to place yourself beyond the power of Rosas; for even if I could save her from the insults of the Mashorca, or from some despotic act of the tyrant, I should be unable to save her from the tyranny of her own organization, if any misfortune should befall you. Amalia loves you passionately. Her sensitive nature and her exalted imagination would make the knowledge fatal to her life or to her health were she to know that but a single drop of your blood had been shed."

"And what must I do, Daniel, what must I do?"

"In the first place, give up the thought of seeing Amalia for a few days."

"Very well."

"If political events take the turn we desire, then you have nothing more to fear."

"True."

"If, on the contrary, they do not take that turn, then it will be necessary for you to emigrate."

"Alone?"

"No, you will not go alone."

"Will Amalia go with me? Do you think Amalia will be willing to accompany me?"

"Yes, I am certain she will. But in addition to Amalia, there are others of your friends who will go with you."

"Oh, yes, let us go to another land, Daniel; the air of our country is fatal today to her children; it stifles us."

"No matter; we must breathe it as best we can until all hope is lost."

"But what if the issue should be long delayed?"

"That would be impossible."

"It might easily happen, however. Some unlooked-for occurrence may interrupt the operations of Lavalle, and then—"

"Then everything will be lost; for delay in the present condition of affairs would be ruin for Lavalle."

"May I come in for a moment, my dear and esteemed pupil?" said Don Cándido, putting the tassel of his white cap in at the study door, which he had partly opened.

"Come in, my dear and esteemed master," returned Daniel.

"Something has happened, Daniel; an event, an occurrence—"

"Will you do me the favor to tell me at once what it is, Señor Don Cándido?"

"You must know, then, that I was walking up and down the hall just now—for when I have a headache, as I have at present, it relieves me to walk up and down, and also to apply a poultice of orange leaves to the temples. For you must know, my sons, that orange leaves smeared with tallow, have on my organization the specific virtue—"

"Of making you well and everybody else ill. What has happened?" asked the impatient Daniel.

"I am coming to that."

"Come to it at once, then, in the name of all the saints!"

"I am coming to it, hothead, I am coming to it. I was walking up and down the hall just now, as I said, when I heard someone stop outside the street door. I approached it, undecided, hesitating, doubtful. I asked who was there. I assured myself of the identity of the person who answered me, and then I opened the door, and who do you suppose it was, Daniel?"

"I don't know, but I should be glad if it had been the devil, Señor Don Cándido," said Daniel, controlling his impatience by an effort.

"No, it was not the devil, for he seems to have been holding me by the coattail for a long time past, Daniel. It was Fermin, your loyal, your faithful, your—"

"Fermin is outside?"

"Yes, he is in the hall; he says he wishes to speak to you."

"Will you finish, in the devil's name!" exclaimed Daniel, starting to his feet and hurrying out of the room.

"What a temper! It will be his ruin yet. Listen, Eduardo, you who seem to be more circumspect—although since you left school, where you were peaceable, quiet and studious, I have not had the pleasure of meeting you often—it is necessary for you to exercise a great deal of caution in the present situation. Tell me, why do you not go this very day to study with the Jesuits, and devote yourself to the ecclesiastical career?"

"Señor, will you do me the favor to leave me in peace?"

"Ah, wicked man! So you too are like your friend? And what is it you seek, misguided youths, in the tortuous path, on the steep descent on which you have launched yourselves? What do you desire—"

"We desire that you shall leave us alone for a moment, Don Cándido," said Daniel, who had entered the room just as his worthy master was beginning the valiant apostrophe he had interrupted.

"Does any danger threaten us, Daniel?" asked Don Cándido, looking timidly at his pupil?

"None whatever. They are matters that concern no one but Eduardo and me."

"But we three form today a single and indivisible body."

"No matter, we will divide it temporarily. Do us the favor to leave us alone."

"Remain alone," said Don Cándido, extending his hand toward the two young men and slowly leaving the room.

"The affair is becoming more serious, Eduardo."

"What is it?"

"Something about Amalia."

"Oh!"

"Yes, about Amalia. She has just been notified that within an hour the police will make her a domiciliary visit; and she has sent me word of it by Fermin, whom I sent to Barracas before coming here."

"What are we to do, Daniel? But oh, how can I ask what we are to do! Daniel, I am going to Barracas."

"Eduardo, this is no time for follies. I love my cousin too well to allow anyone to bring misfortune upon her," said Daniel, in a tone and with a look so serious that they impressed Eduardo's mind strongly.

"But I am the cause of the insults to which that lady finds herself exposed, and it is I who ought to protect her," answered Eduardo coldly.

"Eduardo, let us not act foolishly," repeated Daniel, resuming the affectionate manner with which he was accustomed to treat his friend; "let us not act foolishly. If the question were to defend her against a man, against any number of men, sword in hand, I would leave to you with a tranquil mind the pleasure of fighting them. But it is against the tyrant and all his followers that we must defend her; and against them your valor is powerless; your presence would furnish them with stronger weapons against Amalia, and you would be able neither to secure my cousin's tranquillity nor to save your own head."

"You are right."

"Leave me to act. I will go to Barracas at once; and to force I will oppose strategy; with the intelligence of the man I will endeavor to throw the instinct of the beast off the scent."

"Very well, go; go quickly."

"It will take me ten minutes to go home for my horse, and in a quarter of an hour more I will be in Barracas."

"Very well; and you will return?—"

"Tonight."

"Tell her—"

"That you will be prudent for her sake."

"Tell her whatever you wish, Daniel," said Eduardo, walking to the other end of the room, perhaps because there was something in his eyes which he did not wish his friend to see. When he turned round Daniel had left the room.

It was now eleven o'clock and Don Cándido began to dress to go to Don Felipe's private office.

XXVI

AMALIA IN PRESENCE OF THE POLICE

O n reaching his house Daniel mounted his spirited sorrel and set out for Barracas, taking the shortest road and riding at full speed all the way; but his efforts were in vain, for he was destined to arrive late at the villa.

Shortly after his departure from Barracas that morning Amalia had received a letter announcing a visit from the police, and she had at once sent Daniel word of this occurrence by Fermin, distrusting her own prudence in face of the insult which was to be offered to her house. Five or six minutes after Fermin's departure, and much earlier, consequently, than Amalia had expected, the noise of horses stopping at the door of the villa reached her ears.

Alone and surrounded by dangers which menaced also the beloved of her heart, Amalia gave frank expression to the feelings natural to her sex; she threw herself, pale and trembling, into an armchair, struggling however, to master her emotion.

Don Bernardo Victorica, a police officer, and Nicolas Mariño presented themselves in the parlor, ushered in by Pedro.

Victorica, that man abhorred and feared by all who did not share in the degradation of the epoch, was less vile, however, than was generally supposed. And, without ever failing in the severity prescribed to him by the Dictator's orders, he behaved, whenever he could do so without compromising himself, with a certain civility, a sort of semi-tolerance, which would have been criminal in the eyes of Rosas, had he known it, but which was manifested, nevertheless, by the chief of police, more especially, in the exercise of his functions toward persons whom he believed to be compromised by information prompted by self-interest or by the excessive rigor of the Government.

Holding his hat in his hand he said to Amalia with a profound bow:

"Señora, I am the Chief of Police; I have to perform the painful duty of making a rigorous search of this house; it is the Governor's express order."

"And have these other gentlemen also come to search the house?" asked Amalia, pointing to Mariño and the police officer.

"Not this gentleman," answered Victorica, indicating Mariño by a gesture; "the other gentleman is a police officer."

"And may I know whom or what it is that you have come to seek in my house, by the Governor's orders?"

"I will tell you that in a moment," answered Victorica, with a very serious countenance; for he and his companions were still standing, not having received from Amalia any invitation to be seated.

Amalia pulled the bell and said to Luisa, who appeared on the instant:

"Go with this gentleman and open for him all the doors he may indicate to you."

Victorica with a bow to Amalia followed Luisa through the interior apartments.

As soon as Victorica and the police officer had left the room Amalia, without deigning to raise her eyes to Mariño's face, said to him:

"You may be seated if it is your intention to wait for Señor Victorica."

Amalia was not rosy, she was scarlet at this moment. Mariño on the contrary was pale and ill at ease in the presence of this woman whose beauty fascinated him and whose imperious and aristocratic manners, it might be said, awed him.

"My intention," said Mariño, seating himself a few steps away from Amalia, "my intention was to render you a service, señora—a great service in the present circumstances."

"A thousand thanks," answered Amalia, drily.

"Did you receive my letter this morning?"

"I received a paper signed by Nicolas Mariño, whom I suppose to be you."

"Well," answered the Chief of the Night-Watchmen, controlling by an effort the displeasure which the young woman's scornful reply caused him, "in that letter, that paper, as you call it, I hastened to inform you of what was going to take place."

"And may I know with what object you took that trouble, señor?"

"In order that you might take such measures as a regard for your safety might suggest to you."

"You are very good to me; but very bad to your political friends, since you act with treachery toward them."

"Treachery!"

"So I think."

"That is a very hard word, señora."

"That is the word, however."

JOSÉ MÁRMOL

"I always try to do all the good I can. Besides, I know that there could be no man in this house, after Cuitiño's visit last night. But Doña María Josefa Ezcurra, who is resolved to persecute this house, while I am equally resolved to protect it, went this morning to inform the Governor that a person was concealed here for whom the authorities have been looking for a long time past. His Excellency sent for Señor Victorica and gave him the order which he is now executing, and as I had the good fortune to know what was passing I did not lose an instant in informing you of it, determining, at the same time, to accompany Señor Victorica, thinking I might be so fortunate as to be able to save you from some danger. That is my conduct, señora, and if I act treacherously toward my friends the motive which I have for doing so is my justification. That motive is a sacred one; it springs from an instantaneous sympathy which I conceived for you when I first had the happiness of seeing you. Since that time, my whole life has been devoted to the task of finding a means of approaching this house; and my position, my fortune, my influence—"

"Neither your position nor your influence will prevent me from leaving you alone, however, since you cannot comprehend that your presence annoys me," said Amalia, rising and drawing away her chair from Mariño's and then passing through the library into her bedroom, where she sat down on the sofa, her beautiful face glowing with outraged pride.

"Ah! I will have my revenge, Unitarian!" exclaimed Mariño, pale with anger.

The haughty châtelaine had been only a few moments in her room when Victorica, returning with Luisa from his investigation, found himself once more in Amalia's presence.

"Señora," he said to her, "I have now fulfilled the first part of my orders; and fortunately for you I can say to his Excellency that I have not found here the person I came to seek."

"And may I know who that person is, Señor Chief of Police? May I know why I am insulted by having my house searched?"

"Will you order that child to leave the room?"

Amalia made a sign to Luisa, who left the room, but not before darting an angry glance at Victorica.

"Señora, I am obliged to take your declaration, but I desire to avoid in your case all the customary formalities, and that it shall be rather a loyal and frank conference."

"Speak, señor."

"Do you know Don Eduardo Belgrano?"

"Yes, I know him."

"How long have you known him?"

"Two or three weeks," answered Amalia, red as a newly-blown rose, and lowering her eyes, ashamed of having, for the first time in her life, to tell an untruth.

"He was seen in this house before that time, however."

"I have given you my answer, señor."

"Can you prove that Don Eduardo Belgrano has not been concealed in this house from last May up to the present time?"

"I shall not attempt to prove anything of the kind."

"Then it is true."

"I have not said that."

"But you say that you will not attempt to prove that he was not here."

"Because it is your place, señor, to prove the contrary."

"And do you know where he is at present?"

"I do not know, señor; but if I did I would not tell you," answered Amalia, lifting up her head, happy and proud that an opportunity had presented itself to her to speak the truth frankly.

"Are you aware that I am executing an order of the Governor's," asked Victorica, beginning to repent of his indulgence toward Amalia.

"You have already told me so."

"Then you should be more respectful in your answers, señora."

"Señor, I know very well the respect I owe to others, and also the respect that others owe to me. And if the Governor or Señor Victorica desires informers, it is not in this house, assuredly, that they will find them."

"You do not betray others but you betray yourself."

"What do you mean?"

"You forget that you are talking with the Chief of Police and you are very frankly revealing your Unitarian zeal."

"Ah, señor, there would be nothing very strange in my being a Unitarian in a country where there are so many thousands of them."

"To the misfortune of their country and their own," said Victorica, rising to his feet, furious; "but the day will come when there will not be so many of them, I swear it to you."

"Or when there will be more."

"Señora!" exclaimed Victorica, looking menacingly at Amalia.

"What is the matter, señor?"

"You take advantage of your sex."

"As you do of your position."

"Are you not afraid to speak as you are doing, señora?"

"No, señor. In Buenos Ayres only the men are afraid; the women know how to defend a dignity which the men have forgotten."

"True; the women are the worst," said Victorica to himself. "Come, let us finish," he continued, addressing Amalia; "have the goodness to open this writing-desk."

"What for, señor?"

"I must comply with this final formality; open."

"With what formality?"

"I have received orders to examine your papers."

"Oh, this is too much, señor; you have come to my house in search of a man; that man is not here; and I must tell you that I will consent to your doing nothing further in it."

Victorica smiled and said: "Open, señora, open of your own accord."

"No."

"You will not open?"

"No, no."

Victorica was walking toward the writing-desk, the key of which was in the lock, when Mariño, who had heard the interrogatory from the library, hurried into the room, in the hope of conquering, by a coup de thêater, the heart of the haughty Amalia.

"My dear friend," he said to Victorica, "I will guarantee that there is nothing among the papers of this lady which compromises our cause."

Victorica was drawing away his hand from the key of the desk, and Mariño thought he had won the right to the gratitude of this heart, rebellious to his tenderness, when Amalia hurried to the desk, opened it noisily, took from it four small drawers containing letters, jewels, and money, and with a marked expression of displeasure, confronted Victorica, turning her back on Mariño, and said to him:

"Here are the contents of that desk; examine them all."

Mariño bit his lip till the blood came.

Victorica glanced at the objects which Amalia showed him, and without touching any of them said: "I have finished, señora."

Amalia answered only by a slight inclination of the head and returned to her seat on the sofa; for after the violent effort she had just made she felt dizzy and faint.

Victorica and Mariño, bowing profoundly, left the room and went to join the police officer, who was waiting for them outside the house.

And it was just as they were remounting their horses that Daniel dismounted from his, and, after a polite salutation to Victorica and Mariño, entered his cousin's house, saying to himself:

"Bad; I begin to arrive late; that is a bad omen."

Victorica, on his part, said to Mariño:

"That man must know all about it. That man is a Unitarian, in spite of his father and of all he is doing."

"Yes; it will be necessary to keep a watch upon him."

"And the dagger ready to strike," added Mariño; and they set off at a gallop for the city.

XXVII

Manuela Rosas

Next to her father Manuela Rosas is the most striking figure in the grand historical picture of the Argentine dictatorship.

In 1840 she was not even the shadow of what she became later, but at this period she began to be her father's chief victim and the best instrument, without knowing it and without desiring it, of his diabolical plans.

Manuela was now in the most smiling period of life—she was not more than twenty-two or twenty-three years of age. Tall and slender, with a rounded figure and graceful and delicately outlined proportions, an American type of countenance, pale, with dark shadows under the eyes, which were light gray; an animated and intelligent expression; a forehead not high, but well shaped; dark chestnut hair, abundant and fine; a straight nose; a mouth large but fresh and piquant—such was Manuela in 1840.

In disposition she was gay, easy and communicative. But for some time past there had been noticeable in her a tinge of sadness, of melancholy, of discontent, and her sparkling eyes were at times veiled by reddened lids; she wept, but she wept in secret, like all who truly suffer.

Her education had been neglected but her natural endowments made up for her want of culture.

Her mother, a woman of ability but of an intriguing and vulgar disposition, had done nothing to improve Manuela's natural gifts; and, left motherless two years before the period at which our story opens, there was no human being to take an interest in her but her father, for her brother was an ignorant and evil-disposed churl; and her relatives paid a great deal of attention to Juan Manuel, but none at all to Manuela.

Twice already had her heart heard at its closed doors the tender serenade of love, but on each occasion her father's hand had drawn the bolts upon them, and the unhappy girl had to see only in the mirror of her imagination the fairest charms of a woman's life.

Her father had doomed this girl, who was acquainted with all his baseness, all his intrigues and all his crimes, to eternal celibacy, for, with the young girl's heart, he would have had to deliver up all these important secrets.

She was, besides, his guardian angel; she took note even of the movements of the eyelids of those who approached her father; she watched over the house, the doors, and even the food. We approach this unfortunate woman at the hour, after the candles are lighted, when her salon is thronged with people; and she is there the empress of that strange court.

The principal members of the Sociedad Popular make their customary visit at this time. And they smoke, swear, blaspheme and stain the carpet with their muddy boots and with the water that drips from their wet ponchos.

Here the democracy of the Federation—Gaetan, Moreira, Merlo, Salomon, Cuitiño, Parra, smoke and converse side by side with the deputies García, Balaustegui, Garrigós, Lahitte, Medrano, and with Generals Mancilla, Rolon and Soler. In a group apart Larrazabal, Mariño, Irigoyen and Gonzalez Peña are conversing together, while their wives, enthusiastic Federals, their sisters and their other female relatives and friends surround Manuela and Doña María Josefa Ezcurra.

Larrazabál had just declared loudly that he is waiting only for the authorization of His Excellency to be the first to wet his dagger in the blood of the Unitarians.

"This is to speak like a good Federal," responded Doña María Josefa, in the same tone. "It was owing to the tolerance of Juan Manuel that the Unitarians, who are now coming back with Lavalle, were able to leave the country."

"They are coming to their death, señora," answered a Federal brother, "and we should congratulate ourselves upon their having gone away."

"No, señor; no," replied Doña María Josefa. "They will only be imprisoned; it would have been better to have killed them before they went away."

"Just so!" cried Salomon.

"Yes, señor; just so," continued the old woman. "And Juan Manuel's clemency is not the worst of it; for when he gives an order to arrest some Unitarian, the police stand gaping like idiots and let the Unitarian escape."

The old woman's eyes, small, red and piercing, were fixed on Cuitiño, who, standing within two paces of her, was sending a volume of smoke from between his lips.

"And the worst of it is not that they let the Unitarians escape," she continued; "for when the good servants of the Federation tell the police where some Unitarian is concealed, they go there and the Unitarians themselves hoodwink them as if they were children."

Cuitiño turned his back upon her.

"Are you going, Commandant Cuitiño?"

"No, Señora Doña María Josefa; but I know what I am about."

"Not always."

"Yes, señora, always. I know how to kill Unitarians, and I have given proofs of it. Because the Unitarians are worse than dogs, and I am never happy except when I see their blood. But you are making insinuations."

"I am glad that you have understood me."

"I know what I am about."

"Commandant Cuitiño is our best sword," said Garrigós.

"But this is not a time for swords," returned Doña María Josefa, "but for the dagger. It is by the dagger that all the filthy Unitarian savages, traitors to God and to the Federation, ought to die."

"Just so," assented several voices in chorus.

"Apropos of dying," said Mariño, in an undertone to Soler, "do you know, General, that we are going to lose the Rector of La Piedad?"

"I heard that he was very ill."

"He was a good Federal."

"And a better drunkard."

"In any case, if Lavalle should triumph the devil would have the friar within a couple of hours."

"And a great many others with him."

"You and me, for instance."

"Possibly."

"Everything is possible."

"What do you mean, General?"

"I mean that the worst of the matter is that we cannot be certain that he will not triumph."

"True."

"Lavalle is brave to rashness."

"But we have three times as many men as he has."

"I took the hill of Victoria with a third of the forces that defended it."

"But they were Spaniards."

"Just so! They were Spaniards, which means, Señor Mariño, that they knew how to fight and how to die fighting."

"Our soldiers are as brave as they are."

"I know it. And they may be conquered, as the Spaniards were, in spite of their bravery."

"But justice is on our side."

"On the battlefield there is no such thing as justice, Señor Mariño."

"We have enthusiasm."

"So have they."

"So that—"

"So that there is going to be a battle and the devil only knows who will win it."

"General, we are of the same opinion."

"I know it."

"I am not surprised at your perspicacity, General; you have had a great deal of experience in revolutions."

"I have grown up among them."

"But none of them could ever have resulted in a greater catastrophe than that which would overwhelm us Federals if Lavalle should triumph."

"It would be all over with us."

"With all of us."

"Especially with you and me, Señor Mariño."

"Especially?"

"Yes."

"And why so, General?"

"Frankly?"

"Yes, frankly."

"Because they hate me, why I do not know, and you, because you are a Mashorquero."

"Oh!"

"I know they have no reason to love me."

"And I know that I am not a Mashorquero, in the real meaning of the word."

"That may be, but as we are not going to be judged by a tribunal we must either let ourselves be killed or go into exile."

"And exile must be a terrible thing, General Soler!" exclaimed Mariño, shaking his head.

"That is precisely the word; I have gone into exile several times and I know that it is terrible."

"We must all resist to the death, then."

"Who knows whether all are to be relied upon."

"I too have my doubts as to that."

"Defections are to be looked for in all revolutions."

"Ah! secret enemies are the worst!"

"The hardest to contend against."

"But they don't deceive me. There you have one of them."

"Who?"

"That man who is coming in."

"Why, he is only a boy."

"Yes, a boy of twenty-five. Everyone believes him to be the best of Federals, but my opinion is that he is nothing but a Unitarian in disguise."

"He is of no consequence."

"I know it, but he is a Unitarian."

"What is his name?"

"Bello; Daniel Bello; he is the son of a true Federal; a planter; a partner of the Anchorenas and a man of great prestige in the plains."

"Then he is well protected."

"The young man is, besides, a great protégé of Salomon's, and comes and goes when and where he chooses."

"Then, my friend, we must salute him," said General Soler.

"Yes, but he is a marked man," answered Mariño, as they went to join the others.

XXVIII

Continuation of the Preceding

It was, in fact, Daniel Bello who had, a moment before, entered the salon, and was now making his way through the crowd, giving handshakes to right and left, to pay his respects to Manuela and the Federal ladies of her court.

Manuela was leaning her arm on one of the elbows of the sofa and Daniel, who had taken the chair beside the corner in which she was seated, by bending slightly toward her could talk to her without being heard by the others.

Beginning with a few complimentary phrases, to which Manuela responded with the amiability and the simplicity that were natural to her, Daniel adroitly led the conversation to the subject which he had come to speak to her about; and Manuela herself opened the way directly to it, saying, in answer to a remark of Bello's concerning the Federal enthusiasm displayed by her court and their devotion to herself:

"They weary me, Señor Bello. I lead the most tiresome life in the world. I hear all these men and women speak only of bloodshed and death. I know that the Unitarians are our enemies. But what need is there to keep constantly repeating it, with those maledictions that sicken me, and above all with the expression of a hatred in which I do not believe, for these people are incapable of real passion. Besides, what necessity is there for them to come here to torment my mind with these things, keeping away from me persons of my own sex and the men friends whom I should like to have?"

"True, señorita," said Daniel, in the most natural tone in the world. "True; you need the companionship of girls of your own class, with tastes congenial to your own to divert your mind and make you forget for a time the terrors amidst which you live in these days, terrible for all."

"Ah, how happy I should be then!"

"I know a woman whose disposition would agree perfectly with yours; she would understand you and love you."

"Yes?"

"A woman who sympathized with you from the first moment she saw you."

JOSÉ MÁRMOL

"Truly?"

"Who does not let a day pass without asking me some question about you."

"Oh! who is she?"

"A woman who is as unfortunate as yourself, if not more so."

"As unfortunate?"

"Yes."

"No, there is no woman in the world as unfortunate as I am," said Manuela, with a sigh, lowering her eyes, to which the tears had started.

"You at least are not calumniated."

"I am not calumniated!" exclaimed Manuela, raising her head and fixing her sparkling eyes on Daniel. "That is the only thing which I cannot forgive my father's enemies; they have pulled my reputation to pieces, through a spirit of political revenge. And what calumny, my God!" exclaimed the young girl, covering her eyes with her hand.

The conversation carried on in the various groups around them was so animated that the dialogue between the two young people was not heard by Doña María Josefa and Mariño, but it was followed by their watchful glances.

"Time will rectify all that, my friend," said Daniel, in so gentle and sympathetic a tone that Manuela could not refrain from thanking him with a sweet glance. "But time is perhaps the worst enemy of the person of whom we were speaking."

"How is that? Explain yourself."

"Time is her worst enemy because every moment that passes aggravates her situation."

"But what is the matter? Who is she?" asked the young girl, with the frankness and impetuosity which were natural to her.

"They calumniate her politically. They make her appear to be a Unitarian and they persecute her."

"But who is she?"

"Amalia."

"Your cousin?"

"Yes."

"And they persecute her?"

"Yes."

"By papa's orders?"

"No."

"By those of the police?"

"No."

"And by whose, then?"

"By the orders of a man who is in love with her and whom she scorns."

"And—"

"Pardon me—and they employ the Federation and the respected name of the Restorer of the Laws as the instruments of an ignoble and personal revenge."

"Ah! who is he, who is the man who persecutes her?"

"Forgive me, señorita, but I cannot tell you that yet."

"But I wish to know it in order to tell it to papa."

"You will know it one day. But I must tell you that he is a person of great influence."

"He is all the more criminal then, Señor Bello."

"I know it."

"Listen to me."

"Speak, señorita."

"I wish you to bring Amalia here."

"Here?"

"Yes."

"She would not come."

"She would not come to my house?"

"She is a little eccentric; and she would find herself very ill at ease in so numerous a company as that which surrounds you, señorita."

"I will receive her alone—but no, I am not free to be alone."

"Besides, since her house has been searched she is afraid of receiving some further insult."

"But it is unheard of!"

"In addition, she has had to abandon for the time her beautiful villa at Barracas; and although she lives in the greatest retirement she is in constant terror."

"Poor girl!"

"You might render her a great service, however."

"I? Name it, Bello."

"You might write her a letter which she could show to anyone who should present himself in her house without an order from the Governor."

"And is there anyone who would dare do that without an order from papa?"

"Someone has already done it."

"Very well, I will write the letter tomorrow."

"I will venture to ask you, when you are writing it, to make it understood that no one shall use the name of General Rosas or the Federation as a shield for the commission of injustice, or the gratification of private revenge."

"Very well, very well; I understand," returned Manuela, radiant at having an opportunity of wounding the pride of those who annoyed her unceasingly. "Our conversation," she continued, "in which I have taken so much pleasure, has lasted too long already not to have awakened the jealousy of these people, to all of whom, without distinction, I am obliged to show the same attention, in accordance with papa's desire."

"Your wishes are for me commands. But you will promise me not to forget the letter?"

"Yes; tomorrow you shall have it."

"Very well. Thanks."

XXIX

The Solitary House

To the left of the road following the course of the river, going from Buenos Ayres to San Isidro, and about three leagues distant from the city, there stands, crowning a small eminence, a group of some forty or fifty olive trees, the remains of an ancient wood, from which the place takes its name of Los Olivos. Fronting this grove, to the right of the road, stood, in 1840, on the barranca overlooking the river, a small and solitary house, long uninhabited, and in part fallen into decay. It was in this house, transformed, as if by magic, in the space of a few days, into a comfortable, and even elegant abode, inside, while outside it presented the same ruinous appearance as before, that Amalia had taken refuge from the persecution of which she had been the object at Barracas; and here, at about nine o'clock on a bright moonlight night a few weeks after the domiciliary visit of the police, she and Eduardo, who had arrived about half an hour before, were sitting in the little parlor, in the center of which stood a table laid for three persons, waiting for Daniel's arrival to sit down to dinner.

In accordance with Amalia's orders the windows were all darkened and the doors of all the rooms closed, with the exception of those facing the river, as on that side no one ever passed at night.

Eduardo and Amalia were discussing with mingled hope and anxiety their plans for the future, when Pedro, who had been standing at the window of his room, watching the road, put his head in at the door and said:

"They are coming now."

"Who are coming?" asked Amalia with a start.

"Señor Don Daniel and Fermin."

"Ah! very well; see to their horses."

Animated, gay and careless as usual, Daniel entered his cousin's parlor, a few moments later, enveloped in a short poncho, with the points of his collar turned down over a black necktie, leaving bare his well-shaped throat.

"We have been waiting for you," said the young woman, with a smile.

"For me? Ah, many thanks! You are the most amiable creatures in the world. And how tired you must have been waiting for me! How heavy the time must have hung on your hands."

"Oh, very heavy!" answered Eduardo, nodding.

"Naturally! You tire so soon of each other's company. Pedro!"

"What do you want, madcap?"

"Dinner, Pedro," said Daniel, taking off his poncho and his beaver gloves, seating himself at the table and pouring out a glass of wine.

"Have you heard from Barracas, Daniel?" asked Amalia later, when, dinner over, the conversation took a more serious turn.

"Yes; they have not yet made an attack upon the house, which is something wonderful in these times of the sacred Federal cause."

"Have they ceased to watch it?"

"For three nights past no one has been there, which is strange also. I went to the villa this morning. Everything is just as we left it two weeks ago. I have had a new lock put on the door of the grating, and your faithful negroes who are taking care of the villa sleep a great deal in the daytime in order to keep watch at night; if anyone goes there they pretend to be asleep; but they both hear and see, which is what I wish."

"Oh, my old servants! I will recompense them some day!"

"Yesterday Doña María Josefa sent for them; they were with her this morning early, but the poor creatures could tell her only what they knew themselves—that is to say, that you were not at home, and that they did not know where you were."

"Oh, what a woman, what a woman, Eduardo!"

"No; she is not the one who is to be held responsible."

"There is one thing, however, in our favor."

"What is that?" they both asked eagerly.

"The situation of affairs. The Liberating Army is still encamped at Lujan, but tomorrow, the 1st of September, it will resume its march; Rosas can give his attention only to great dangers, and no one will venture to annoy him now with personal gossip; the persecution of which you are the object and which still continues in the case of Eduardo, is a private affair entirely, and comes from a low quarter. Rosas has given no orders for it; and the Mashorca and the leaders of the Federation do not wish to assume a more decided attitude until they know the result of the invasion; so that in the past fortnight no event of any importance has occurred. But when these terrible times are past," he continued, "and you and Eduardo, my Florencia and I are living all together I will tell you horrible things, my noble cousin, which have taken place very near you and of which you are utterly ignorant. It is true that we shall then be so happy that we may not care to speak of past misfortunes. Let us drink to that moment."

"Yes, let us drink to our future happiness," responded Eduardo and Amalia, raising their glasses to drink with Daniel.

"You have scarcely tasted your wine, Amalia, but Eduardo and I have drunk for you; and we have done well, for wine strengthens and we have a ride of three leagues along the shore before us."

"My God! That ride terrifies me!" exclaimed Amalia; "at this hour—"

"Thus far no harm has come to us; nor will there in the future," said Eduardo.

"But what if you should prove to be mistaken in your confidence?"

"No, my friend, no. The soldiers of Rosas never go alone, it is true, but their parties never exceed six or eight in number."

"But you are only three."

"Precisely, Amalia; and it is because we are three that the Mashorqueros would need to be at least twelve—four to one; then the matter might be doubtful," answered Eduardo, with so much confidence in his manner that he almost succeeded in inspiring Amalia with confidence also; but only for the moment—a woman in love never doubts the courage of her lover, but neither does she ever wish to see it put to the test; and Amalia said quickly:

"You will avoid any encounter, however, will you not?"

"Yes, unless Eduardo's old passion for fencing should return. Rather than bear the weight of the sword he wears every night I would take my chance of being wounded by one like it."

"I do not use mysterious weapons, señor," answered Eduardo smiling.

"That may be so; but they are the most effectual ones; and above all, the most convenient to carry."

"Ah! I know what you are alluding to. What is that weapon which you use, Daniel, and with which you have at times done so much harm?"

"And so much good, you might add, cousin."

"True, true, forgive me. But answer my question; it is one that I have often before desired to ask you."

"Wait; let me finish this jam first."

"I shall not let you leave the house tonight until you tell me what I wish to know."

"I am almost inclined to refuse to tell it to you, then."

JOSÉ MÁRMOL

"Tease!"

"Well, then, here is the mysterious weapon, as Eduardo calls it."

And Daniel took from his coat pocket and laid on the table a slender osier wand a foot in length, with an iron ball, weighing at least six ounces and covered by a fine close network of Russia leather at either extremity; a weapon which, held by one of the balls, could be wielded without breaking the osier, the other ball acquiring triple weight and force from the slightest movement of the hand.

Amalia took the weapon in her hand, as if it were a toy, but as soon as she comprehended its deadly power, she laid it down again.

"Have you examined it already, Amalia?"

"Yes, yes; put it away. A blow given with one of those balls must be terrible."

"It would be fatal if given with full force either on the head or the chest. Now I will tell you its name. In English it is called Life-preserver; in French casse-tête; in Spanish it has no special name, but we call it by the French name, which is the most expressive, for it means, as you know, head-breaker. In England this weapon is very common; it is used also in one of the provinces of France; and Napoleon caused it to be carried by several cavalry regiments. It has for me two recommendations—one that it saved Eduardo's life, the other that it is ready to save his life again, if the occasion should arise."

"Oh, it will not arise! Is it not true that you will not expose yourself again to danger, Eduardo?"

"No, I will not expose myself to danger; I should be too much afraid of being unable to return here."

"And you are right, for it is the only place that you are not turned out of," said Daniel.

"He?"

"Why, did you not know that, my dear cousin? Our respected schoolmaster did not put him out of his house, but he talked him out of it. My Florencia gave him shelter for a night, but I turned him out of that house. A friend of ours wished to keep him for a couple of days, but his worthy father would consent to shelter him for only a day and a half; and finally, I have been willing to keep him for only two days, or, counting tonight, three."

"But I spent one night in my own house," said Eduardo, with a certain emphasis.

"Yes, señor, and that was enough."

Amalia tried to smile, but her eyes filled with tears. Daniel perceived them and taking out his watch, said:

"Half-past eleven; we must return to the city now."

They all stood up.

"Your poncho and your sword, Eduardo?"

"I gave them to Luisa when I came; I believe that she took them to one of the inner rooms."

Amalia passed through the adjoining apartment into a room beyond it; both of which were dark, except for the moonlight which entered through the windows that looked out on the road lying between The Olives and the solitary house.

Eduardo and Daniel were talking together when they heard a cry from Amalia and then the sound of her footsteps hurrying toward the parlor.

The two young men were about to go into the adjoining room when Amalia stopped them at the threshold.

"What is the matter?" asked the two friends simultaneously.

"Nothing—don't go away yet—don't go away tonight," answered Amalia, with an excessively pale and troubled countenance.

"For God's sake, Amalia! what is the matter?" asked Daniel, with the impetuousity natural to him, while Eduardo endeavored to force his way into the room, the door leading into which Amalia had closed, and before which she now stood, saying:

"I will tell you; I will tell you, but do not go in."

"Is there someone in there, then?"

"No, there is no one there."

"But cousin, why did you give that cry? Why are you so pale?"

"I saw a man looking in at the window of Luisa's room, which looks out on the road; I thought at first that it might be Pedro or Fermin; I went to the window to see who it was; the man saw me, turned round quickly, covered his face with his poncho, and hurried away, almost running; but, as he turned from the window the moonlight fell upon his face and I recognized him."

"And who was he, Amalia?" asked both young men simultaneously.

"Mariño."

"Mariño!" exclaimed Daniel, while Eduardo clenched his hands.

"Yes, it was he; I am sure of it. I could not control myself and I gave a cry."

"All our labor is lost!" exclaimed Eduardo, walking with agitated steps up and down the room.

"There is not a doubt of it, he followed me here," said Daniel, thoughtfully.

The young man then went to the door facing the river and called to Pedro, who had just finished removing the dinner dishes.

The veteran immediately appeared.

"Pedro, where was Fermin while we were at dinner?"

"He has not stirred from the kitchen since we took the horses to the stable."

"And neither you nor he heard anything on the road or near the house?"

"Nothing, señor."

"It seems, however, that a man was standing for a long time at Luisa's window, looking into her room."

The soldier raised his hand to his gray mustache and, pretending to twist it, gave it a sharp pull.

"You did not hear him, Pedro. That might very well have happened, but it is necessary to be more vigilant for the future. Call Fermin, and, meanwhile, saddle the horse he rides."

Pedro left the room without answering a word and a moment afterward Daniel's servant appeared.

"Fermin, I wish to know if there is a party of horsemen among the olives; and if they are not there I desire to know what direction they have taken and how many there are. If they have left the grove it cannot have been more than a few minutes ago."

Fermin retired, and Daniel, Amalia and Eduardo went immediately into Luisa's room where Daniel opened the window, from which they could see the road and the group of trees, three hundred yards from the house, that looked like so many ghosts revisiting this solitary scene.

They had been watching the road skirting the grove for a few moments when Amalia said:

"But why does Fermin delay so long in leaving the house?"

"Oh, he is already several hundred yards away from it, Amalia."

"But he has not passed by, and this is the only way to the road."

"No, child, no; Fermin is a good gaucho, and he knows that the runaway horse is not to be overtaken from behind. I am sure that he has descended the barranca and ascended it again, three or four hundred yards farther on, to return to The Olives by the upper road. There he is, do you see him?"

And in fact, a couple of hundred yards from the solitary house, keeping well to the right and leaving The Olives a little to the left, a man mounted on a dark horse was seen galloping up the road, and a moment afterward the man's voice was heard singing one of the melancholy and expressive songs of our gauchos, all differing in words but resembling one another in air.

Shortly afterward they saw him halt and return at a trot toward The Olives, still singing. Then he disappeared among the trees and a few moments later they saw him issue from the grove like an exhalation and retrace in a minute the road he had traversed.

"They are pursuing Fermin, Daniel."

"No, Amalia."

"But look; he is no longer to be seen."

"I understand it all."

"But what do you understand?" asked Eduardo, who lacked that genius for observation which Daniel possessed in so remarkable a degree, and by means of which he had acquired the learning of the gaucho as well as the learning of civilization.

"What I understand is that Fermin found no one among the olives; that he descended the barranca in search of a clue; that he found tracks leading him to believe that horses had passed recently along the road that he has taken and that he is following it to ascertain if his supposition is correct."

They then returned to the parlor, and before they had been ten minutes standing at the door facing the river, they descried Fermin galloping rapidly toward them along the beach. He ascended the barranca at a slow trot, rode up to the door, and dismounted.

"There they go, señor," he said with the indolence which is characteristic of the gaucho.

"How many?"

"Three."

"By what road?"

"The upper road."

"Did you observe the horses?"

"Yes, señor."

"Did you recognize any of them?"

"Yes, señor."

"Which?"

"The one in the lead is the horse with the two white forefeet of Commandant Mariño."

Amalia looked with surprise at Eduardo and Daniel.

"Good; take the horses down to the shore."

Fermin went away, leading his own horse by the bridle.

"Are you going, then?" asked Amalia.

"Without losing an instant," answered her cousin.

"But how can we leave her alone, Daniel?"

"Fermin will remain, and he and Pedro will answer to us for her safety. I am to accompany the officer of the day on his rounds tonight and you will sleep in my house."

"My God! Fresh troubles!" exclaimed Amalia, covering her face with her hands.

"Yes, fresh troubles, my Amalia. This house is no longer safe, and we must seek another."

"Come quickly, Daniel," said Eduardo with such marked impatience and so stern an expression in his brilliant black eyes, that Amalia fancied she divined his intention and catching him by the hand she said:

"For my sake, Eduardo, for my sake," with so much sweetness, so much tenderness in her glance and in her voice, that Eduardo, for the first time, was obliged to turn away his eyes from hers, lest his resolution should give way before their soft enchantment.

"Leave everything to me, my Amalia," said Daniel, kissing her on the forehead, as his custom was when parting from her.

As Eduardo pressed Amalia's hand Pedro gave him his poncho and his sword, swearing inwardly because he had not been able to salute with his carbine the man who had come to spy into the windows of the house of his Colonel's daughter.

At the foot of the barranca Daniel and Eduardo vaulted upon their horses, Fermin having received orders to remain with Amalia until six on the following morning.

XXX

The Officer of the Day

"I t is useless, Eduardo; we shall only kill the horses without succeeding in what you desire," said Daniel, while the horses flew along the road.

"And do you know what it is that I desire?"

"Yes."

"What?"

"To overtake Mariño."

"Yes."

"But you will not do it."

"No?"

"You will not succeed in doing it; and that is the reason why I have humored your caprice that we should fly along this road like two demons, as we are doing, at the risk of stumbling and breaking our necks."

"We shall see whether I will succeed in overtaking him or not."

"He has twenty minutes the start of us."

"Not so many."

"More."

"We have made up two of them, at least, already."

"And how if we should overtake him?"

"All roads lead to Rome."

"What do you mean by that?"

"That I will provoke a quarrel with him and run him through the body."

"A magnificent idea."

"If it is not magnificent it is at least conclusive."

"Do you forget that there are four to fight against?"

"Even if there were five. But there are only three—he and his two orderlies."

"There are four—Mariño, his two orderlies and I."

"You?"

"I."

"You against me?"

"I against you."

"Very good."

Such was the dialogue that took place between the two young men as they made their gallant steeds fly along the road like the wind; and they had already traversed a league and a half of the three leagues they had to cover when Daniel, who was beginning to fear that Eduardo would carry out his mad idea, a thing which must at all costs be prevented, availing himself of the appearance of two men on horseback, whom he perceived riding along the road, to the right, in the same direction as themselves, said:

"Look there, Eduardo, there go three men—to the right—about two hundred yards away—do you see them?"

"But there are not three, there are only two."

"No, I saw three—it is that they are in line with us."

Eduardo waited to hear no more, but, crossing the road, galloped after the horsemen, who were now about five hundred paces away, thus losing some minutes, which was all that Daniel, who kept at his side of the road, desired.

The strangers, seeing two men riding after them at full speed, reined in their horses and waited for what was to follow.

The young men halted at a few paces' distance from them and Eduardo bit his lip vexed to see that it was a poor old man and a boy who had taken them out of their course and made them lose five or six minutes; more especially when he comprehended that it had been a ruse of Daniel's.

To perceive his mistake, turn his horse's head, and gallop on again, was the work of a second.

Daniel, certain that Eduardo could not now overtake Mariño, allowed him to urge on his horse without further remonstrance, persuaded that the only risk they now ran was that of a fall, as he had said. But the poor beasts, powerful and swift as they were, could not keep up the rate of speed at which they had been going for three leagues and they were beginning to falter and refuse to obey the spur when suddenly, to Daniel's great relief, the "Who goes there!" of a sentinel fell upon their ears. They were at the foot of the Barrancas del Retiro, where General Rolon was quartered, with a picket of cavalry and half a company of the naval battalion commanded by Maza, which was guarding the barracks, as the troops had marched to Santos Lugares whither the Dictator had preceded them by a few hours, on the 16th of August.

"Thank Heaven!" said Daniel to himself. "Our country!" he said aloud, in answer to the sentinel's challenge, stopping his own horse and the horse of Eduardo, which he reined in with such force as almost to unseat its rider.

"Who goes there?" demanded the sentinel.

"Good Federals," responded Daniel.

"Pass on."

Eduardo was about to put his horse to a gallop again when a deep, resonant voice cried out:

"Halt!"

The young men stopped.

A party of ten horsemen were descending the barranca from Maza's quarters.

Three of the horsemen rode forward to examine the men who were riding up the Bajo road; and they were observing them attentively when the rest of the party joined them.

"You owe me a horse, General," said Daniel, with that confident manner which he knew how to assume in the most difficult circumstances and with which he disarmed the most clear-sighted and suspicious, as he recognized in the leader of the party, General Mancilla, who, as officer of the day, was now making the nightly rounds.

"You here, Bello?" answered the general.

"Yes, señor, I am here, after riding for more than a league along the coast in the hope of meeting you, as I could not find you at any of the barracks in the city. There is not a word to be said—you owe me a horse, for mine is done up from all he has galloped in search of you."

"But you agreed to be at my house at eleven, and I did not leave it until a quarter past."

"Then it is I who am to blame?"

"Of course."

"Well, I confess my fault, then, and I will not claim the horse."

"Agreed."

"And is there nothing new, General?"

"Nothing."

"But I told you that I desired to see our soldiers in their barracks."

"I began with those of the Retiro; all the others are yet to be inspected."

"And you are going now—"

"To the fortress."

"I wager they are all asleep there."

"Well, what can you expect! Alcaldes and justices of the peace! What sort of soldiers are they?"

"Well, General, what road are you going to take?"

"The Bajo, as I am going first to the battery."

"Well, then, I will meet you at the fortress."

"But are we not going together?"

"No, General; I am going to accompany my friend here to the city first; he had intended to spend the night with us, but he has been taken suddenly ill."

"That's the way with you! Deuce a thing you young men of the present day are good for."

"That is just what I was saying to you this morning."

"You can't pass a bad night without suffering for it."

"So you see."

"Well, go quickly, and meet me at the fortress and we will take supper there."

"Good-bye for a while, General."

"Make no delay."

Eduardo, bowing slightly to General Mancilla, rode with his friend up the Barranca del Retiro.

Ten minutes later Daniel opened the door of his house and entered it with Eduardo; a few moments afterward he left it again, alone, closed the door behind him, and mounted his horse—a fresh and spirited horse, the best of the many in his father's stables.

Passing the grand arch of the Recova, he saw the officer of the day and his party riding toward him across the Plaza of the 25th of May, and the general and Daniel exchanged salutations again, beside the moat of the fortress which, after the customary military formalities, they entered together.

The night continued beautiful and calm and in the large courtyard of the fortress and the corridors of what had formerly been the Ministerial Departments were crowded together, smoking and talking, all the alcaldes and justices of the peace of the city, with their lieutenants and orderlies, half of the corps of Night-Watchmen and a large part of the staff; amounting in all to between four hundred and fifty and five hundred men.

This heterogeneous garrison was commanded on this night by Mariño, in accordance with the orders of General Pinedo, inspector of arms.

It would be impossible to describe the amazement of the Commandant of the Night-Watchmen on seeing Daniel in the company of General

Mancilla, believing him, as he did, to be in the solitary house, three leagues distant from the city.

Daniel had not known that Mariño was on this night in charge of the fortress but he showed no surprise in his countenance, and comprehending the surprise that Mariño must feel at seeing him he said to the officer of the day:

"This is what may be called serving the state, general. Señor Mariño lays down the pen to take up the sword."

"That is only fulfilling my duty, Señor Bello," answered Mariño, who had not yet recovered from his surprise.

"And this is what may be called vigilance. Everybody is awake here," said the officer of the day.

"A thing we have seen nowhere else," added Daniel, completing the perplexity of Mariño, for if Daniel had been accompanying the officer of the day in his rounds it could not have been he whom the editor had followed to the solitary house, three hours before; and perhaps the woman who had uttered a cry in a dark room of that house was not Amalia, either. Thus Mariño lost himself in conjectures, and when the general had gone upstairs to one of the rooms in which a table was spread with cold meats and wine, to talk with some of the justices of the peace, Mariño could not refrain from asking Daniel, with that indiscretion into which one is apt to be betrayed by a sudden surprise:

"Then you were not riding alone this evening?"

"I was for a while."

"Ah!"

"I was in the house of the Deputy Governor until seven, and before going to meet General Mancilla I took a turn through that part of the Retiro."

"Through the Retiro, toward San Isidro?"

"Yes, toward San Isidro. But I suddenly remembered that I had some business to attend to near El Socorro, and I gave up my ride, envying a man who was riding in front of me and who continued on his way without having any business to attend to."

"Riding in front of you?"

"Yes, toward San Isidro, on the upper road," returned Daniel, with such naturalness that Mariño was completely bewildered and began to think that after all he had been deceiving himself.

"What would you have?" continued Daniel; "we have not a moment that we can call our own."

"That is true."

"Oh, but if I had your genius, Señor Mariño, if I could only write like you, my vigils might then be of some service to our cause; but I go about all day and all night, and devil a thing I do to serve the Restorer."

"Everyone does what he can, Señor Bello," answered Mariño, on whose soul, more distorted than his eyes, not even flattery could make any impression.

"When shall we be at peace and see those brilliant Federal principles established which you are disseminating in the *Gaceta?*"

"When there is not a single Unitarian left, either open or concealed," responded the Federal writer.

"That is exactly what I was saying this evening to the Deputy Governor."

At this moment an adjutant of the officer of the day came for Bello and Mariño and they went upstairs together.

Standing around the table of the room in which Mancilla was awaiting them were thirteen or fourteen men drinking with the officer of the day. But strange to say, though they were now emptying their glasses for the third or fourth time, no enthusiastic Federal toast had yet resounded under the vaulted roof of this Palace, which in other days had rung with toasts to liberty and country! Mariño arrived in time to drink with them, but he too drank in silence.

"Come, Bello, what will you have?" said General Mancilla.

"Nothing, señor, nothing to eat; but I will drink a glass to the speedy triumph of our arms."

"And the eternal glory of the Restorer of the Laws," added Mancilla; and all present emptied their glasses, but in silence.

"Commandant Mariño!"

"At your service, señor," answered Mariño, approaching General Mancilla, who said to him aside:

"Let all these people go to bed; the affair may be long, and it is not well for them to fatigue themselves so much."

"Shall I order the drawbridge to be raised?"

"There is no occasion."

"Do you think, General, there will be any trouble tonight?"

"None."

"Are you going now?"

"Yes; I am going to visit some of the other barracks, and after that I am going to bed."

"You have a good companion."

"Who?"

"Bello."

"Ah, that boy is a jewel!"

"Of what metal, General?"

"I don't know whether it is of gold or of gilded brass, but it shines," said Mancilla, smiling and giving his hand to Mariño.

Then they descended the great staircase together, and while Mancilla went to mount horse again with his party Daniel went over to Mariño and said to him:

"I envy you, Commandant—I should like to have some position, too, in which I could distinguish myself."

"And would you suffer the anxieties that I suffer for the Federation?"

"Everything; even to the calumnies."

"Calumnies?"

"Yes. Only just now I heard some persons here criticizing you."

"Me?"

"They were saying that you did not come to the fortress until eleven when you ought to have come at seven."

Mariño looked away, turning as red as a tomato.

"And who said that, Señor Bello?" he asked, in a voice trembling with rage.

"That is not to be told, Señor Mariño; the miracle is related without mentioning the saint; but they were talking about it, and it would be very disagreeable if this should reach the Restorer's ears."

Mariño turned pale.

"Gossip," he said.

"Gossip, of course."

"Don't repeat it to anyone, however, Señor Bello."

"I give you my word of honor, Señor Mariño. I am one of the most ardent admirers of your genius, and I have special reasons for being grateful to you for the service you wished to render my cousin."

"And is your cousin well?"

"Very well, thanks."

"Have you seen her lately?"

"I was with her this afternoon."

"I hear that she has left Barracas."

"No. She has come to the city for a few days, but she will return soon to Barracas."

"Ah, she is going back to Barracas?"

"She may do so at any time."

"Come, Bello," cried General Mancilla, who had already mounted his horse.

"I will be with you in a moment, General. Good-night, Señor Mariño."

"I recommend you to forget that gossip, Señor Bello."

"I have already forgotten it; good-night."

And Daniel vaulted on his horse and rode out of the fortress with the officer of the day, leaving Mariño full of perplexity and disquietude and unable to classify rightly this young man who everywhere eluded him and who was forever interfering in his private affairs; whom he hated by instinct, but in regard to whom he could not discover a single piece of evidence, a single indiscretion, by means of which to ruin him.

XXXI

Continuation of the Preceding Chapter

The party of the officer of the day turned into the Calle de la Reconquista, which led to the quarters of Colonel Ravelo.

Although it was only twelve o'clock, the streets were already deserted; not a soul was to be seen but the night-watchmen standing at their posts, ready to march to the fortress to join their chief at the signal of alarm. Of gay and noisy Buenos Ayres whose young men in former times waited impatiently for the night to give expansion to their spirits, avid of adventures and pleasures, there now remained not a single vestige. Every house was closed at nightfall, and the simple act of walking through the streets of Buenos Ayres, in this reign of terror, after eight o'clock at night, was of itself sufficient to prove that the person doing so had in his Federalism the assurance of his security. A terrible school in which for two years past the young men who remained in Buenos Ayres had been learning effeminate habits, taught by the absence of personal security, which made those who feared at every step, the dagger or the rope of the Mashorca, seek within the walls of their houses the only guarantee possible.

But did sleep, at least, come to the relief of the anxious and heavy hearts of the inhabitants of this unhappy city? Their desires were too intense and their feelings at this critical period too poignant to make it possible for them to find forgetfulness in sleep. And no sooner did the hoofs of the horses of the cavalcade of the officer of the day resound on the pavement of the streets than some shadow would be projected from a roof, or the shutter of some darkened room would be cautiously opened to give passage to an uneasy and searching glance.

"Our good city does not sleep, General," observed Daniel, who was riding at Mancilla's side; "have you not noticed that this is the case?"

"They are all waiting, my friend," answered General Mancilla, from whose lips a word rarely fell that was not either malicious, satirical, or ambiguous in its meaning.

"But are they all waiting for the same thing, General?"

"All."

"It is amazing what unanimity of opinion there is under our Federal Government!"

Mancilla turned round and glanced furtively at the jewel at his side, as he had called him, and then answered:

"Especially in one thing. Can you guess what that is?"

"Upon my honor I cannot."

"There is a wonderful unanimity in the desire which there is that this should end as soon as possible."

"This? And what is this, General?"

Mancilla glanced again at Daniel, for the question was a direct attack upon his confidence.

"The situation, I mean."

"Ah, the situation! But the political situation will never end for you, General Mancilla?"

"What do you mean?"

"You are not the man to lead a domestic life; it is a necessity with you to engage in public affairs, and whether in support of or in opposition to the Government, you will always play a prominent part in our country."

"Even if the Unitarians should come into power?"

"Even so. There are many of our Federals who will figure among them."

"Yes; and some in very eminent positions—on the gallows, for instance; but in any case we should always be on the side of the Restorer."

The equivocal meaning of the phrase did not escape Daniel's observation, but he continued with infantile naturalness:

"Yes, he deserves that we should all stand by him in this emergency."

"Do you not think that man's good fortune is wonderful?"

"That is because he represents the Federal cause."

"Which is the best of causes, is it not?" said Mancilla, looking fixedly at Daniel.

"So I learned in the sessions of the Constituent Assembly."

Mancilla bit his lip; he had been a Unitarian in the Assembly, but the expression on Daniel's countenance was so candid that the astute old man could not be sure whether the words were a sarcasm or not.

"A cause," continued Daniel, "that will never be ruined by the Unitarians. We must make no mistake—it is only the Federals who can destroy General Rosas."

"One would think you were fifty, Señor Bello."

"That is because I pay a great deal of attention to what I hear talked about."

"And what do you hear talked about?"

"The popularity which some of the Federals enjoy; you, for instance, General."

"I?"

"Yes, you. If it were not for the family ties which unite you to the Governor he would keep a close watch upon you, for he cannot be ignorant of the popularity that you enjoy, and especially of your ability and your valor. Although I have heard it said that, speaking on one occasion of this last, in 1835, he said you were good for nothing but twopenny riots."

Mancilla, pushing his horse close to Daniel's, said in an angry voice:

"That is just like what that brutal gaucho would say. But do you know why he said it?"

"Perhaps he said it in jest, General," answered Daniel, with the utmost composure.

"He said it because he fears me," replied Mancilla, pressing Daniel's arm and muttering the name of Rosas, coupled with an epithet not to be uttered in polite society.

This brusque declaration was in keeping with Mancilla's character, a mixture of courage and petulance, of daring and indiscretion. But the situation was so serious that he at once became conscious that he had gone too far in his confidences with Daniel; but it was now too late to retreat and thinking his best course would be to draw similar confidences, if possible, from his companion, he said to him with his natural astuteness:

"I know that if I were to call upon them, I should have all the young men on my side, for there is not one of you who likes the present order of things."

"Do you know, General, that I think so too," answered Daniel, as if the idea had now occurred to him for the first time in his life.

"And you would be the first to be on my side?"

"In a revolution?"

"In—in anything," said Mancilla, not venturing to pronounce that word.

"I think you would have many to join you."

"But would you be one of them?" asked Mancilla, persisting in his attempt to draw some confidential expression from this young man, who had just become the depositary of an enormous indiscretion of his.

"I? Well, you see, General, I could not be one of them, for a very simple reason."

"And what is that?"

"Because I have sworn never to join the young men of my age in anything, since most of them have become Unitarians, while I follow and profess the principles of the Federation."

"Bah! bah! bah!"

And Mancilla drew his horse away from Daniel's, trying to persuade himself that the latter was only a talkative boy, whose ideas were of no importance whatever, since a vain scruple like this could not find place in a superior mind.

"Besides, General," continued Daniel, as if he had observed nothing, "I have a horror of politics; my tastes lean more to literature and the ladies, as I told Agustinita this afternoon, when she asked me to accompany you tonight."

"So I believe," answered Mancilla drily.

"What would you have? I wish to be as true a son of Buenos Ayres as General Mancilla is."

"How so?"

"I mean that I wish to stand as high in the favor of the ladies as he does."

The tender passion had always been the weak point of General Mancilla, as his strong point had been an aptitude for political intrigues; and Daniel proceeded to humor it.

"But those days are over," said Mancilla, smiling.

"Not for history."

"Bah, history! And what do we gain by that?"

"Nor for the present time, if you choose."

"That is not true."

"It is true. There are a thousand Unitarians who hate General Mancilla because they envy him his wife."

"My wife is beautiful, is she not?" said Mancilla, almost coming to a halt and looking at his companion with a face beaming with gratified vanity.

"She is the queen of beauty; even the Unitarians themselves confess that; and I think if that has been your latest conquest it is worth all the rest put together."

"As for being the latest—"

"There, I wish to know nothing, General; I am very fond of Agustinita and I do not desire to hear about your infidelities to her."

"Ah, my friend, if you have as cajoling a way with the women as you have with the men you will have more adventures in the course of your life than ever I had."

"I don't understand you, General," answered Daniel, feigning the utmost surprise.

"Let us drop the subject; we are at Ravelo's quarters."

They had, in fact, arrived at the barracks, where a hundred aged negro soldiers, under the command of Colonel Ravelo, were asleep; and having made the prescribed inspection they proceeded to the quarters of the fourth battalion of patricians, commanded by Ximeno; and those of some other reserves.

But, strange to say, the champagne of the Federation did not now seem to effervesce in the bosoms of its enthusiastic sons; for the questions, the answers and the remarks which passed between the officer of the day and the chiefs whom he visited, were without spirit. And what happened there was happening everywhere and among all classes. A cause without faith, without conscience, without genuine enthusiasm, which trembled and grew faint at the first menace of its political adversaries; priests without religion who prostrated themselves before an idol that was already tottering to its fall upon its altar of skulls.

Daniel saw and noted all this and he said to himself at every step:

"With two hundred men at my back I would deliver all these people bound hand and foot to General Lavalle."

It was three in the morning before General Mancilla turned his horse's head in the direction of his house, in the Calle del Potosí.

Daniel accompanied him to the door. But he did not wish that the brother-in-law of Rosas should go to sleep uneasy on account of his confidences and he said to him on reaching the house:

"General, you have doubted me and I am sorry for it!"

"I, Señor Bello!"

"Yes; knowing that all our young men have allowed themselves to be led away by the madmen of Montevideo, you wished to sound me, saying things you did not mean; for I know well that the Restorer has no better friend than General Mancilla; but happily you have discovered nothing in me but Federal patriotism. Is not that true?" asked Daniel, assuming the most anxious expression in the world.

"Perfectly true," answered Mancilla, shaking hands with him and smiling at the poor simple boy, as he called him in his own mind at that moment.

"So that I may count upon your protection, General?"

"Always and at all times, Bello."

"Very well; good-bye until tomorrow."

"Until tomorrow; thanks for your company."

And Daniel turned his horse around, inwardly laughing and saying to himself:

"I would not have given a straw for my life so long as you believed I possessed your secret; now you have allowed me to redeem it and I have not returned you your pledge. Good-night, General Mancilla."

XXXII

Country, Love and Friendship

When Daniel reached his house he took his horse to the stable himself, as the faithful Fermin was not expecting him and the other servants knew nothing of their master's nocturnal excursion. He called one of them, however, and desired him to hold himself in readiness to receive his orders.

Then, lighting a candle, after visiting the bedroom in which Eduardo was asleep and which adjoined his own, Daniel entered his study and threw himself into a chair.

But suddenly, pushing back his disordered hair from his forehead, he rose and going to his desk seated himself before it, took several letters from a secret drawer, read them, one after another, made a note of the date of one of them, and then wrote the following letter, which he read over afterward with perfect composure:

> Señor Bouchet Martigny, etc., etc.
> Buenos Ayres, September 1, 1840.
> At four o'clock in the morning.

My dear Señor Martigny:

"I have received your letters of the 22nd and the 24th ult. and that of the latter date confirms me in the flattering belief that the righteous cause of my country is finding proselytes, not only among her sons, but also among men of heart, whatever the land of their birth; and the solicitations which, as you inform me, have been addressed by compatriots of yours to the French Government concerning the affairs of the Plata, and in favor of the Argentine cause, are so many titles to our gratitude to those noble exceptions among the peoples of Europe, who understand us so little and who love us even less.

"But in acquitting myself of my share of this debt of gratitude, I must say to you frankly that in the extremity at which matters have arrived, any intervention that might come from Europe, whether favorable or adverse to our cause, would come too late to influence the issue of events, for the question between the two political parties will soon be decided by force of arms.

"To my mind, the situation involves a plain and conclusive dilemma in this respect—either the city will be taken before a fortnight is over, and the power of Rosas will be forever destroyed, or the Liberating Army will retreat, and then all will be lost for years to come, and so utterly lost as to preclude all possibility of recovery, even with the aid of a foreign power.

"To give General Lavalle all the aid possible, is the only advisable course in the present situation; but to give it to him without loss of time; for otherwise, from the moral effect which a sudden invasion of the city rather than an attack on the redoubts of Santos Lugares would produce, there might result only the triumph of an army which does not number three thousand men of whom two-thirds are cavalry, which has to fight against a force numerically twice as strong as itself, and which cannot and ought not to count upon the slightest coöperation from the inhabitants of Buenos Ayres, until the din of its arms and its vivas for the country resound in the streets of the city itself.

"This apparent contradiction in a people the majority of whom execrate the chains that bind them and who ardently long for the rebirth of their country's liberty, the Unitarians, I am well aware, are resolved to take no account of; because they will not acknowledge that the people of Buenos Ayres are not in 1840 what they were in 1810. This is an error that does them honor; but it is, after all, an error, and since the events, now become a part of history, that have occurred in the northern part of the province, have destroyed half the hopes of the Unitarians, and argue strongly against those which they have founded on the city, I believe it to be undeniably expedient to count upon no other resources than those which the army has in itself.

"It is a material impossibility to establish today an association of ten men in Buenos Ayres; individualism is the cancer that is eating away the vitals of this people. This phenomenon is explicable, is even justifiable, I might say, but this is not the time for philosophical disquisitions, but to take facts as they are, good and bad together, and make them a basis of calculation for fixed operations. And it is upon the fact of non-revolution in Buenos Ayres, that the Liberating Army must calculate its operations.

"Without any other resources than his own ought General Lavalle to proceed against Rosas or not?

"Before answering this question, however, I should like to make General Lavalle, and all the world, understand that the power of Rosas is not in the marshes, the trenches, the cannons and the soldiers of Santos Lugares; that it is in the capital; that it is in the fortress. Buenos Ayres, I might say, is the head; the rest of the country only subordinate members. It is in Buenos Ayres that the reaction must set in, in the revolutionary current which is to flow thence throughout the whole republic. And in this case the problem to be solved is simply whether it is expedient or not to march upon the capital, flanking the camp of Rosas, and take possession of it, leaving him master of the plains.

"Were I in General Lavalle's position I would not hesitate to decide upon the former course; for I have the firm conviction that if the army retreats, both the cause and the army are lost; and at this juncture I should prefer to risk this immense loss on the only ground which offers a possibility of victory.

"In this city there can be no resistance; the Federals are depressed by the mere uncertainty of events; and half of them, at least, would willingly desert to General Lavalle, to seek in their treachery to Rosas a guarantee for the future.

"In the letter preceding this I gave you all particulars in regard to the barracks, troops of the line, etc., in the city; and if the present one will contribute to induce you to consider the plan I advise, I shall have attained my object, for I do not doubt but that on examination it will meet with your approval.

"Accept, Señor Martigny, the assurance of my profound consideration.

B.

Daniel sealed this letter with a special seal; and then, writing an address upon it for Mr. Douglas, put it into a secret drawer of his desk.

Then he wrote the following letter:

"Amalia: The apparition was no other than Mariño. I have succeeded in mystifying him completely. He does not know whether or not to believe that he followed me and discovered your abode. But that very doubt will irritate him all the more and he will endeavor to set it at rest.

"From this day forth my footsteps will be dogged more persistently than ever.

"There is no help for it; in the difficulties that surround us the only course is boldness, which, in difficult situations, is prudence.

"You must return to Barracas, and that soon.

"Make all your arrangements and hold yourself in readiness to do so at any moment.

"Events are hastening to a crisis, and everything must be swift, as will be the collision between our good and our evil fortune.

"God guard the right!" This letter finished, the young man wrote, finally, to his Florencia, as follows:

"Soul of my soul: I may still count myself fortunate, very fortunate, since, depressed and exhausted as I am, by a barren though terrible struggle, of which you as yet know nothing, I have your heart as a refuge for my spirit, your name, to draw me nearer to God and the angels, as I write.

"Today I have suffered a great deal, and my only consolation is the hope I have that you will lend me your aid to attain my desire—you must persuade your dear mother to make the journey to Montevideo; but soon—tomorrow, if possible. And if it be necessary for your tranquillity that you should be my wife before your departure tomorrow, the church will unite us, as God has already united our hearts, forever.

"In the sky above us, in the air we breathe, there is today misfortune and perhaps—Who can tell!—All is today ominous. I do not desire your hand, that is to say, my happiness, my pride, my paradise, in these moments, but I will claim it if it be necessary to your departure.

"Ask me nothing. All I can tell you is that I would like to lift you above the stars that the air of these times might not blow upon your brow. Do not ask me to follow you. I cannot—Fixed as doom, my fate is already decided. I am bound to Buenos Ayres, and—But we shall soon see each other—within a week, within a fortnight, at farthest. It is a century, is it not? No matter; in the clouds, in the air, in the light, you will speak to me, Florencia, and I will treasure your words in the shrine which holds your image in my soul.

"Will you please me in this?

"Madame Dupasquier will refuse you nothing.

"And I have never asked anything from you, that was not for your happiness and mine.

Daniel

The young man closed this last letter, placed it in his breast and waited for the morning to address it with the others.

XXXIII

Don Cándido Rodriguez Appears
as he Always Appears

At ten o'clock, on the morning of the 3rd of September, Don Cándido Rodriguez, with his inseparable bamboo cane, was walking down the Calle de la Victoria with a surprisingly firm gait, while the saffron hue of his countenance and the vagueness of his gaze might make one believe for a moment that he wore a false face, seeing portrayed in his countenance a feeling exactly the reverse of the feeling expressed in his walk.

Arrived at his destination, which was the house in which our readers first made his acquaintance and which, as may be remembered, was Daniel's house, he stopped and knocked for admittance.

A few moments later our luckless secretary was entering the parlor of his former pupil, whom he found seated in a comfortable rocking-chair, tranquilly reading the *Gaceta Mercantil*.

"Daniel!"

"Señor?"

"Daniel! Daniel!"

"Señor! Señor!"

"We are on the brink of destruction."

"I know it."

"You know it and you will not save us."

"That is what I am trying to do."

"No, Daniel, no; there will not be time."

"So much the better."

"What do you mean?" asked Don Cándido, opening wide his eyes and seating himself on a sofa near Daniel.

"I say, señor, that in difficult situations the best thing to do is to end them quickly."

"But to end them well, you mean?"

"Or end them ill."

"Ill?"

"Yes; for, well or ill, it is always better than to live one day anticipating good and the next day evil fortune."

"And the evil would be—"

"That they should cut off our heads, for instance."

"Let them cut off your head, and that of every other conspirator, if they like, but not mine. I am a peaceable, innocent, quiet man, incapable of doing wrong designedly, with premeditation, with—"

"Sit down, my dear master," said Daniel, cutting short the discourse of the schoolmaster who, as he spoke, had been gradually rising from his seat on the sofa and was now standing erect.

"What have I done or what have I ever thought of doing that I should find myself now, as I do, like a frail bark tossed about on the waves of a tempestuous sea?"

"What have you done?"

"Yes, what have I done?"

"Oh! what you have done is a trifle; a mere nothing."

"I have done nothing, Señor Don Daniel; and it is time now that our partnership should cease, should come to an end, should be dissolved forever. I am an ardent defender of the most Illustrious Restorer in the world. I love every member of the respectable family of his Excellency, as I love and am the defender of the other governor, Dr. Don Felipe, of his ancestors and of all his children. I have desired—"

"You have desired to emigrate, Señor Don Cándido."

"I?"

"You; and that is a crime of lèse Federation which is paid for with the head."

"The proofs."

"Señor Don Cándido, you are determined that someone shall hang you."

"I?"

"And I am only waiting for you to tell me whether you wish to be hanged by the hand of Rosas or by the hand of Lavalle. If the former, I will oblige you on the instant, by paying a visit to Colonel Salomon. If the latter, I will wait for three or four days until Lavalle enters the city, and at the first opportunity I will speak to him of Don Felipe's secretary."

"I am a drowning man, then?"

"No, señor, a hanging man, if you will persist in talking the nonsense you have been talking."

"But Daniel, my son, do you not see my face?"

"Yes, señor."

"And what do you read in it?"

"Fear."

"No, not fear; distrust, the effect of the terrific sensations by which I have been just overcome."

"And what is the matter?"

"On my way here from the Governor's I met twice those men who look like—who look like—"

"What?"

"Who look like devils dressed as men."

"Or men dressed as devils, is it not so?"

"What countenances, Daniel; what countenances! And above all, those knives they carry! Do you believe that one of those men would be capable of killing me, Daniel?"

"No. I do not think so. What have you ever done to them?"

"Nothing, nothing. But, fancy, if they should mistake me for someone else, and—"

"Bah, let us drop the subject, my dear friend. You told me that you left Arana's house to come here, did you not?"

"Yes, yes, Daniel."

"Consequently, you had some object in coming here?"

"Yes."

"And what was it, my friend?"

"I don't know; I don't wish to mention it now. I want no more politics, nor confidences."

"Ah, then it is a political secret you have come to confide to me?"

"I have not said so."

"And I wager that you have some important document in your coat pocket."

"I have nothing."

"And I wager that if some Federal brother should take it into his head to search you when you leave this house, to see if you carry arms, and should find that document on your person, that he would despatch you in the twinkling of an eye."

"Daniel!"

"Señor, will you give me the documents you have brought me or not?"

"On one condition."

"What is it?"

"That you will not require from me that I shall continue longer to be false to my duties."

"That would be so much the worse for you; for before four days are over Lavalle will be in Buenos Ayres."

"Well, and would you not in that case bear witness to the immense services I have rendered to liberty?"

"Not if you stop halfway on the road."

"And do you think that Lavalle will enter the city?"

"That is what he has come for."

"Well, now, between ourselves, I think so too; and it is for that reason that I have come to see you. There has been an encounter."

"Where?" asked Daniel, quickly, a flush mounting to his face, in which the various emotions that had shaken his soul during the last few days had made notable ravages.

"Read this."

Daniel, unfolding the paper which Don Cándido had given him read as follows:

San Pedro, September 1.

"Two days ago Mascarilla, with a thousand men, assaulted the town, which displayed extraordinary valor, repulsing him vigorously. He had with him a piece of ordnance, one hundred and fifty foot soldiers and about six hundred horsemen. He made the attack from two sides simultaneously. They penetrated at one time as far as the plaza, but they were repulsed by a hot fire from us. The loss exceeds one hundred men.

"I enclose copies of the communication which I received from the general.

"Tomorrow I will write to you in detail.

JUAN CAMELINO

"Señor D."

"Let me see the document to which he refers," said Daniel, after a silence of more than ten minutes, during which he kept his eyes fixed on the paper he held in his hand, while his expressive countenance was clouded by sorrow and dejection.

"Here it is," said Don Cándido. "They are both documents of importance, which were found in a boat taken last night. I copied them hastily to bring them to you."

Daniel took the paper, without hearing Don Cándido's words and read what follows:

Liberating Army, General's Quarters,
on the march.
"August 29, 1840.
Señor Don Juan Camelino,
Military Commandant of San Pedro.

The General-in-Chief has the satisfaction of informing you, in order that you may communicate the news to the troops under your command, that through communications which have been intercepted from Don Felix Aldao to the tyrant Rosas, it has become known that the feeling of the towns of the interior is most favorable to the cause of liberty. The Provinces of Córdoba, San Luis and San Juan have refused to give Aldao the aid which he solicited. The Province of Rioja has risen en masse against the tyranny of Rosas and has armed a force of cavalry and eight hundred infantry. General La-Madrid, who entered the territory of Córdoba at the head of an army of the brave friends of liberty, will soon come to support the operations of the Liberating Army.

"The Vega division routed completely at Navarro the militia which Chirino had assembled. The army counts upon a squadron of this militia.

"The General-in-Chief has learned that the militia of Magdalena have revolted, abandoning their leaders on receiving from them the order to join the army of Rosas. The cause of liberty is making rapid progress, and the General-in-Chief hopes that victory will soon crown the efforts of the soldiers of the country, among whom the brave defenders of San Pedro will occupy a distinguished place.

"You will inform the troops under your command of the news which I communicate to you, with the assurance that the Liberating Army does not imitate the systematic lying by which the tyrant endeavors to conceal his critical situation.

"You will send a copy of this communication to the Justice of the Peace of Baradero.

"God guard you.

JUAN LAVALLE

"What do you think of it?" asked Don Cándido when Daniel had finished reading the document.

The young man did not answer.

"They are coming, Daniel; they are coming."

"No, señor, they are going," responded the young man; and crushing the paper between his hands he rose and began to pace the floor, impatience and disgust stamped upon his countenance.

"Have you lost your senses, Daniel?"

"It is others who have lost their senses, not I."

"But if they have defeated Lopez, my dear and esteemed Daniel!"

"That is of no consequence."

"If they are already in Lujan!"

"That is of no consequence."

"Do you not see by what ardent, fiery, tremendous enthusiasm they are animated?"

"That is of no consequence."

"Are you in your senses, Daniel?"

"Yes, señor; those who are not in their senses are those who are thinking about the provinces, showing thereby that they do not confide in their own resources, nor see the opportunity that presents itself to them, two steps away. Strange fatality, that which pursues this party and with it our country!" exclaimed the young man, who continued pacing the floor with agitated steps, while Don Cándido looked at him in amazement.

"Then we Federals were right in saying—"

"That the Unitarians are not worth a rush; you are right, Señor Don Cándido!"

At this moment a loud double knock was heard at the street door.

XXXIV

Pylades Angry

Don Cándido trembled.

Daniel's countenance changed as suddenly and as completely as if another face had been substituted for his own; before, visibly altered and disturbed, it was now tranquil and almost smiling.

A servant appeared to announce a lady.

Daniel gave orders to show her in.

"Shall I retire, my son?" asked Don Cándido.

"There is no need, señor."

"It is true that I do not wish to do so; I would prefer to wait until you are going out and go in your company."

Daniel smiled. And at this moment a woman whose skirts rustled as if they were made of tissue paper, with a Federal topknot half a yard long, and stiff, brown, glossy curls falling down either side of a round, plump, swarthy face, appeared at the parlor door.

"Come in, Misía Marcelina," said Daniel, rising; "you have something to say to me; let us go into my study;" and he led the way into his study, followed by Doña Marcelina.

"Douglas has arrived," said the latter, after closing the study door behind her.

"When did he arrive?"

"This morning."

"And he left?"

"The day before yesterday. Here is the letter."

Daniel, seating himself at his study table, read the letter handed to him by Doña Marcelina—one of his private couriers, as the reader already knows—and then remained sunk in thought for more than ten minutes; a period employed by Doña Marcelina in examining the titles of the books on the shelves, smiling and nodding, as if she were saluting old friends.

"Could you find Douglas before three in the afternoon?"

"Yes."

"With certainty?"

"At this moment the intrepid mariner is sleeping."

"Well, then, I wish you to go to his house."

"I will go on the instant."

"And tell him that I wish to see him before night."

"Here?"

"Yes, here."

"I will do so."

"Let us fix an hour—I will expect him between five and six in the afternoon."

"Very good."

"Lose no time, Doña Marcelina."

"I will fly on the wings of fate."

"No, walk; nothing more; it is not well to make one's self conspicuous in these times, by going either very fast or very slow."

"I will follow the flight of your thoughts."

"Good-bye, then, Doña Marcelina."

"The gods be with you, señor."

"Ah! and how is Gaëte?"

"Destiny has spared him."

"Is he up?"

"He still remains in bed."

"So much the better for my friend Don Cándido. Goodbye, then, Doña Marcelina."

And while the latter left the study by the door leading to the parlor, Daniel left it by another door leading to his bedroom, carrying in his hand the letter which Doña Marcelina had brought him from Douglas and which he gave to Dr. Alcorta, who was there with Eduardo, saying:

"I have just received this by way of Montevideo."

Dr. Alcorta took the letter and read:

Paris, July 11, 1840

"Vice-Admiral Mackau has been named to command the expedition of the Rio de la Plata, in place of Vice-Admiral Baudin. He will sail immediately. Señor Mackau, who belongs to a distinguished French family, has the honor of having terminated satisfactorily the questions which France had with Santo Domingo and Cartagena.

"He is noted for his bravery, and those who are familiar with the naval history of France will remember his glorious fight with the *Critie,* an English man-of-war. In the recent unfortunate war between France and England Señor Mackau, at that time barely seventeen years of age, was serving on a French brigantine in the capacity of midshipman. A pestilence had decimated the crew of the French vessel and the only officer who survived its ravages was Midshipman Mackau. Filled with noble pride at finding himself in command of a French warship he resolved to justify the selection which fate had made by some daring feat of arms. Shortly afterward he fell in with an English man-of-war—it was the *Critie*. After a desperate conflict Mackau took the enemy's vessel, which was commanded by a veteran naval lieutenant. When this honest sailor entered the presence of his conqueror, seeing that the latter was a midshipman of seventeen, in command of a crew decimated by pestilence, his grief was so intense that it killed him.

Cordially yours, etc.

"Everything combines to hurry events to an end, my friends," said Dr. Alcorta, after reading the letter.

"Yes, to an end, but what will that end be?"

"Have you not heard that an expedition is coming, Daniel?"

"Which will arrive too late, and which meantime inspires the letters that are written to General Lavalle from Montevideo not to expose his army but to wait for the expedition, which will either not come at all, or, if it comes, will make Rosas compromise with the French before the troops arrive at Rio Janeiro."

"But that would be infamous on the part of France!" responded Eduardo.

"Political actions are not measured by the same standard as personal morality, Eduardo."

"And is it certain that such counsels are given to General Lavalle?" asked Dr. Alcorta.

"Yes, señor; they are given by the greater number of the Argentine commissioners, who will see no hope except from a large army."

"Ah! if I were Lavalle!" exclaimed Eduardo.

"If you were Lavalle you would be insane by this time. The General is thwarted by everyone and everything. The refusal of Commandant Penau to land the army in El Baradero, instead of taking it to San Pedro, has caused the General to lose not only time but the horses that were waiting for him at the former point. Rivera's hostility has hampered all his movements for a year past. The illusions of the Unitarian wiseacres make him conceive a world of flattering hopes, of brilliant anticipations in regard to the ready support which he will find in the provinces, and the General comes and sees the actual state of things, and finds no such support. A hundred contradictory letters come every day from Montevideo to him, to his chiefs, to his officers, advising him to advance and not to advance, to wait and not to wait. There are not ten men who are of the same opinion. And the General doubts and hesitates; he fears to march, contrary to the advice of men worthy of respect from the names they bear; and he marches slowly, dissipating his forces, pursuing today one insignificant leader, tomorrow another; and it is now the 3rd of September, and he is less than a league distant from Lujan, and meantime Rosas is recovering himself, morally; his men are recovering from their first fright; and he will approach the city to take a look at it, perhaps, and go away again; or, perhaps, that there may be a great deal of bloodshed which a fortnight ago, a week ago, might have been avoided," said Daniel, in melancholy and dejected accents which visibly impressed his friends.

"That is all true, and the city will feel the full weight of the anger of Rosas, as it has already begun to feel it," responded Dr. Alcorta.

"Yes, the city, señor, the city, the accomplice, up to a certain point, of the barbarous tyranny that oppresses it, will pay with its blood, with its liberty and with its reputation for its fear of the armed enemies of the tyrant and for the egotism of its citizens, indifferent alike to their country's fate and to their own. Much blood will flow if Lavalle retreats, and all thought of the fall of Rosas must be abandoned for years to come."

"But we are reasoning on conjectures," responded Eduardo. "Up to this, the army continues to advance. Tomorrow, or the day after, at farthest, we shall have some certain knowledge. Meantime, Dr. Alcorta thinks with you and me that our private plan is excellent. Is not that true?"

"Yes, at least I think it is very prudent," answered Dr. Alcorta.

"There was another project which you were to communicate to him."

"I know it already. Regarding that I have some doubts."

"No, señor; have no doubts; it is true that we are few; I have been able to assemble only fifteen men, but we shall be fifteen determined men. The roof we are to occupy, at the same time that it will serve as a place of meeting, will also be an admirable position from which to keep the Calle del Colegio free from obstructions, if the General invades the city on the side of Barracas, as I have urged him to do and leads his troops up the Barranca de Marcó, which is the most important point. The place which I have chosen is the best in all that long, straight street; and with twenty-five men more, whom the General should leave me, I would answer for the retreat, should the necessity for a retreat arrive."

"Arms?"

"I have forty-six muskets and three thousand cartridges which I purchased in Montevideo, and which are now safe in Buenos Ayres."

"The signal?"

"That which they shall communicate to me from the army, if they decide upon the attack."

"The communications are safe?"

"Perfectly safe?"

"Well, then, I approve with all the more reason of the second plan, as it will be necessary that you should be disembarrassed of domestic affairs to be ready for whatever may occur. The only thing I fear is the moment of embarkation."

"That is what is least to be feared, Doctor; there will be no risk. I have just sent for one of my agents, in order to send a letter by him to the commander of one of the blockading vessels informing him of our purpose, and asking him for an armed boat, for the only danger would be in meeting one of the government boats that patrol the coast."

"Well thought of."

"I will tell the commander also to name himself the night, and the hour, and the signal which he will give me from on board."

"The embarkation will be at San Isidro?"

"Yes, señor. Eduardo will have already given you all the particulars concerning it."

"He has done so."

"And do you think that Madame Dupasquier will be able to bear the journey?"

"What I think is that she will not be able to bear a fortnight more of Buenos Ayres. Hers is one of those maladies that reside in no one of the organs but are diffused through the springs of life itself which they rapidly exhaust and dry up. The moral malady of that lady is so deep-seated that it has already affected the heart and lungs, and her life is wasting away. But the air of freedom will restore her to health with the same rapidity with which the want of it is killing her in Buenos Ayres."

"And is she entirely willing to go?" asked Eduardo.

"Last night she agreed to everything," answered Daniel.

"And today she eagerly desires to go," added Dr. Alcorta; "and she is willing that Daniel shall remain. She loves you already, my friend, as if you were her son."

"I will be so, señor; and if I do not become so tomorrow, today, it is because she refuses to consent. She is superstitious, like every woman of heart, and she would fear for a marriage contracted in these most sorrowful moments."

"Yes, yes, it is better as it is. Who knows what fate may await us! Let the women at least escape," said Dr. Alcorta.

"With the exception of my cousin, señor. There is no one who can persuade her to do so."

"Not even Belgrano?"

"No one, señor," answered the latter, into whose heart Dr. Alcorta's question had sunk deeply.

"It is two o'clock, my friends. Are you going to San Isidro today?"

"Yes, señor, this evening; and we will be back before daybreak."

"Be cautious, be very cautious, for Heaven's sake!"

"This is almost our last journey there, señor," said Eduardo. "As soon as Madame Dupasquier sails for Montevideo the house at The Olives will be left vacant."

"Until tomorrow, then."

"Until tomorrow, señor."

"Until tomorrow, my dear friend."

And the two young men embraced their former professor of philosophy, whom Daniel accompanied to the street door.

XXXV

The Smuggler of Men

D r. Alcorta had hardly left the room when a double knock was heard at the door of Daniel's study, which, as the reader knows, adjoined the parlor.

"Wait here," said Daniel to Eduardo. And he entered the study, a little surprised to hear a knock at the door of a room which no one entered without his express orders.

"Ah, it is you, my dear master?" said the young man, finding himself face to face with Don Cándido.

"It is I, Daniel, I. Forgive me, but, the fact is, that seeing that you delayed so long I began to fear that you might have left the house by some secret door, some private passage which was unknown to me; and, as for some time past I shun solitude— For you must know, my esteemed Daniel, that solitude affects the imagination, a faculty, which according to what philosophers say, works both for good and for evil; for which reason I prefer the faculty of memory which, according to the opinion of Quintillian—"

"Eduardo!"

"What is the matter?" asked the latter, entering.

"How! Belgrano here?"

"Yes, señor, and I have called him in to listen to your disquisition."

"So that this house is a nest of dangers for me?"

"How is that, my worthy master?" asked Eduardo, sitting down beside him.

"What does this mean, Daniel? I desire a frank, conclusive and clear explanation," continued Don Cándido, addressing Daniel, and drawing away his chair from Eduardo's. "I wish to learn one thing that shall fix, determine and establish my position; I wish to know what sort of house this is?"

"What sort of house this is?"

"Yes."

"Why, a house like any other house, my dear master."

"That is no answer. This house is not like any other house. For here Unitarians conspire and Federals conspire."

"How is that, señor?"

A quarter of an hour ago you received in your house a woman whom I have urgent reasons for believing to be a spy of the Federals; and now I behold in your private, your innermost apartments this mysterious young man who has fled from his home and who goes from one house to another with all the appearance of a masked and secret conspirator."

"Have you finished, my dear master?"

"No, I will not finish without telling you once, twice, and three times that in the exalted and delicate official position which I occupy, I cannot continue to maintain relations with a house for which I can find no perfect grammatical definition. And since I do not know what sort of house this is I wish to abstain from all association and connection with it."

"But the thing is, Señor Don Cándido," responded Daniel, "that you have called my friend a conspirator, and that does not seem to me very courteous among colleagues."

"Colleagues! I was this gentleman's teacher when he was an innocent and tender child. But since that time—"

"Since that time you have had him concealed in your house, my dear master."

"That was an act in which my will had no part."

"No matter."

"But I have never been his colleague in anything," said Don Cándido.

"But you are so now, Señor Don Cándido," replied Daniel. "Are you not the secretary of Señor Arana?"

"I am."

"Very well; this gentleman is the secretary of General Lavalle."

"Secretary of General Lavalle!" exclaimed Don Cándido, rising slowly to his feet and staring at Eduardo with eyes that seemed starting from their sockets.

"Just so," continued Daniel; "and as you are the secretary of Arana and this gentleman is the secretary of Lavalle, it follows that you are colleagues."

"Secretary of Lavalle! And conversing with me!"

"And your guest a few days ago."

"And my guest!—"

"And very grateful to you, besides, for your hospitality," added Eduardo. "So much so that the first visit I make, which will be within two or three days, will be to you, my dear colleague."

"You in my house? No, señor, I will not, I cannot be at home to you."

"Ah, that is another matter. I had intended to go visit my old master, in company with some of his former pupils who are coming here in the Liberating Army and who might serve him as a guarantee in the just reprisals which we intend to take on all the supporters of Rosas and Arana. But if you object, why, everyone is free to let himself be hanged if he chooses."

"But, Señor Secretary," responded Don Cándido, who in truth found himself in a state of pitiable perplexity, "I do not say this in case the brave and intrepid defenders of his Excellency General Lavalle should come here; but—Daniel—speak for me, my son—my head is like an oven."

"There is nothing to say, señor," responded the other; "your colleague has understood you perfectly. We all understand one another, or rather we shall understand one another."

"Except me, my dear Daniel, who will go down to my grave without understanding, without comprehending, without knowing either what I have done or what I have been, in these calamities and abominable—"

A double knock at the street door arrested the words on Don Cándido's lips, and while the two secretaries remained in the study Daniel went into the parlor and himself opened the door leading into the courtyard, to see who his visitor was, unable yet to master in his mind or in his countenance the impression produced by Don Cándido's news.

"Ah! it is you, Mr. Douglas!" said the young man to an individual who was already in the courtyard.

"Yes, señor," answered the latter. "Doña Marcelina has just spoken to me—"

"And she told you that I wished to see you?"

"Yes, señor."

"It is true. Come in, Douglas. You left Montevideo the day before yesterday?"

"Yes, señor, the night before last."

"Great excitement there, eh?"

"There everybody is preparing to come here, and here everybody wants to get away," answered the Scotchman, with a shrug.

"So that you are making money?"

"Not much. Last month I made seven trips and I took over sixty-two persons, at ten ounces each."

"Ah, that is not bad."

"Bah! My head is worth more, Señor Don Daniel."

"Yes, of course. But it would be easier to catch Satan himself than to catch you."

The Scotchman laughed.

"Well, señor," he said, "do you know that I often wish that they might catch me to see if I should be frightened. For all this is a diversion for me. In Spain I smuggled tobacco; here I smuggle men."

And the Scotchman laughed like a boy.

"But they don't pay much," he continued. "You gave me more for the boxes I brought from Montevideo than others have given me for saving their lives."

"Well, Mr. Douglas," said Daniel, "I need your services again."

"At your orders, Señor Don Daniel—my boat, four men who know how to shoot and to row, and I, who am worth all four together!"

"Thanks."

"If there is anyone to be taken over I have discovered another spot, so safe that not even the devil himself would be able to find anyone concealed there."

"No; there is no one to be taken over. But first, when do you intend to return to Montevideo?"

"The day after tomorrow, if I complete the number."

"Well, don't go until you hear from me."

"Very good."

"Tonight you will take a letter for me to the blockading squadron."

"Very well."

"You will bring me the answer by ten tomorrow morning."

"And before that, if you wish."

"Tomorrow at dusk you will be in your house to receive two small trunks which you will put in the cellar in which the two boxes of arms are. Those trunks will contain jewels and articles of ladies' apparel, and you yourself will take them on board the vessel which I shall designate to you when you have brought me the answer to my letter."

"Everything shall be done as you wish."

"Do you know the coast at Los Olivos?"

"As well as I know this," answered the smuggler, opening his large hand and showing the palm to Daniel.

"Could a boat put in there easily?"

"That would depend upon the state of the river. But there is a little creek called El Sauce, where a boat could put in, even when the water is low, and lie hidden among the rocks, without any risk whatever. But that is a mile beyond Los Olivos."

"And at Los Olivos?"

"If the river is high. But there is one danger there."

"And what is that?"

"That the two government boats patrol the coast after ten at night."

"Both together?"

"No. Generally they go separately."

"What crews have they?"

"One has eight, the other ten men; and they are swift boats."

"Very good, Mr. Douglas. It was important that I should know all this. Let us recapitulate:

"You are not to sail until you hear from me.

"You are to go to the squadron tonight, and to bring me back an answer to the letter which I will give you presently, between eight and ten o'clock tomorrow morning.

"You will receive two trunks tomorrow evening, which you are yourself to take on board one of the vessels of the squadron, when I send you word to do so.

"The price, whatever you name."

"That is the best of all," answered the Scotchman, rubbing his hands together, "that is the best of all. That is the way a man should speak. Now all I want is the letter."

"You shall have it at once," returned Daniel, rising and going into his study; while the smuggler of tobacco in Spain and of men in Buenos Ayres remained calculating the price he should set upon his services.

And he was not the only smuggler of men. There were many who carried on this business between 1838 and 1842 in Buenos Ayres. And although it is very possible that they may have been actuated chiefly by the reward which their daring brought them, it is none the less true that hundreds of good and patriotic citizens owed to them their lives, who, without the assistance of this novel species of smuggler, would have fallen by the bullet or the dagger of Rosas.

The most distinguished of the refugees from Buenos Ayres escaped in contrabandist boats; and almost all the young men who left the country left it in the same way as did Paz, Agrelo, Belgrano, and others, that is to say, under the protection of men like Mr. Douglas. And one fact, which goes far to explain this circumstance, must be borne in mind, and that is, that when denunciations were so lavishly rewarded, and when not a day passed in which the police of Rosas did not receive such denunciations from natives of the country, among all the foreigners—Italians, Englishmen and North Americans—who had in their power the secrets and the persons of the refugees, and knowing, as they did, the high rank of many of them which would have ensured them a large reward from Rosas, there was not a single one who betrayed the secret or the confidence reposed in him.

XXXVI

The Chief of the Night-watchmen

Two days after that on which the events recorded in our last chapter took place, that is to say, on the 5th of September, all was confusion and anarchy in Buenos Ayres, in its ideas, its fears and its hopes. Silence and reserve prevailed everywhere among the enemies of the dictatorship; while the Federals were in a state of nervous excitement that kept them in continual movement—for since eleven in the morning it had been known that the Liberating Army was within a league of La Capilla de Merlo, and consequently, that on the following day it might be before Santos Lugares, or in the city itself.

The whole of the block on which the house of Rosas was situated was obstructed by the horses of the Federals, their tails adorned with red ribbons, their heads with feathers which waved in the breeze.

The courtyard, the inner yards, the office, the whole house, with the exception of the dictator's rooms, were like a veritable ant hill.

The whole Federal world kept passing in and out of the house all day. What for? Anything. There the triumph or the defeat of Lavalle would be known sooner than anywhere else.

There was, however, one class of persons who entered the house of Rosas and sought the presence of Manuela with an avowed and express object; these were the negresses.

One of the social phenomena most worthy of study in these times of terror was that presented by the African race—African in its origin, but notably modified by the language, the climate, and the habits of America. Africans in color; populace of Buenos Ayres in everything else.

At the very beginning of our revolution the great law decreeing the freedom of all born after its enactment was passed in protection of that unfortunate portion of humanity that had been brought to the vice-royalty of Buenos Ayres, also, by the cupidity and the cruelty of the European.

Buenos Ayres was the first country on the continent of Columbus which covered with the ægis of liberty the brow of the African; for where the waters of baptism had been she did not wish to see stamped the degradation of the human species. And liberty which thus regenerated and which struck from his wrists the fetters of the slave had in the reign of terror no more bitter nor more open enemy than this very African race.

That the negroes should be the partisans of Rosas was not strange; it was even natural that they should endure all manner of privations and make all manner of sacrifices for his sake; since he, more than anyone else, flattered their instincts and encouraged in them sentiments of vanity hitherto unknown to this class, which occupied from its condition and from its very nature the lowest round on the social ladder.

To promises and flatteries Rosas added acts; and the members of his family, the chief men of his party, his daughter herself, mingled as fellow-Federals, and even danced with the negroes.

It is not to be wondered at, then, that this part of the populace of Buenos Ayres should manifest enthusiasm, fanaticism, even, for the government which thus favored it.

But what is to be wondered at, what is matter for serious reflection, and what ought, later, to engage the attention of the regenerators of this unhappy land, are the perverse instincts which revealed themselves in this class with extraordinary rapidity and frankness.

The negroes, and especially the women of that race, were the principal organs of information, the chief spies of Rosas.

The sentiment of gratitude seemed to have withered in their hearts, without taking root in them.

To the houses in which their children were supported, where they themselves had received their wages and the lavish gifts of a class who err, it may be said, on the side of generosity, indulgence, and familiarity toward their domestics, they brought calumny, misfortune and death.

An insignificant letter, a gown or a ribbon with a thread of blue in it was a weapon for future use; and a cross look, a reprimand of the master or mistress of the house, or of one of their children was cause sufficient to use that weapon. The police, Doña María Josefa, any justice of the peace, or agent or leader of the Mashorca could receive a denunciation in which communications with Lavalle or something of the kind, figured, that meant ruin and mourning to a whole family; for to be classified as a Unitarian in Buenos Ayres was to be placed beyond the pale of the law, to be exposed to every indignity, every outrage, every crime.

Since the departure for Santos Lugares of the Dictator and with him of the negro troops who had occupied the fortress, the negresses too had begun to go to the camp on their own account, leaving the families with whom they had been at service to depend altogether upon their own resources.

But before leaving the city they presented themselves in bands at Manuela's or Doña María Josefa Ezcurra's, announcing that they too were going to fight for the Restorer of the Laws. And on the day of which we speak a large number of them crowded the courtyards and halls of the house of Rosas, noisily taking leave of Manuela and of everyone present.

It was a day of jubilee in this house, so famous in the annals of tyranny.

Doña María Josefa had arrived at eleven in the morning, and now at eight in the evening she was still there, waiting for some messenger from Santos Lugares bringing word whether Lavalle had passed Merlo and was advancing on the city or whether the Federal army had gone to meet him and had utterly annihilated him by the irresistible power of its arms and by the brilliancy of its genius.

Suddenly the distant report of a cannon thrilled every heart.

Manuela changed countenance. It was not fear for the political cause, it was fear for her father's life that oppressed her heart with a weight of painful emotions.

For a long time all listened with every faculty concentrated in the sense of hearing, but in vain.

Manuela sought with her gaze someone from whom she might learn the truth. But she knew so well those who surrounded her that she did not dare to question any of them.

Suddenly a movement which had begun in the courtyard reached the parlor, and all eyes were turned toward the door where through the dense clouds of tobacco smoke that filled the room, appeared the face of the Chief of Police, while his voice was heard saying, in answer to the questions of those around him:

"It is nothing, it is nothing; it is only the cannon fired at eight o'clock by the French."

Manuela relieved with a sigh her oppressed heart and impatiently asked Victorica, who had approached to salute her:

"Has no one come?"

"No one, señorita."

"For pity's sake! and since eleven o'clock I have not heard a word!"

"But it is probable that within an hour we shall know everything."

"Within an hour?"

"Yes."

"And why within an hour, Victorica?"

"Because at six I sent a police officer with the despatch of the day to the Governor."

"Very well; thank you."

"He will be here at nine, at the latest."

"Heaven grant it! And do you think they are now very near Santos Lugares?"

"It is not likely. Last night Lavalle encamped at Bravo's farm. At half-past ten this morning they were within three leagues of Merlo; and at this hour they will be at the most a league from that place; that is to say, two leagues distant from our camp."

"And tonight?"

"What do you mean?"

"How if they do not march tonight?" responded Manuela, hanging on Victorica's words.

"Oh! they will not march tonight," answered the latter; "nor perhaps tomorrow either; Lavalle has only a small force, señorita, and he will have to prepare it very well."

"And how large is Lavalle's force? Tell me the truth, I entreat you," continued Manuela, who spoke to the Chief of Police almost in a whisper.

"The truth?"

"Yes, yes; the truth."

"The thing is that the truth is not to be had for the asking in that way, señora; in these times it is very difficult to discover it. But, according to what appears to be the most reliable information, Lavalle has three thousand men."

"Three thousand men! and they told me he had hardly a thousand!" exclaimed the young girl.

"Did I not tell you that you could not discover the truth?"

"Oh, it is terrible!"

"They deceive you in a great many things."

"I know it. In everything; and everyone deceives me."

"Everyone?"

"Except you, Victorica."

"And why should I deceive you now?" responded the Chief of Police with a brusque shrug that seemed to say: We are staking our all; the decisive moment has come, and there is no one to deceive now, unless it be ourselves.

"And papa, what force has he? The truth also."

"Oh, that is easy to answer! The Governor has in Santos Lugares from seven to eight thousand men."

"And here?"

"Here?"

"Yes, here in the city."

"Everyone and no one."

"What do you mean?"

"That according to the news that reaches us from the camp tomorrow or the day after, we shall either have a world of soldiers or we shall find ourselves without one."

"Ah! yes, yes; I know it," responded Manuela quickly, as she caught the meaning of what had at first seemed a paradox of Victorica's. She knew better than anyone how little faith was to be placed in the words of the vile beings who surrounded her, who were brave only when they held the dagger at the throat of the defenseless victim.

"And you will bring me the news tonight," she continued, "as soon as you have received it, if papa does not write to me?"

"I cannot promise, señorita, for I am going now to the Boca, and I have left orders for the commissary to follow me there."

"To the Boca! And are you not needed more in the city?"

"I think, señorita, that I am needed nowhere," answered Victorica, with an expression on his countenance that would have resembled a smile, and that was doubtless intended for one, if those stern and rigid muscles that lent themselves only to the expression of violent and profound passions had allowed it.

"What do you mean by that, Señor Don Bernardo," asked Manuela with some seriousness, for the young girl's character had naturally begun to be affected by the regal authority exercised by her father, and she was displeased at seeing symptoms of discontent in one of his servants.

"I mean to say," answered Victorica, "and it is better to say it frankly, that formerly I received my orders directly from the Governor, and for some time past I have been receiving them from others, in his Excellency's name."

"And do you think that anyone would dare to make an unauthorized use of my father's name?"

"What I think, señorita, is, that one cannot go to Santos Lugares and return in half an hour."

"Well?"

"And this afternoon, for example, I received in his Excellency's name an order to watch the coast at San Isidro tonight; and twenty minutes or half an hour later I received a counter-order, also in the Restorer's name, to patrol the Boca."

"Ah!"

"And you see, Manuelita, that one of the two orders is not from the Governor."

"Certainly. This is very strange!"

"For me there have never been either good or bad epochs in the service of General Rosas, nor shall there ever be. But I am not equally willing to serve other people, who are acting for private interests and not for the cause."

"Believe me, Victorica, I will speak to papa about this at the first opportunity."

"That lady gives me more to do than the Governor."

"That lady! What lady?"

"Have you not understood that I am referring to Doña María Josefa?"

"Ah, yes;" and yet Manuela had understood nothing of the kind; for she had in truth paid little attention to anything that did not concern her father's situation at the present moment.

"That lady," continued Victorica, "has a particular interest in having the coast watched to prevent the Unitarians from going away, but if I had anything to say in the matter, I would let them all go."

"And so would I," said Manuela, quickly.

"Today she sent me an order to have a house watched for the second time in which I know very well that even the walls are Unitarian. But what do we gain by watching it? They neither tell me what I am to watch for nor what I am to do in case I should discover such or such a thing."

"I see."

"And immediately afterward another order in his Excellency's name to keep a watch upon the movements of a hare-brained boy."

"What an idea!"

"A boy who goes hither and thither, like a mountebank; and who in reality is known to have only Federal associations."

"And who is he, Señor Victorica?"

"Someone who often comes here."

"Here? And you have received an order to watch him?"

"Yes, señorita."

"But who is he?"

"Bello!"

"Bello!" exclaimed Manuela, who had a sincere friendship for the young man.

"Yes, in the name of the Governor," continued Victorica.

"Oh, that cannot be."

"Nevertheless, Doña María Josefa herself told me to do so."

"To arrest Bello," responded Manuela; "why, I repeat that it is impossible. Papa can have given no such order. Bello is an excellent young man; he is a good Federal, and his father is one of my father's oldest friends."

"I was not told to arrest him, but to watch him."

"He is perhaps one of the few sincere men around us," added Manuela.

"He does not seem to me to be bad. But I must say that he has either a great many enemies, or some very powerful ones."

"Señor Victorica, take no step whatever against that gentleman, except by papa's express orders."

"If you desire it—"

"I desire it, unless the order be given by Corvalan."

"Very well."

"I know something about this matter. Let us not allow papa's name to be used as a screen."

"Very well, very well," returned Victorica, delighted to have revenged himself on Doña María Josefa; and, as if he desired to reward Manuela for the satisfaction she had just given him, he promised to send the police officer to her immediately on his arrival with the news from the camp.

"But I request," he added, "that whether the news he brings be good or bad, you will not tell it to anyone until I report it to you myself, as is my duty."

"I give you my promise."

"Good-night then, Manuelita."

And the Chief of Police made his way again through the groups that crowded the parlor and the courtyard without anyone venturing to stop him to ask him the news, as they always did with one another.

The seat he left did not remain vacant for an instant, for a new personage of the epoch came to congratulate the young girl in advance on the approaching Federal triumph.

And while Manuela was requesting her new interlocutor to go ask the negresses in the courtyard to make less noise and to tell them that her father would receive them with a great deal of pleasure in the camp, Doña María Josefa was shaking hands with a well-built man of about thirty-eight or forty years of age, with fine eyes, a dark complexion and a heavy black mustache, attired in a red cloth jacket, black trousers with a scarlet stripe, and a waistcoat and cravat of the same color, and who displayed an enormous badge and a no less enormous dagger in his belt.

"Well, then, early," Rosas' sister-in-law was saying to him.

"Yes, señora, before seven I will be at your house to report to you."

"But if there should be any news before that time you will send at once to let me know?"

"Yes, señora."

"I will remain here all night, or at least until we hear from Juan Manuel. But, remember, give no quarter. You know that all who escape will go to Lavalle."

"No fear of that," answered the other, with a slight smile which seemed to say: I do not require that recommendation.

"Victorica is going to patrol the coast from the fortress to the Boca," continued María Josefa.

"I know it, señora; and I am going to relieve Cuitiño, who is patrolling from the Batería to San Isidro."

"Good. There is a rat that escaped once before from the trap, but I fancy we shall catch him again sooner or later. Go at once. You know that in these matters I act for Juan Manuel. Go take your leave of Manuelita, and good-bye until tomorrow."

And the personage who was going to relieve Cuitiño took his leave of the Dictator's sister-in-law. This individual was Martin Santa Coloma, one of the chief leaders of the Mashorca, whose hands were in 1840 imbrued in the blood of his defenseless compatriots.

XXXVII

The Launch

I

THE NIGHT WAS FOGGY BUT mild; the river calm; a fresh, but gentle breeze curled the surface of the water, which now at high tide covered the rocks on the coast and flowed noiselessly into the little inlets bordering it. Occasionally a star could be seen shining through the gray clouds that veiled the firmament.

At nine o'clock on this evening a boat had put off from one of the blockading corvettes, with a young French officer, the coxswain and eight sailors on board.

For an hour the boat sped along, standing far out from shore, her prow west-by-north, with swelling sail, light and graceful as a vision of the night borne on the wings of the breeze; while the young officer, wrapped in his cloak and stretched on the stern bench, with that indolence which is characteristic of the sailor, lowered his eyes from time to time to look at a small chart spread out at his feet, on which fell the light from a lantern by which he examined from time to time a small mariner's compass, which kept the chart in place, indicating afterwards by a gesture of the hand, without uttering a word, the direction which the coxswain, who was steering, was to give the boat. And by the light of the lantern placed at the bottom of the boat could be distinguished also the muskets of the sailors, laid athwart it.

At the end of about an hour the officer looked at his watch and then examined again, more attentively than before, the compass, the chart and the course taken by the boat, after which he gave orders to lower the sail and row in the direction which he indicated, after placing the lantern under a bench in the stern. The upper part of the oars was wrapped in canvas, and the faint noise made by the blade cutting the water was scarcely perceptible.

The lights of the city were now completely lost to view, and on the left appeared, vaguely distinguishable, the dark outlines of the coast rising higher and higher as the boat advanced more rapidly at the impulse of the oars than she had done before under sail.

At last the officer gave an order to the helmsman, and the boat veered three points around toward the land, and, at another order from the coxswain, the sailors began to row gently, hardly touching the surface of the water with the tips of their oars, and the boat decreased its speed by more than one-half.

The officer then seated himself on the floor, in the stern of the boat, took the lantern in his hand, examined attentively the compass and the indications of the chart, and after a few moments raised his arm, without removing his eyes from the compass or the chart.

At this action the sailors gave a single back stroke with their oars and the boat stopped suddenly, remaining as if riveted to the surface of the water, in the midst of the silence and darkness of the night.

They were now within a hundred yards of the shore.

The officer then obtaining from two of the sailors their oilcloth caps placed the lantern between these so that the light should be projected in a straight line, leaving the surrounding space in darkness, and rising to his feet, lifted the lantern thus protected, to a level with his face, with the light shining in the direction of the shore.

He remained thus for some minutes, while the eyes of all sought on the land the answer to this mysterious signal. But in vain.

The young man shook his head, and putting the lantern back in its former place gave orders to row on again.

Five minutes later the same operation was repeated with the same precautions. But this time also in vain.

The officer, now with something of ill-humor, again examined the course taken by the boat, and having ascertained that it was in the place and following the direction marked on the chart, he gave orders to put a little further off from shore so as to get out of the shadow cast by the neighboring barranca.

After a few minutes' progress the boat passed in front of a small headland, and about two hundred yards from its last station the signal was again repeated by the officer.

The floating light had been sending its mysterious rays toward the land for less than a minute when a light appeared on the neighboring barranca somewhat brighter than seemed to be called for by the light on the river, which was surrounded by so many precautions.

"There it is," exclaimed all in the boat, but in a voice scarcely audible even to themselves.

The lantern was then raised and lowered twice in succession by the officer, and the light on the land was immediately extinguished.

It was now eleven o'clock.

II

AT ABOUT SEVEN O'CLOCK ON the same evening a carriage, driven by Fermin, had stopped at the door of Madame Dupasquier's house, and that noble lady, looking pale and thin, had entered it shortly afterward, followed by her daughter.

The carriage had driven off at once, taking the direction of the fortress, reaching which it had crossed the Plaza del 25 de Mayo, and descending to the Bajo proceeded rapidly northward.

As they were passing the Recoleta a little after nightfall, two horsemen overtook the carriage and after examining it attentively followed it at the distance of a few paces.

From time to time, disregarding the night air, Madame Dupasquier herself directed her daughter to open one of the carriage windows to see if their friends were following them. And each time the young girl complied with this order, not a very disagreeable one for her, as may be imagined, a pair of watchful and loving eyes descried her beautiful head and in an instant one of the two horsemen was at the carriage door, and a brief colloquy of the most tender character took place between the young girl and the young man, between the mother and her son, for the young man, as will be easily understood, was no other than Daniel, the affianced husband of Florencia.

Returning from one of these journeys to the carriage door Daniel, riding close to his companion's side, in whom the reader will have recognized Eduardo, and putting his hand on his shoulder said to him:

"Do you wish me to make a confession which perhaps another man would be ashamed to make?"

"Perhaps you are going to tell me that you are in love? Well! I too am in love, and I would not be ashamed to say so."

"No, it is not that."

"What is it, then?"

"That I am afraid."

"Afraid."

"Yes, Eduardo, afraid. But only at this moment, on this solitary journey, in view of the dangerous step that we are about to take. I, who risk my life every hour of the day; who from a child have loved darkness and peril and adventure, who learned to break in the colt for the pleasure of running a danger, who have traversed the waters of our river, angrier and more mighty than those of the ocean, in a frail boat, without any other aim or object than the pleasure of coming face to face with nature in her wildest and most savage moods, I who have a strong heart and a skillful arm, would tremble like a child if at this moment any accident should occur that would place us in danger."

"Well, that is a pretty way to be valiant! When do you want courage for if not for the time of danger?"

"Yes, but danger for me; not for Florencia, not for her mother. It is not fear of losing my life, it is fear of causing her to shed a tear, of making her suffer the horrible tortures that she would suffer if we should suddenly find ourselves in the midst of a conflict. It is fear that she should be left alone, her father absent, her mother almost expiring, and without my protection, in this tempest of crime which is gathering above our heads. Do you understand me now?"

"Yes, and the worst of it is that you have inoculated me with the fear which had not occurred to me, by my faith—the fear of death, not for its own sake, but because of those who remain behind. But we are near our destination now, Daniel; in ten minutes more we shall be there. My poor girl! Your Florencia at least has our company; but she, she has been alone since yesterday. Ah! to think that the day after tomorrow, tomorrow, perhaps, this horrible life that we are leading may cease! Fugitives, pariahs in our own country, in our own houses! See Daniel, I think that when I smell the powder, when I hear the advance guard of Lavalle approaching, and we twenty men, as we are now, sally out with our muskets to meet them, I think, I say, that I shall begin to fire in the air solely for the pleasure of smelling powder, if that canaille of Rosas does not give us the chance to fire at their breasts. Do you think that they will be here the day after tomorrow?"

"Yes," returned Daniel, "that is the order of march. The attack may begin the day after tomorrow, and it is for that reason that I have so strongly urged the journey which is to take place tonight. I know myself. With Florencia here I should not be worth half what I shall be worth alone in that fateful moment."

"And to think that Amalia should refuse to accompany them!" exclaimed Eduardo.

"Amalia is more courageous than Florencia, and besides, her nature is different. No human power could make her separate her fate from yours. Here you are and here she will remain. She is your shadow."

"No, she is my light, she is the star of my life!" answered Eduardo with an accent of pride that seemed to say: That is what I desire the woman I love to be!

"There is the house," said Daniel, and riding a little in advance he gave orders to Fermin to take the carriage around to the other side of the building as soon as the ladies should have alighted.

A minute later he was at the door of the solitary house. Not a light was to be seen; not a sound was to be heard but the murmur of the wind among the trees.

No sooner had the carriage and the horsemen stopped at the door, however, than this was opened, and the eyes of the travelers, habituated to the darkness for the past two hours, were able to distinguish clearly the forms of Amalia and Luisa standing at it, while, looking through the slats of one of the windowblinds they saw old Pedro, the veteran soldier who guarded the daughter of his Colonel with the same vigilance with which, twenty years before, in the vanguard of the armies of his country, he had guarded his post and his watchword.

Madame Dupasquier alighted from the carriage greatly exhausted by the fatigue of the journey. But every preparation had been made by the thoughtful and hospitable Amalia, and, after taking a glass of cordial and resting for a little the invalid recovered her usual strength. Besides, the thought that she should soon cease to breathe this air that was stifling her, and save her daughter, was the best tonic for her present debility.

In accordance with Daniel's instructions only Amalia's bedroom, whose one window looked out on the small courtyard of the house, had been lighted. The parlor and the dining-room, whose windows faced the river and whose doors faced the road, were completely dark.

Daniel left the room to give some orders to Fermin, and a few minutes later returned, saying:

"It is almost ten. We must go to the dining-room to await there the signal from the boat, which cannot now delay. But Luisa must remain here to bring the light to the parlor the instant I ask for it. Do you understand, Luisa?"

"Yes, yes, señor," answered the little girl, with ready comprehension.

"Come, then, mamma," said Daniel, taking Madame Dupasquier's hand. "You too will help us to watch the river."

"Yes, let us go," answered Florencia's mother, with a smile which sat ill upon her wasted features. "And here is something that could never have occurred to me."

"What is that, mamma?" asked Florencia, quickly.

"That I should ever have to become a Federal even for a moment, using my eyes to spy in the dark. And above all, it could never have occurred to me that I should one day have to embark upon a journey in such a way as this and at such an hour."

"But you will disembark to return home in your carriage within a week, señora."

"A week! And will it take as long as that to expel that rabble from Buenos Ayres?"

"No, señora," answered Eduardo; "but you will not return from Montevideo until we all go there to escort you back."

"And that will be the day on which the power of Rosas shall be ended," added Daniel, who was rewarded by a slight pressure of Florencia's hand, that had remained in his since they had left Amalia's room; for they were now in the dining-room, which was dark, save for the light that entered through the windows facing the river, toward which the eyes of all were turned.

As the minutes passed the conversation became more and more difficult to sustain, for the same thought occupied the minds of all— the hour had arrived and the boat did not appear. Madame Dupasquier could not remain here. The battle might take place on the following day; and it would take three days at least to make a new arrangement with the French squadron.

Suddenly Amalia, who was standing beside Eduardo, exclaimed, pointing to the river:

"There it is!"

Daniel opened the window, mentally calculated the distance from the house to the edge of the water, guided by the noise of the waves, and assuring himself that the light was on the river, he closed the window, and cried:

"Luisa!"

The hearts of all beat with violence.

Luisa, who had been standing with her hand on the candlestick ever since she had received the order, brought the light before the sound of her name had died away in the room.

Daniel placed the candle in front of the window and after seeing the light on the water move twice up and down, as had been agreed upon, he closed the blinds and said:

"Come."

Florencia was as pale as marble and trembled in every limb; Madame Dupasquier was tranquil and serene.

Outside the house Daniel made them stop for a moment.

"What are we waiting for?" asked Eduardo, who had given his arm to Florencia, while Madame Dupasquier leaned on that of Daniel.

"This," replied Daniel, pointing to a figure which was seen ascending the barranca.

Daniel dropped Madame Dupasquier's arm and went forward.

"Is there anyone in sight, Fermin?"

"No one, señor."

"What is the distance?"

"About four hundred yards from side to side."

"Is the boat visible from the shore?"

"It is now, señor; for it has just put in among the rocks; the river is very high, and you can go on board without getting wet."

"Very well, then. You remember everything?"

"Yes, señor."

"Take my horse to the White Rock, which is about three-quarters of a league from here. Keep well in the water, so as to remain concealed from view by the large rock. I will land there within two hours. But for greater security, mount your horse at once and go there to wait for me."

"Very well, señor."

The others were now beginning to be impatient, and a little puzzled at Daniel's delay. But he soon tranquilized them and they all began to descend the barranca.

The night air seemed to invigorate the invalid, who walked with notable serenity leaning on the arm of her future son.

In front of them walked Florencia with Eduardo; and Amalia, holding little Luisa by the hand, headed the party.

Twice Eduardo had begged her to take his other arm, but wishing to inspire the others with courage she had each time refused, saying she was the chatelaine of the place and it was proper that she should lead the way.

In a few minutes they reached the shore, where the boat had put in and was being held in place by two robust sailors, who had jumped on land for the purpose.

When the ladies appeared the French officer sprang on shore with all the gallantry of his nation to assist them on board.

There was something indescribably solemn in this parting, amid the silence and darkness of the night, and on these desert and solitary shores.

Madame Dupasquier took leave of Amalia, saying only:

"Good-bye for a little, Amalia."

But Florencia, who rarely sought relief from her sorrows in tears, at last felt the fountains of her heart unsealed and wept freely on the shoulder of her friend.

Amalia wept inwardly, while the most gloomy and sinister images tortured her vivid and unhappy imagination.

"Come," said Daniel at last, and taking Florencia by the hand he separated her from Luisa, who was crying also, and lifting her by the waist, he placed her at a bound in the boat, where Madame Dupasquier was already seated beside the officer.

Once more Florencia exchanged adieus, with Amalia and Eduardo, and at a command from the officer the boat put off from shore, then tacked south and ran along the coast with its sail unfurled and without any of the precautions with which it had approached the land a quarter of an hour before.

Amalia, Eduardo and Luisa followed it with their eyes until it disappeared from view in the darkness.

Eight minutes might have elapsed when a sudden flash of light and the detonation of a volley of musketry on the shore, from the direction which the boat had taken, thrilled like an electric shock the hearts of all there.

XXXVIII

The Federal Patrol

E duardo's head was still turned in the direction from which the sound of the firing had proceeded, and his hands were instinctively seeking the pockets in which he carried his pistols, when Amalia's voice broke the silence of the melancholy region crying:

"Come up! come up! for Heaven's sake," while she caught her lover by the arm and tried to drag him away with all the force of her feeble hands. Eduardo, comprehending everything and understanding the danger which Amalia incurred by remaining a moment longer in this place, clasped her tightly around the waist, saying:

"Yes, quick, there is not a moment to be lost;" while Luisa, pulling her mistress by the skirt, endeavored also to hurry her up the ascent.

They had been walking for about two minutes when a second report caused them to stop mechanically and turn their eyes in the direction whence the sound had proceeded, and then they saw distinctly, although at a considerable distance, a sudden flash of light on the river, which was followed by another report.

"My God!" exclaimed Amalia.

"No; that last is from the boat which is answering them," responded Eduardo, with a smile of mingled rage and satisfaction.

"But they may have wounded them, Eduardo?"

"No, no; that is hardly possible. Come up, there is another danger to be avoided."

"Another?"

"Come up; come up."

They were within a few steps of the house when they saw Pedro coming toward them, ramming a bullet into his carbine, while he held his saber under his arm.

"Ah, here you are at last," he said, when he saw them.

"Is that you, Pedro?"

"Yes, señora; it is I. But this is no hour for you to be walking here." This was perhaps the first time that the good old man had ever addressed a reproach to his Colonel's daughter.

"Did you hear, Pedro?" asked Eduardo.

"Yes, señor; I heard everything. But this is no hour for the señora—"

"Well, well, it is the last time, Pedro," said Amalia; who understood how deep an interest this faithful servant of her family had in her welfare.

"I want to ask you, Pedro," continued Eduardo, as they entered the house, "if you were able to distinguish with what arms the first and second shots were fired."

"Bah!" exclaimed the veteran with a smile, closing the door.

"Let us hear, then."

"The first and second were with a carbine, and the third with a musket."

"That is my opinion, also."

"Anyone who has ears could tell that," answered Pedro, who seemed to be in a very bad humor with everyone, on account of the danger to which his mistress had just been exposed; and, as if to escape further questions, he went to put a light in the room in which Eduardo and Daniel slept when they remained overnight in the solitary house, and which was at the other end of the building from that in which Amalia's rooms were situated.

When the latter entered the parlor and took off the silk handkerchief which covered her head, Eduardo was surprised by the extreme pallor of her face.

The young woman sat down in a chair and resting her elbow on the table leaned her forehead on her hand, while Eduardo went into the unlighted dining-room and, opening the window, listened intently, for the increasing darkness of the night rendered it impossible for him to see anything.

Not a sound was to be heard.

When he returned to the parlor Amalia was still sitting in the same attitude.

"There, my Amalia, there, it is all over now, and Daniel will be going on his way laughing, at this moment," he said, sitting down beside her and smoothing the glossy tresses of his beloved, which the pressure of her hand had disordered.

"But so many bullets! It is impossible that they should not have wounded someone."

"On the contrary, what is impossible is that a bullet from a carbine could have gone within fifty yards of the boat. They saw its shadow on the water, and fired at random."

"But the whole coast must be watched, then? And Daniel? How will Daniel disembark? My God!"

"He will disembark at daybreak when the patrol have retired."

"And has Fermin taken his horse to him?"

"Yes, señora," answered Luisa, who just then entered the room with a cup of tea for Amalia.

At this moment Eduardo rose from his seat and went again to the dining-room to listen once more at the window. For some time past one thought—the only one that now troubled him—had been tormenting his mind.

He had been leaning for about three minutes against the window bars when he fancied that he heard a noise coming from the direction of the Bajo.

A moment later this noise was clearly audible and there could not be a doubt that it was made by the tramp of many horses.

Suddenly the sound of the march of the cavalcade ceased, but the confused noise of voices conversing at the foot of the barranca could be distinguished. Then the tramp of the horses could be heard again.

"There is not a doubt of it," said Eduardo to himself; "that is the patrol that fired. They have stopped at the foot of the barranca and they have probably been talking about this house. There is not a doubt of it; they are going to make a detour and come here by the upper road. What a fatality! What a fatality!" and the young man bit his lip until the blood came.

When he returned to the parlor Amalia, who could interpret so well every change in her lover's countenance, comprehended that he was agitated by some profound emotion and she herself opened the way for him to speak, saying:

"Tell me what it is, Eduardo; I am always resigned, for I am always expecting misfortune."

"No; misfortune, no," responded Eduardo, as if ashamed that his beloved should have perceived in his face even a transitory expression of fear.

"And what is it, then?"

"Perhaps—perhaps nothing—a foolish thought of mine," said the young man, smiling.

"No, no; something is the matter and I desire to know what it is."

"Well, then, the matter is this—that a patrol has just passed by at the foot of the barranca and that it is probably the same patrol which fired on the boat. That is all."

"All? Well, you shall see that I have understood what you have not wished to tell me. Luisa, call Pedro."

"And what for?" asked Eduardo.

"You shall hear presently."

The veteran appeared.

"Pedro," said Amalia, "it is possible that an attack may be made upon the house tonight; they may attempt to search it, or something of the kind; make all the doors secure and prepare your arms."

Eduardo was astonished at the valor and serenity of his beloved; admiring her in his inmost soul, knowing that this was not constitutional courage, but the courage of love, exalted to the height of self-sacrifice. For at this time armed resistance, any resistance, indeed, to a command of the agents of Rosas was a certain sentence of death, or of misfortune of all kinds, and Amalia dared to brave this, in the attempt to save the beloved of her heart.

"Everything is ready, señora; I have twenty charges, and my saber," answered Pedro.

"And I four and mine," said Eduardo, suddenly rising to his feet; but still more suddenly, as if he had been transformed into another man, he sat down again saying:

"No; here no blood shall be shed."

"What do you mean?"

"I mean, Amalia, that if the worst should come my life is not worth your witnessing a scene like the one which we have imprudently desired to prepare, and which would result only in the ruin of everyone."

"Pedro, do as I have ordered you," responded Amalia.

"Amalia!" cried Eduardo, seizing her hand.

"Eduardo," replied the young woman, "I have no life apart from the life of him I love; and if his destiny should hurry him on to disaster, I would join my fate to his so that we might both share it together."

While she was still speaking a sound of horses galloping toward them came from the upper road.

Eduardo rose calmly, went out to the courtyard, where Pedro was walking up and down, and crossing it, entered his room. Here, without haste, he took off his poncho, which he had not before removed, took his double-barreled pistols from his trousers' pockets, examined the priming and then, unsheathing his sword, returned to the courtyard and placed it in a corner.

At this moment Amalia also appeared in the courtyard, with Luisa clinging to her skirts.

Amalia had hardly exchanged a few words with Eduardo and Pedro when the sound of voices outside the door was heard and shortly afterward the clanking of the swords and spurs of men dismounting; then all four entered the parlor, the door of which opened into the hall.

A moment later a dozen loud knocks sounded in quick succession on the street door.

"Pedro and I have already formed our plan," said Eduardo to Amalia; "we will neither open the door nor answer. If they get tired and go away so much the better. If they try to break down the door, they will find it a difficult task, for it is stout and strongly barred, and even if they should succeed in doing so, they will be already fatigued when we receive them."

The knocking at the door was repeated, and was soon followed by knocks at the windows of the parlor and dining-room.

"Break it down!" cried a loud, harsh voice, that had already made itself heard several times above the voices of those who accompanied with oaths and obscene words the blows which they showered in vain on the doors and windows.

"Shoot away the lock!" continued the same voice, all the efforts of the men to break down the door having proved unavailing.

Pedro looked round with a smile at Eduardo, who was standing with Amalia, holding her hand clasped in his, in the middle of the room.

At the same instant, four shots were fired from the outside, and the lock fell at the feet of Pedro, who with admirable coolness walked over to Amalia, and said to her:

"Those rascals may fire through the windows; it is not well for you to be here."

"True," said Eduardo; "go into Luisa's room."

"No, I will stay where you are."

"Señorita, if you don't go in, I will take you in my arms and carry you in," said Pedro, in so quiet but so determined a voice that Amalia, although she was surprised, did not venture to answer him, but went into the bedroom with Luisa; while Pedro and Eduardo placed themselves between the two windows in the shelter of the wall.

These precautions were not useless, for they had scarcely taken this position when the windows were shattered into a thousand fragments, and several bullets whizzed through the room.

Suddenly a tremendous blow, an almost irresistible shock, made the hinges of the door grate and its framework creak; it seemed as if the door was about to fall in entire for even the walls trembled as if they had been shaken by an earthquake.

"Ah, I know now what it is, and for this there is no remedy!" said Pedro, leaving the shelter of the wall, cocking his carbine and going toward the hall, while Eduardo, who had also got his pistols ready, walked beside him with flashing eyes and parted lips, convulsively grasping his weapons.

A second dull but powerful blow given full on the door shook the house again, and a shower of splinters and fragments of mortar fell from the framework of the door.

"It will not stand another," said Pedro.

"But what the devil are they battering it with?" asked Eduardo, trembling with rage, and wishing that the door might fall in at once.

"With the haunches of two or three horses simultaneously," answered Pedro; "we broke down the door of a barrack in Peru in the same way."

At this moment, for the whole scene had passed as quickly as thought, Luisa, who was clinging to Amalia's knees, trying to prevent her from leaving the room, said to her mistress:

"Señora, the Virgin has reminded me of something—the letter; I know where it is; with that we shall be safe, señora."

"What letter, Luisa?"

"The letter that—"

"Ah, yes; Divine Providence! It is the only means of saving him. Bring it, bring it."

Luisa flew to a table, took a letter from a little box which stood upon it, and returning to Amalia handed it to her.

Amalia then ran to the parlor door and said to Eduardo and Pedro, who were in the hall expecting every moment to see the door fall in:

"Don't stir, for God's sake; listen to everything, but do not speak nor come into the parlor;" and without waiting for an answer she closed the door, and, flying to one of the windows, she drew the bolt and opened it.

At this noise ten or twelve of the men who had dismounted, leaving the door, rushed to the window and instinctively took aim with their carbines at the grating.

Amalia did not retreat; she did not even change countenance but in a firm and dignified voice said to them:

"Why do you attack a woman's house in this way, gentlemen? Here there are neither men nor treasures."

"Eh, we are not thieves!" answered one of the men who pushed his way through the others to the window.

"Well, if this is a military patrol, it ought not to try to break down the doors of *this house.*"

"And to whom does *this house* belong?" asked the man who had approached the window, parodying the emphasis which Amalia had laid on the italicized words.

"Read this, and you will know. Luisa, bring a light."

Amalia's voice, her youth, her beauty, and the mysterious confidence and menace involved in her last words together with the paper which she handed the man to whom she spoke, at this epoch in which everyone feared to incur, through a mistake or through any trifle, the anger of Rosas, naturally perplexed these men who had never suspected that in this house, abandoned for so many years, there could be a woman like the one they saw before them.

"But, señora, open the door," said the person who had taken the letter, with embarrassment, and who was no other than Martin Santa Coloma at the head of his band.

"Read first and I will open afterwards if you wish," responded Amalia in more assured tones, into which she had infused a tinge of reproach; while Luisa, feigning courage like her mistress, held the light, protected by a glass shade, close to the window bars.

Santa Coloma unfolded the letter without taking his eyes off this woman who seen by the light of the candle, and in this melancholy and deserted spot, exercised a sort of spell over his imagination. Then he looked at the signature of the letter and surprise was depicted on his countenance, which had in it something manly and interesting.

"Have the goodness to read aloud so that all may hear," said Amalia.

"Señora, I am the leader of this party, and it will be enough for me to read it," he answered, acquainting himself with the contents of the letter which it is proper that the reader should know also, and which were as follows:

Señora Doña Amalia Saenz de Olabarrieta.

My distinguished compatriot:

"I have learned with great displeasure that certain persons have dared to annoy you in your solitude, without cause and without any order from papa, which is a great abuse and one that he would censure if he were to know of it. The life you lead can excite the suspicions of none but those who use the Governor's name for their own private ends. You are one of those whom I esteem most highly, and I request you as a friend to send me word if you should be again annoyed; for if it be without an order from papa, as I do not doubt, I will inform him of it immediately, so that the use of his name may not be again abused.

"Believe that the moment in which I can be useful to you will be a happy one for

Your obedient servant and friend,
Manuela Rosas
August 23, 1840

"Señora," said Santa Coloma, taking off his hat, "I had no intention of doing you any injury, nor did I know who lived here. I supposed that some of the persons who embarked from this coast a short time ago might have left this house, for I have just had a fight with one of the enemy's boats not far from here, and as there is no other house but this—"

"You came to break down my doors, is it not so?" interrupted Amalia, to complete the subjugation of Santa Coloma's mind.

"Señora, as no one opened the door and I saw a light—but excuse me. I did not know that it was a friend of Doña Manuelita's who lived here."

"Very good; will you come in now and search the house?" and Amalia made a movement as if to go and open the door.

"No, señora, no. I will only ask you the favor of allowing me to send tomorrow to repair the door, which has perhaps been injured."

"A thousand thanks, señor. Tomorrow I intend to go to my country house and this is a matter of no consequence."

"I will go in person," resumed Santa Coloma, "to present my excuses to Doña Manuelita. Believe me, this was unintentional."

"I believe everything you say, and there is no need for excuses, for no one shall ever learn from me of what has taken place; you made a mistake, and that is all there is to be said about it," responded Amalia, speaking as sweetly as it was possible for her, in the circumstances, to do.

"Gentlemen, to horse; this is a Federal house," cried Santa Coloma to his followers. "I ask your pardon once more," he continued, turning to Amalia. "Good-night, señora."

"Will you not rest a moment?"

"No, señora, a thousand thanks; it is you who require to rest after the disagreeable moments I have made you spend."

And Santa Coloma retreated from the window without having yet put on his hat.

"Good-night," said Amalia, closing the window.

A moment later she was lying in a swoon upon the sofa.

XXXIX

Of Forty only Ten

O n the night succeeding that of the attack on the solitary house, a number of men, who had been arriving one by one for two hours previously, were assembled in a large wholesale warehouse adjoining a handsome two-story dwelling-house which commanded a view of almost the whole length of the Calle de la Universidad.*

Each one on arriving had knocked in a particular manner at the door of the warehouse, which opened immediately to close behind him the instant he had entered.

At the further end of the warehouse could be distinguished the dim light of a candle that stood behind a pile of wine boxes, around which the men gathered as they arrived.

"Ten o'clock," said one of the number, holding his watch to the light.

"So much the better," responded another, rising and taking a few turns up and down the room.

"Yes, true," added a third, "if anything had happened we should have known it before this."

"I think the entry will not take place before daybreak," observed another, rising also; for they had all been sitting on boxes around the candle.

"But how is it that the others do not come?"

"But we do not know how many of us there are."

"Did not Belgrano tell you?"

"No."

"Nor did Bello tell me how many of us were to meet here."

"And what does the number signify?"

"Of course it signifies. Do you suppose that with those who are here now we could do a great deal?" responded a man of military bearing, who seemed to be the oldest of the party, although he appeared to be hardly thirty-five.

"But—"

---

* Throughout this work, the names which the streets had in 1840, when the events related in our story took place, have naturally been retained.

JOSÉ MÁRMOL

A knock at the door interrupted the answer, holding the attention of all while the door was being opened; for the knock had been given in the manner agreed upon.

An instant later Daniel and Eduardo were surrounded by the ten men who were present.

The two young men wore ponchos and had large Federal badges in their hats. But the faces of both, and especially Daniel's, expressed the deepest grief and disappointment.

"The face of each of you is a bulletin of Rosas in which he informs us of the defeat of Lavalle;" said one of the party.

"No," answered Daniel, "no; Lavalle has not been defeated. It is worse than that."

"The devil! It had never occurred to me until now that there could be worse than that."

"And yet so it is," replied Daniel.

"But explain yourself, in the name of all the saints," cried another.

"Nothing is easier, my friend," answered Daniel; and he continued:

"Lavalle began his retreat from Merlo at six o'clock this evening. And in my opinion that means the defeat of our cause for many years to come; a thing which is undoubtedly of more importance than the defeat of an army."

A long silence followed this announcement. An icy chill froze the blood in the hearts of all. This news was precisely what they had least expected to hear.

Eduardo at last broke the silence.

"However," he said, "Bello has not told all. It is true that Lavalle has retreated. But I understand, according to Daniel's own information, that he has done so in order to give a blow to Lopez, who is molesting his rear; and to return afterward, free from that annoyance, to direct his operations against Rosas."

"Of course," responded another. "Now I understand. That is to say that what Bello has just told us means nothing more than the delay of our triumph for a few days."

"Undoubtedly," they all responded.

"Think as you choose, gentlemen," replied Daniel. "For me this is ended. General Lavalle's enterprise, to be successful, should be directed rather against the moral than the material strength of Rosas. The moment has been lost. A reaction will take place in the minds of the Federal party and, once recovered from their first fright, they will be ten times stronger than we. Within two hours, now, General Lavalle could take Buenos Ayres. Tomorrow he will be powerless. Lopez will draw him out of the province. And meantime Rosas will raise another army at his rear."

"But how do we know that he has retreated?" asked one of the party.

"Do you believe me or do you not? If you believe me then refrain from asking questions whose answer would lead to nothing," answered Daniel drily. "Let it suffice you to know that today, the 6th of September, he has begun his retreat, after having advanced as far as Merlo; and that I received the news of his retreat half an hour ago."

"Well, we must communicate this news to the others."

"To what others?" asked Eduardo.

"Why! is there not in the neighborhood another meeting of our friends?"

Daniel smiled bitterly and a look of scorn and contempt crossed his expressive countenance.

"No, gentlemen," he answered; "there is no other meeting than the present one. A fortnight ago I had the promise of forty men for this event. Afterwards they were reduced to thirty. Yesterday to twenty. I count you now and I find only ten. And do you know the explanation of this? The philosophy of the dictatorship of Rosas. The habits of disunion among our cultured class; our want of association everywhere and in everything; our life of individualism; our apathy; our neglect; our selfishness; our ignorance regarding the value of the collective strength of men—these keep Rosas in power, and will enable him tomorrow to cut off our heads one by one, without there being four men to join hands for mutual protection. Liberty will always be a lie; justice a lie; human dignity a lie; and progress and civilization lies also, where men do not unite in purpose and in will to become all sharers in the misfortunes of each, to rejoice all in the good of each; to live all, in a word, in the liberty and in the rights of each. But where there are not twenty men who will united give their lives and their fortunes the day on which the liberties and the destinies of their country, their own liberties and their own destinies are at stake, there must of necessity be a government like that of Rosas; and there such a government is fitting and proper. Thanks, my friends, honorable exceptions among our puny generation who have all the faults without any of the virtues of their fathers. Thanks, once more. Now we shall not have a country tomorrow, as we had hoped. But we must have a country within a year, within two years, within ten—who can tell! We must have a country, if only for our children. And for this we must begin from today with another programme of incessant and laborious work and of slow results, but work which will bear its fruits in time. The work of emigration. The work of the propaganda everywhere and at all times, without cessation. The work of the sword in military movements. The work of speech and of the pen, wherever there are half a dozen men to listen to us in another land; for some one of our words will return to our country, in the air, in the light, in the waves. My presence is necessary in Buenos Ayres for a few weeks longer, but not yours. Up to this I have tried to be the dyke of emigration. Now circumstances have changed and I will be its bridge. Emigrate, then. But always haunting our country's doors; always knocking at them; always making the tyrant feel that the name of liberty still has an echo in our souls; always harassing him, to exhaust his strength, his resources, even his terror. This must be our programme for many years to come. It is a war of blood, of mind, of life on which we are about to enter. Let him who survives among us when liberty has been won teach our children that this liberty will last for a very short time if the nation does not unite as one man to defend it; that they will have neither a country nor liberty, nor laws, nor religion, nor public virtue until the spirit of association shall have destroyed the cancer of individualism which has made and which still makes the misfortune of our generation. Let us now embrace one another and bid one another good-bye until we meet in a foreign land."

Tears coursed down the cheeks of those who a few moments before had been so full of hopes and dreams of liberty and triumph; and a moment later there remained on the scene of so bitter a disillusion only the man who was entrusted with the task of closing the doors and concealing the arms.

XL

English Sanctuary

A few days after the meeting which we have just described had taken place a carriage drawn by two spirited horses drove at a quick pace down the Calle de la Reconquista in the direction of Barracas, until it reached the villa of Sir John Henry Mandeville, her Britannic Majesty's Minister, at the door of which it stopped.

The coachman opened the door of the carriage and two men alighted from it.

One of them, however, with his foot still on the carriage-step turned round, and putting his head in at the door said to another individual who had not moved from the front seat which he had occupied during the journey:

"Are you sure that you remember everything, my dear master?"

"Yes, Daniel, but—"

"But what?"

"Would it not be better to inquire if the minister is at home before I set out on this solitary and lonely journey through these lugubrious streets, at this hour and shut up in this vehicle?"

"That does not matter—if he is not at home we will wait for him, and when you return you will find us here."

"And if the Prior should ask me—"

"I have already told you a hundred times—you are not to give a direct answer to any question. Whether they will consent or not to what you ask, cost what money it may—that is all."

"And it is necessary that he should be my nephew?"

"Or your son."

"I, sons, Daniel!"

"Or your cousin."

"What an idea!"

"Or your godson, or whatever else you choose. You can be back within an hour."

"Farewell, Daniel. Farewell."

"Good-bye for a little, my dear friend," and the young man shut the carriage door and made a sign to the coachman, who was no other than Fermin, and who drove off immediately.

The minister was at home, and Daniel and his companion, in whom the reader will have already recognized Eduardo, were shown into the drawing-room where the candles were just being lighted.

Sir John Henry Mandeville did not keep his visitors waiting long, for Buenos Ayres never had a European Minister more affable and democratic than he to all who came to his house with the insignia of the epoch.

The minister entered the room, his distinguished countenance, fresh looking still, notwithstanding his years, his coat closely buttoned, his linen cuffs falling over his white and well cared-for hands; and with that polished ease of manner which is acquired only by constant contact with the best society, he gave his hand to Daniel and exclaimed:

"Ah, what a pleasure! You cannot imagine, Señor Bello, what an honor and what a happiness it is for me to see you in my house."

"Señor Mandeville," answered the young man, shaking the hand which the diplomat extended to him, "the honor and happiness I have in being here are infinitely greater than any I could confer. I have the pleasure of presenting to you my intimate friend, Señor Belgrano."

"Ah! Señor Belgrano. I have long desired the pleasure of knowing this gentleman."

"It is a happiness for me," responded Eduardo, "that my name should be known to Señor Mandeville."

"What would you have, my young friend? I am an old man and I enjoy so much of the society of the beautiful ladies of Buenos Ayres that I have learned in it by heart the names of her distinguished young men."

"Every word of yours is a compliment, Señor Mandeville," answered Eduardo, who, sought in vain to join in this exquisite fencing with words which is one of the special attributes of cultured society and of European diplomacy, and which was not in consonance either with the young man's character or his habits.

"No, no, justice, nothing more, Señor Belgrano—And tell me, have you seen Manuelita lately, Señor Bello?"

"Not today, Señor Mandeville."

"Ah, what an enchanting creature! I never weary of talking to her and admiring her. Many people think that my visits to his Excellency have a political object, but nothing could be further from the truth. I go to his house to find in the society of that spirituelle creature something to cheer my spirit, fatigued with affairs. In London, Misia Manuelita would make a furore."

"And her father?" asked Eduardo, upon whom a look from Daniel fell like a blow.

"Her father—General Rosas—well, you see, in London—"

"In London the Governor would not enjoy good health;" interposed Daniel, to extricate the minister from the dilemma in which his friend had just placed him.

"Oh, the climate of London is detestable. Have you ever been in Europe, Señor Belgrano?"

"No, señor, but I intend to spend a few years traveling there."

"And is your journey a sudden one?"

"Not so sudden as Señor de Mackau's journey here," returned Daniel, desiring now to give another turn to this insubstantial conversation.

"What! Has Vice-Admiral Mackau arrived already?"

"Did you not know it, Señor Mandeville?"

"No, indeed."

"Well, he has arrived."

"Here?"

"No; at Montevideo. He arrived the day before yesterday, at one o'clock."

"And does his Excellency know it?"

"And how do you suppose that I could know it and his Excellency the Governor not know it?"

"True; true. But it is strange that the Commodore should have said nothing to me about it."

"An English brig was in sight at dusk."

"Ah!"

"The wind has been unfavorable, Señor Mandeville," observed Eduardo, "and it was only at five this afternoon that the news was brought by a sailboat."

"So that the crisis has now arrived," said Mandeville, playing with his nails, as was his habit when he was preoccupied with anything.

"And that is not the best part of the news."

"Is there more?"

"A trifle, Señor Mandeville! You know that up to this we all expected the French envoy to arrive in a hostile attitude, did we not?"

"Yes, yes; well?"

"Well, he comes with the soundest and most pacific intentions possible."

"Ah, what happiness!"

"For us."

"For everyone, Señor Bello."

"Except in so far as regards the Eastern Question."

"Yes, there may be something in that."

"A difficulty the less for France is an obstacle the more to the peace of Europe at this juncture. Fortunately, the relations existing at present between England and France guarantee us, to a certain extent, the result of the Mackau mission."

"The British Government would not hesitate," observed the minister, "to offer its good offices in that question."

"That is not what I meant to say," replied Bello. "I meant to say that if England had any interest in diverting for a moment the attention of France from the question of the Plata, the present is a brilliant opportunity. Señor Belgrano and I were talking of that just now as we were coming here."

"Nevertheless—if Baron de Mackau's instructions are to arrange this affair at all costs, I confess that I do not see how England could well interfere with that arrangement, in the supposition, which is an entirely imaginary one, that she had any interest in doing so."

"Here, no; but in France she might interfere with the ratification of the treaty, since there will be in it a defect which fortunately will not be perceived in France, but which would ruin everything if the English Ministry should take the trouble to draw the attention of the French Opposition to it. Of that danger precisely Bello and I were talking as we came here," said Eduardo, while Sir John Henry Mandeville turned his keen eyes from one to the other of the young men, whose real thoughts he constantly endeavored to grasp, and which as constantly eluded him.

"And in what would that defect consist?" he asked, ingenuously.

"In nothing less than the signature of the Governor," answered Daniel.

"What do you mean?"

"That the Unitarians who are in Montevideo have prepared a representation to Señor Mackau, which, to a certain extent, is a rather strong argument."

"And that is, Señor Bello?"

"That the signature of the Governor is invalid, my dear Señor Mandeville. Imagine that they reason in this way—that even if Señor Mackau brings instructions to make a treaty at any cost, there is no power with whom to treat in the Argentine Republic; for General Rosas has no power or authority whatsoever to conclude treaties in the name of the Argentine people."

"But he is a power in fact," replied the minister; "and the Plenipotentiary is not to question his legitimacy but to recognize and to treat with him."

"But to that argument the Unitarians answer," continued Bello, "that if the admiral had come to treat with General Rosas, as Governor of Buenos Ayres simply, and with relation to this province alone, he might then treat with him, as Admiral Le Blanc and Señor Martigny treated with the Government of Corrientes. But that, coming to treat with a Government representing abroad the National Sovereignty, no such Government was found to exist."

"There is something in that, indeed," answered the minister, with an abstracted air.

"The Unitarians maintain," continued Daniel, "that the Argentine Provinces never delegated the power of treating of foreign affairs, making treaties, etc., to the Government of Buenos Ayres in perpetuity, but specially to the Governor, at each legal gubernatorial election. That General Rosas, appointed Governor for five years, on March 7, 1835, entered into office on April 13, and that his term expired on the same day of 1840, and that with it expired also the powers delegated to him by the Provinces; that, re-elected for an equal period, he accepted office only for six months; but that his re-election did not produce *ipso juri* the continuation of that special trust, and therefore that it was indispensable that it should be renewed. But far from this being the case, it was withdrawn from him explicitly by those who had conferred it upon him."

"I have read something of that in the Montevidean newspapers," replied the minister, growing more and more thoughtful.

"That is to say that you have read in the newspapers the official documents."

"Not precisely the documents; at least my memory is not very clear in the matter."

"Nor mine either; but I believe that the Chamber of Representatives of Tucuman issued, on April 7, a decree by which it withdrew the authorization that it had conferred on General Rosas, on the part of the Province, to maintain and preserve relations with foreign powers.

The legislature of Salta issued a similar decree on April 13. On May 5, the Province of Rioja revoked by a decree the authority which it had conferred on General Rosas to intervene in the relations with foreign powers. The Province of Catamarca issued a similar decree on May 7. The Province of Jujui declared itself in terms equally positive on April 18. And as for the Province of Corrientes, no other evidence is needed than the stand it has taken. Thus, then, the Unitarians show that out of the fourteen provinces which form the republic, seven have withdrawn from General Rosas the power to treat in their name."

"And Admiral Mackau is in possession of these facts?"

"How is it possible to doubt it? And if his instructions lead him to the extreme of treating with General Rosas, notwithstanding his legal incapacity, it is easy to foresee that, this radical defect in the negotiation being brought to the knowledge of the French Opposition, either the treaty would be rejected, or the minister would find himself in a very embarrassing position. And I am certain that, even if the frank policy of the British Government could admit of the sacrifice of a friendly power, like the Argentine Republic, for the sake of embarrassing the action of the French Government, we should gain little, Señor Mandeville, by the treaty which Baron de Mackau will probably eventually conclude. But I am sure that the British Government will not sacrifice the friendship of the Argentines, either to hostilize the French Government or to correspond to the reaction in favor of England which is about to take place in the Eastern Republic."

"What, what! Señor Bello!"

"I mean to say that if the Eastern Republic, with the large number of Argentine emigrants who are in it, should be abandoned by France after her former solemn promises, it is very probable that, a reaction unfavorable to French influence taking place in public sentiment in those countries, as a logical consequence public sympathy would turn toward England, which labored so loyally in another epoch for Eastern independence."

"Ah, yes; true. The independence of the Eastern Republic is due, to a certain extent, to the good offices of England."

"So that," continued Daniel, "French influence being destroyed in these countries, should the independence of the Eastern Republic be in danger the action of England would not only be efficacious, but would also be a master stroke to win for herself all the ground lost by France in countries with so promising a future as those of the Plata."

"Señor Bello, you would be a dangerous ambassador for General Rosas," said the minister, who had not lost a single word that his interlocutor had uttered.

"I think that my friend has not given expression to his own opinions, nor has such been his intention," observed Eduardo with a smile.

"And so true is it that I have not spoken in my own name that I am inclined to believe that I have talked a great deal of nonsense, repeating from memory what they say in Montevideo and what I read in the newspapers."

"Señor Bello," said the astute Englishman, "I am not so much obliged to you now for your visit as I was before; for it will keep me from my sleep for a couple of hours tonight, while I make some private memoranda for my own use. And to begin to drive away sleep let us take a little wine." And going over to the sideboard he poured out some sherry from a decanter, and the three men, after taking a little of the wine, continued the conversation, walking up and down the room with the respectful familiarity of well-bred men which neither goes beyond nor falls short of the proper limits.

"I accept the wine, but not the memoranda," Daniel answered.

"Will you explain to me what you mean by that, my dear Señor Bello?"

"Nothing more easy, Señor Mandeville— In these times, only the foreign ministers can make memoranda. No one is safe from an enemy, a calumny, an accident. Happy you, Señor Mandeville! To live in this house is the same as to be in England."

"These immunities are reciprocal. The Argentine Legation in London is the Argentine Republic."

"And do you know that there is one thing that surprises me, Señor Mandeville?" said Daniel, stopping short and looking at the minister with an expression of well-feigned surprise.

"What is that, Señor Bello?"

"That England being in Buenos Ayres, and there being so many here who would walk a thousand leagues to get away from this country at the present moment, they have not walked a few hundred yards and come to this house.'"

"Ah yes, but—"

"I beg your pardon; I wish to know nothing. If there are some unfortunates protected by the English flag in this house it is a duty and an act of humanity on your part, Señor Mandeville, to have received them; and I would not be guilty of the indiscretion of wishing to know it."

"There is no one; I give you my word of honor, there is no one sheltered in my house. My position is exceptional. My instructions are decisive to act with the utmost circumspection. With the best will in the world I could not disobey my instructions."

"Then this house is neither more nor less than any other house?" said Eduardo in a tone so impertinent that Daniel hastily interposed:

"We all understand your position, Señor Mandeville. In these moments of popular excitement our own Government could not render the immunity of this house effective; and you wish to avoid the diplomatic difficulties which would necessarily arise if the people should forget the respect due to the Legation."

"Exactly so," answered the minister, sincerely rejoiced that his interlocutor should himself have extricated him from the embarrassing position in which Eduardo's abrupt inquiry had placed him; "exactly so, and I have found myself in the necessity, the harsh necessity, of refusing the shelter of my house to several persons who have solicited it; for I could neither answer to them for its safety, nor is it permitted to me to act in a manner that might entail further difficulties on this country, for whose people I have the sincerest regard and with which my Government is solicitous to maintain the most friendly relations."

"I think, Daniel, that I have just heard the carriage stop at the door and that it is time for us now to take our leave of Señor Mandeville, who must wish to go make his usual visits," said Eduardo, whose ears were burning.

"There is no pleasure comparable, Señor Belgrano, to that which I have in being with you."

"My friend is right, however, and we must make the sacrifice of leaving Señor Mandeville and his excellent sherry," said Daniel, filling two glasses with wine, one of which he handed to the minister, whom he saluted with the most polite smile in the world as he drank with him.

A moment later the two young men were bowing themselves out in the ante-chamber, leaving the Englishman unable to decide in his own mind what they had come for, to which party they really belonged, or what was their opinion of him, as they went away.

XLI

Mr. Slade

Although Eduardo's ill-humor had mastered him so completely that his farewell bow to Sir John Henry Mandeville was rather an impertinence than a salutation, his ear had not deceived him when he announced to his friend the arrival of the carriage.

It was at the door, in fact, and in it was our Don Cándido Rodriguez, who drew a deep breath of relief at seeing himself once more in the company of Daniel and Eduardo when the carriage drove off again, taking the same road as that by which it had come, in accordance with the orders which Daniel had given his faithful servant on entering it.

And no sooner had the carriage begun to jolt over the rough paving stones of the Calle de la Reconquista than Daniel said to Don Cándido:

"To which of the two?"

"What do you mean, Daniel?"

"To Santo Domingo or to San Francisco?"

"I must first inform you of everything, deliberately, with every detail, with—"

"I desire to know everything; but we must begin at the end, in order to give directions to the driver."

"You positively desire it?"

"Yes."

"Well, then—But you will not get angry?"

"Finish, or we will throw you out of the carriage," said Eduardo, with a look which terrified Don Cándido.

"What tempers! what tempers! Well, then, hot-headed youths, my diplomatic mission has failed!"

"You mean to say," returned Daniel, "that they will receive him neither in Santo Domingo nor in San Francisco?"

"In neither."

Daniel leaned forward, opened the front window and said a few words to Fermin, who put his horses to a quick trot, driving still through the Calle de la Reconquista, in the direction of the fortress.

"To continue," resumed Don Cándido; "I ordered the carriage to stop at Santo Domingo, alighted, entered the monastery, crossed myself, and walked to the end of the dark and solitary cloister; there I stopped and clapped my hands, and a lay brother, who was lighting a lantern, came to meet me. I inquired after everybody's health and then asked for the reverend father whom you told me to ask for. The brother took me to his cell, and, after the usual salutations and compliments had passed between us, I could not but congratulate him on the tranquil, happy and holy life which he led in that mansion of rest and peace; for you must know that from my earliest years I have had a taste, an inclination, a vocation for the cloister; and when I think that I might have been living tranquilly today under the sacred roof of a convent, free from political agitations, and with the doors closed at dusk, I cannot forgive myself for my want of prevision, my negligence. In brief—"

"Yes, my dear master; and let it be as brief as possible."

"I was about to say then, that I at once formulated my first propositions."

"In which you did wrong."

"Why, was not that what I went there for?"

"Yes, but you should never begin with what you wish to obtain."

"Let him speak," interrupted Eduardo, settling himself comfortably in a corner of the carriage as if he were preparing to go to sleep.

"Proceed," said Daniel.

"I will proceed. I explained to him in clear and precise terms the position of a nephew of mine who, although an excellent Federal, was persecuted through personal spite, through the envy and jealousy of certain bad supporters of the cause, who did not respect, as they should, the exalted fame and honor of the patriarchal Government of our Illustrious Restorer of the Laws, and his respectable family. I narrated with eloquence and enthusiasm the biography of all the members of the illustrious families of his Excellency the Governor and of his Excellency the Deputy Governor; concluding that for the honor of these illustrious branches of the Federal trunk religion and politics alike were interested in preventing an outrage to the nephew of an uncle like me, who had given notable proofs of valor and constancy in the Federal cause; and that in order not to distract the attention of the Illustrious Governors and the other exalted and distinguished personages at present occupied in preserving the independence of America, I asked from the convent of Santo Domingo sanctuary, protection and shelter for my innocent nephew, offering to donate to it for charitable purposes a large sum of money, either in bank notes or in gold, as the Reverend Fathers should determine. Such, in brief, was the discourse with which I opened my conference. But, contrary to all my expectations and preconceived ideas the Reverend Father said to me:

"'Señor, I should be glad to be of service to you, but we cannot mix ourselves up with political affairs; and something there must be when your nephew is persecuted.'

"'I protest once, twice and three times,' I answered, 'against whatever may be said against my innocent nephew.'

"'No matter,' he replied. 'We cannot run any risk with Señor Don Juan Manuel; and the only thing we can do for you is to pray that God will protect your innocent nephew, if he be indeed innocent.'"

"Amen," said Eduardo.

"So I answered too," continued Don Cándido, "rising and begging a thousand pardons for having taken up so much of his Reverence's time. And now I will pass on to my conference in San Francisco."

"No, no, no; enough of friars, for Heaven's sake; and enough of everything, and enough of life, for this is not life, but a hell!" cried Eduardo, striking his forehead violently with the palm of his hand.

"All this, my dear friend," said Daniel, "is only one act, one scene in the drama of life; of this life of ours and of our epoch, which is a drama unique on earth. But only cowardly hearts give way to despair in the difficult crises of fate. Remember that those were Amalia's last words to you. She is a woman, but by Heaven! she has more courage than you."

"Courage to die is what is easiest. But this is worse than death, for it is humiliation. Since yesterday morning I have been refused admittance everywhere. My servants fly from me; my few relations disown me, other lands, and even the house of God, close their doors against me; and that is a thousand, a million times worse than the stab of a dagger."

"But love and friendship still watch over you, and it is not everyone who can count upon these in Buenos Ayres. Three days ago you lost your house, you lost everything you had. They have destroyed, sacked, confiscated all your possessions, as they believe. And yet I have been able to save more than a million dollars for you. And with a bride as beautiful as the day, a friend like me, and a handsome fortune, you have no reason yet to complain so greatly of fate."

"But I go about from door to door like a beggar."

"Let us stop talking nonsense, Eduardo."

"Where are we going, Daniel? I perceive that we are approaching the Retiro."

"Precisely, my dear master."

"But are you in your senses?"

"Yes, señor."

"Do you not know that General Rolon's regiment and a part of the troops of Maza are in the Retiro?"

"I know it."

"Well, then, do you wish them to arrest us?"

"As you wish."

"Daniel, what I wish is that we should not sacrifice ourselves so soon. Who knows what happy days may await us in the future. Let us turn back, my son; let us turn back. Observe that we are now approaching the barracks. Let us turn back."

Daniel again put his head out of the front window, spoke a few words to Fermin, and the carriage turned to the right, and in two minutes more stopped at the door of the handsome house occupied by Mr. Slade, the United States Consul. The great iron gate was closed, and the building, which stood back about a hundred paces from the railing, was entirely dark, with the exception of the rooms on the ground floor.

Daniel gave a loud double knock with the knocker at the gate and waited for someone to appear, but in vain; while Don Cándido kept calling to him at every moment, "Let us go, Daniel; let us go"—without alighting from the carriage or taking his eyes off the barracks, which at this hour—near ten o'clock—was buried in profound repose.

Daniel knocked again, this time more loudly; and a few minutes later a man appeared coming slowly toward the gate. The man approached him, examined him coolly and then asked in English:

"What do you want?"

With equal conciseness Daniel answered:

"Mr. Slade."

The servant took a key from his pocket and opened the gate without uttering a word.

Don Cándido immediately alighted and placing himself between Daniel and Eduardo, followed the footsteps of the servant with them.

The latter introduced them into a small ante-chamber and, motioning to them to wait went into an adjoining room.

Two minutes later he returned and employing the same language of signs as before, invited them to enter the apartment he had just left.

The room was lighted only by two tallow candles.

Mr. Slade was lying on a horsehair sofa, in his shirtsleeves, without waistcoat, cravat or boots; and standing on a chair beside the sofa were a decanter of cognac, a carafe of water and a glass.

Daniel knew the United States Consul by sight only, but he knew his country very well.

Mr. Slade sat up, without showing the slightest embarrassment, bade his visitors good-evening, motioned to the servant to place chairs, and then put on his boots and his coat, precisely as if he had been alone in his bedroom.

"Our visit will not be long, citizen Slade," said Daniel to him in English.

"You are Argentines?" asked the consul, a man about fifty years of age, above the medium height, with an open and honest countenance and of an ordinary rather than a distinguished type.

"Yes, señor, all three of us," answered Daniel.

"Good. I am very fond of the Argentines," and he signed to the servant to help them to some brandy.

"I believe it, señor; and I have come to give you an opportunity of manifesting your good-will toward us."

"I know it."

"You know what we have come for, Señor Slade?"

"Yes; you have come to seek an asylum in the Legation of the United States, have you not?"

Daniel was perplexed by this strange frankness, but comprehending that he ought to follow the lead given him he answered quietly, after drinking half a glass of brandy-and-water:

"Yes, that is what we have come for."

"Well, you are here now."

"But Señor Slade does not yet know our names," interposed Eduardo.

"What does it signify to me what your names are? The flag of the United States is here and here every man, no matter how he may be called, receives protection," answered the consul, lying down again very unceremoniously on the sofa, without troubling himself to move when Daniel rose from his seat, approached him and taking his hand and pressing it warmly, said:

"You are the most perfect type of the freest and most democratic nation of the nineteenth century."

"And the strongest," added Slade.

"Yes, and the strongest," repeated Eduardo, "for it could not be otherwise with citizens like hers," and the young man crossed over to the window that looked out upon the river to conceal the emotion which he could no longer control.

"Well, Mr. Slade," continued Daniel, "we have not all three come to ask an asylum from you, but only the gentleman who has just left his seat, who is one of the most distinguished young men of our country and who is at present pursued by the police. I do not know whether I may not myself have to seek the protection of this house, later, but for the present we ask it only for Señor Belgrano, the nephew of one of the leaders in our War of Independence."

"Ah, very good. This is the United States."

"And will they not dare to enter here?" asked Don Cándido.

"Who?" and as he asked this question Mr. Slade frowned, looked at Don Cándido, and then laughed. "I am a great friend of General Rosas," he continued. "If he asks me who are here I shall tell him. But if he orders them to be taken away by force, I have those," and he pointed to a table on which lay a rifle, two revolvers and a large knife, "and up there is the flag of the United States," and he raised his hand and pointed to the ceiling.

"And me to help you," said Eduardo, returning from the window.

"Good; thanks. You make twenty."

"You have twenty men in this house?"

"Yes, twenty refugees."

"Here?"

"Yes; in the other rooms on this floor and upstairs, and I have been spoken to for more than a hundred."

"Ah!"

"Let them all come. I have neither beds nor the means of providing for so many people but here are the house and the flag of the United States."

"Good; we shall want for nothing, nothing. Your protection will be sufficient for us, noble, frank, and loyal compatriot of Washington, for I too will remain here," said Don Cándido, holding his head erect and striking the floor with his cane with so serious and determined an air that Daniel and Eduardo looked at each other and then burst out laughing, which obliged Daniel to give Mr. Slade in English some idea of his ex-master's character and peculiarities. And this slight account put the simple Mr. Slade into so good a humor that he could not refrain from pouring out some brandy and drinking with Don Cándido, saying to him:

"From this day forth you are under the protection of the United States; and if they kill you I will burn down Buenos Ayres."

"I do not accept that hypothesis, Señor Consul. I would prefer that Buenos Ayres should be burned down before I had been killed, rather than that I should be killed first and Buenos Ayres burned down after."

"Come," said Daniel, "all this is only a jest, my dear Don Cándido, and you must return with me."

"No; I shall not go with you, nor have you now any rights over me, since I am in foreign territory. Here I will pass my life watching over the precious health of this worthy man, whom I already love devotedly."

"No, Señor Don Cándido; you must go with Daniel," said Eduardo. "Remember you have something to do tomorrow."

"It is useless to talk. I will not go. And from this moment all relations are at an end between us."

Daniel rose, and calling Don Cándido aside, held a brief but animated conversation with him, in the course of which he employed every argument he could think of to persuade the ex-schoolmaster to return with him to the carriage. But all his arguments would have been in vain had he not added to them the promise of leaving Don Cándido absolutely free to return to the United States, as soon as he should have brought him from the Deputy Governor's office some information which he desired to have.

"Finally," said Don Cándido, "it shall be an express condition that I am to sleep tonight at your house, and tomorrow night also if I do not return tomorrow to this hospitable and secure abode."

"Agreed."

"Señor Consul," said Don Cándido, turning to Mr. Slade, "I cannot have tonight the honor, the pleasure, the satisfaction of seeing wave above my head the glorious North American banner. But I will do all in my power to be here tomorrow."

"Very good," answered Slade. "I will never give you up alive."

"How diabolically frank this man is!" said Don Cándido, looking at Eduardo.

"Come, my friend," said Daniel.

"Come, Daniel."

Mr. Slade rose lazily, bade Daniel good-bye in English, and shaking hands with Don Cándido, said to him:

"If we do not see each other again here, I hope we shall meet in the other world."

"Yes? Well, then, I will not stir from here, Señor Consul;" and Don Cándido made a movement as if to sit down again.

"It is only a jest, my dear master," said Eduardo.

"Come, come; it is already late."

"Yes, but it is a jest that—"

"Come. Good-bye until tomorrow, Eduardo."

And the two young men separated with an eloquent embrace.

The same servant who had admitted them conducted them to the street door and as he opened it Don Cándido asked him:

"Is this door always closed?"

"Yes," answered the servant.

"And would it not be better to leave it open?"

"No."

"What diabolical conciseness! Look at me well, my friend. Would you know me again?"

"Yes."

"Come, Señor Don Cándido," said Daniel, entering the carriage.

"I am going. Good-night, honest servant of the most illustrious of consuls."

"Good-night," answered the servant, closing the gate.

XLII

How Don Cándido was a Relation of Cuitiño

At eight o'clock one morning toward the close of September, Daniel's former master was drinking deep draughts of hot and foaming chocolate from an enormous china cup while his pupil was occupied in reading, folding and sealing papers, both men bearing traces in their countenances of having spent the night in vigil.

"Daniel, my son, would it not be well for us to lie down to rest for a little, a brief period, a few moments?"

"Not yet, señor; later. I need you for a few minutes longer."

"But this must be the last time, Daniel; for I am resolved upon going today to the United States. Do you know that it is five days since I gave my word to that honorable and worthy consul to go and reside in his territory?"

"That is because you do not know what has happened," said Daniel, sealing a package of papers.

"And what has happened?"

"Or what may happen, in that territory."

"No, no, you cannot deceive me. Last night, while you were writing, I read five treatises on international law and the chapters in two diplomatic manuals which treat of the immunities of public agents and the houses in which they reside. And do you know, Daniel, that even their carriages are inviolable, from which I deduce that I may drive about in the worthy consul's carriage without fear, without anxiety, without risk, without—"

"Let me have the list of dead which you have brought me," said Daniel, folding the paper which he had just finished reading, and taking up another.

"Stay, wait, my dear and esteemed Daniel; let us leave the dead in peace."

"No, it is only the number I wish to see."

"The number is here, Daniel—fifty-eight in twenty-two days."

"That is it—fifty-eight in twenty-two days."

And Daniel folded these papers as he had folded the others, and put his seal upon them.

JOSÉ MÁRMOL

"Don't forget the marches of the army in Santa Fé."

"This is what I shall do with them, my dear master," and Daniel held the paper to the candle and burned it. Then he put away all the packages in a secret drawer of his desk.

Presently he took his pen and wrote:

My dear Eduardo:

"Last night I remained with Amalia from dusk until eleven o'clock. She is ill. The surprise of our visit the night before last, and her anxiety after we left her, have made her ill. And when I reflect on my complacency toward you I confess that I reproach myself.

"The Mashorca continues to perpetrate its atrocities. The prison, the barracks and the camp are scenes of bloodshed which increases every moment; and I have reason to believe that all this is only a preparation for the greater crimes which are in contemplation for October.

"Everyone is talking of the house in which you are, and it is whispered that it is to be attacked. I do not believe this; but it is necessary to be prepared for everything. The rumor has reached Amalia's ears. She desired earnestly that the marriage should take place on the first of October, since you are resolved not to leave the country until you are united to her; but I have shown her that Mr. Douglas cannot be here before the 5th, and she has had to resign herself to wait.

"Everything is ended, my dear friend. The result of the conferences with Mackau will be peace. I will wait, however, until the last moment, and then I will take your Amalia to you, as we have agreed.

"I have concluded all my arrangements and I am momently expecting my dear father.

"I shall not go to see you before the day after tomorrow.

"This letter will be taken to you by our dear master, who is resolved not to stir again from that house; let him remain with you.

Your

Daniel

"You are to deliver this letter, Señor Don Cándido," said the young man, sealing the letter which the reader has just read, and handing it to his master.

"This letter has no direction, Daniel?"

"No matter. It is for Eduardo; take good care of it."

"Shall I take it now?"

"Take it whenever you please. But you are to go in my carriage, and that is not ready yet."

"Ah, good! A good idea!"

Daniel was about to ring, when a knock was heard at the street door, and a moment afterward a servant appeared, saying in a disturbed voice:

"Commandant Cuitiño."

Don Cándido leaned back in his chair and closed his eyes.

"Show him in," said Daniel. "Courage, my dear master," he continued, "this is nothing."

"I am a dead man, Daniel," answered Don Cándido, without opening his eyes.

"Come in, Commandant," said Daniel, rising and going forward to receive Cuitiño, while Don Cándido, hearing him enter the room, by a reaction purely mechanical rose, opened his lips in a convulsive smile, and extended both his hands to take the hand of Cuitiño, who sat down at a corner of the table at which master and pupil had just spent so many hours in vigil.

"When did you receive my message, Commandant?"

"About two hours ago, Señor Don Daniel."

"And were you ill, that you delayed so long in coming?"

"No, señor, I was on duty."

"Ah! I thought so! When it is a question of serving the cause I wish that everyone was like you. And that is what I was saying yesterday to the president; for if we mean to go creeping along like the chief of police, it would be better to say so at once and not to go on deceiving the Restorer. For my part, Commandant, I don't even know now what it is to sleep. I have spent the whole night with this man folding *Gacetas* to send them everywhere; for the Restorer wishes that the enthusiasm of the Federals should be known everywhere. And a little while ago this gentleman" (and Daniel pointed to Don Cándido, who was gradually returning to himself on learning that Cuitiño had come at a summons from Daniel), "called my attention to something which you must have already noticed, Commandant."

"What is that, Don Daniel?"

"That the *Gaceta* does not mention a word of you or of the Federals who hourly risk their lives in support of the cause."

"Why, they do not even publish the despatches!"

"To whom do you send them, Commandant?"

"I send them now to the chief of police, as the Restorer is in the camp. I have observed what you say only too well, Señor Don Daniel; and this man is quite right."

"Oh, Señor Commandant," said Don Cándido, "who would not be surprised at the silence that is observed regarding a man of your antecedents?"

"And antecedents that are of no recent date, either."

"Of course they are not of recent date!" returned Don Cándido. "Before you were born you were already deserving of public consideration, for Señor de Cuitiño, your honored father, belongs to a branch of one of our oldest families. One of your illustrious uncles, Señor Commandant, married, as I have heard my elders say, one of my mother's cousins; for which reason I have always had for you the sympathy of a relation, at the same time that we are bound together by the close and Federal bonds of our common cause."

"Then you are a relation of mine?" asked Cuitiño.

"A relation, and a near one," answered Don Cándido. "The same blood flows through our veins and we owe each other affection, esteem and mutual protection, for the preservation of our race."

"Well, if I can be in any way useful to you—"

"So then, Commandant," interrupted Daniel, in order that Don Cándido might not end by betraying himself, "so then, they do not even publish the despatches?"

"No, señor. Just now I sent the despatch about the Unitarian savage Salces, and you'll see they won't publish it."

"Salces?"

"Yes, old Salces. We have just put him to death."

Don Cándido closed his eyes.

"He was in bed," continued Cuitiño, "but we soon dragged him out of bed and killed him in the street. The other day I sent another despatch, when we put La-Madrid, of Tucuman, to death. Last Saturday we killed Zanudo and seven more and they have not published those despatches either. As far as I am concerned, my Cousin—what is your name?"

"Cándido," answered Daniel, seeing that the owner of that name did not appear to be in possession of his faculties.

"Well, my Cousin Cándido, as I was saying, is quite right; and now that the thing is going to begin in earnest, I don't intend to render an account to anybody."

"What! is it only going to begin now?" asked Don Cándido in a voice that seemed to proceed, not from a human breast, but from a sepulchre.

"Yes. The best of the business is going to begin now. We have received the order already."

"Did you receive it direct, Commandant?"

"Yes, Señor Don Daniel. I communicate now with no one but the Restorer. I wish to have no more dealings with Doña María Josefa."

"She has given you trouble enough already!"

"Now she has got hold of Gaetan and Badia and Troncoso; and she still keeps harping on Barracas, and still talking about that savage who escaped, as if he were not already with Lavalle."

"Why, that lady hates even me!"

"No, she has said nothing to me about you. It is your cousin she dislikes."

"I will tell you why some day, Commandant."

"Today she was shut up a long time with Troncoso and a young negress from the neighborhood of the villa."

"While you, Commandant, occupy yourself in rendering real services to the Federation see how Doña María Josefa occupies herself!"

"Yes! in setting spies on women."

"Of course. The negro girl must be a spy. What will you take, Commandant?"

"Nothing, Don Daniel, I have just breakfasted."

"And tell me, have you heard nothing?"

"What about?"

"Have you not received a certain order yet?"

"I don't know what order you refer to."

"About the Retiro?"

"The Retiro?"

"Yes, the big house, you know."

"The consul's?"

"Yes."

"Ah, no. An order, no; but we know what we are to do."

"So!" and Daniel clenched his right hand and raised it to a level with Cuitiño's eyes; while Don Cándido's hair stood on end and his eyes seemed about to start from their sockets; for he thought he saw before him in Daniel Judas himself.

"I know," answered Cuitiño.

"But there is no order?"

"None."

"So much the better, Commandant."

"How, so much the better?"

"Yes, I know what I am saying; and it was to say it to you that I sent for you. Your cousin is to be trusted and he is in all these secrets."

"But, what is it you mean, then?"

"That it is not yet expedient."

"Ah!"

"There are not enough yet. By the time the thing begins in earnest the house will be full. So that about the 8th or the 9th—do you understand?"

"Yes, Don Daniel," answered Cuitiño, whose face shone with ferocious joy as he grasped Daniel's meaning.

"Just so! All of them together."

Don Cándido thought that he must have lost his senses, for he could not believe that he had heard aright.

"Precisely!" answered Cuitiño, "that would be the best way. But we have no order, Don Daniel."

"Ah, yes, without an order, God forbid! But I am taking steps in the matter."

"And Santa Coloma?"

"Yes, I know."

"He has a strong hankering after the gringo."

"I know it, Commandant."

"He has probably had some dispute or other with him."

"Just so. So that if I obtain the order, you know what you are to do."

"With all my men, Don Daniel."

"And if Santa Coloma obtains it you will let me know?"

"Of course."

"For there is this. It will be necessary for me to be there to prevent them, in the ardor of their Federal enthusiasm, from touching the papers of the consulate."

"Ah!"

"For in that case the Restorer would be angry on account of the difficulties in which that might involve the country; you understand?"

"Yes, Don Daniel."

"But even if Santa Coloma should receive the order, I am of opinion that we ought to wait until there are more; until the 8th or 9th, say."

"You are right, that would be better."

"What a stroke, Commandant!"

"So they all know about it?"

"All; but so long as there is no order, we will not venture to do anything."

"You are right; that is to be a Federal. But do you know what we have thought of doing?"

"Tell me, Commandant."

"We are going to set a watch upon the house, from tonight on."

"A good idea; but take care of one thing."

"What is that?"

"Take care not to stop any carriage. Stop only those who go on foot."

"And why not the carriages?"

"Because they might be the consul's, and those cannot be touched."

"And why not?"

"Because they are his, and everything belonging to the consul is under the protection of the Restorer."

"Ah!"

"So that to touch his carriage is the same as to touch the consul himself."

"I did not know that."

"You see! It is always well to talk about things. Imagine how angry the Restorer would be if we should commit any act of rashness that should involve him in new wars."

"I will go at once and warn my comrades."

"Yes, lose no time; these matters are very delicate."

"Of course."

"So then, nothing without an order."

"Heaven forbid, Señor Don Daniel."

"And when the order comes, we will manage to delay until there are more assembled?"

"Just so."

"We understand each other, then, Commandant?"

"Perfectly, Don Daniel. And I will go now, lest they should stop some carriage."

"Yes, see them all."

"Well, Don Cándido, if I can serve you in any way, remember I am your cousin."

"Thanks, my dear and esteemed cousin," answered Don Cándido, more dead than alive, rising mechanically, and taking the hand which Cuitiño held out to him.

"Where do you live?"

"I live—I live here."

"Well, I will come to see you sometime."

"Thanks, thanks."

"Good-bye, then."

And Cuitiño left the room with Daniel, who, as he was bidding his visitor good-bye in the parlor, took a roll of bank-notes from his pocket, and said:

"This is for you, Commandant; it is five thousand dollars which my father has sent me to distribute among the poor Federals, and I will ask you to do it for me."

"Very good, Don Daniel. And when is Señor Don Antonio coming to the city?"

"I expect him from one moment to another."

"Send to let me know as soon as he arrives."

"I will do so, Commandant. Good-bye, and serve the cause."

And Daniel returned to his study, took a sheet of paper without noticing Don Cándido, who was looking at him fixedly with eyes in which there was an indescribable mixture of anger and stupefaction, and wrote these lines:

Eduardo, I know positively that the rumors regarding an immediate attack on Mr. Slade's house are unfounded; no order whatever has been given to that effect. But it is necessary for the consul to warn those who have solicited an asylum in it on no account to go there on foot, as the house is going to be watched; they may go, however, in a carriage without any risk, and it would be best for them to go in Mr. Slade's own carriage.

Adieu

"Now my dear master, instead of one letter you will have two to take," said Daniel, holding out the note to Don Cándido. But the latter answered:

"No. Or perhaps you wish to involve me too in your base treachery?"

"What is the matter now! Have you lost your senses, my respectable cousin of Cuitiño?"

"The cousin of Satan, that cutthroat must be!"

"But you told him you were his cousin."

"How do I know what I am saying? I think I must have lost my senses, in this labyrinth in which I find myself, surrounded on all sides by crime, by treachery, by deceit. Tell me who you are. Define your position. How is it that you speak in my presence of attacking the house in which I am going to seek an asylum, in which that young man is sheltered whom you call your friend, in which—"

"For the love of Heaven, Señor Don Cándido! I must explain everything to you, then, it seems!"

"But what explanation can there be of what I myself have heard."

"This," said Daniel, opening the last of the two notes which he had written and which he had not sealed, and giving it to Don Cándido, in whose face and eyes there was an expression that was in truth appalling.

"Ah!" he exclaimed, after reading it over twice.

"This, Señor Don Cándido, is to build upon the foundation laid by others; it is to catch men in their own traps; it is to destroy them by their own machinations; it is to make our enemies serve us; it is, in short, the whole science of Richelieu, applied to little things, for there is neither a Rochelle nor an England here, and even if there were, it would still apply. Now go and repose tranquilly in North American territory."

"Come to my arms, admirable youth, who have just made me pass the most cruel moment of my life!"

"Embrace me, and then depart in my carriage, illustrious cousin of Cuitiño."

"Do not insult me, Daniel."

"Very well; good-bye until tomorrow—no, until the day after tomorrow. The carriage is at the door."

"Good-bye, Daniel."

And poor Don Cándido again embraced his pupil who, half an hour later was courting sleep, while Don Cándido walked about with head erect in the territory of the United States, as he said, and while Eduardo read his friend's letters.

XLIII

The Warning of the Soul

On the evening of the 5th of October a carriage might have been seen to stop at the door of a modest looking house in the Calle de Corrientes, from which issued at the same moment a venerable priest, who entered the vehicle saluting, as he did so, two men who were in it. The carriage drove off again at once, entered the Calle de Suipacha and turned south. Crossing the Calle de la Federation, the driver was obliged to pull up his horses to avoid a collision with three horsemen who were coming from the plains, their horses unshod and with all the appearance of having traveled many leagues. One of the horsemen seemed advanced in years and was apparently the leader or the master of the others, to judge by the respectful distance at which they kept from him, and by the costly trappings of his horse.

Eight o'clock had just struck.

The Calle Larga of Barracas was deserted.

But in the midst of this solitude there was a hidden animation, and amid the obscurity a torrent of light, concealed within the walls of Amalia's villa.

In the salon the light of fifty tapers was reflected from the mirrors, from the polished surface of the furniture and from the facets of the cut glass vases filled with flowers.

Radiant with beauty, youth and health Amalia, standing before the mirror in her dressing-room was putting the last touches to her toilette, while Luisa gazed at her in an ecstasy of admiration.

A clock struck eight, and from the first stroke every succeeding one might have been counted in the palpitation of Amalia's heart, beneath the lace which covered her bosom, and suddenly the pomegranate of her lips and the May rose of her cheeks took the hues of the pearl and the jasmine.

"You have turned pale again, señora; and just now, too, when the clock struck eight," said Luisa.

"It is precisely for that reason," answered Amalia, passing her hand over her forehead and sinking into a chair.

"Because it is eight o'clock?"

"Yes; I don't know why it is, but since six this evening every time I hear the clock strike I suffer horribly."

"Yes, I have noticed it three times since six o'clock; and do you know what I am going to do?"

"What, Luisa?"

"I am going to stop the clock, so that when it is nine you may not become ill again."

"No, Luisa, no; it is over now; it was nothing," returned Amalia, rising, while the color returned slowly to her cheeks.

"It is true, it is true; now you are as beautiful as ever; more beautiful than I have ever seen you before, señora."

"Hold your tongue, silly child; go and call Pedro."

A few moments later Luisa returned with Pedro, so carefully shaved and combed, with his coat buttoned up to the chin and with so martial an air that he seemed to have grown twenty years younger on this day on which his Colonel's daughter was to be married.

"Pedro, my good friend," said Amalia, "nothing will be changed in this house; I wish to be for you always what I have been up to this day; I wish you to care for me always as for a daughter; and the first proof of affection which I desire to receive from you, in my new state, is your promise that you will never leave me."

"Señora, I—I cannot speak, señora," said the old man, shaking his head, as if with rage, or as if he wished by this movement to restrain the tears which filled his eyes and paralyzed his tongue.

"Very well; all you need say is yes. I wish you to accompany me next week to Montevideo; for he who is to be my husband must leave Buenos Ayres tonight and it is my duty to share his fate. Will you come, Pedro?"

"Yes, señora; yes, of course," answered the old man, affecting to be perfectly self-possessed and capable of uttering any number of words.

Amalia went over to a table, opened an ebony casket which stood upon it, took from this a ring, and returned to her father's old companion in arms.

"This ring," she said, "was made from my hair when I was a child. That is its only value, and it is for that reason that I give it to you to keep forever. My father wore it when he was in the army."

"Yes; this is it, I know it; I know it well!" said the soldier, stooping down and kissing the ring which his Colonel had worn, as if it were a holy relic.

"One thing more, Pedro," continued Amalia, whose eyes were moist with tears.

"What is that, señora?"

"I wish you to be one of the witnesses to my marriage. No one will be present but you and Daniel."

The soldier for sole answer approached Amalia, took her hand in both of his, that trembled with emotion, and imprinted a respectful kiss upon it.

"Have the two men servants left the villa already?"

"I sent them away at dusk, as you directed me to do."

"You are alone then?"

"Alone."

"Good. Tomorrow you will distribute this among the servants, without telling them why;" and Amalia took a roll of bank-notes from the table and gave it to Pedro.

"Señora," said Luisa, "I think I hear a noise on the road."

"Is everything closed, Pedro?"

"Yes, señora. But the iron door leading to the street—I don't know how it is, but I have twice found it open in the morning, as I have already told you, although I close it every night myself and keep the key under my pillow."

"Well, let us not speak of that tonight."

"Señora," repeated Luisa, "I hear a noise and I think it is a carriage."

"Yes, I hear it too."

"And it has stopped," added Luisa.

"Yes, it must be they. Go, Pedro, but do not open until you learn who it is."

"Have no fear, señora. I am alone, but—have no fear," repeated the veteran as he left the room.

XLIV

THE BRIDAL VEIL

A malia had not been mistaken, for the persons who had just arrived were in fact those whom she had been awaiting for so many hours and with so much anxiety.

From her dressing-room she heard the door of the salon open and at once recognized Daniel's step approaching through the outer rooms.

"Ah, señora," said the young man, standing still at the door of the dressing-room and regarding Amalia, "I expected to have the pleasure of finding here a beautiful woman, and I have the delightful surprise of finding a goddess!"

"Truly?" answered Amalia, with an enchanting smile, as she finished drawing on a white kid glove that fitted her beautiful hand to perfection.

"Yes, truly," replied Daniel, approaching his cousin with a look of genuine admiration, and pressing a kiss upon her forehead—"But come; Eduardo and the priest are outside; and the latter must not remain even ten minutes."

"And why not?"

"Because while he is here the carriage must remain at the door."

"Well?"

"Well, a party of soldiers might pass by; the carriage would attract their attention; they would watch, and—"

"Ah, yes, yes—I understand you—Come, Daniel—but—" and Amalia leaned her hand on the table beside her and was silent.

"But what?"

"I don't know—I should like to laugh at myself, but I cannot do that either—I don't know what it is that oppresses my heart—but—"

"Come, Amalia."

And the young man took his cousin's hand and passing it through his arm led her through the bedroom and the ante-chamber into the salon where the priest and Eduardo were awaiting them.

The latter was dressed entirely in black and wore white gloves. His hair, black as ebony, seemed blacker from the contrast it formed with the pallor of his face, and the velvety shadows under his fine eyes imparted a tinge of romantic sadness to his manly countenance.

He and Amalia exchanged volumes in their first glance.

And the priest, who had been informed by Daniel of the necessity of concluding briefly the ceremony that was about to take place, all the arrangements for which had been made beforehand by Bello, prepared himself at once for the most solemn act, perhaps, of his mission on earth—that which unites two lives and two souls.

The priest offered up a prayer, asked that question the response to which influences for time and for eternity the fate of the man and the woman who pronounce it, and which no human lips can pronounce without the heart beating more quickly, and then, in the name of the Trinity, Indivisible and Eternal, Eduardo and Amalia were united for earth and for heaven.

No sooner was the ceremony ended than Daniel approached Pedro and whispered to him:

"Is your horse in the stable?"

"He is."

"I shall need him for an hour."

"Very well."

Then, taking Amalia by the hand and leading her to a sofa in the ante-chamber, while Eduardo was thanking the priest, he said to her:

"The priest is going now and I am going also."

"You?"

"Yes, Madame Belgrano; I; because it is my fate to be at rest nowhere, in order that your husband may be at rest at last in Montevideo."

"But what has happened? My God! what has happened? Did you not tell us that you would stay with us until the moment of embarkation?"

"Yes, and it is for that reason that I must leave you for a short time now. Listen to me; you know that the place of embarkation is the Boca, for the reason that no one will think of it; but Douglas and I agreed to meet tonight between nine and ten o'clock at one of the little frame houses in the port, lest anything should in the meantime have occurred to render necessary any change in our plans; and as the Englishman is even more punctual than an Englishman I am certain that before a quarter of an hour he will be at the place of meeting, for it is now on the stroke of nine. I will be back within an hour; and meanwhile, Fermin, who is acting as coachman, will drive the priest to his house and will come back here on horseback, bringing my horse with him for me to return to the city."

"And to go to the Boca?" asked Amalia, who was hanging on Daniel's words.

"No, when I go with Eduardo we will go on foot."

"On foot?"

"Yes; for our way lies between the villas of Somellera and Brown, and then by the bathing ground, and we shall be as safe as if we were in London."

"Yes, yes; I think that is better," answered Amalia; "but Fermin and Pedro will go with you?"

"No, we two will go alone; leave all to me. Now we must part, for I shall not be easy in my mind until the carriage has driven away from your door."

"Do you carry arms?"

"Yes; come and say good-bye to the priest."

They returned to the salon and a moment afterward Amalia and Eduardo accompanied to the hall-door the minister of the church who exposed himself in the fulfillment of the duties of his ministry to all the dangers of the place and the hour in those times.

And at the same moment in which the carriage started for the city and Eduardo closed the street door, Daniel rode slowly through the gate of the villa, enveloped in his poncho, humming one of the melancholy songs of the plains, like the best and most careless of gauchos.

XLV

THE NUPTIAL COUCH

A s the clock of the villa was striking ten, Pedro opened the gate to admit Daniel, whose voice he had heard and recognized singing in the dark and solitary Calle Larga.

"Heaven protects us, my child," said Daniel to Amalia, joining Eduardo and his cousin in the salon. "All the arrangements are completed and everything is now ready. Only, that instead of waiting for daybreak, Douglas has fixed the hour of embarkation for twelve o'clock; that is, within two hours."

"And why this change?" asked Amalia.

"That is what I cannot tell you; but I have so much confidence in the foresight and sagacity of my famous smuggler, that when he named that hour I asked him no questions, because I was certain that it must be the hour most suitable for the embarkation."

Eduardo took Amalia's hand in his and it seemed as if he wished to transmit his soul to her in the contact.

Daniel regarded them tenderly for a moment and then said:

"Fate has not granted my most ardent desire—I had wished to behold your happiness in the light of mine. Involved in the same misfortunes, I had wished that at the same hour we might snatch from fate a moment for our common happiness; and if Florencia were now at my side, I should be the happiest of mortals. But at least I have obtained already half of my desires. As to the other half—God will dispose—. But come, let us be satisfied with these moments which are ours, and think only of the days which we shall soon spend together in Montevideo, and speak only of them."

A few moments afterwards Pedro entered with the tea-tray and placed it on a table in the library which, as we know, was between the salon and Amalia's bedroom, and into which Amalia now passed with her husband and her cousin, having first told Pedro to retire, for she would never allow the old man to wait on her.

Before ten minutes were over Daniel had brought cheerfulness back to his friends.

But suddenly a cry from Luisa fell like a thunderclap on the ears of all three.

It was a shrill, horrible, strident cry, while at the same instant they saw the terrified girl running toward them from the inner room and at the same instant, also, a shot sounded in the courtyard, accompanied by a loud and confused noise of cries and hurried steps.

And before Luisa had had the time to utter a word, before anyone had asked her a question, they all divined what had happened and, simultaneously with this instinctive divination, the reality appeared before them, through the glass door of the library, at the further end of the room from which the girl had run; for a number of sinister figures were precipitating themselves through Luisa's room into Amalia's dressing-room. And all this, from the girl's cry to the appearance of those men, passed in a space of time as brief as the duration of a flash of lightning.

But with the same swiftness, also, Eduardo drew his bride to the salon and took his pistol from the mantelpiece.

And at the same instant, for all was simultaneous, and swift as light, Daniel dragged the table to the door leading from the library into the bedroom and overturned it with the lamp, teatray, and everything else upon it, in the doorway.

"Save us, Daniel!" cried Amalia, throwing herself upon Eduardo as he was taking his pistols.

"Yes, my Amalia, but it must be by fighting; there is no time now for talking."

These last words were lost in the report of the pistols of Eduardo who fired at a number of the ruffians who were already in the bedroom, while Daniel piled up chairs in the doorway, and another shot sounded in the courtyard and a roar like that of a lion rose above the cries and the detonations.

"My God! they have killed Pedro!" cried Amalia, clinging to the left arm of Eduardo, who tried in vain to free himself from her clasp.

"Not yet," cried the soldier, entering the salon through the door that opened into the hall, his face and breast bathed in the blood that streamed from a wound which he had received in the head, and throwing into the library, as he spoke, Eduardo's sword, that fell beside them where they stood together behind the barricade improvised by Daniel. And while with his left arm he wiped the blood from his eyes, with his right, in which he held his saber, he tried to push into its place the bolt of the door of the salon.

The voice of Eduardo saying to his bride, who was clinging to him "You will ruin us, Amalia; leave us; go into the salon," was lost in the noise of the demoniac shouts of the men in the courtyard and the dressing-room, and of those who were entering the bedroom, one of whom had already fallen, killed by a shot from Eduardo's pistol.

The glass of the mirrors in the dressing-room was shattered into a thousand fragments by the saber-strokes showered upon them as well as upon the furniture, the window-panes, the china on the washstand, upon everything in the room, each stroke being accompanied by savage cries which rendered still more frightful this scene of terror and death.

When Eduardo had fired some of the men who had invaded the bedroom had retreated a few paces while others had stopped suddenly, not venturing to advance toward the barricade in front of the door. But at this instant two men precipitated themselves into the bedroom.

"Ah, Trancoso and Badia!" cried Daniel, throwing down another chair, placing himself with his back against the jamb of the door, and drawing from his bosom the weapon with which he had saved his friend's life on the night of the 4th of May, the only one he carried and which could be of little avail in the unequal struggle that was about to begin.

And as these two men rushed into the room, like two demons, the one with a pistol in his hand, the other with a sword, Eduardo threw his arm around Amalia, lifted her up and carrying her into the salon, placed her upon a sofa, and returning to the library, took up the sword which Pedro had thrown in. And the latter, who had just succeeded in bolting the door of the salon, attempted to follow Eduardo into the library, but he had hardly taken two steps before his strength failed him, his knees bent beneath him, and he fell, trembling with rage, beside the sofa on which his mistress lay. There he clung to her feet, bathing with his generous blood this young creature whom he still endeavored to save, holding her tightly in order to prevent her from moving.

Meanwhile, swift and fatal as the lightning, Eduardo's saber fell on the head of the nearest of the ten or twelve ruffians who, at the command of their leader, had attacked the frail barrier opposed to their further progress by the overturned table and chairs. And at the same instant, Daniel, reaching across it, struck another of them a powerful blow with his *casse-tête* on the shoulder, dislocating his arm.

"Take his saber!" cried Eduardo, while Pedro, who had attempted in vain to rise, for he had received a wound in the breast and another in the head, either of which of itself would have proved fatal, had only strength sufficient to clasp Amalia's feet, and voice to keep repeating to Luisa, who was also clinging to her mistress:

"The lights, extinguish the lights, for God's sake!"

But Luisa either did not hear him, or if she heard would not obey him, fearing no doubt to be left in the dark—if it were possible for her to be more afraid than she already was.

But the well-aimed blows of Daniel and Eduardo only served to draw the assassins upon them in greater numbers; for, at the command of one of their leaders the men who were pillaging and smashing furniture in the dressing-room came to the assistance of their companions. As they rushed toward the barricade Eduardo himself, impatient at the obstacles which impeded the sweep of his sword, endeavored with his feet to push aside the chairs; and a passage had been almost cleared from the one room to the other when Daniel brought down his terrible weapon upon the back of one of the men who was stooping in the bedroom, to push aside a chair, and the body of the ruffian filled up the space which Eduardo had cleared.

"Save Amalia, Daniel, save her; leave me to myself; save her!" cried Eduardo, trembling with rage, less because of the unequal struggle he was maintaining than because of the obstacles which he was unable to remove with his hands, obliged as he was to defend himself with his sword against the daggers and sabers on the other side of them, while he feared to stumble and fall if he should try to push them aside with his feet.

All this might have lasted some ten minutes, when six or eight of the ruffians left the bedroom and retreated through the dressing-room while the others continued, at the command of their leader, who remained with them, to endeavor to drag away the overturned articles of furniture, but so timorously that they had succeeded only in removing two or three chairs that were out of the reach of Eduardo's sword.

Neither of the two young men had been wounded and Eduardo, while he was resting his arm for a moment, turned his head to look through the glass door of the library at Amalia, guarded by a dying man and a child, and then, turning to his friend, he said to him in French:

"Escape with her through the door of the salon to the road; gain the ditch on the opposite side; and in five minutes I shall have broken all the lamps, and I will cut my way through this rabble and join you."

"Yes," said Daniel, "it is the only way; but I did not wish to leave you alone nor do I wish to do so now. I will try to take her out and be back with you in a few minutes; but meanwhile, do not cross the barricade."

And Daniel passed, swift, as lightning, into the salon; but just as he threw down one of the lamps and one of the two candelabra that were burning there, a tremendous blow delivered on the door of the room forced the bolt, the door flew open, and a band of the ruffians rushed into the room.

A terrible cry, a cry that seemed to tear with it the fibers of her heart, issued from the breast of the unhappy Amalia, who, releasing herself from the cold hands of Pedro and from the weak arms of little Luisa, ran to shield Eduardo with her body, while Daniel took his sword from the now expiring Pedro and ran also into the library.

But the assassins entered it with him, and when Eduardo pressed Amalia to his heart, to make a last rampart for her with his body, all were confounded together; Daniel received a cut from a knife in his right arm and a dagger pierced the breast of Eduardo, who, by a superhuman effort, still maintained himself upon his feet, and at this moment in which Amalia's arm supported him with difficulty, in a corner of the library, while his right hand was raised at the impulse of the blood to strike his assailants, and while Daniel, in the opposite corner, with a saber in his left hand, was defending himself like a hero, a succession of tremendous blows fell upon the street door. Luisa, who had run terrified into the hall, recognized Fermin's voice, drew the bolt and opened the door.

Then a man of venerable aspect, enveloped in a dark poncho, rushed in, crying in a voice of thunder, but full of anguish, like the cry which nature tears from the heart:

"Hold! hold! in the name of the Restorer!"

And all heard this voice but Eduardo, whose soul had at that instant taken its flight to God; his head dropped on the breast of his Amalia, who, sinking with him unconscious, as he fell, lay bathed in blood, beside the body of her husband, of her Eduardo.

At that instant the clock struck eleven.

"Here, father, here; save Amalia," cried Daniel, who had heard and recognized his father's voice.

And at the same instant the young man, who had received another wound, a deep wound in the head, fell into the arms of his father, who by a single word had suspended the dagger which the same word had raised to be the instrument of so much misfortune and so many crimes—!

Epilogue

History, which has much of interest to say later regarding the fortunes of certain personages who have figured in this long narration, relates only, for the present, that on the day succeeding that on which this bloody drama was enacted those of the neighbors who through curiosity entered the villa at Barracas that had been attacked by the Federal soldiers, found there only four dead bodies—that of Pedro, and those of three members of the Sociedad Popular Restauradora; all of which remained there until the evening of the same day, when they were taken away in a police wagon, at which time also the articles that still remained in the presses, on the tables, and in the wardrobes were carried off.

It is related also that Don Cándido Rodriguez, on the death of Mr. Slade, which occurred a few weeks after the events just narrated, was compelled by a justice of the peace to leave the consul's house, for he had positively refused to quit the territory of the United States, even after the consul's death and when the house was no longer a consulate.

Of Doña Marcelina it is only known that one day she went to offer her hand to Don Cándido, as a living reminder of the dangers they had together passed through, which Don Cándido rejected with horror.

The End

A Note About the Author

José Mármol (1818–1871) was an Argentine poet, novelist, and journalist. Born and raised in Buenos Aires, he left law school for a career in politics. In 1839, he was arrested by the regime of Juan Manuel de Rosas and was forced to flee within two years for his political opposition. In Montevideo, he befriended a vibrant community of fellow exiles including Esteban Echeverría and Juan Bautista Alberdi. Several years later, Mármol fled to Rio de Janeiro following the siege of Montevideo by Manuel Oribe, an ally of Rosas. He returned in 1845 and remained in Uruguay for seven years. In the Uruguayan capital, he founded three journals and gained a reputation as a prominent political poet. His twelve-canto autobiographical poem *El Peregrino* (1847) and a collection of his lyric poems placed Mármol at the forefront of the Latin American Romantic school. He is perhaps remembered most for his Costumbrist novel *Amalia* (1851), which was recognized as Argentina's national novel following the defeat of Rosas in 1852. Mármol returned after thirteen years in exile to serve as a senator, national deputy, and diplomat to Brazil. From 1858 until his retirement due to blindness, Rosas served as the director of the Biblioteca Nacional de la República Argentina, a position later held by his fellow countryman Jorge Luis Borges.

A Note from the Publisher

Spanning many genres, from non-fiction essays to literature classics to children's books and lyric poetry, Mint Edition books showcase the master works of our time in a modern new package. The text is freshly typeset, is clean and easy to read, and features a new note about the author in each volume. Many books also include exclusive new introductory material. Every book boasts a striking new cover, which makes it as appropriate for collecting as it is for gift giving. Mint Edition books are only printed when a reader orders them, so natural resources are not wasted. We're proud that our books are never manufactured in excess and exist only in the exact quantity they need to be read and enjoyed.

bookfinity™

Discover more of your favorite classics with Bookfinity™.

- Track your reading with custom book lists.
- Get great book recommendations for your personalized Reader Type.
- Add reviews for your favorite books.
- AND MUCH MORE!

Visit **bookfinity.com** and take the fun Reader Type quiz to get started.

Enjoy our classic and modern companion pairings!

Classic & Modern